Praise for *New York Times* bestselling author Christina Dodd

"If Lisa Jewell, Ruth Ware and Lucy Foley are on your Mount Rushmore of suspense writers, Dodd's latest release definitely needs a spot on your shelf."
—*E! News* on *Wrong Alibi*

"As with all her fiendishly clever suspense novels, Dodd's latest should come with a warning label: may cause sleeplessness even after the reader reaches the last page."
—*Booklist* (starred review) on *Wrong Alibi*

"Christina Dodd reinvents the romantic thriller. Her signature style—edgy, intense, twisty, emotional—leaves you breathless from first page to last. Readers who enjoy Nora Roberts will devour Dodd's electrifying novels."
—Jayne Ann Krentz, *New York Times* bestselling author

"Featuring an unforgettable protagonist, who makes Jack Reacher look like a slacker, Dodd's latest superior suspense novel builds on the well-deserved success of *Dead Girl Running.*"
—*Booklist* (starred review) on *What Doesn't Kill Her*

"Action-packed, littered with dead bodies, and brimming with heartfelt emotion, this edgy thriller keeps the tension high."
—*Library Journal* (starred review) on *What Doesn't Kill Her*

"Dodd's gripping voice will appeal to fans of Sandra Brown, Nora Roberts, Linda Howard and Jayne Ann Krentz."
—*Mystery Tribune* on *What Doesn't Kill Her*

"Dodd is at her most wildly entertaining, wickedly witty best."
—*Booklist* (starred review) on *Dead Girl Running*

"Complex, intense, and engrossing, this riveting romantic thriller has a chilling gothic touch and just enough red herrings and twists to keep readers on edge."
—*Library Journal* (starred review) on *Dead Girl Running*

**Also available from
Christina Dodd
and HQN**

Right Motive (ebook novella)
Wrong Alibi

Cape Charade

Hard to Kill (ebook novella)
Dead Girl Running
Families and Other Enemies (ebook novella)
What Doesn't Kill Her
Hidden Truths (ebook novella)
Strangers She Knows

For additional books by Christina Dodd,
visit her website, www.christinadodd.com.

CHRISTINA
DODD

POINT LAST SEEN

Recycling programs for this product may not exist in your area.

ISBN-13: 978-1-335-62397-3

Point Last Seen

For questions and comments about the quality of this book, please contact us at CustomerService@Harlequin.com.

HQN
22 Adelaide St. West, 41st Floor
Toronto, Ontario M5H 4E3, Canada
www.Harlequin.com

Printed in U.S.A.

To my mother, Virginia Dodd, who read to me,
listened to me, laughed at my corny jokes
and believed I could do whatever I set my mind to.
I miss our travels together, the sound of your voice, your gentle hands,
your raucous humor. Your gritty determination in the face of adversity
taught me everything I know about surviving the tough times
and coming out on the other side. When I'm cold, I snuggle under
the afghan you crocheted for me, and you're beside me.
Thank you for being the best mother I could ever have.
I miss you every day, and I love you forever.

POINT LAST SEEN

1

TWO PRIMAL ELEMENTS DOMINATED this remote area of Big Sur, California: the Santa Lucia Mountains to the east, and the Pacific Ocean to the west. Their legendary battles gave rise to the storms, the sparkling blue days and the interesting legend of Gothic, City of Lost Souls.

The plaque outside the Live Oak Restaurant read:

On stormy nights, Gothic is said to disappear, and on its return it brings lost souls back from the dead.

The myth was nonsense, of course, but local shops encouraged its belief.

A legend or two is always good for business.

Historic buildings lined the seven hairpin turns that formed Gothic's backbone, a hodgepodge collection of restaurants and art shops that catered to whatever hardy tourists made the trip from the Salinas Valley along the narrow, winding

Nacimiento-Fergusson highway on its way west to the coast, or north and south on the Pacific Coast Highway.

Today there was no traffic in Gothic; the Nacimiento-Fergusson highway was open, but the Pacific Coast Highway was washed out *again* and had been for months, and when it was closed, the village businesses saw bleak times.

Gothic residents were a hearty bunch of loners and eccentrics, artists and fortune-tellers. People who came to Gothic and stayed…and stayed for a reason.

Adam Ramsdell's reasons were his own.

2

A Morning in February
Gothic, California

THE STORM OFF THE Pacific had been brutal, a relentless night of cold rain and shrieking wind. Adam Ramsdell had spent the hours working, welding and polishing a tall, heavy, massive piece of sculpture, not hearing the wailing voices that lamented their own passing, not shuddering when he caught sight of his own face in the polished stainless steel. He sweated as he moved swiftly to capture the image he saw in his mind, a clawed monster rising from the deep: beautiful, deadly, dangerous.

And as always, when dawn broke, the storm moved on and he stepped away, he realized he had failed.

Impatient, he shoved the trolley that held the sculpture toward the wall. One of its claws swiped his bare chest and proved to him he'd done one thing right: razor-sharp, it opened a long, thin gash in his skin. Blood oozed to the surface. He used his toe to lock the wheels on the trolley, securing the sculpture in case of the occasional California earth tremor.

Then with the swift efficiency of someone who had dealt with minor wounds, his own and others', he found a clean towel and stanched the flow. Going into the tiny bathroom, he washed the site and used superglue to close the gash. The cut wasn't deep; it would hold.

He tied on his running shoes and stepped outside into the short, bent, wet grass that covered his acreage. The rosemary hedge that grew at the edge of his front porch released its woody scent. The newly washed sunlight had burned away the fog, and Adam started running uphill toward town, determined to get breakfast, then come home to bed. Now that the sculpture was done and the storm had passed, he needed the bliss of oblivion, the moments of peace sleep could give him.

Yet every year as the Ides of March and the anniversary of his failure approached, nightmares tracked through his sleep and followed him into the light. They were never the same but always a variation on a theme: he had failed, and in two separate incidents, people had died...

The route was all uphill; nevertheless, each step was swift and precise. The sodden grasses bent beneath his running shoes. He never slipped; a man could die from a single slip. He'd always known that, but now, five years later, he knew it in ways he could never forget.

As he ran, he shed the weariness of a long night of cutting, grinding, hammering, polishing. He reached the asphalt and he lengthened his stride, increased his pace.

He ran past the cemetery where a woman knelt to take a chalk etching of a crumbling headstone, past the Gothic Museum run by local historian Freya Goodnight.

The Gothic General Store stood on the outside of the lowest curve of the road. Today the parking lot was empty, the rockers were unoccupied and the store's sixteen-year-old clerk lounged in the open door. "How you doing, Mr. Ramsdell?" she called.

He lifted his hand. "Hi, Tamalyn."

She giggled.

Somehow, on the basis of him waving and remembering her name, she had fallen in love with him. He reminded himself that the dearth of male teens in the area left him little competition, but he could feel her watching him as he ran past the tiny hair salon where Daphne was cutting a local rancher's hair in the outdoor barber chair.

His body urged him to slow to a walk, but he deliberately pushed himself.

Every time he took a turn, he looked up at Widow's Peak, the rocky ridge that overshadowed the town, and the Tower, the edifice built by the Swedish silent-film star who in the early 1930s had bought land and created the town to her specifications.

At last he saw his destination, the Live Oak, a four-star restaurant in a one-star town. The three-story building stood at the corner of the highest hairpin turn and housed the eatery and three exclusive suites available for rent.

When Adam arrived he was gasping, sweating, holding his side. Since his return from the Amazon basin, he had never completely recovered his stamina.

Irksome.

At the corner of the building, he turned to look out at the view.

The vista was magnificent: spring-green slopes, wave-battered sea stacks, the ocean's endless surges and the horizon that stretched to eternity. During the Gothic jeep tour, Freya always told the tourists that from this point, if a person tripped and fell, that person could tumble all the way to the beach. Which was an exaggeration. Mostly.

Adam used the small towel hooked into his waistband to wipe the sweat off his face. Then disquiet began its slow crawl up his spine.

Someone had him under observation.

He glanced up the grassy hill toward the olive grove and stared. A glint, like someone stood in the trees' shadows watching with binoculars. Watching him.

No. Not him. A peregrine falcon glided through the shredded clouds, and seagulls cawed and circled. Birders came from all over the word to view the richness of the Big Sur aviary life. As he watched, the glint disappeared. Perhaps the birder had spotted a tufted puffin. Adam felt an uncomfortable amount of relief in that: it showed a level of paranoia to imagine someone was watching *him*, but…

But. He had learned never to ignore his instincts. The hard way, of course.

He stepped into the restaurant doorway, and from across the restaurant he heard the loud snap of the continental waiter's fingers and saw the properly suited Ludwig point at a small, isolated table in the back corner. Adam's usual table.

Before Adam took a second step, he made an inventory of all possible entrances and exits, counted the number of occupants and assessed them as possible threats and evaluated any available weapons. An old habit, it gave him peace of mind.

Three exits: front door, door to kitchen, door to the upper suites.

Mr. Kulshan sat by the windows, as was his wont. He liked the sun, and he lived to people-watch. Why not? He was in his midnineties. What else had he to do?

In the conference room, behind an open door, reserved

for a business breakfast, was a long table with places set for twenty people.

A young couple, tourists by the look of them, held hands on the table and smiled into each other's eyes.

Nice. Really nice to know young love still existed.

There, her back against the opposite wall, was an actress. *Obviously* an actress. She had possibly arrived for breakfast, or to stay in one of the suites. Celebrities visits happened often enough that most of the town was blasé, although the occasional scuffle with the paparazzi did lend interest to the village's tranquil days.

She wasn't pretty. Her face was too angular, her mouth too wide, her chin too determined. She was reading through a stack of papers and using a marker to highlight and a ballpoint to make notes… And she wore glasses. Not casual *I need a little visual assistance* glasses. These were Coke-bottle bottoms set in lime-green frames.

Interesting: Why had an actress not had laser surgery? Not that it mattered. Behind those glasses her brown eyes sparked with life, interest and humor, although he didn't understand how someone could convey all that while never looking up. She had shampoo-commercial hair—long, dark, wavy, shining—and when she caught it in her hand and shoved it over one shoulder, he felt his breath catch.

A gravelly voice interrupted a moment that had gone on too long and revealed too clearly how Adam's isolation had affected him. "Hey, you. Boy! Come here." Mr. Kulshan beckoned. Mr. Kulshan, who had once been tall, sturdy and handsome. Then the jaws of old age had seized him, gnawed him down to a bent-shouldered, skinny old man.

Adam lifted a finger to Ludwig, indicating breakfast would have to wait.

Ludwig glowered. Maybe his name was suggestive, but the

man looked like Ludwig van Beethoven: rough, wild, wavy hair, dark brooding eyes under bushy eyebrows, pouty lips, cleft in the chin. He seldom talked and never smiled. Most people were afraid of him.

Adam was not. He walked to Mr. Kulshan's table and took a seat opposite the old man. "What can I do for you, sir?"

"Don't call me *sir.* I told you, call me K.H."

Adam didn't call people by their first names. That encouraged friendliness.

"If you can't do that, call me Kulshan." With his fork, the old guy stabbed a lump of breaded something and handed it to Adam. "What do you think *this* is?"

Adam had traveled the world, learned to eat what was offered, so he took the fork, sniffed the lump and nibbled a corner. "I believe it's fried sweetbread."

Mr. Kulshan made a gagging noise. "My grandmother made us eat sweetbread." He bit it off the end of the fork. "This isn't as awful as hers." With loathing, he said, "This is Frenchie food."

"Señor Alfonso is Spanish."

Mr. Kulshan ignored Adam for all he was worth. "Next thing you know, this Alfonso will be scraping snails off the sidewalk and calling it *escargots.*"

"Actually…" Adam caught the twinkle in Mr. Kulshan's eyes and stood. "Fine. Pull my chain. I'm going to have breakfast."

Mr. Kulshan caught his wrist. "Have you heard what Caltrans is doing about the washout?" He referred to the California Department of Transportation and their attempts to repair the Pacific Coast Highway and open it to traffic.

"No. What?"

"Nothing!" Mr. Kulshan cackled wildly, then nodded at

the actress. "The girl. Isn't she something? Built like a brick shithouse."

Interested, Adam settled back into the chair. "Who is she?"

"Don't you ever read *People* magazine? That's Clarice Burbage. She's set to star in the modern adaptation of Shakespeare's...um...one of Shakespeare's plays. Who cares? She'll play a king. Or something. That's the script she's reading."

Clarice looked up as if she'd heard them—which she had, because Mr. Kulshan wore hearing aids that didn't work well enough to compensate for his hearing loss—and smiled and nodded genially.

Mr. Kulshan grinned at her. "Hi, Clarice. Loved you in *Inferno*!"

"Thank you, K.H." She projected her voice so he could hear her.

Mr. Kulshan shot Adam a triumphant look that clearly said *See? Clarice Burbage calls me by my first name.*

The actress-distraction was why the two men were surprised when the door opened and a middle-aged, handsome, casually dressed woman with cropped red hair walked in.

Mr. Kulshan made a sound of disgust. *"Her."*

3

***HER* WAS ANGELICA LINDHOLM.**

Angelica had inherited the Tower and, by extension, most of the property in Gothic. After a brief career as a model and minor actress, she seized the moment to tell women how to organize their lives. When that proved to be a success, she taught crafts, cooking, gardening, housekeeping and decorating.

Who knew women wanted to be told how to properly arrange a pantry? Certainly not Adam. Yet Angelica —a woman in her sixties, fit, well-dressed, with impeccably cut and styled red hair—had made herself and her operation a brand name.

A harried-looking, twentysomething woman carrying a clipboard, computer tablet and briefcase trailed after Angelica. She took her burdens to the table against the back wall and placed them on one of the two chairs, then went to consult with Ludwig.

Angelica took the occasion to tour the restaurant, speaking to the young couple who looked startled and confused (the man) and thrilled (the woman.)

To Mr. Kulshan Angelica said, "I hope the arthritis in your feet has improved. Did you use the balm I made for you?"

Mr. Kulshan virtually sprouted porcupine's quills. "Yes, yes, I use it." He added grudgingly, "Helps. Thank you."

"Let me know when you need more, and I'll have Veda deliver it to you." Angelica smiled in self-congratulation. "Mr. Ramsdell, good to see you out and about." She moved toward Clarice's table.

Mr. Kulshan muttered, "Why don't you ask a little louder so everyone in the place knows I've got toes that look like knobby tree roots?" Only, as before, he was louder than he realized.

Angelica stiffened and paused.

She might be able to tell women how to live their lives, but every man in Gothic got his back up when she spoke in tones that insinuated they must be fans…or idiots. That patronizing comment about being *out and about*… Adam read it as a criticism of his private lifestyle. And who was she to talk? After speaking with Clarice, she made her way to the back table and seated herself, and while Veda carried boxes of flower arrangements to the conference room, Angelica poured coffee, ordered breakfast and scanned her notes.

Adam stood. "Good chatting with you, Mr. Kulshan. Enjoy your sweetbread." As soon as he returned to his table, Ludwig disappeared into the kitchen, then reappeared with a large pot of strong coffee, a small pot of heated cream and a bowl of cubed brown sugar. He poured the coffee into the waiting mug, added the exact amount of cream Adam required and dropped in one sugar cube. He examined Adam's face, then added another cube.

"Why did you do that?" Adam asked. "Now it'll be too sweet."

Ludwig stirred the brew, lifted the cup, put it in Adam's hands and again disappeared into the kitchen. He returned with two plates piled with food. "This morning Chef has prepared a Spanish tortilla of potatoes, eggs and onions with a skewer of fruit and fried sweetbread."

"Sounds good." Adam sipped the coffee. It *was* too sweet, yet the coffee and the food were exactly what his exhausted body needed. Simple food, but prepared so well that, if Adam was given to displays of emotion, he would groan with pleasure.

Angelica got the continental breakfast: a basket of rolls, a small orange juice and an assortment of jams. She ate sparingly, although Adam knew the pastries were top-notch. As Veda worked, she glanced wistfully at Angelica's table. Did she ever get to eat? Angelica could have at least tossed her assistant a *mollete.*

When two vans pulled up in front of the restaurant, Angelica pushed her breakfast away and marched to the door.

Veda joined her, tablet in hand, and opened the restaurant door while the vans discharged eighteen people of various genders, ages and skin colors...and yet, they were alike: clean, alert and dressed in the Angelica style. Adam appreciated that ethics meant hiring diversely, paying according to skills and not discriminating by gender. But there should be a law against hiring people who all dressed the same.

Angelica welcomed each one with a handshake and a restrained smile. When the last of the line had passed, Angelica consulted her tablet. "Where are Noah and Jill?"

As she spoke, a man and a woman stumbled off a van looking pale and shaky. Motion sickness. The shade and sunshine of the windy road did have that effect.

"Oh, dear." While the other employees filed into the conference room, Angelica walked two Angelica Lindholm–brand bottles of water out to the unfortunates and shepherded them inside.

Ludwig whipped into the conference room carrying pitchers of orange juice, baskets of pastries, and tea and coffee: the employees would eat like the boss. Except for Noah and Jill, who hastily vacated the room… Sometimes the smell of fresh-baked bread could be fatal to one's composure. When Ludwig finished placing the food on the table, Veda shut the door behind him. The meeting had begun.

The street door opened, and Adam looked up to see Rune of Madame Rune's Psychic Readings and Bookshop. Six feet tall with a darkly stubbled chin and flowing gray hair, she wore clothes that proclaimed her profession: long skirts, shirts with asymmetrical hems and coins affixed to the fringe of a tie-dyed scarf. As she made her way across the restaurant she fluttered her fingers at everyone in the place, spoke in her fluting Julia Child voice and took the table next to Clarice Burbage, who welcomed her warmly. They were, apparently, old friends.

How did a fortune-teller from Gothic know a movie star? More ominously, why were they chatting and glancing at Adam?

As soon as Ludwig whisked away Adam's plates and refreshed his coffee, Clarice wove her way through the tables and indicated the empty chair opposite. "May I?"

Up close, she was striking but not beautiful. Young but not a teenager. Tall but not…well, no. She had legs that rose to the moon. Adam couldn't imagine that any man ever said no to her. Still, she waited for him to grant permission before seating herself.

Of course, he did grant permission.

Mr. Kulshan said to no one, "Well, he's a good-looking-enough boy."

Clarice smiled, gently amused. "Rune told me to wait until

you'd eaten. She said you weren't such a grump when you'd been fed."

Adam still felt like a grump. "I imagine that's true of most men. And women."

"Eating always works for me. Smooths out my temperament." She seemed so calm, so unassuming, Adam found he couldn't imagine her showing temperament. "As K.H. told you, I'm here studying for a part. I need privacy. I've got one paparazzo who stalks me everywhere I go. Rune says that because of the roads, and because the sheriff and his deputies have a lot of county to cover, it can sometimes take them thirty minutes plus to answer a call in Gothic. Rune indicated to me that you're the unofficial law enforcement in town."

"Rune is wrong. I am absolutely not the law enforcement, unofficial or otherwise."

"I can't call the sheriff about a paparazzo. Bruno doesn't do anything criminal. He takes my picture for profit." Clarice took a quavering breath. "What he really enjoys are photos of me glaring, or sobbing in frustration, or threatening him, so when Bruno finds me, he gets in my face. Pops out and scares me. He's a stalker who uses a camera as an excuse to terrify. Worse, I'm his special target. He's told me so."

At one time Adam had been a target of the press. They were ruthless, but once the scandal had passed, they were on to the next story, indifferent to the pain they left behind. If this guy stalked Clarice specifically…he was dangerous.

"Señor Alfonso promised that Gothic was off the beaten track…and so far, it is. But it's also known among insiders as a place to stay to study a part."

Adam remembered the flash of binoculars from the hill above Gothic. Perhaps not binoculars, maybe a long-range lens. "Let's assume Bruno won't find you." Because Adam didn't want to get involved. Not with her, not with anyone.

Even now, a vast weariness weighed him down, and to think that he needed to protect someone when five years ago, he had proved to be so lacking…

He couldn't do it. He just couldn't.

Clarice knew she had been refused, and she laughed an ugly laugh. "Bruno is a slug. He crawls out of the mud and consumes everything he touches, leaving only the memory of what once bloomed, and a trail of slime to mark his passing. If you ever hear me say anything less, you'll know somehow he's got his claws in me."

"Is that what you fear?" Adam understood her in ways he wished he did not. "That he'll gain power over you?"

"Yes." She stood and with an audible flick of scorn, she said, "But as you said, Mr. Ramsdell, we'll hope he doesn't find me here." As she strode away, her long legs stretched and reached.

Adam made a point of not watching. She was too young, he wasn't going to help her, and he needed sleep. Mindless sleep that never ended. He dug for his wallet, flung cash on the table—and jumped.

Rune stood by the recently vacated chair. "May I sit?" she asked and sat.

"No." How had such a large-framed woman snuck up on him?

She tsked and brushed at the air around him. "Your aura. Wisps of anger, guilt and frustration are working their way out like slivers of pain. You've been flushing your soul, I can tell. Like…floosh!" Rune vocally imitated a toilet.

Adam caught her wrist. "Leave my aura alone, and tell me what you want."

"Let's talk about the spring festival."

"What spring festival?"

"The Gothic Spring Psychic Festival." With her other hand, Rune made a final plucking motion near Adam's right shoulder. "The GSPF is in three weeks, and our knight in shining armor canceled. He got hemorrhoids from the jousting saddle. We need you to step in."

"You are kidding. Have you ever *met* me? You want me to clank around a festival in metal chatting up the tourists?" Adam dropped Rune's wrist and stood. "I live below the road for a reason. I can hear the ocean and not my neighbors."

"I need your help. *Gothic* needs your help."

Adam debated. He really debated. But no character flaw dismayed him as much as his weakness for people he liked and respected.

He liked and respected Rune. He sat. "You've got five minutes."

"You don't have to chat up the tourists. In fact, the festival committee would prefer you didn't go within *ten feet* of a tourist, and I know because I'm the head of the festival committee. What we'd like is for you to perform a sword demonstration. We know you can do it. We've seen you work out with what looks like a medieval sword."

Unease prickled Adam's spine. "Who's *we*, and how have *we* seen that?"

"Mr. and Mrs. Hardling's house sits on the second corner from the bottom, and Mrs. Hardling has a clear view down to your place."

"A clear view?"

Rune met Adam's cynical gaze and conceded, "With binoculars. A sniper in Tucson severed her spine, she's in a wheelchair, and she watches her neighbors. So sue her. She's a nice lady. The committee meets in her parlor. When we got the cancellation, she threw out your name. She wasn't embarrassed about spying on you. Because you know what they say—a woman who likes younger men is a cougar, and a guy who likes younger women is…a guy."

"It's not the age difference. I thought I was unseen." To know someone was watching as he fought invisible demons… Adam could hardly bear the thought.

"If you wanted to be unseen, you should have stayed in Denver."

There was justification in that. Mrs. Hardling's hobby also explained his ongoing sense of being observed, and that blessed him with a sense of relief. "A sword demonstration is a great way to get hurt." Then, "What does a medieval knight have to do with a psychic fair, anyway?"

"You won't get hurt. Mrs. Hardling assures me you know what you're doing."

Rune had not answered the second question, Adam noted. "I can dress in shorts and a T-shirt?"

"We know you have a chain-mail shirt, as well as a chain-mail coif to cover your head. Which you made. Like the sword."

Of course they knew. It appeared they knew everything.

"You've got leather boots. We would provide breaches. Just one little exhibition," Rune pleaded. "Adam, the GSPF needs you. You know I wouldn't ask otherwise."

Adam did know it. In his five years in Gothic, no one had ever asked him to do anything. "All right. No breeches. No pumpkin pants. Let me know the schedule."

"Another reenactor will be here for you to spar with."

Adam stood and leaned across the table, and his voice grew deeper and quieter. "Another reenactor?"

"There had been arrangements for jousting. That takes two." Rune obviously knew she had left out an important element of the agreement, and she waited for Adam to knock her to the wall or go with it.

For a moment, Adam debated, then chose to go with it.

"I'll be there. Now, why am I here listening to you when I could be in bed and snoring?"

"No use. Your aura is turbulent. A lost soul is coming to challenge your being." Rune sounded bedrock-certain. "Go down to the sea and find what you need."

Adam was weary to his bones and sick of imagining things. Up all night creating a wickedly sharp sculpture that recalled its time in the ocean's depths and lamented its dark past and the pain only death could erase. "*A lost soul.* Sometimes, Rune, I think you're as barking as everyone else in this town. I swear I'm going to bed."

Not to the sea. To bed.

If only Adam had kept his promise…

4

ADAM STEPPED OUT OF the Live Oak Restaurant into the sunshine, scanned the distant olive grove at the top of the hill and saw no flash of binoculars or camera lens. Must have been a birder earlier, and whoever it was had found new aviary life to study.

As it turned out, he *was* being watched, but by Mrs. Hardling, and when a man lived in a hamlet this small, what else could he expect? The neighbors were nosy and eager for entertainment, and apparently he wasn't as boring as he had hoped.

On the run downhill, he spoke to every person he saw. This part of Big Sur was sparsely populated—he'd lived here five years, and he knew the names. But he made it a point never to discuss their kids or their dogs, whether the economy was recovering or failing, when the next storm would arrive...or where he was from, what he'd done in the past, why he had come to Gothic, why he stayed. Human nature being what it was, he knew his reticence made him all the more interesting. He just didn't care.

Bed. He really ought to go to bed.

Yet his brain yammered with hateful memories, the Pacific Ocean called his name, taunting him with the promise of treasure brought up from the deep by the wind and tide, and Rune's comments about his aura and finding what he needed from the ocean resonated with the songs of seabirds and the rhythm of the waves.

Damn it, Rune, why did you put the thought into my head?

Except Rune hadn't put the thought into his head. The Pacific called to Adam, endlessly, persistently, and sooner or later Adam would return forever to the depths. He was, after all, the lost soul Rune predicted. Why not return now?

Go to the beach. Look for another scrap of metal brought forth by Mother Ocean. Maybe, just maybe, fling himself in to drown.

At home, he donned his leather duster and his broad brimmed hat, got in his ATV and drove down the road to the Pacific Coast Highway.

The ocean and the mountains might be hereditary enemies, but they were united in their determination to destroy their common nemesis—California State Route 1. The Pacific Coast Highway was famous, or infamous, depending on who you were or how you looked at it. It snaked between LA and San Francisco through dry hills to the south, then sliced across spectacular cliffs that cartwheeled into the ocean.

The road was never more than two lanes with the occasional passing lane. Storms blasted wind and rain onto the land. The land gathered the rain in dry creek beds that swelled to destructive rivers and roared down to the sea, undermining the highway's bridges and leaving the way open for the waves to tear at concrete and asphalt.

Last spring, one storm after another had shut the highway to traffic. The California Department of Transportation had erected gates, closed them and spent months trying to get the road repaired. So far, no luck.

Phone in hand, Adam took photos of a new, deep gash in the pavement and sent them to the Caltrans head of repairs. When he got a single-word response, he winced.

He parked on the left lane of the highway above Nora Pocket Beach. Not another human soul was in sight. From the head of the path, he hiked down the cliff, skidding as sand shifted out from underfoot, and when he set foot on the white sand, he smelled sea, salt and loneliness. The sun shone, heating his shoulders and back, while the cold wind whistled off the water and slapped at his face, demanding attention.

Here after the last storm, he'd found the metal that he'd formed into last night's brutal art. But although high tide had covered the beach and ripped at the base of the cliff, today he saw nothing imbedded in the sand. He climbed to the top of the promontory that separated this beach from the next. That sand, too, was clear. The ocean giveth, the ocean taketh away. No man could predict the Pacific. No man should try.

Turning west, he surveyed the horizon, the restless water, the fast-moving clouds, the swooping seagulls whose flight mocked the earth. Weary, he walked out to the farthest point on the rocks, found a sunny spot and sat, arms propped up on his crooked knees, watching the waves break and retreat, break and retreat. The endlessness of the Pacific, the promise that it would remain restless and in motion and cleansing, hypnotized him. The ocean had given life before he arrived on this earth, and it would provide life when he was gone. When he was gone…

When he was gone, he wouldn't have to remember the people whose trust he had betrayed, who had paid with their lives for his stupidity. Mesmerized by the ocean's promise of forgetfulness, he stood and took a step toward the edge that plunged into the ocean's maw. He took another, and another—

What was that?

Something long and black rolled in on the swells. So not a fish or any other living thing. It was a long parcel of…plastic? It disappeared under the first line of breakers, then appeared again, battered by an insistent ocean. As the bundle moved, it undulated, probably a tangle of plastic ripped from the massive raft that polluted the Pacific.

He wavered, looked at the deadly plunge that enticed him, then back at the hateful toxic bomb.

Someone else would find it. Someone else would retrieve it. It was not his responsibility.

But in the meantime, a seabird would ingest it and die, a fish would nibble at it and turn into a stinking corpse on the beach, a curious child would find it and…

He shuddered. At one time, it had been his job to figure out every possible consequence for any given situation, and he knew only too well what could happen in this worst-case scenario.

The edge and the death it offered would be there tomorrow.

He made his way off the rocks, down to the sand.

The ocean rocked the black plastic, pulling the parcel back out into the deep, then shoving it farther onto shore to the spot where the foam gathered and the waves grew shallow. As he walked, a wave rolled the bundle lengthwise.

And a female arm flopped out.

5

SHIT!

Adam broke into a run. He splashed into the water, grabbed the arm—it was icy—and the plastic—it was a long rain poncho—and dragged the corpse all the way onto the beach. Because it had to be a corpse, didn't it?

Yet in the quest for life, he flipped the body out of the poncho and onto her back.

Among other things—seaweed, driftwood, a severed crab claw—there was an orange-and-white life preserver tangled in the plastic.

With the sun on her cold, colorless face, his feeble, unrecognized hope faded and he knew the truth. She was dead.

He pressed his fingers to her throat, to her artery, to confirm her heart did not beat. Then he saw them: the marks of a man's fingers ringing her neck.

She'd been dead before she went in the water. A young woman. A pretty woman. A violent crime… Adam kept his fingers over her artery, knowing he would feel nothing.

And he did not.

But he couldn't leave her down here for the seabirds to feed on and the ocean to retrieve. He had to get the body up to the road, onto his ATV and up to the village. From there, he could call the authorities and—

He looked up the cliff toward the road. What a helluva climb. But he wasn't a man to shirk his duty. Bending at the knees, he grasped the body around the waist, threw it over his shoulder and stood.

The woman explosively emptied her stomach down his back, gave a gasp, another, another, and when he flipped her back onto the sand, she opened her eyes, looked at him—and screamed.

She screamed as if all the screams in the world had been pent up inside her, as if she had given terror and horror a voice.

He jumped back and held up his hands in a *not going to touch you* gesture.

She rolled over onto her hands and knees, coughed up more seawater, took a long breath as if preparing to scream again… and slowly let the air out. She turned her head. The braid of her dark drenched hair hung over her shoulder. Her eyes… one was blue, one was brown.

Just out of reach, he knelt on the sand. "Can you speak?"

She stared as if she didn't understand. Maybe she didn't. Maybe she spoke another language. Maybe she'd suffered brain damage from lack of oxygen. Maybe—

"Yes," she said. "I can speak." She was hoarse. She put a hand up to her throat and held it there, cupping her injuries as if she didn't understand what had caused them.

"What's your name?" he asked.

She stared harder at him, and if she hadn't already spoken, he would again wonder if she spoke English at all. Keeping his voice pitched low, trying hard to present an unthreatening appearance, he asked again, "What's your name?"

Slowly, moving with the care of someone battered and bruised, she changed positions. She sat on the sand and concentrated on him, her hand still on her throat.

Again he began to ask.

"I don't know." Her unusually colored eyes were wide with confusion and terror.

He sat back on his heels.

Adam Ramsdell had found his first lost soul.

6

ADAM STOPPED THE ATV by his outdoor shower, the one he utilized to wash off the salt and sand of every beach visit. He set the brake and turned to the woman beside him.

The seat belt was the only thing holding her in the seat. The climb up the cliff had taken whatever strength she could summon and had left him drenched with sweat and cursing his luck. Not that he was unhappy about bringing a woman back to life, but with vomit down his back and in his shoes, and a trembling awareness that his own stamina was close to failing him, too… Well, as if he needed another reminder of what had happened five years ago.

At least this time, he had saved the woman.

"Let's get you in the shower. While you wash the worst of the ocean away, I'll call emergency medical. They'll transport you to the hospital—"

The woman came alive in a way he could never have imagined. She grabbed his arm, squeezed it, looked at him with wide, terrified eyes. "No. No. I beg you, no. He'll find me. He'll kill me. He's insane."

"Who'll find you?" Adam asked urgently.

"I don't know." She lifted a trembling hand to the bangs on her forehead. She pushed them aside, and he saw another bruise forming on her temple. "I don't know who he is. I only know—" She stared into the air as if she could see something he could not. "He was big. Like a football player. He choked me. I wanted to scream and he— I hit him."

"With something?" He couldn't imagine her fists would have done a lot of good, not if the guy was as big as she said. "With what?"

She squinted. "A pole. It was shiny and slippery in my hand. And it..." She squeezed Adam's arm again, harder. "I thought I hurt him. I was sure I... He came at me again. He was silhouetted against the light. I *couldn't* hurt him. Couldn't stop him. Nothing could hurt him." Fiercely she turned on Adam. "You can't let him have me."

He believed she was frightened, but now he wasn't so sure about her memory. Remembering just that much and no more, well—darned convenient. "I won't let him have you, but you're in bad shape. We need to have you checked out. Maybe if you had your memory..." He let that dangle.

"The doctors, the hospitals, they have to make records. He has power. He'll find me. This time he'll kill me."

"Is he your husband?"

"No?" She thought. She shook her head definitely. "No. But he is..."

"Powerful, you said. Rich?" It sounded like someone from up the coast in Carmel.

"I don't know. Yes, I think so. Please, I'm safe with you."

"How do you know that?" God, he was cynical.

She looked at him, and the clouds lifted from her eyes leaving them clear and unafraid. "You brought me back."

He didn't see what that had to do with it. "I don't keep women at my house." Actually, he didn't keep anyone at his house.

"Please let me stay here. I won't tell anyone where I am."

"You need medical attention for the beating the ocean gave you. The hypothermia." *The dying.* "Not to mention you don't know your own name. Possible concussion!"

"I'm Elle—" She froze, breathless.

He leaned forward. "Elle. That's good."

"There's more."

"Your last name. What's your last name?"

"It's not just Elle, it's—" She tried to speak, to force words out of her mouth. She trembled with the effort.

The strain she put on herself made him fear a stroke or seizure. "Come on." He placed a gentle hand on her shoulder. "Let's get you in the shower."

"Promise me you won't turn me over to the authorities." One tear rolled down her cheek. Then another.

He was such a sucker. "I won't. But how do you know you can trust me?"

"You didn't kill me when you found me."

"You've got low standards."

"No. But I am such a sucker."

The echo of his own thought shook him. "Why do you say that?"

She touched her throat. "I let the wrong person get close to me."

"That doesn't mean you're a sucker." Or maybe it did. "What do you remember?"

"It's like a series that reruns the same clip over and over." She lifted one hand to rub her temple, then winced when she encountered a bruise. "It's surreal. It was raining. Storming. The wind was shrieking in my ears."

"Yes. You *are* remembering, because last night's storm was violent." Full of voices calling him to join them in hell.

"The storm didn't matter. I was happy. Excited!"

For a moment, he thought she was going to say she was pregnant.

Instead, she said, "I had found it." Tears filled her eyes, as if that last memory of joy could not erase what followed.

"Found…what?"

"I don't know, but it was important, and *he'd* made it possible. I was almost hopping up and down in excitement. I told him, then I saw his face—"

Adam leaned forward. "You remember his face?"

"A broad face in shadow. A hulking silhouette. Broad shoulders, long arms and fists like an old boxer."

"Skin? Black or white or brown or—"

"White."

"Hair?"

"Brown? Dark and wet. Eyes that glinted in the darkness, like a jaguar on the prowl. Rain slapped my face. Lights swayed and swung."

"Where were you?"

She frowned intently, looked around as if the answer was outside herself, then shook her head. "I don't know."

He thought she was tired of saying that. "Go on. Tell me what you do remember. Tell me about him."

"He turned toward the light. I saw his expression, and I realized he was so angry. I was confused. Why would he be angry?" A tear slid down her cheek. "His big hands reached for me, but I didn't move. Stupid, I know. But no one has ever hurt me."

Adam noted that she knew that.

"Of all people, I never thought he would… He wrapped his hands around my throat. For a split second, I didn't realize how much trouble I was in. Then…then I tried to scream." She gasped as if she needed oxygen. "I pulled at him. Shoved him. I couldn't breathe! Everything was rolling, lights were sliding and shaking." She talked faster and faster. "Starbursts exploded behind my eyes, and I think I lost consciousness—"

It took a moment before he realized she was finished. "How did you get into the ocean?"

"I don't know."

He remembered his first impression, that she'd been dead when she was thrown in. But that wasn't possible. After so many hours, she couldn't return from the dead. "What you described was an unprovoked assault."

"I was stupid. I know better. Always listen to your instincts."

"Yes." He knew that all too well. "We all have moments of stupidity that we regret."

"I don't want regrets. I don't want to be afraid!" In a lower tone, she added, "I don't know if I can walk."

"Let's get some more water in you." He passed her his canteen.

She sipped, and sipped again.

"Can you eat something?" He unwrapped and offered one of the energy bars he carried in the ATV.

She tried to break off a piece. Her hands shook too much.

He broke it for her. It was painful to watch as she chewed and swallowed. And swallowed again as if the swelling in her throat made it all too difficult.

The bruises on her throat were getting darker, more pronounced. Her eyes were more haunted, more afraid. She looked at the wooden shower structure with both longing and fear. "I want… I need to wash. I'm crusty with salt, and

I want… I want to be clean. I want to clean away the night." Her voice wobbled.

"I'll help you. Come on." He slid out of the seat. "I'll help you shower." He thought she might sensibly refuse.

Instead she waited for him to come around and lift her out.

When she put her weight on her feet, she sagged, then straightened. She leaned on him, pushed herself off the ATV and staggered like a drunk.

He pulled her arm over his shoulder and half carried, half dragged her toward the shower.

He owned an acre adjacent to the highway. His four-room house was old, square and tiny. One small bedroom, one cramped bath, a miniature kitchen and a living area large enough for a love seat, a recliner, an end table and a TV he seldom used. Years of salt and wind and rain had given the house that sad, slumped look, like an old woman who remembered better times.

His workshop was new. He'd created a flat space inside a retaining wall and built a garagelike structure, with high ceilings, two large doors, one on each side to let the breeze through, room for his tools, a well-protected kiln—fire was always a terrifying concern in Big Sur—and a small loft with a bed and bath for those times when he drove himself too hard and needed a place to collapse.

Adjacent to the shop, the outdoor shower was enclosed in rough cedar. A toilet and sink were in a separate enclosure, and to make it all work to the satisfaction of the California environmental inspectors, he'd been forced to spend a fortune on a pump to carry the waste up the hill to the Gothic sewage station.

It was worth it: he was self-sufficient here, and he lived days and days without seeing anyone. And now he had somewhere for Elle to clean up.

He helped her up the steps and into the shower stall.

The outer cedar boards fit together like a fence, tight in spots but with long, narrow gaps. The floor was a fiberglass shell. The ceiling was the sky. And right now the sun shone into the stall with cheerful indifference to her trauma.

He leaned her against the wall, turned the shower on, waited until the instant hot-water heater kicked in, then stood with his back under the water to wash away the vomit, and he studied her.

Her face and arms looked as if every piece of driftwood in the ocean had taken the opportunity to beat on her. Or maybe the guy who'd throttled her had also been free with his fists. She wore jeans, a T-shirt, hoodie, boat shoes. He wished that guaranteed she'd been aboard a boat. But her clothes were the kind of clothes any sensible woman would wear outside in a storm. "Can you wash yourself?" he asked.

She opened her eyes, and sighed and straightened away from the wall…and sank down on her knees.

"Okay." He didn't want to do this, but he didn't see a choice. "We're going to have to take off your clothes." He expected to hear her choke out an emphatic *no*.

She nodded.

Well, hell.

He knelt beside her, pulled off her shoes and unzipped her jeans.

She rolled back on the floor, lifted her hips and inched her damp, salty jeans off her hips. She did not remove her panties.

He was more relieved than he wanted to admit. "We'll shampoo your hair first."

She sat up and bent her head, waiting for him without protest.

He loosened her braid, washed gently, barely touching the spots on her scalp that were raw and torn.

She winced anyway.

He removed the handheld shower nozzle from its hook and rinsed, then gathered a washcloth and his bar of unscented soap. "Now we'll, um..."

Slowly, creakily, she removed her T-shirt.

She wasn't wearing a bra.

He closed his eyes, trying to unsee the girls, then opened his eyes again and went to work washing her back, her arms, her feet, her legs... This injured woman, this lost soul had come into his care, and lascivious thoughts seemed the ultimate in selfish and off-color. Was this his punishment for withdrawing from the human race? He couldn't express his relief when she took the cloth and soap and said, "I'll do the rest."

"I'll find you clean clothes." He gave her the handheld, took her clothes and dashed out to avoid watching her wash...more.

He stopped halfway between the shower and the house and scanned the horizon. He couldn't forget this morning's uneasy sense of being observed. A man with his history did well to always be constantly vigilant. Elle's appearance in his life reminded him that he paid the price for failing to protect himself, but when he had vowed to care for another and failed, the sin, the guilt and the sorrow stained his soul forever.

He would not fail again.

7

ELLE DIDN'T SO MUCH go to bed as collapse onto the bed, asleep.

Adam stood and stared down at her morosely. His whole day—breakfast, the beach, discovering her body, seeing her revive, helping her up the cliff, that shower, dressing her in one of his old T-shirts and boxers, feeding her sips of broth… All of it had taken hours. Hours and hours, which had been exhausting to a man who hadn't slept the night before.

Now it was nine in the evening, she was unconscious in his California queen bed, and he was doomed to find whatever sleep he could on the diminutive love seat in his miniature living room.

But not yet. First he needed to establish her identity, where she came from and if someone was looking for her. He left the door open to allow him to hear her if she stirred. He took her pile of clothes and put them in the compact washing machine on his back porch. Her T-shirt gave him pause. The print across the chest declared *Machu Picchu Rocks*.

What could he deduce from that? That she'd been to Peru, eight thousand feet up in the Andes, and visited the Incan citadel, Machu Picchu? Or (more likely) that someone she knew had visited Machu Picchu and brought her a T-shirt?

He headed into the living room and to the compact desk where he'd set up his computer and monitor. He got online and typed in *Missing persons, Monterey and Carmel.* Of course, there were lost persons, but no one matched Elle's photo or description. He moved south, searching in Santa Barbara and—

From the bedroom, a low moan started, a sound so unearthly that for a moment he couldn't figure out what it was. It built, then he knew and bolted toward the bedroom in time to see her sit up and release a full-bodied scream.

The scream went on and on.

He didn't know what to do. He had experience with physical emergencies, but this... Her eyes saw him, silhouetted against the light. They widened in terror, she pushed with her hands as if to force him away. The scream became more intense, louder, of a soul in fear and anguish.

Perhaps it was the wrong thing to do, but he flipped on the overhead.

He saw the moment she snapped awake out of her nightmare. She collapsed back against the headboard, bumped her skull and moaned, "I thought you were him." Her voice rasped from the bruising on her throat and probably from the force of the scream.

In a low, reassuring voice, he said, "No. I'm not him. You're safe."

She started crying painful, wrenching sobs and tears.

He moved toward her, holding his hands palms up where she could see them. He made shushing noises, the way people did with a baby, and offered her a box of tissues. She didn't take one or two, she took the whole box. "I'm okay," she kept saying. "I'm okay."

Oh, definitely. "You need water." He picked up the water bottle he'd left at her bedside and offered it.

She took it and fought to stop crying so she could drink. She drank sips of water, looked at him with eyes drooping. "Thank you."

"Who is he?" Adam asked.

She froze, staring. She paled, and the bruises burned purple and black against her skin. She trembled, as did her voice. "He's coming at me…out of the darkness. Tall. Eyes glinting. His big fists…they're reaching for me. He has me!" Her voice rose to a shriek. "I can't breathe! I can't scream!"

He sat on the bed, grasped her hands. "Shh. Shh. Elle, you're not there. You're with me."

Her hands jerked in his. She didn't seem to hear him. "I can't see. Nothing but explosions of light. I'm dying. Dying…"

"You're with me. Stay with me." At last, his urgency seemed to reach her.

Her gaze returned to his. She saw him. She nodded, slid sideways and just like that, she was asleep.

He caught the bottle as it tipped. He put it and the tissues on the bedside table and eased her back onto the mattress.

Right. Neither of them had slept last night. He was starting to think his chances of sleeping tonight didn't look promising, either. When he thought of how she'd fought the storm, the cold, the waves, he was in awe of her stamina—even if she was dead when she hit the beach.

He heard the beep-beep-beep of the washer, went out to the porch and put her clothes into the dryer, then returned to the computer and his search for *Missing persons, Santa Barbara and vicinity.*

Nothing.

He widened the search to Coastal California.

This time, when the moan began, he was on his feet and moving fast. "Elle," he called, "Elle!"

She was faster with the scream, too. By the time he flipped on the overhead, she was up and shrieking like a soul clutched tightly in a monster's claws. That pale face marked by bruises, those wide, staring eyes, that hopeless terror...

This time Adam touched her shoulder.

She smacked at him, a good solid fist thump on his forearm.

Then she was awake. She stopped screaming, thank God, but she was breathing hard, staring at him, haunted, disillusioned, broken. Like him.

"I'm okay," she said.

"You don't have to say it if you're not."

"I'm okay as long as I'm awake. But I can't..." She started to droop again. "Each time I go to sleep, he comes at me again."

"You're dreaming." He didn't believe that. She was reliving. He knew. He understood. The monsters came at night for him, too, and when they captured him, sleep was nothing but a desperate hope.

"I want to scream, *want to*, but he chokes me, and the screams build up inside, and then it all comes out, and I'm not there anymore. I'm in the dark alone and... I'm so afraid."

"I know." He kept his hand on her shoulder.

"Would you stay with me? Sit here for a while? Until I go to sleep." With that, she fell asleep.

He figured he'd better sit a little longer. He pulled his book out of the bedside drawer, a well-worn copy of *Good Omens*, and read a couple of chapters while keeping his hand on her shoulder. But the search for a missing person waited, so when she seemed to be peacefully sleeping, he lifted his hand and tiptoed away. This time, he did not turn off the light.

He seated himself at the desk, although he didn't pull his chair in, and searched for persons missing from vessels offshore.

Nothing.

He supposed this figured. Some guy had choked Elle almost to death, flung her into the water and was satisfied she was dead. Probably not a husband. A spouse would report her missing in case her body washed up on shore and give some bullshit reason she had fingerprints on her throat. But if it was a random guy, a date or an unlucky (for her) encounter with someone who enjoyed inflicting pain and violence on another person, no report would be filed.

Maybe she'd run into a serial killer.

If only she could tell him who she was.

Maybe she didn't want to. Victims were embarrassed by the violence inflicted on them.

He heard her stir. He leaped up and ran into the bedroom.

Not soon enough. The scream bubbled up in her, ear-piercing and anguished. She saw him, woke, tried to stop, did stop and started sobbing while saying, "I'm okay, I'm okay."

"No, you're not." He was almost sure that none of his neighbors lived within earshot, but if this continued, someone would hear Elle's anguish and come to investigate. He sat next to her, stroked her head while she cried.

With surprising strength, she gripped his forearm in both hands. "Tall. Strong. Coming after me out of the darkness. Why does he hurt me? Why?"

"Some people, some men…they're cruel and…" He was taking her question literally when in fact he didn't know the answer. "Do you remember the name of your attacker?"

"I don't even remember his looks." She reached for the tissues and blew her nose. "I'm sorry. I can't believe this is me. Afraid like this. Consumed by this terror, not able to escape…" Her gaze strayed to the window, to the darkness that stretched forever.

He stood, fetched the trash can, offered it to her. "I can't sit here with you. I'm tired. As tired as you. Do you want me to lie down with you?"

She tossed her tissues and nodded, big-eyed and teary.

"I can sleep on the outside of the blankets—" although the nights got cold this time of year "—and be here to wake you before you scream."

"You can get under the covers." She scooted over and lifted the blankets. "We're both exhausted. And please, I want you to hold me."

Five years he'd been alone, deliberately alone, paying penance for his mistakes, and now in a single day he'd bathed a young woman who wanted him to sleep with her. Nothing more, just sleep. Sturdily he told himself she was right, that they were both too worn out to entertain so much as a thought of anything… Yet today, he'd entertained a striped circus tent of thoughts.

He eased onto the mattress. He was so tired, uncurbed instinctive reactions leaked through his usual controls. He thought longingly of that time earlier today when he'd been unhappily alone, dealing with his own problems… Okay, not dealing. Thinking of ending his troubles with a permanent dip into the Pacific Ocean.

"You can take off your pants," she said.

But surely that was better than *this*. This torture involving an attractive woman who had washed up on the beach and dragged him into a painful semblance of life… "No."

"At least your belt."

He thought about that. Of necessity, they would be close, and yes, maybe his belt and its buckle would be touching her person. He removed and coiled it and placed it neatly on the nightstand.

Still she held the blankets up, waiting for him, her eyes anxious.

She wanted him in that bed with her. She thought human contact would keep the terrors away.

He hoped to hell she was right—about her terrors and his—and climbed in. He rested on his back, his arms outside the covers.

She reached for his wrist and tugged, brought him onto his side and placed his arm around her waist, spooned her.

This night was one torment after another. He might as well bid slumber farewell.

Then, unexpectedly, he fell into the dark, warm depths of sleep.

8

Aboard the Research Vessel Arcturus.
Off the Central California Coast.

"WHAT'S THE HELICOPTER DOING here?" DeAnna stepped out into the morning sun and watched it spill onto the deck of the *Arcturus*.

Liam whipped around to face her. "Did you not hear what happened?"

"When?"

"Last night!"

"No. Those rough seas… I don't know how you guys drink and party when it's that rough. I was downstairs tossing my cookies."

"We've got a disaster on our hands." Liam's face was grim. "Last night around nine, Stephen disappeared from the party."

"Stephen Penderghast?"

"Yes, Penderghast!"

EMTs leaped out of the helicopter with a stretcher. Someone in the dining room was waving them in the door. The crew ran into the dim depths.

DeAnna leaned forward. "Tell me."

Because Stephen Penderghast was the man who funded this research vessel. The hundred-and-sixty-meter *Arcturus* carried sixty scientists, interns and students who studied, among other things, marine biology, undersea currents, meteorology and, because of the lack of light pollution on the high seas, astronomy. The vessel supported a removable lab van, multibeam sonar, a subbottom profiler (subject to much humor among the younger researchers) and an excellent telepresence that brought in land-bound researchers. The accommodations were luxurious and included a gym and cruise-ship-quality mess hall. All this, and the only thing they had to do was keep Stephen Penderghast up-to-date on developments in their fields.

Scientists no longer got to be nerdy, pocket-protector-wearing, unsociable lab masters. To be on this ship, they had to present Stephen with explanations about how their research would add to the base of knowledge and forward the progress of humanity. He would check up on them, too, requiring face-to-face meetings to ask them questions and listen closely to the answers.

What amazed the researchers was how much from every field he understood, how well he put them at ease and how he never took advantage of his power.

"He'd been gone about a half hour when Lily decided to call it quits. When she came back in, she was sopping wet, sobbing and carrying on, and we couldn't understand her. Then we didn't believe what she was saying."

"You guys are such jackasses," DeAnna said contemptuously.

"You know she gets hysterical about nothing."

"Finding the rubber rat you planted in her desk is *not* nothing."

People were appearing on deck, gathering in small groups, talking anxiously.

"Yeah, well..." Liam moved his shoulders as if they were tight. "Miller from Marine Studies went out to check."

"Check on what?"

"On *Stephen*. He was unconscious on the deck. The waves were crashing over the rails." Liam didn't seem to notice DeAnna had turned pale. "Miller touched Stephen, but he was cold, and Miller realized the stain on the deck was blood. The rain kept washing it away, so he turned him over. Stephen had been stabbed in the back."

DeAnna gasped and put her hand to her mouth.

"Miller rushed into the party and announced Stephen was dead."

She could only imagine the uproar that created.

"Someone got smart and called the doctor. Who was drunk in his cabin."

"Figures." The doctor was the only incompetent on the ship.

"He staggered up on deck and said Stephen wasn't dead and for us to move him inside."

"No kidding!" That seemed obvious to DeAnna.

Defensively, Liam said, "We were afraid of internal injuries."

"Sounds like he *had* to have internal injuries. Was he in shock?" DeAnna might get seasick, but she knew a few things about first aid from Girl Scouts and some courses before she'd come onboard.

"Yes. We carried him into the mess and placed him on a table. He was waxy white. I thought he was dead for sure." At the memory, Liam looked ill. "We covered him in blankets. The doctor examined the wound, and he said it looked like he'd been shot with an arrow, then it had been torn out."

"Does someone have arrows on the ship?" DeAnna doubted that.

"Nope, but you know Gunner from Operations? He came in carrying a boathook. It had come loose from the wall, and he said he guessed Stephen had tripped and fallen on it."

"Huh." DeAnna doubted that even more.

Liam nodded. "I agree. Sounds lame. But who would hurt Stephen?"

"You're right." Yet she was troubled. Was somebody on-board disturbed enough to try to kill Penderghast? Without him, this ship might never sail again.

The EMTs appeared. Stephen was strapped to a wheeled stretcher. IV lines ran from a bottle into his arm. Oxygen tubes were taped to his pale face. The little DeAnna could see convinced her it would take a miracle to save him. Yet, his eyes were open and alert.

Liam went right to the heart of the matter. "If he dies, what happens to the funding for this ship? I'm in the middle of my weather-influenced current changes study, and to stop now before I have results—"

"Oh, shut up."

"Like you're not worried about your undersea geologic features."

She was, of course. But to talk like that when a man could be dying… How crass. "I'd suggest that you pray that Stephen lives."

"I'm a scientist. I don't believe in prayer."

"I'm a scientist, too. You have a better suggestion?" Turning on her heel, she headed for the chapel on deck two.

Liam joined her.

9

ELLE WOKE TO BRIGHT sunshine shining into the east-facing bedroom windows in Adam's house. She didn't remember much before she'd landed on the beach: nothing but cold saltwater, cold shrieking wind, cold brutal waves and cold dark panic.

But she remembered the last twenty-four hours perfectly.

Right now, she was alive and snuggled up to Adam Ramsdell's back and glad to be there. He was strong and capable of protecting her, and he had helped her with a shower and slept all night with her without making any moves. She had somehow landed in the right place.

Now to find her way back to her old place, her other place. All she had to do was recover her memory, discover who had assaulted her and why, serve justice on that dark threat that made her want to curl up and hide and…

No. She would not curl up and hide. The nightmares would not overcome her, and the man who had killed her would pay for his crime. She would see to it. In the bright warmth of daylight, she believed anything was possible.

She had to pee, so she rolled onto her back. She planned to sit up, but holy hell, the mere act of rolling hurt. The side she rolled on, the back she rolled to, the ribs she breathed with, the hands she clenched against the pain, her head… She lifted one hand, a motion that made her wince and touched her forehead. "Wow," she said out loud.

Adam sat up, turned to put his feet on the floor and looked at her. Either he had woken instantly or he'd been lying there awake, waiting for her to move.

"Something hit you hard," he said. "You've got a knot that's purple and a black eye that's—"

"Black?"

He didn't smile. His mouth did quirk. "Purple. Today you sound less—"

"Manic?"

"Scared."

She noted he could be tactful. "I'm alive, and I slept well. Reasons for optimism."

"Do you remember when I came to sleep with you?"

"I was having a nightmare." She took a hard breath. Which hurt her ribs. "The man. He had me by the throat. I couldn't scream." The words made the nightmare real. Panic began to build in her veins.

Adam's voice was calm, instructional. "You did scream. You screamed loudly. More than once. Scared the hell out of me, and I'm surprised the neighbors didn't come to investigate."

She squinted, reaching for yesterday's memories. "When you brought me here, I wasn't fully functioning, but I don't remember neighbors."

"I have neighbors. Just not close. Still, you were…vocal."

"I know. I'm sorry. I have to use the bathroom." With

painful motions, she lifted herself onto her elbows. "It's of the utmost urgency."

He stood, leaned over her, slid his arm under her shoulders and eased her into a sitting position while she whimpered a low, continuous moan. In between the stabs of pain, the muscle aches and the increasing need to go, she noted that Adam Ramsdell wore a T-shirt that fit nicely over broad shoulders and a pair of stretchy midcalf exercise shorts that fit nicely over muscular thighs.

The T-shirt must be a long fit, because she couldn't eyeball the good stuff.

While his head was bent to hers, she took a moment to note that he shaved his head, and the stubble was blond with hints of red. Every bit of skin she could see was tanned, or maybe a Viking ancestor had roamed into the Mediterranean seeking more than loot. Also, he smelled good. He used an unscented soap, so that scent was pure Adam Ramsdell. Nice. Very nice.

Somehow, she was now on her feet beside the bed, no longer whimpering, but still far too smashed up to be thinking lascivious thoughts... Yet here she was.

He looked into her face. "You're smiling."

"I'm not quite dead yet." She hobbled toward the door.

Gently he turned her toward the other, narrower door. "You'll find your jeans and underwear on the hook, and one of my button-up shirts."

She kept moving, this time in the right direction. "Did my T-shirt not survive the ocean?"

"It did. But a button-up shirt will hide the marks on your neck. You look rough enough without everyone in Gothic knowing you were throttled."

"When will I see everyone in Gothic?"

"Let's discuss that at breakfast."

"Good idea." Her gotta-go situation was desperate.

He said, "I don't have any women's bras. Sorry."

Now over her shoulder, she shot him a smile. "I don't really need a bra, anyway."

For one second, his gaze flashed toward her. "I know."

Right. He did know. In the strangeness of the morning, she'd lost track of last night's communal shower. But he didn't sound or look at all interested.

Hm.

She managed to shut the bathroom door behind her, take care of her immediate needs, look at herself in the tiny old silvered mirror and shudder at the sight. She dressed in his shirt and her jeans, came out and followed the sounds and the smells to the kitchen, where she found ham, toast, boiling eggs, orange juice, sliced peaches and percolating coffee.

How long had she been in that bathroom?

Probably a long time. She was moving slowly...

"Sit down. Drink your juice. Once you eat, you can have a pain reliever."

"First, let me..." She hobbled over to the kitchen sink and looked out the front window. The house faced west into the waving grasses, a few twisted cypress trees and, down over the edge of the hill, the eternal blue of the ocean and sky. Whatever had happened yesterday was past; here she could faintly hear the sea and again marvel at its beauty. "The Pacific is so primal," she whispered.

From beside her, he said, "The sea promises much, and in its own way, it gives what it promises."

She couldn't quite decide what he meant, and he stared with such concentration at the horizon he seemed to have forgotten her. Until he looked at her, his eyes alert. "Ready for breakfast?"

She shambled back to the table and eased herself into an old straight-backed wooden chair. "The bruises are one thing, but all my joints and muscles hurt. Why do I feel as if I have the flu?"

"Hypothermia. Recovery is always fraught—and sometimes includes loss of memory." The timer went off, and he fished the eggs out of the pan and rinsed them under cold water. "I looked it up. In your case, add the trauma of being strangled, and it's not surprising you're suffering from amnesia. I had hoped you'd remember more this morning."

"I have. I know I'm a scientist."

He turned away from the counter and stared. "How do you know that?"

"Because I know no matter what my feelings, it's illogical to possess the rock-solid belief that the man who tried to kill me…is invulnerable."

He flipped the ham onto a plate, piled toast on top, and brought it to the table. "Feelings are feelings. They deserve respect, too." He seemed to doubt her claim to the title of scientist.

"Sure about the feelings. But I know stuff. About ocean currents, rock formations, how caves are formed. Archaeology. Particularly—" she wrinkled her brow as she thought "—archaeology in the Andes."

Gently, he pointed out, "Those subjects are popular with lay people, too."

"Scoff if you want. Science is bred into me." She wanted to convince him, but without her memories, how? "Anyway, I'm hungry."

"The eggs are soft-boiled. Do you need me to open one for you?"

She shot him a withering look, took an egg, took her knife, slashed the top off and spread the golden inner goodness on her toast. "What's the plan for the day?" The ham was thick and salty, the peaches were perfect, ripe and sweet and golden, and the food filled the emptiness in her belly.

"We're going to take you to the doctor."

"Kicking and screaming." Although from the little she knew of this man, she hoped he wouldn't deem that necessary.

"I know a fair amount about first aid." He opened three eggs with considerably less dash than she had. He spread his butter methodically, placed his bacon precisely. "I suspect you have at least one cracked rib."

She took a painful breath. "Me, too."

"There's nothing to be done. The old belief was to wrap them. The new belief is to leave them to heal."

"If wrapping will make them hurt less, let's wrap them." *Soon.*

"As you wish. In your judgment, do you have other broken bones?"

She rotated her shoulders, wiggled her toes, moved from side to side in her chair. "No. When I was a kid, I broke my wrist rollerblading." She looked at the wrist. "How do I remember that?"

"Traumatic event. They tend to imprint themselves on your consciousness." He pushed two blue pills toward her. "Take your pain relievers."

She did as she was told, then in a voice so bright, so perky, she could be from a teen sitcom, she said, "So no need for a doctor!"

"You're suffering from the remnants of hypothermia. Quite serious."

She started to argue.

He raised a hand to stop her. "Yes, if your appetite is anything to judge by, you're on your way to recovery." He seemed to choose his next words deliberately. "But unless you're lying, you still suffer from amnesia."

She put her fork down. "I'm not lying. I don't remember anything but… I'm Elle. Elle Something Something."

"Elle Marie?"

"No. But more than just Elle. I remember flashes of that man, coming at me again after I'd killed him. And every time I remember that…" Heart pounding, she stared at Adam and lived it again.

She screamed and screamed, but his hands gripped her throat in a killer's hold, and not a sound escaped.

The square of light from the window slid across the glistening floor as if it was slick. From inside the cabin the music throbbed, there was laughter and singing. She knew her friends and colleagues were in there, drinking, partying, interested in each other and not in her.

They couldn't hear her, silently screaming…dying.

Out here, the storm lashed the two struggling figures with rain and wind.

He held her against the wall, choking her with increasing force.

"Elle." Adam knelt beside her, his arm around her shoulders. "My God, Elle. When this happened, *where were you?*"

She breathed in with a gasp and realized she'd been holding her breath. "I don't know. If I could remember…"

"No wonder you were screaming. All those pent-up screams clamoring for release." Adam pressed her fingers. "I will not let him kill you."

"I know. I trust you. I know you'd do your best to keep me safe."

"I have locks on the doors. I have surveillance cameras. I have electronic sensors on the perimeter." He lifted his wrist and showed her his watch. "When someone crosses onto my land, I am warned. No one will surprise us."

He did allay her fears, but why would someone who lived

in such a lonely spot take such precautions? Did something or someone threaten him? Who haunted Adam's nightmares?

"I am going to take you to the doctor I used when I was injured and needed to be put together long enough to get to a hospital. Dr. Brocklebank is sensible and trustworthy, and he's not required to report your case to anyone except a ewe."

"A *you*?" she repeated cautiously.

"A female sheep." He was, she realized, being funny. Or at least...funny for him. "Dr. Brocklebank is the area veterinarian. He deals with all kinds of animals—sheep, cows, hamsters, dogs, cats. Whatever ranchers raise and people keep as pets. I'd like his opinion about that bump on your head and your amnesia."

"Okay. We'll risk that." She turned her hand under his and pressed his fingers in return. "Thank you so much. You never signed up for this." She meant it with all her heart.

"When you live in the City of Lost Souls, you take what life excretes."

Wow. After being choked, drowned and now basically called a big ol' pile of poo, she felt special. Maybe she didn't know her full name, and maybe she didn't know her background, but she did know some things about the bedrock of her nature: she was a fighter, a survivor, and somehow she would get to the bottom of who tried to kill her, where she came from, and what was going on with Adam Ramsdell and his buttoned-up version of reality.

After all, she was a scientist. She knew how to ask the right questions.

10

“CITY OF LOST SOULS? Calling it a city is a bit of a stretch, wouldn’t you say?” Elle observed.

“I’m not the one who named it. And yes.” Adam drove his ATV through Gothic, up the main street with its seven curves, past Ye Olde Antique Shop, featuring *the finest junk in Gothic*, past Mrs. Santa’s Gifts and Tea Shop, past the Hair on Your Chest Coffee Shop and Firm Buns Bakery. And past what seemed like every person in town standing on the street, staring, mouths open.

“Everybody’s staring,” she observed. “Don’t you ever have company?”

“No.”

“Relatives? Friends?”

“No.”

“Okay, then.”

She was looking at him, he could tell.

He didn’t look back.

“Do you not like these people?”

"Like them? I suppose. Why?"

"You're not exactly smiling and waving."

No, he was not. If he nodded to one, they would all shout out a greeting and want him to stop and introduce the woman at his side, and he didn't want to discuss who she was (he didn't know) or where she'd come from (he didn't know) or whether or not she was his girlfriend/wife/sister (that at least he knew—no, no and no).

They took one of the hairpin turns, and Elle saw the Tower and pointed, although it was more of a flick of her finger than a full-fledged gesture. "What's that thing? Dracula's castle up on the hill?"

He was more than glad to change the subject. "That's the home of Angelica Lindholm. Ancestral home, actually."

"I'm not familiar with the name. Should I be?"

"Most people seem to be. Angelica is a personality. Online, television, magazine, lecture, you name it."

"She sounds busy. Is she popular?"

Remembering how intensely Mr. Kulshan disliked Angelica Lindholm, Adam said, "That's one way of putting it. She's well-known, at least. Also, she owns a good part of Gothic."

"*Owns* it?" Elle looked from side to side as they passed Runs with Scissors Needlework and Quilting and on the opposite side of the street the Encore! Vintage Clothing Shop (motto: Not responsible for Haunted or Possessed Items) in what looked like a glamorous former movie theater.

"Angelica Lindholm owns and runs the General Store. That's a pet project of hers. She stocks it with her clothing line, her organic health food, her make-at-home meals—which are good, by the way." He'd eaten them many times when he couldn't leave his shop because the cruel madness of creation took him and he had to reveal his past in a sharp-edged piece of art that spoke of death. "She owns both gift shops in town but allows her managers to run those. She owns most of the commercial buildings and leases the space."

"So she leases to—" Elle read the signs "—Sadie and Hartley's Rock and Mineral Emporium and the Eat, Drink, Gossip Saloon?"

"Yes."

Mr. Kulshan was sitting in front of the rock shop, and he waved.

Moving with great care, she waved back. "Dracula's castle is her home? Her ancestral home? Is she the equivalent of British nobility?"

"Around here, she is. Fifth-generation Gothic resident. Or sixth. I've only heard the gossip." Overheard, actually; he knew what it was to be gossiped about, and he didn't indulge. "The Tower was modeled on a French château."

"Is it haunted?"

He hesitated.

Elle perked with the expected enthusiasm. "It is, isn't it?"

"At least one tragedy occurred up there. Ghosts are good for local businesses, especially in Gothic. What tragedy I'm not sure. I never cared enough to buy *Gothic, California: A Haven for Lost Souls.* That's the book they sell at the Gothic Historical Museum."

"The one down by the cemetery. We passed it first."

"Right. The only museum in town. The book was written by Freya Goodnight, who is none other than the same Freya who sells maps and books of local interest out of the museum's gift shop, guides the haunted twilight tours and owns the jeeps that give driving tours of Gothic and the vicinity."

"This is a happening place."

He glanced at Elle, thinking she had to be sarcastic, but no. She looked pleased and satisfied. "Adam, what do *you* do out here in the middle of nowhere?"

"Do?" Not a question he wanted to answer.

"For a living. Unless you're independently wealthy, you must do something to earn a living, and even in the case of riches, most people do *something* to keep themselves busy."

"I work with metals. For the most part, I create chain-mail armor and weapons for medieval reenactments and the active warrior-fantasy market."

"Wow. That's impressive." She sounded awed. "I can't imagine doing that kind of precision work. Does it keep you busy?"

"I have more work than I have time for. I also—" *Wait. No. Shut up.*

"You also?"

He didn't answer. He didn't look at her.

"No, no, no." She sounded exasperated. "You can't stop now. What activity would make you, a stoic guy, so uncomfortable you don't want to admit it?"

He still didn't answer. Surely she'd get the message.

"You *also* knit baby booties? You *also* translate French pornography? You *also* create art out of tin cans?"

Startled, he glanced sideways at her. How had she come so close?

"Really? This determinedly unfeeling guy is an artist?" She gestured at him, up and down. "You create art out of—"

He had to stop her. "Not tin cans. Out of scrap metal. Occasionally."

She rolled her hand to keep him going.

"Scrap metal that I find on the beach, a piece of iron from some old internal combustion engine someone dumped there. Or steel from an old shipwreck that the ocean deposits on the sand."

"The ocean burps up pieces of ships?" She sounded interested.

Okay, she was interested. In one short morning, he'd figured out she had a keen interest in, well, everything. Made her claim of being a scientist seem solid.

"The area off this coast has powerful crosscurrents, variances in ocean depth—for all I know, the kraken might lurk in those depths. But the ocean floor is littered with shipwrecks, old and new, and those powerful currents, helped sometimes by an earth tremor, can carry heavy objects to shore."

"Not just wood from the shipwrecks? Metal, too?"

"Most of the time there's nothing big. A manacle from a prison ship, or the frame of a porthole. Evocative pieces on their own. But more than once, I've retrieved parts of a hull, and I..." He should stop talking.

"Make art?" She was *so* interested.

"I listen until it speaks to me, then I shape it into what it asks to be." He shot her a humorous glance, the first humor she'd seen him display. "That is to say, I shine it up and sell it to someone so they can brag about their good taste."

He wasn't really being humorous. He meant what he first said about listening until the metal spoke, but he didn't like the earnestness of that so he tried to shift the mood. Something to remember. The man had a sensitive side that he hid with the care of a miser for his gold. And she wondered, was there anyone on earth who really knew Adam Ramsdell? Or was he as friendless and solitary as he seemed?

11

AS SOON AS ADAM drove past Gothic's last house, he pointed at a narrow paved road that turned off to the left, barricaded by an ornate iron gate topped by patinated copper finials. "That's the way to the Tower. Angelica Lindholm holds seminars there, and this time of the year, during the Gothic Spring Psychic Festival, she rents rooms to properly vetted tourists."

Elle took a quick, delighted breath. "There's a Spring Psychic Festival?"

Adam wished he'd thought before speaking. Twenty-four hours ago it wouldn't have mattered, but now he'd agreed to make an ass of himself pretending to be a knight.

"What happens at a psychic festival?"

"Pretty much what happens at every renaissance festival in the country."

"Fried churros, kissing wenches, puppet shows, jousting demonstrations?"

"Add palm readers, horoscopes, crystal-ball gazers, aura

readers, all led by Gothic's own fortune-teller, Madame Rune, and you've got the picture."

"How fun!" Elle clapped her hands, then glanced around as if the sound of her own enthusiasm startled her.

"That's one way to put it."

She slid down in the seat. "We're certainly exposed up here on the road, aren't we?"

He, too, glanced around and saw what she saw: below them, the vista of the ocean, grassy rolling hills dotted with live oaks, a mature olive grove that could provide cover and the road stretching before and behind them like an arrow pointing them out to a sinister observer. In town, she had had the sense of being among friends. Here, they were alone and, as she said, exposed.

He didn't make the mistake of telling her she was imagining trouble where none existed. His own uneasiness had been growing. Why? Had he subconsciously noted something ominous? Pulling over, he studied their surroundings. "I see no evidence of a watcher," he told her.

"Really? That's good, because for a minute, I forgot how scared I am, and I…should never, ever forget. I should be vigilant because…maybe that's why I was hurt. Because I wasn't paying attention." She shrank farther and farther down into the seat as if trying to make herself invisible.

After her pleasure in seeing Gothic, enjoying the sights and the people, Adam hated this return of fear in her. He tried to infuse his voice with comfort and warmth. "I'm here to be vigilant when you aren't." Did he succeed? No telling. Comfort and warmth wasn't his forte. He texted Dr. Brocklebank, then handed Elle his phone and started driving again. "That is who I am, and it would grieve me if that's who you became."

In a small voice, she said, "You're smart. Always being vigilant saves you from peril."

God. She made him feel, *live* the pain and sorrow all over again. "I wish that was true," he said and changed the subject before she could ask questions. She did that, he knew. "It's spring. That brings a burst of life in the form of lambs, kids, calves and colts. When Dr. Brocklebank pings me with his location, we'll find him in some barn or kennel where there'll be no possibility of trouble." A lie. There was always a possibility of trouble, but he wanted Elle to feel safe.

She did relax as she stared at the lump of black metal in her hand. "What is *this*?"

"It's my phone."

"You own a flip phone?" She flipped it open and closed. "Why don't you have a real phone?"

"A smartphone? They're too fragile."

"There's some tough ones." Under his gaze, Elle grew uncertain. "Aren't there?"

"I got a tough one. It broke. I need a military-grade phone that I can use to communicate in case of emergency, with a good keyboard, clear speaker, bright screen, and that's waterproof. Oh, and a camera. In an emergency, it takes decent photos. And I can text."

She looked at the traditional numerical keyboard.

"I use voice-to-text," he said.

"You don't seem like the kind of guy who would carry his phone with him everywhere. I would have thought you didn't need to be always connected."

"I like to be prepared."

"For what?"

"In case I find someone on the beach who needs emergency care."

"Yes, but you didn't call for help."

"You can't get cell service down on the beach." Adam opened up the ATV and headed up the highway toward the area ranches. The phone honked like a goose. "That's a text," he told her.

Elle flipped it open and consulted the screen. "The text is *Goat's Beard.*"

"It's the Beard family's operation, not far. They raise goats. Dr. Brocklebank is probably checking out the new arrivals."

"Baby goats." She smiled. "I love baby goats."

"Then, you'll have fun." He turned onto the Beard acreage, flush with spring-green grass and ancient oaks, and drove up the gravel road to the barn. He parked between Dr. Brocklebank and the wall of the barn, in the shade, protected from sight. Coming around, Adam offered Elle his arm. "Slowly," he cautioned.

"No kidding. I can barely move." She got out and leaned on him heavily.

Dr. Brocklebank stuck his head out of the barn. "Come in. Mama just delivered a healthy kid." He looked at them together, gave Elle a swift visual examination and said, "Oh, this is going to be good." He disappeared inside.

Dr. Brocklebank had brown hair, hazel eyes, a rotund upper body and stout, stubby legs. He was sensible, never spoke unless he had something to communicate, ate with the concentration of someone who seldom had time to finish a meal and liked animals better than people. The only advice he had ever given Adam was to get a dog who would teach him to socialize, and he had been unconcerned when Adam ignored him.

The barn smelled of animals and manure. Sun leaked through the spaces in the board walls and lit the swirls of straw and dust. The penned pregnant goats bleated, the penned baby goats romped, the male goats were nowhere to be seen, and Dr. Brocklebank knelt in a pen drying a shaky, damp black-and-brown kid with a towel while the mother urged her baby to feed. "Baby was early, and she's not sure if she can do what she needs to for it to survive."

Adam could almost see Elle's worries evaporate. She was instantly intent on the exhausted mama, the tentative baby. She leaned into the pen and said to the kid, "Life is pretty great when you get to know it. Give it a try."

God, Elle was cute.

In a damned swift hurry, Adam straightened his spine.

Not cute as in he liked her, wanted her, but cute like a wet goat kid.

Dr. Brocklebank finished wiping Baby and urged her toward her mother.

The kid nuzzled, found a teat and did what baby goats do.

"Makes you want to sing 'Circle of Life,' doesn't it?" the vet said to Adam.

"Sure."

"You don't know what I'm talking about, do you?"

"No."

"When you were a child, did nobody ever show you a Disney movie?"

"No."

"Your parents didn't believe in Disney?"

"My parents didn't believe in modern civilization."

"That explains a lot." The veterinarian offered his hand to Elle. "Young lady, I'm Dr. Fred Brocklebank. What happened to you?"

"Young man, you can't be much older than me." She wasn't snappish, exactly, but she wasn't going to be patronized.

Adam grinned, relaxed and propped his shoulder against a post.

Dr. Brocklebank laughed. "I look young. Most times, I feel old."

"What do you have to feel old about?" Now she didn't sound snappish at all. She sounded interested. Again. Always.

"The usual. I always wanted to be a doctor. Did my four years in college and got into a medical school, but the cost choked me so I decided to do the smart thing." Dr. Brocklebank sneered at his younger self. "I joined the military so I could earn the GI Bill. I was a medic in the Marines, did two tours in the Middle East, one of them on the fringes of that Syrian ethnic annihilation, and a third in Korea."

Adam had never heard any of this.

"That sounds awful." Elle examined Brocklebank as closely as he had her. "You must have been devastated."

"Every day. Every damned day." Brocklebank stepped out of the pen, but he didn't take his gaze off the suckling kid. "By the time I finished my stint, I was done with pain and death. I swore I wasn't going to stitch people up so they could be medevacked to a hospital where they died in agony or from blood loss or a lost limb. Instead I became a veterinarian, and now I deliver baby goats."

She touched his arm and smiled into his face. "That sounds like the perfect solution."

"Yes. Yes, it was." He cleared his throat, and when he spoke, he once again sounded like a concerned medical professional. "So I repeat, young lady, what happened to you?"

12

“OH. WHAT HAPPENED. I don’t know. I know it wasn’t as bad as a whole bunch of months spent in battle trying to put people back together, but I—” Elle’s voice caught for a moment, and she put her hand to her throat.

“Open your collar and show him,” Adam instructed.

Her fingers trembled so much Dr. Brocklebank stepped closer—Adam noted he didn’t crowd her—and opened the first two buttons. He spread the collar, and as the bruises were revealed, he muttered, “Bastard.”

“I don’t remember what happened, but I’m pretty bruised and battered.” She stepped away from him. “I think someone’s hunting me.”

“You *really* don’t remember?” He seemed to have his doubts.

That made Adam’s own doubts seem a little less callous, and for that Adam felt a profound relief.

Brocklebank continued. “As in, you got yourself into a risky situation, got hurt and you don’t want to admit it? Because I would never—”

"No! I don't even remember my whole name, and I want..." Once again, she was on the verge of tears. "I don't want to hurt in my body, I don't want to be afraid to drive up the road, and I don't want to glance around in my brain and see a shadowy shape lurking."

Dr. Brocklebank stepped into the pen filled with older, bleating, romping kids, picked out a wobbly-legged baby and handed it to Elle. "Hold this little guy. He needs some love."

Elle clutched the kid to her chest.

"Sit there." He pointed at a long, narrow box filled with feed.

She sank down and smiled tremulously at the baby nudging her face.

"Probably ought to feed that guy." The vet reached into a small refrigerator, found a full plastic bottle, warmed it in a microwave, topped it with a goat-sized nipple and handed it to Elle.

The kid didn't have to be persuaded. It latched onto the nipple and sucked and wiggled with delight, and Adam could see Elle's anxiety dissipate under the onslaught of baby-goat cuteness.

"Adam, do you want to feed one?" Brocklebank asked.

"No, I've had experience with goats and I...don't need more."

"A baby goat's not going to hurt you."

"Make no mistake, everything in this world has the capacity to hurt you."

"Right. When you care, that's true." The doctor examined the pregnant goats, looked over the kids and, when the bottle was empty, he came back and took it out of Elle's hand.

The kid had subsided into her lap, asleep with a full belly. For the first time since Adam had pulled her from the ocean, Elle was fully relaxed.

Brocklebank stepped back to stand with Adam. "Those are quite the marks on her neck. Fingerprint bruises."

"Yes."

"Why?"

"Don't know. Found her on the beach yesterday. I brought her to you because she doesn't remember her name, what happened to her, where she came from—comes from."

"Temporary amnesia. Sure, trauma. Makes sense."

Adam tried to find the right words, but that wasn't possible. "She had hypothermia. She died of hypothermia. Or she drowned. But she was dead."

"Died." Brocklebank slashed a look at Adam, then at Elle. "A strong word for someone who is holding a goat and cooing."

"I know how to take a pulse. She was facedown. I flipped her back on the sand—"

"Thumped her heart."

"No. She was cold and white. Dead. I threw her over my shoulder and knocked the seawater out of her, and she returned to life."

Brocklebank choked out a laugh. "Gothic, City of Lost Souls. Makes you believe, doesn't it?"

"No." Adam was firm. "But that death, that loss of oxygen, explains why she doesn't remember who she is. Nothing more than her first name, and she insists there's more to it than just Elle."

"She's got a hell of a bump on her forehead. I can't treat that. I can't treat her." Urgently, Brocklebank said, "She needs to see a doctor. A family physician. Someone with a diploma to treat, you know, humans."

"I know that. But she won't go. She's afraid of the man who tried to kill her. She's convinced he's powerful and could eliminate her, so—"

"So you came here for advice. Okay, here it is. Take her to Rune."

Adam reared back in disbelief. "Rune? Madame Rune? What's she going to do? Sell her a crystal?"

"Maybe. Sure. But back in the day, Rune was a hugely successful Hollywood psychiatrist."

Adam had trouble believing that Rune had ever been a hugely successful anything. "Why would a Hollywood psychiatrist live in Gothic?"

"Why do any of us live here?" The vet sounded tired and more than a little disillusioned. "What is here that heals the wounds, makes the pain tolerable, keeps us putting one foot in front of the other? We don't know, and we don't ask." He wiped his hand across an invisible blackboard. "Rune understands people, motivations, evasions. That's why she's such an intuitive psychic."

"That's not being psychic. That's paying attention."

Brocklebank shrugged. "Same difference."

Adam wanted to argue, but...maybe. Yeah. "Fine. I'll take Elle to Rune."

"Not right now, you won't." Dr. Brocklebank sounded amused.

Adam looked and couldn't believe what he saw. Somehow Elle had shifted the kid onto the box, curled up beside it and was fast asleep with the kid tucked into her arms. "Again? She's asleep again?"

"She got strangled, beat-up pretty good, and she's traumatized. She needs time to recover."

Adam burst out, "God, she's trouble!"

"What else do you have to do besides work alone in your shop making sharp, pointy weapons and disturbing art?" Brocklebank made Adam's work sound like pornography. "It won't hurt you to take care of someone for a while."

Adam didn't point out that Dr. Brocklebank worked alone most of the time, too. They had both taken responsibility for people and failed to save them. Loneliness was the price a person paid for surviving the world's horrors. "She didn't sleep well last night."

"Nightmares?"

"Yeah." Until he'd gone to bed with her. But he didn't say that. Brocklebank would draw the wrong conclusions.

In fact, after one trip through Gothic, he was pretty sure the entire town had already drawn the wrong conclusions.

His own conclusions were unformed. All he knew was that he hadn't enjoyed a good sleep for five years, and last night... he'd slept through all the hours of darkness. He didn't understand it. He figured sleeping with someone, anyone, would disturb him. And her, Elle... Even with all the bruises, she was pretty. When he lay down with her, he had been convinced he would doze at best, and every time she turned over or snored or, yes, screamed, he'd be awake. But he didn't remember a thing until this morning when he woke to sunlight and a woman's body pressed against his back. He racked it up to too many hours of wakefulness and a helluva exhausting day.

Not that that had ever mattered before...

"I suspect you've noticed the eyes," Brocklebank said.

"It's hard to miss one blue and one brown."

"That's a condition known as heterochromia iridum, fairly common in the animal world, a lot more unusual among humans. It is usually genetic and harmless but can also be an indicator of a physical problem."

"Possibly a result of strangulation?"

"Or hypothermia. Keep an eye on that, and if there's any change...keep an eye on it. God, what a pun." Brocklebank chuckled, shook his head and stepped into the pen of pregnant goats. "Anyway, get her to a physician if you observe a change in the color. As for the other—we all have nightmares, all of us who live through the carnage." He went back to work examining the weary, waiting mothers.

No. Adam rejected that for Elle. He didn't want her to suffer forever. She was kind. She was hopeful. She deserved better than a guy who'd tried to kill her, and she deserved better than Adam, a man who had broken apart, never to be healed.

"Trying to find balance between present life and past horrors takes a lot of work." Dr. Brocklebank glanced back at Adam. "You should attempt that sometime."

Adam didn't want to find balance. If he did, who would mourn his dead?

He settled down to wait for Elle to wake up.

13

STEPHEN PENDERGHAST HEARD THE hospital door swing open.

The light tap created by well-made shoes came closer and closer. They stopped beside his bed.

In a low voice, the doctor asked, "Are you the one he's been waiting for?"

Through the throbbing in his head, Stephen didn't hear the answer.

"Good," the doctor said, "because if I don't get him into surgery, he's going to die. The hook destroyed his kidney, he's bleeding internally and I don't know what other damage I'll find when I get in there. Hell, he's probably going to die, anyway. But his best chance is in speed. He's in agony, but he won't take morphine because he wants to talk to you. Find out what he wants." Footsteps moved away. Before the door closed again, the doctor spoke loudly and with irritation. "Let's get this show on the road. I am a busy man."

Of course that was the doctor's real concern. He was the

best, and he didn't have time to hang around. Except if he saved Stephen Penderghast's life, he would have fame and fortune.

Stephen opened his eyes a slit and saw the person he'd picked, when he was four years old, out of five candidates his wealthy father had purchased as possibilities for best friend. Short, thin, with black hair and swimmer's shoulders, Zsóke hid incredible skills beneath that unassuming guise. For forty-seven years, he and Zsóke had been master and servant. Demands had been made. Jobs had been done. Companionship and, when Stephen felt the need, sex had been provided. Now Stephen needed one more thing.

Possibly one last thing. He spoke softly, so softly his friend leaned over him. "The girl found it. Elladora Varela. She found it."

"Bad move on her part."

"She told me I'd been mistaken in my search."

"Stupid and asking for trouble."

Because no one ever told Stephen Penderghast he was wrong. Not if they knew what was good for them. "She told me what she found, and where."

A nod. "Very good. Stupid girl. She didn't know you'd kill her to claim the credit."

"I tried."

Eyes widened, then narrowed. "Tried… What? Tried to kill her? You tried, and she's still alive? I have trouble believing that."

"This time I failed, and she did this to me. To me!" The room spun, and Stephen stopped speaking to suck oxygen through the tubes in his nose.

"She was lucky." Zsóke sounded certain.

He remembered that silver pole in Elladora's hand, the

agony when she sank the hook into his back, his disbelief at her unexpected courage and at his own failure. "Yes. Lucky."

"But you are alive, and she was short, thin, trusting. She didn't know the real you. No one knows what you're capable of. No one knows the things you've done." Time and again, Zsóke had witnessed Stephen's ruthlessness. "How is it she's not dead?"

"She jumped overboard."

"Ah." Zsóke relaxed. "Then, she's dead."

"I want her body found. Her body—or her."

"If she went into the sea that far offshore, there's no way—"

"Find her."

Stephen knew his best friend wanted him to be logical. His friend wanted to talk about sharks and riptides and the impossibility of surviving in the Pacific in a raging storm. His friend wanted to point out that Elladora would be talking to the police or the coast guard, and if Stephen survived this surgery, he would spend the next weeks in a prison ward.

But Zsóke understood duty and vengeance and what was owed to Stephen. "Right. If she's alive, I'll find her."

"If she's alive," Stephen said as he shut his eyes, "kill her. Kill her slowly. Make her suffer." That he would relinquish the right to murder Elladora Varela was an admission he believed he would not survive.

"Of course. You'll go to surgery now?"

"Yes." For the first time, Stephen gave in to the blast of pain. The doctor might be right. Stephen might not survive.

But he'd made sure that Elladora would die with him.

14

THE NIGHTMARE PULLED ELLE into the depths, below the waves, below the light… If only she could scream…but the weight of the ocean crushed the breath from her lungs. She struggled, fighting for freedom…and woke with a baby goat tap-dancing on her shoulder, its tiny pointy hooves finding every bruise in the vicinity. Before she could react, the goat was lifted away, and she opened her eyes to see it wiggling in Adam's arms, stretching its skinny neck up to look into his eyes. He pressed its head to his chest, carried it to the pen and deposited it with the other kids. "It's feeding time." He indicated the schedule penned on the wall.

She sucked in oxygen—had she been holding her breath?—and with an aching difficulty, she rose to lean on her elbow. "Sorry. Did I sleep long?"

"An hour."

Her mouth felt like she'd been eating cobwebs. "What happened to Dr. Brocklebank?"

"He's got a colt up on Cabrillo's Dude Ranch that's not arriving as it should." Adam offered his hand. "Come on. We've got things to do."

"Go to the psychic?"

Adam didn't look surprised, exactly. More puzzled that distracting her with a baby goat hadn't deafened her to two men's robust voices.

She let him hoist her up. "I need to eat first." About that she was decisive. It wasn't merely the kids who were impatient for their meal. "There's that restaurant I saw on the way up here. The Oak?"

"The Live Oak." He didn't quite groan, but she got the impression he didn't wish to be seen in the restaurant. Or not be seen in public with her. She did look pretty rough. Or maybe he was broke. After all, she didn't know what chain metal, weapons and artwork earned. "We can go back to your house and make lunch," she added hastily.

He viewed her as if he knew what she was thinking. "We can go to the Live Oak." He herded her toward the ATV, helped her in, and stopped and looked around.

"What is it?" *What...is...it?* She scanned the area: the barn, the pen, then up at the hills.

"Nothing." He paused. "You know me. I'm wary."

Alarmed, she paid particular attention to the wide oaks that stood, their branches bowing to the ground. "Do you think it could be—"

"Your attempted murderer? How could he have found you? He choked you, he pushed you in the water, he left you to drown. He believes you're dead."

Adam looked so knowledgeable, and he made sense. She felt a lifting of anxiety within herself...and a lowering of fear for Adam. "You're right. But why would anybody hate you? You're great."

That brought his attention back to her. For the first time

since she'd regained consciousness on that beach, he smiled. "Great? That's not usually the term I hear about myself. But everyone who lives on this planet for long collects a few enemies and ill-wishers." He glanced around again. "No one is in sight. Perhaps what I sense is nothing but a hungry bobcat watching the kid barn."

"Oh, no!" She clutched her arms as if she was cradling the baby goat.

"Bobcats have to feed their young, too." He came around and got in the driver's seat. "Don't worry. The Beards keep close watch. Let's go back to town."

He may have dismissed his feeling, but the way down the hill was speedy and without the care he'd previously shown for her aches and pains.

She didn't complain. Her own fears were amplified by his unease.

He parked in a space on the side of the restaurant marked *For Customers of the Live Oak* and came around and helped her out.

As before, she leaned heavily on him. "Did you bring the painkillers?"

"I did."

"I would like some with my meal." Hand tucked in his arm, she shuffled around to the front of the restaurant.

Across the street stood Madame Rune's Psychic Readings and Bookshop with a door sign that said *We're away for an hour. Madame Rune predicts you'll come back soon!*

Halfway to the next curve, a three-story house had men, women and children on each balcony staring at them. She asked, "Doesn't anyone have anything to do in this town but gossip?"

"Everybody's got secrets here. Speculation passes the time." He glanced at her. "You're with me, which is unusual. You're obviously injured. Why? By whom? Am I protecting you? Or am I the one who hurt you?"

She snorted. "No one who knows you would believe that."

"No one knows me."

"I am sorry to hear that, for their sake."

"You make a lot of assumptions on twenty-four-hour acquaintance."

"Look." She turned on him fiercely, finger in his face, and winced. "In twenty-four hours, you found me and pulled me out of the ocean, dead, if what I heard you tell Dr. Brocklebank is true."

"Your hearing is extraordinary." He frowned as if trying to remember exactly what he'd said to the veterinarian.

"You dragged me up a cliff, bathed me, cared for me, let me sleep in your bed—"

"Shh!"

"—fed me and kept your word to me about the doctor. I've got a pretty good idea about your character."

"You shouldn't be so trusting."

"You shouldn't be so cynical."

"Right. We're attracting a bigger audience." Which was clearly abhorrent to him. "We'd better go in." He held the door for her.

Inside the restaurant was quiet and safe, without curious eyes watching Adam and Elle, and without that restless feeling of a nearby hostile presence.

Clarice Burbage sat at her table, head in her hand, tablet at her elbow, papers spread out in front of her, reading aloud in a low, intense mutter.

Mr. Kulshan sat at his table, head lolling on the back of his chair, napping. The click of the door woke him, and he sat up as if he'd been awake. He stared at Elle. "Who hurt that girl?" He looked directly at Adam.

Adam shook his head. "Not me."

Elle said, "Don't worry, sir. I'm recovering because of Adam."

"I knew it." Mr. Kulshan knocked his knuckles on the table. "He'd better take care of you." Leaning his head against the chair again, he went back to sleep.

Clarice observed Elle. "Ouch! No wonder people are talking," she said sympathetically and went back to studying her script.

Ludwig walked out of the kitchen, bristling with irritation, and snapped, "We're not open. Lunch is over. We seat for dinner in two hours."

"We'll go to the General Store." Adam helped Elle turn around. "They have a good section of takeout."

"Thank you, anyway." Elle smiled into Ludwig's grumpy Beethoven face. "Adam said the food is magnificent. I hope to eat here another time."

Grumpy Ludwig looked startled and smiled back. At least, one side of his mouth rose, so Adam counted it as a smile. "Wait! We can seat *you*." He went into the conference room and came out dragging a padded armchair. He placed it against the back wall at a four-person table. He pulled the side of the table away from the easy chair to allow Elle to seat herself without pain, and when Adam had helped her lower herself into the seat, Ludwig pushed the table close. From the wait station, he brought a white linen tablecloth and napkins, two small plates, a carafe of water and two glasses. "As always, Señor Alfonso will rise to the occasion. I'll consult with him and return with the details."

Adam seated himself next to Elle. Ludwig had always treated Adam as a favored customer. But this…this was a welcome!

The kitchen door swung open, and Señor Alfonso himself bustled out. Everything Ludwig was not, Señor Alfonso was:

effusive, balding, smiling. One shoe was untied, and a series of stainless-steel toothpicks decorated one lapel of his white chef's jacket. He held out his hands to Elle. *"Señorita! Bienvenida a mi restaurante!"*

"Gracias, señor. Estoy contenta y honrada."

Señor Alfonso's mouth dropped.

Adam was flabbergasted. He had spoken Spanish well before he settled in Gothic. Now he had little chance to practice, but he recognized Elle was fluent.

Where had she come from?

"You speak my language!" Señor Alfonso said. "With a delightful New World accent. Where did you learn?"

Beside him, Adam felt Elle tense. "In the New World, I suppose."

"South America, I think. What an honor to serve you today." In an obvious aside, Señor Alfonso added, "And you, of course, Mr. Ramsdell. Lunch has been consumed. Dinner is not yet prepared, but Ludwig—ah, here he comes. Ludwig is bringing you a selection of tapas. We start with a few cold small plates, *aceitunas* and *papas arrugadas con allioli.*"

On the table, Ludwig placed a small bowl of marinated olives and a plate of small potatoes with a creamy sauce.

"These are what we eat in the kitchen to give us strength. You like shrimp?"

Elle relaxed into her chair. "I love it."

"I will return to the kitchen and prepare *gambas y setas al ajillo.* The *setas*, the mushrooms, Ludwig himself gathered nearby. Spring! Local mushrooms! You will be delighted." Señor Alfonso hustled back into the kitchen, Ludwig trailing behind.

"If I had known speaking Spanish to him would result in tapas, I would have done it myself." Adam spooned olives and potatoes onto the plates, added a dab of creamy sauce to Elle's and pushed it toward her.

Elle dipped the potato in the sauce, took a bite and inhaled with delight. "So much garlic!"

Adam tried it, too. "It's a good thing we're not—" He stopped. *Don't say* kissing.

Clarice saved him. She stepped to the table and, as before, asked, "May I?"

"Of course!" Elle indicated the chair opposite. "You're Clarice Burbage, aren't you? I'm Elle. I saw you on stage in New York in the revival of *The Miracle Worker.* You were phenomenal!"

Adam tensed. She remembered that? A play?

Clarice lit up. "You remember? So long ago. I was sixteen."

"I was twelve, and afterward I wanted to be an actress like you. Then I read how you were bruised every night after the performance—"

"The folding-Helen's-breakfast-napkin scene," Clarice explained to Adam, who still didn't understand.

"I decided I'd rather watch." Elle's smile faded. "I'm a coward when it comes to pain." She flexed her hands as if trying to ease the tension.

Gently, Clarice said, "The staging was a bitch, but it was worth it. That kind of acclaim and your long memory doesn't often come to a stage actress."

"My long memory..." Eyes wide and stunned, Elle turned to Adam. "I remember it all so clearly. The theater. The seats. The shock when Annie Sullivan told the Kellers she'd grown up in a poorhouse."

Adam waited, barely daring to hope.

Elle sat very still, as if concentrating, delving into her mind for more. Shaking her head, in a choked voice she said, "That's all. That's all."

Ludwig stepped out of the kitchen and, seeing Clarice at their table, sighed heavily and brought a plate to set in front of her.

"Thank you, Ludwig." Clarice helped herself to a few olives and a potato. As she dabbed the potato in the *allioli*, she said, "Elle, I hear you washed to shore and Mr. Ramsdell saved you."

Adam exploded in exasperation. "How do you know that?"

15

CLARICE LAUGHED IN ADAM'S face. "Everybody's talking about it."

"How do they *know* anything?" he asked.

"You drove through town with her. That's what started it." Clarice thought for a moment. "No, not quite. Mr. Hardling said last night when he was out on his back porch smoking his cigar, he heard a woman screaming down at your house. He was ready to call the cops when it finally stopped. Nobody wants to believe you were beating a woman, so they had to figure out what else it could be. One guy thought you'd bought a peacock, because peacocks scream like a woman."

Being the object of attention brought Adam an upswell of horror. People were gossiping about him. People were staring at him. With Elle in tow, the situation could only get worse. "I didn't want a dog, and now I own a peacock?"

"You didn't want a dog?" Elle sounded appalled.

Her surprise and the implication of heartlessness set his teeth on edge. "I live alone."

Awkward silence.

Elle looked down at the table as if he'd rebuked her for being alive and a burden on him. Which he hadn't meant at all.

But before he could find the words to explain, to backtrack, to take away any hurt, Clarice jumped in. "It's Ludwig who remembered overhearing Madame Rune tell Adam to go to the beach and there find a lost soul."

How was this possible? How could a stupid random prediction from a fake seer get this kind of attention...and respect? Didn't anyone in this town, besides Adam, know the difference between reality and woo-woo? "She's not a lost soul. She was just..."

Dead.

Don't say that.

Ludwig appeared with more olives and potatoes and a platter of warm, crusty bread. Like the showman he was, he swept his arm toward the kitchen.

Señor Alfonso burst through the door carrying a sizzling platter of shrimp and mushrooms in garlic olive oil. The sound, the smell, the joy of his presentation made Elle smile, and that smile gave Adam a sense of relief. He wasn't trying to hurt her feelings, he just... He lived alone. That was all. And he didn't want to talk about the reasons.

When Señor Alfonso placed the platter on a red-glazed tile trivet on the table, Elle and Clarice gave him a round of applause. Elle tore off a piece of bread, dipped it in the bubbling hot oil, scooped up a mushroom and a sliver of garlic and conveyed it to her mouth. As she chewed, her fascinating eyes closed, and she moaned.

Señor Alfonso and Ludwig beamed, overcome with joy.

"Next," Señor Alfonso said, *"chorizo al vino."*

"And *huevos rotos,*" Ludwig said.

"Are you the cook?" Señor Alfonso touched his chest. "I am the cook!"

"Eggs," Ludwig informed him. "She needs strength."

"Yes." Señor Alfonso shook his finger at Ludwig. "You're right. Eggs!"

The two men headed back into the kitchen.

"Is it really that good?" Clarice asked Elle.

"No. You shouldn't eat any." Elle pulled the trivet away from Clarice.

Laughing, Clarice tugged it back into the center of the table, tore off a chunk of bread and dug in. When she ate a shrimp she, too, made a moaning sound.

Sitting at this table with these two women, who had barely met and yet immediately bonded…it felt weird to Adam, as if he was a sociable creature who could casually spend time with the rest of the human race. He needed to remember how miserably he had previously failed interacting with some parts of the human race. "Clarice? All that speculation you mentioned, the people in Gothic gossiping—it's all come about since we drove up the hill?"

"Please. There's more!" Clarice lifted one finger. "Elle is your daughter/sister/lover who needs to escape an abusive relationship, and she came to you."

Elle took his plate and served him mushrooms, shrimp and bread. "Don't fuss. Eat. It's good."

Clarice continued. "You have a reputation, Adam, as a man who people ask for help. After all, I did."

"Did he help you?" Elle nudged his plate closer to him.

"Not yet. But after seeing him with you, I have faith in him."

"I can't help you. I can't help anyone." Fiercely he battled this surge of faith and friendship. Normal was not for him.

"All I'm doing with Elle is giving her shelter until she can figure things out. Like where she comes from."

"She doesn't know where she comes from? That's interesting." Clarice transferred her gaze to Elle. "Amnesia?"

"I guess. It's not fun."

Adam cursed himself. This was what came of socializing. He had said too much. "Miss Burbage, please don't repeat that."

"I don't have to. Ludwig has his ear pressed to the kitchen door."

Adam looked toward the kitchen door. It was rocking slightly. A nightmare. This was his nightmare.

"It's okay, Adam. Señor Alfonso and Ludwig aren't out to get me. Or you." Elle tapped his plate. "Eat!"

Adam gave in to Elle's urgings, and after a couple of bites, he relaxed. Amazing what comfort food could bring. "Any sign of your predator, Miss Burbage?"

"No, and I've got a training team coming from Hollywood—a guy to teach me to fight, use weapons. A voice coach. An acting coach. I think that's it. The studio has a lot invested in this picture, so the team will stay in the suite with me, and we'll work day and night until the filming starts."

With satisfaction, Adam said, "Your coaching team will give this town something better to gossip about than me and Elle."

"You underestimate the good people of Gothic. They're able to keep two story lines separate." Clarice lifted her chin and smiled. "An added benefit of the team—I'll be safe. The nasty little slug of a paparazzo won't be able to get close."

"Bruno, right?" Adam asked.

"Right." Clarice stood. "This has been lovely, a much-needed break. I really hate to leave before the next course, but I've got to memorize this script."

"Mr. Kulshan said it's Shakespeare." Had the old man got that right?

"Shakespeare updated. We're bending *King Lear.*" In a deliberate excess of drama, Clarice put the back of her hand to her forehead. "Such a risk. Elle, I hope you recover your memory soon."

Adam watched her walk back to her table. "Bending?"

"Gender-bending. Meeting her was interesting. She's one of my heroes, and she's nice. You never know, do you? About people." Elle's head drooped, and her usually sparkling eyes grew sad.

"What do you remember? Something more than a play?" He didn't have much hope, but he prompted, "How you got into the ocean would be helpful."

"In my mind, there's a stain of disappointment, and it seems to be growing darker, clearer." Elle patted Adam's arm. "We've done what we can. We've met with Dr. Brocklebank, and as far as he was able, he gave me a clean bill of health. I can breathe more freely, and I remember the weirdest stuff, like seeing *The Miracle Worker.* I need time and quiet and a place to heal. Maybe talking to your psychic friend will help me, too. I know you want me out of your life—"

More awkwardness. "It's okay. I'm fine with you staying with me."

"I'm glad you can say that." Although she didn't sound as if she believed him. "Let's enjoy this meal and—"

Across the restaurant, Clarice Burbage stood up, scattering papers in an excess of distress. "He's there! He's found me." She pointed at the window where a man in his late thirties, handsome in a careless way, had a long camera lens pressed to the window. Her voice grew shrill. "Make him go away."

Mr. Kulshan woke with a snort and a start.

As if they'd been listening to every word uttered in their

dining room, Ludwig and Señor Alfonso appeared, and together they bundled up Clarice, her manuscript, all trace of her presence and escorted her to the door marked *Private*.

Clarice's hands shook as she tried to fit the key in the lock.

Ludwig took the key away and unlocked the door, and the three disappeared into the room beyond.

Bruno ran toward the restaurant entrance.

Adam stood. He hated opportunists with a fiery passion that only the anguish of his past could provide. As Bruno barreled into the unguarded restaurant, Adam ran and blocked him with a casual shoulder slam to the chest.

The paparazzo staggered backward.

Mr. Kulshan stuck out his leg.

Bruno fell over it and flat onto this back. The heavy camera thumped on his chest, and when he got his breath back, he sucked in a long, pained breath.

After a prolonged, satisfied look, Mr. Kulshan collapsed onto the floor shouting, "My knee, my knee! He broke my knee!" proving that he was more than a bothersome old fart, he was also an actor of consummate proportions.

Bruno climbed to his feet, turned on Mr. Kulshan, and in a rage he shouted, "You pathetic excuse for human refuse!" He raised his fist, but Adam caught his arm.

"I'm the Gothic community law enforcement. Do you really wish to strike this elderly gentleman who you gravely wounded in your rush to trespass on this establishment?"

"You'd better arrest him, Adam. He hurt me. Hurt me awful." Mr. Kulshan put his hand to his chest. "I'm having a heart attack!"

Bruno swelled like a speckled toad. "Because I tripped over your leg?"

"Trespassing and injury to an aged man." Adam grabbed

Bruno's shoulder and turn him roughly as if to put handcuffs on his wrists.

Bruno had obviously dealt with handcuffs before. He put his hands behind his back, then bolted out the door.

Mr. Kulshan extended his hand up to Adam and in a normal tone said, "Good riddance."

Adam reached his arms around Mr. Kulshan's body and hefted him to his feet. "Excellent work."

Mr. Kulshan cackled, bent and rubbed his knee. "The bastard really did hurt me." He nearly toppled.

Suddenly Elle was there, her arm under Mr. Kulshan's arm.

Señor Alfonso and Ludwig marched back in, looked around, and in his most menacing, Beethoven-deep voice, Ludwig asked, "Where is he?"

"Gone. Chased away by these two," Elle said. "They were magnificent."

Adam found he liked being called magnificent. He also felt compelled to say, "He'll be back, and soon."

16

AS ADAM AND ELLE walked toward the door, carrying to-go boxes loaded with leftovers, Mr. Kulshan asked in a quavering voice, "Could an old man hitch a ride down the hill?"

Adam shot him a sardonic look.

To Elle, Mr. Kulshan said, "I want to visit the missus."

Remembering the cemetery, Elle asked sympathetically, "How long ago did you lose your wife?"

"Lose her?" Mr. Kulshan's quaver dissipated under his blast of sarcasm. "I should be so lucky."

Elle was shocked into silence.

Mr. Kulshan charged on. "The old bat is still alive and kicking. We can't stand to live in the same house, so she has her place and I have mine. When we bought the two houses, I was more spry. Now I can't hobble down and hobble back, not in one day, anyway."

Elle still didn't know what to say.

"We'll take you down, Kulshan." Adam offered his arm.

Then he looked at Elle, struggling to put one foot in front of the other and muttering resentfully to her own damaged body.

Mr. Kulshan saw it, too. "I've got my cane right here." He retrieved it from where it was hanging on the table. "You help her."

Elle said, "I'm fine. Help him."

Adam did the diplomatic thing and offered an arm to each of them.

Mr. Kulshan chuckled and took an elbow. "Between her and me, it's hard to keep up with your invalids."

Elle leaned into Adam and moved even more slowly than the old man.

To him, Adam said, "There's nothing wrong with Elle that time won't heal."

"Me, too, boy," Mr. Kulshan said roundly. "Me, too."

When they got to the ATV, Elle insisted Mr. Kulshan sit in the front seat, and Adam silently thanked her for that. He wanted Mr. Kulshan buckled in, and that wasn't possible for the backward-facing seat in the rear.

As they drove sedately down Gothic's main street, Mr. Kulshan yelled back at Elle, "There's my place," indicating the small, Craftsman house with its handkerchief-sized lawn behind the tattered picket fence, two lots down from the restaurant.

Mrs. Kulshan's home bore a remarkable resemblance to her husband's except for a few traditional feminine touches: flower pots on the front walk, bold colors of trim paint and a pile of yarn on the table beside the porch swing. As Adam pulled up, Elle looked back and realized Mr. and Mrs. Kulshan could see each other when they stood on their front porches.

Huh. Interesting arrangement.

Adam had barely set the brake when Mr. Kulshan unbuckled his seat belt and tried to hop out.

Adam jumped toward him, but before he could catch him, Elle got around to steady the old guy. Without taking his gaze off the elderly woman who stood on the front porch, Mr. Kulshan thanked Elle and took his cane from Adam. "There she is," he said. "The bossiest, meanest old woman in the world."

"That's something coming from a creaky know-it-all like you, Rupert," Mrs. Kulshan called.

"Must have new hearing-aid batteries," he muttered and made his way up the narrow concrete walk.

Mrs. Kulshan waited while he labored up the two stairs to the porch, then stepped into his embrace. They kissed affectionately, and she called to Adam and Elle, "Thanks for bringing the old fool down. If you're out tomorrow, stop by and take him home."

"I don't need help getting home," Mr. Kulshan said in irritation.

"You'd get halfway there and they'd have to carry you back down in a coffin. Come in, have dinner and stop complaining. These young people will think we don't like each other." She winked at Elle and Adam, and as she ushered a cranky Mr. Kulshan into the house, they heard her ask, "Did you find out the truth behind what happened to that girl?"

"Yes, and if you made pound cake, I'll tell you," he said.

Mrs. Kulshan laughed and shut the door.

Adam turned to Elle.

She was leaning on the ATV, her face screwed up. When she saw him looking, she said defensively, "He was going to plant it face-first on the pavement. I had to help him. Do you have painkillers on you?"

"Yes." He glanced at his watch. "It's almost time to take it. I had hoped to stop at the General Store for supplies…since I hadn't prepared for a guest." He seemed chagrined at his lack of foresight. "You don't need to go in. You can stay in the vehicle. Can you manage that?"

"If you'll bring me a bottle of cold water so I can take my pills." She let him help her into the ATV.

"I can do that." He drove slowly down the road. He wanted to make sure Elle wasn't jostled unnecessarily, but the leisurely pace made it seem like they were leading a parade and Elle was Miss Congeniality, waving and smiling. When she lifted her arm, only he could hear her wincing.

"People are very friendly here," she said.

"Yes."

"I suppose you know everybody."

"Yes."

"It's good to have friends."

"I don't have friends here."

She thought about that. "Do you have friends anywhere?"

"No."

With humor in her voice, she said, "Don't tell Mrs. and Mr. Kulshan. They'd be shocked to hear you aren't their friend."

"We don't have to be friends for me to do them a favor that's convenient for me."

The Gothic General Store was down all seven curves and four hundred feet of elevation. Built in the 1930s, the large structure had been assembled out of pine logs brought from the Sierra Nevada and stained a rich reddish-brown. The green tile roof and broad windows gave the structure visual appeal, and its wide front porch and series of rockers invited the tourists to sit.

The paved parking lot circled the building, and Adam pulled into a place next to the accessible-parking spots—only one other car, a white Mercedes, was in the lot—set the brake on the ATV and climbed out. He figured in and out in less than five minutes. "Is there anything you don't like to eat?"

"No tarragon. No coconut or coconut milk." She was firm. "Other than that, I'm pretty easy."

"Right. No tarragon. No coconut." He didn't know what tarragon was…and who knew there were people who didn't like coconut? He could live on the stuff.

He stepped onto the front walk.

From the ATV, he heard a shout. "Wait!"

17

ADAM TURNED BACK TO see Elle struggling to get out.

"They've got clothes! On sale!" She pointed at the hanging rack on the broad front porch. "If you'll front me the money, I can give you back your shirt." She managed to stand erect with a minimum of flailing.

"I like you in my shirt," he said to her.

She seemed unconvinced, or maybe uninterested, and she hobbled around him and toward the stairs.

Sure, the shirt tails hung over her thighs, and the collar, even with the buttons fastened, sagged enough to reveal the marks on her throat. But she hadn't complained. Didn't that mean she was okay with it?

He followed her to the four steps that led up to the porch, saw her hold the banister, take a steadying breath and start up.

Oh, hell. If she wanted new clothes that badly, he'd assist. He put his arm under hers. They got to the top.

Elle veered toward the rack.

Adam glanced to the right and saw a figure stretched out

on the bench. A figure with dramatic fringed shawls, wild gray hair and a pallor to her face.

Rune. What was wrong with Rune?

"There's your clothes rack. Get what you want." He veered off and knelt beside Rune's prone figure. "What's wrong?"

Rune opened her eyes. She had a line of sweat on her forehead that she wiped with a trembling hand. "I'm fine."

Which was what Elle said when she obviously was so not fine.

"I walked down for a few groceries. No big deal, right? But this time—" Rune feebly waved one beringed hand.

From inside the store Adam heard a clatter, a thump, a curse.

Elle said, "I'm so sorry! Let me help you!" She limped inside.

Adam was torn. Elle or Rune? Who needed him most?

"Go on." Rune closed her eyes again. "I'm not going to die this time."

"Make sure you don't." Adam stood and walked into the store.

Because Angelica Lindholm owned the Gothic General Store, it was spotless and well organized, with the original textured wooden floors, log-cabin walls and an open vaulted ceiling. Rows of shelves held an ample grocery section, a selection of vacation clothes and logo sweatshirts, and a gourmet prepared-food aisle.

Tamalyn stood over the pile of clothes and hangers she had dropped, staring at Elle, color fluctuating in her face.

With difficulty, Elle knelt to pick up hangers. "I wanted to shop the clothes, anyway. Now I can look at them one by one."

From deeper inside the store, Adam heard Angelica ask, "Tamalyn, what happened?" She came around the corner carrying two giant Cheery Freeze cups fitted with lids and straws. With a glance, she took in the mess. "How did you—"

Elle looked up at her. "Hello. Wow, I *do* recognize you. Angelica Lindholm! This town is full of celebrities. I'm Elle."

As if her hands had lost their strength, Angelica let loose both cups. They hit the floor flat on their bottoms. The force of the frozen fluids broke the seal on the plastic tops. Frozen red beverages rose like geysers to splatter Angelica's white slacks and the hem of her short apron.

Even though the liquid must have been frigid, Angelica didn't react. She stared at Elle as if she'd seen a ghost. Then, as if coming out of a trance, she exclaimed, "How clumsy of me. I'm not usually so…clumsy."

"Mrs. Lindholm, you—" Tamalyn wrung her hands. "We've got Cheery Freeze everywhere!"

"It's a well-known law that if a frozen beverage is dropped, no matter how distant the far wall, it will reach it," Angelica said, pale yet composed. "It's my mess. I'll deal with it. You pick up the clothes. Our customer should not be doing that while you stand immobile. Make sure to put aside any of the stained clothes."

Tamalyn nodded jerkily.

Angelica knelt and picked up the cups. "I'll clean up this mess first." She smiled toward Elle. "We're not usually so discombobulated. I've cleaned the Cheery Freeze machine, and these are cups for Tamalyn and for Madame Rune, who is not well. If you and Adam would like a beverage, there's plenty left. On the house!"

Adam noted she never quite looked *at* Elle again. He helped Elle to her feet. "She needs a new shirt. And we need to pick up a few extras for dinner." Remembering, he recited, "No tarragon, no coconut."

"A Cheery Freeze would be delightful. I always loved them, but I… I don't think I've had one for years."

"A great number of our clothes are on clearance. We're closing out last season's stock. Adam, you're familiar with our dinner selections." Angelica turned toward the back of the store. "I'll get a caution board to put over the spill, then I'll help you myself."

"You're not going to clean up? Right now?" Tamalyn was clearly aghast. "But you always say—"

"I am going to help our customers," Angelica repeated. "Elle, is it? Is it short for something?"

"Yes. Well, long story. No."

"You don't know your own name?" Tamalyn muttered.

With tried patience, Angelica said, "Tamalyn, finish hanging the clothes."

Tamalyn picked up an armload of hangers and stormed toward the door.

"Get them picked up quickly." Angelica's voice was deadly calm, but it would have taken a braver soul than Tamalyn to argue with her. "Adam, if you need to do something else," Angelica said, "I'm glad to help Elle."

"Thank you, because… How did Rune take ill?"

"I'm afraid I don't know. She walked down, said she was going to rest before she shopped and went out on the porch. Do you really think she's sick? With a fever?" Angelica looked horrified. "Nothing contagious, I hope."

"I don't know." Adam said to Elle, "You'll be all right without me?"

"Yes. Is your friend going to recover?"

"I hope so." Adam didn't think to say Rune wasn't his friend.

But Elle noticed.

18

ANGELICA CAME BACK WITH clean hands and in a pair of ironed linen slacks. She carried a stack of towels, which she used to sop up the spill, and a laundry basket where she deposited the now-stained rags. She stood a sandwich board that said *Caution! Wet surface!* over the remains of the Cheery Freeze disaster. To Elle, she said, "I don't mean to pry, but you look as if you need pain relief."

Elle smiled, but she didn't shake her head. Her neck was getting stiffer, and the muscles in her shoulders were tight. "Adam brought the pills. I'll get them."

"Not at all necessary. Wait here." Angelica returned with a small opened foil package and another giant red Cheery Freeze topped by a cap and straw. She shook pills out of the packet into Elle's hand, and when Elle had put them in her mouth, she handed her the cup. "Careful. It's slick, but the cold will help your throat."

Elle held it in both hands and gratefully took the pills.

"Thank you, and the Cheery Freeze is as good as I remember." *Remember* was the wrong word, but she stuck with it.

"Pardon me for asking, but Adam Ramsdell didn't—"

"No! No." Elle tried to think what exactly to say to this restrained woman, how to explain her circumstances. Strangled by a hulking shadow, a leap into the ocean, washing ashore and being rescued by Adam. Having no memory of her full name or anything else important. She couldn't say all that. "No."

Angelica waited, but when the silence went on too long and more information was not forthcoming, she asked, "Would you trust me to pick out your clothes?"

Elle had seen Angelica on videos, talking about the best paint colors for the kitchen cabinets, cooking with other celebrities, caring for her garden and her pets. "Please. But I'm not able to pay immediately, and I won't be a burden on Adam Ramsdell." She corrected herself. "More of a burden."

"Sit there." Angelica pointed to a seat beside the cash register and walked toward the back of the store.

Elle noticed the stack of newspapers on the counter. She put down her Cheery Freeze, picked up a newspaper. She read the headlines and stared at the pictures. She didn't remember anything about these stories. How could she have lost so much? Would she ever regain her memory?

"Are you all right?" Angelica stood a few feet away.

Tamalyn stood behind her with her arms full of clothes.

Elle couldn't say *I'm afraid and I don't know what I'm afraid of.* "Yes, I just… You have newspapers. Real, paper newspapers!"

"The area includes a fair number of elderly who refuse to break with tradition, so when one of my employees comes in from San Luis Obispo or Sacramento or LA, they bring a stack of newspapers."

"Because Gothic is so boring nothing ever happens, and we don't need our own paper." Tamalyn glowered with hostility, although this time it seemed distributed over the whole of Gothic.

Angelica ignored her. "We put the papers on the counter, and they slowly sell until the next batch arrives."

"That's interesting. I can see reading the news this way would be a tactile experience." Elle could almost hear Tamalyn roll her eyes.

"Go ahead and take it. You can catch up on events, and who knows? Adam might be interested, too." Angelica glanced at the paper upright on the counter and grimaced. "Because it's the wrestler, Big John Hammer."

Angelica had to be kidding. "That's his name?"

"Where have you been?" Tamalyn asked nastily.

I don't know.

Angelica turned smoothly. "Tamalyn, thank you for your assistance. Now, if you'd go help our new customer..."

Tamalyn piled the clothes on the counter while muttering, "It's Mrs. Worcsh and that toddler of hers. He'll wreck the place. Don't put him down, don't put him down..." She rushed toward the woman and her wiry son.

"Yes, Big John Hammer, that's his name, or has been since he legally changed it." Angelica meticulously placed the clothing for a viewing. "He's running for governor of California. His fan base is fervent."

Elle looked harder at the grainy photo of the handsome man and his tall, perfectly proportioned and groomed wife. "They're a handsome couple." She didn't mean it as compliment: they were artificial, created by plastic surgery, hair plugs, Botox, hair color and beauty expectations.

"I've met them." Angelica seemed to be carefully choosing her words. "She's an ornament who always says the right thing."

"That seems like a good gift to have." Elle felt sure she herself wasn't so blessed.

"It is." Angelica sounded as if she knew that for a fact.

Another customer came through the door, a middle-aged man in shorts and flip-flops, carrying a backpack slung over one shoulder.

"Hm." Angelica stepped in front of Elle and shielded her from sight. "Let's step over here." She moved behind a tall display cabinet with lit shelves of butterflies with agate wings.

"Those are beautiful!" Elle almost pressed her nose to the glass, then realized it was Angelica Lindholm's glass and she should not smudge it.

"Sadie and Hartley's Rock and Mineral Emporium markets them. The butterflies are popular, and the display sends people to their store." Angelica lowered her voice. "About Big John Hammer. He's not quite…right."

"Right?"

"He's a vast ego in an expensive suit." Angelica seemed compelled to tell Elle about a man she would never meet. "He's a time bomb set to go off, and when he does, none of us want to be anywhere in the vicinity."

With astonishment, Elle said, "You're afraid of him!" She realized she'd been too loud and lowered her voice to match Angelica's.

"He wanted my endorsement. I don't give endorsements. Politics is bad for business. When I said that—"

"He threatened you?"

"Some people worship him. Men who are…bullies like him. There have been incidents where people have spoken out against Big John Hammer. They were intimidated. *Taught a lesson.*"

Elle was appalled. "Surely you have security?"

"I do. But not a bodyguard. I hired one for a while, but

nothing's happened and—" she gestured around the quaint store "—it's Gothic. It doesn't seem as if..."

"No. It doesn't." Governor of California. That was powerful.

"You never heard me say any of that," Angelica said.

"I understand. But why are you confiding in me?"

"Your Adam Ramsdell and Big John Hammer are acquainted."

"Friends?" That didn't sit with what Elle had seen of Adam. "No."

"No. Not friends. They went on a trip together." Angelica tweaked the stacks of clothing. "No one truly knows what happened between them. We do know two people died. Adam was held responsible. He won't speak up for himself, but I don't believe—"

"Neither do I!" Elle said hotly.

Another customer hurried in, a teenage boy wearing an avid expression and carrying a phone.

Angelica sighed. "Tamalyn lied. There is a newspaper, the *Town Blab*."

"Really? That's what it's called?"

"No. It's called the *Gothic Times*, and Justin Scharphorn puts it together with the help of the English teacher who also teaches journalism. I imagine Justin is here to ask for an interview. We need to get you back into Adam's custody. Justin won't dare approach you then. Now, what do you think of these?" Angelica showed Elle a loose-fitting sheath dress in a bright, tropical-flower print, a lemon-colored T-shirt, a blue cambric button-up shirt, a pink fleece hoodie and two pairs of jeans, one cut short, another ankle length.

"That's too much."

"They were damaged by my appalling failure with the Cheery Freezes."

"I wouldn't call it a failure. More like..." Elle remembered the incident vividly because somehow it seemed so wrong. "I have to ask—have we met?"

Angelica looked her in the eyes. "No. I have a remarkable memory for names and faces. We most definitely have not met."

"Okay." But Elle got the feeling she was standing in the bright sunlight squinting at a truth and unable to see it for the glare.

Angelica pointed to a spray of red on the hoodie. "I can't sell them. Imperfections are not acceptable for the Angelica Lindholm line. Take them. It'll save me the trouble of donating them to a charity."

"If you're sure." Elle lightly touched the soft fleece.

"Very sure. I've included a pair of pajamas. They're undamaged. When you're on your feet, you can pay me for those." Angelica handed Elle her Cheery Freeze. "Go find Adam. I'll wrap the clothes and fetch two dinners to go."

"Thank you. For the clothes, the care, the protection and the information."

"It's the least I can do."

19

ADAM RETURNED TO RUNE, now sitting in one of the rocking chairs on the porch. "What happened?" he asked.

Rune smiled wanly. "It's a recurring problem. I'm better now."

What is wrong? Adam wanted to ask, but he respected Rune's privacy.

Yet Elle had asked Brocklebank about his past, and he had confessed a painful history. She asked Clarice about her acting, and Clarice explained how she got into her career. She asked Mr. Kulshan about his marriage, and he'd told her how it worked and why.

Here Adam sat with Rune. They had known each other for five years. Perhaps… Adam should ask for more information? He saw how people responded to Elle's questions. They told her stuff because she was interested. Was that how this relationship business worked?

Before he had to make a decision, Elle came out of the store and across the porch and extended her hand to Rune. "You must be Madame Rune."

Rune lit up and shook her hand. "You recognized me! You're Elle. Dr. Brocklebank called about you."

"I'm glad he gave you a heads-up." Elle viewed Rune seriously. "Do you have a pronoun you prefer?"

Rune fixed her with a stern glance and said, "I am whatever your instinct tells you I am."

Elle glanced at Adam, a question in her eyes.

"She said the same thing to me. It's her background as a psychiatrist rearing its head." Adam turned to Rune. "Right?"

"What do you think?" Rune asked him.

Adam sighed loudly.

Rune grinned.

Elle looked Rune over. The rings, the clothes, the beard stubble, the complete lack of concern for what anyone else thought. "Okay, I'll go with she/her."

Rune inclined her head.

Elle said, "You're the person who is supposed to help me recover my memory."

"You've *lost* your *memory*?" The wild psychic Rune changed into a person of serious intentions. "That's interesting. Since you were first spotted this morning, I've heard amazing speculation about who you are and what you're doing with, of all people, Adam Ramsdell."

Adam grunted.

"But no one mentioned a loss of memory, not even Brocklebank."

"Dr. Brocklebank is discreet and trustworthy," she said.

"He's a good man," Rune agreed. "He said Adam found you?"

Adam could see what was coming. "I found her on the beach."

"Ha! I was right, was I?" Rune beamed. "Go ahead, Adam. Say it."

"You were right." Adam would have to move away from Gothic or he'd never hear the end of it.

Rune returned her attention to Elle. "You're battered. What can you tell me about your experiences?"

Elle sat down at Adam's side and reached for his hand.

He didn't react. Then he realized he should have reached, too.

But she pulled back, and Adam was discomfited. He should have offered comfort. She needed it, and he was always the strong person.

"Not much. I have impressions, that's all."

"Amnesia is rare and is caused by a number of possible reasons. One is brain trauma, of course, and if the trauma is severe, the damage might be irreparable."

Elle touched the lump on her skull.

"But no seizures, no slurred speech, no blurry vision?" Rune peered inquiringly into Elle's face.

"I feel fine. Sore." She stretched out her leg. "Everything hurts."

"Physical problems which, with the right care, will heal. Apply ice packs. If Brocklebank says you seem to be functioning well, and Adam and I concur, it's wise to look for a psychological issue."

"I agree. I'm so scared. It's a low, constant buzz of terror." Her breathing quickened, and her eyes shifted from side to side as if sensing danger in the shadows. "I see shadows in my peripheral vision, I hear noises that aren't real and when I close my eyes, I want to scream. *I want to scream.* But I can't, and the anxiety is slowing my mind at a time when I need to be alert."

Adam wanted to reassure her. He wasn't going to let anything happen to her. But what words to use?

Rune said, "That's the other cause of amnesia—emotional trauma. I'd have to say being dragged out of the ocean half-dead—"

"She was fully dead," Adam interrupted.

Rune looked up in interest.

"I flung her body over my shoulder, and she vomited and came to life."

Rune nodded, laughed a little and said, "Lost souls back from the dead."

"Shut up," Adam said.

Rune waggled her index finger at Elle. "A murder attempt, a battle with a Pacific storm, long moments of oxygen deprivation followed by an abrupt and shocking return to life… That easily equals amnesia."

Adam hadn't thought about it like that. "I guess so. Sure."

Rune said, "Even if Elle decides she doesn't want to be hypnotized—"

"Hypnotized?" Adam was shocked. "I didn't say you could do that."

"No, you didn't. Because I didn't ask you. Whether I do or don't isn't up to you." With a wave, Rune dismissed Adam and turned to Elle. "You can choose the more conventional question-and-answer method. We will possibly get some knowledge of your past, but it will take longer. Hypnosis is the swifter route."

"I don't think we should do that today." Elle reached across the space between them and rested her hand on Rune's arm. "*You* are looking quite ill. *Are* you? Is there something we can do for you?"

Adam found himself asking, "What happened to you?" Today, he meant.

Rune didn't take it that way. "That's the story, isn't it? How did a Hollywood psychiatrist become a successful psychic? Do you want hear it?"

Elle was surprised. "Of course I want to know."

Adam suspected it was going to involve more wild emotions. In the last twenty-four hours, one trauma had piled on top of another until it felt contagious.

Rune reached into her skirt pocket and pulled out a battered deck of cards. She placed them on a table beside her and pointed to the chair adjoining. "Sit there, Elle. Shuffle the deck. Shuffle it three times."

Elle laboriously changed seats, picked up the cards and looked them over. "Tarot!"

"Oh, for God's sake." Adam sighed.

Elle and Rune grinned at him, identical smirks of undiluted delight.

Elle shuffled the first time.

"I was Dr. Edward Simon, successful Beverly Hills psychiatrist." Rune rubbed her fingers together to indicate cash. "Stars and their traumas, charity work on the east side, 1930s house redesigned by my wife and featured in *Sunset* magazine. Then COVID hit."

Elle shuffled again.

"I'm a physician, right? I understand virus transmission. But I figured I'm healthy, I run marathons, I take precautions, wash my hands. I thought masks might have merit, but they're bad for the patients with trust issues." Rune sighed. "I caught it on the first wave. I was on a ventilator, damned near died in the hospital. Alone, because my wife and parents couldn't visit."

Elle shuffled again, a slow rattle of cards coming together.

"After two months, I went home. In a week, I returned with blood clots. Then a stroke." Rune flexed her right hand.

For the first time Adam realized her little finger and the one next to it were immobile.

"I'm a caretaker." Rune splayed her palm on her chest. "It's a failing, but my wife was always the most hurt, most depressed, sickest. Now she couldn't be the sickest. She *wasn't* the sickest. Six foot one and I weighed a hundred and twenty pounds."

Elle held up the deck. "They're shuffled. What do you want me to do?"

With a shaking hand, Rune patted the table.

Elle pushed the deck of cards across the table. "What happened?"

"My wife left me. There is nothing like being a psychiatrist who realizes he's made the wrong life choices because he assumed he'd always come out on top..." Rune looked sideways at Elle. "My voice changed. Lung damage coupled with respiratory-system collapse and suddenly I was Julia Child."

"Everyone loves Julia Child," Elle said, "and it's a good fit for you."

"Thank you, dear." Rune picked up the deck. "I can feel your vibrations. You're a good person."

"Asking you about your life doesn't make me a good person."

"A caring person. Does that fit better?" Rune asked.

A caring person. Which Adam was not, because he wanted to put his hands over his ears rather than to listen to all this anguish.

"If you were sick, I guess you couldn't work." Elle urged Rune on.

"Right. No income." Rune placed the cards in a simple pattern. "Hm. Look, it's all here. Violence. In the night. And the ocean. See?" She turned over more cards. "My friends slipped away. I was embarrassing to be around."

"You had the wrong friends," Elle said.

"I didn't *have* the wrong friends. I *chose* the wrong friends." Rune laughed her trilling laugh. "Sorry! You can take the psychiatrist out of the office, but you can't stop him from giving the proper responses."

Adam figured if they were ever going to get to the end of this story, he'd better take over. "Rune, how did you get from there to here?"

"I became a wine connoisseur. As in, I drank a lot of it." Rune turned over a card with hanging grapes. "Finally my mom sat me down and said…a lot of things. The important thing she said was 'Figure out what you want.' I said, 'I want to be who I was,' and she said, 'You weren't happy, anyway.'"

"Sounds like that was news to you," Adam said.

"More like enlightenment. I figured out what I wanted. No more therapy, no more Hollywood stars. I like California, and from the first moment I came to Gothic, I was home." Turning to Elle, Rune asked, "Did you ever feel that way? Is there someplace you are at home?"

Elle looked around the porch as if seeking something. *Seeing* something. "Yes. There's an orchard. With peaches. I sit in the tree. I look at the house. It's old. Painted white. The garage behind it—it sags."

Adam started to speak. To say something.

Rune held up a warning hand. "The back door opens. Who comes out?"

Elle smiled. "Grandma."

20

SON OF A BITCH. Adam had been sitting here, feeling like a bad friend, listening and hurting for Rune—and Rune had been leading Elle to a memory.

"What's she wearing?" Rune asked.

Elle's eyes narrowed. "Jeans and a T-shirt. The shirt says, *The sass is strong in this one.* Her hair is platinum blond. She bleaches it every month. Grandpa helps her. He says it's no big deal, he knows how to paint."

Adam couldn't contain himself anymore. "What are their names?"

Elle blinked away her memories and looked at him, clear-eyed and impatient. "Grandma and Grandpa. Adam, don't you think I want to know? It's like unraveling a sweater. I catch a thread and start to pull, and the hole gets bigger and I can almost see everything—and then I hit a knot."

"Perhaps what you remembered makes you feel better," Rune suggested.

"It does." Elle lifted one finger. "Grandma and Grandpa Boedecker."

"There you go." Rune grinned nastily at Adam. "Something to work on."

"It would help to know where Grandma and Grandpa live." Adam knew he was being unfair. What Elle had remembered was amazing compared to her previous blank terror.

"There were chiggers." At the memory, Elle scratched her ankles. "I got them under my socks. Rune, you were telling us how you became a fortune-teller."

"Let's save that for your appointment tomorrow." Rune pulled a battered leather notebook out of her skirt pocket. "How about eleven o'clock? Afterward, Adam can take us to lunch."

Elle sighed and nodded.

Adam looked sharply at her. In addition to the bruises, she had dark marks under her eyes. Time to wind this thing up. "Thank you, Rune, for that miraculous recovery of memory."

He must have sounded cynical, for Rune snapped, "Adam, she recalled one scrap of her life, nothing more. To do more, she has to know me, so I told her a little bit of my life. Surely even you must have been curious how I changed from a washed-up psychiatrist to a fully operational psychic."

Adam shrugged. "We've all got our secrets."

"In other words," Rune said to Elle, "he has no intention of sharing his."

Elle nodded wisely, as if she saw more than he would like. "He's afraid if he touches a single thread of the yarn, it'll all unravel, and he'll be naked."

"That's enough." Adam didn't frown. He knew how to hide the pain.

Tamalyn came out on the porch bearing a grocery bag and

the newspaper. She plopped the bag at Adam's feet and offered Elle the newspaper. "You forgot this. Do you want it?"

"Yes, thank you." Elle took it, unfolded it and looked at the front page. "This is not good," she murmured.

Adam saw the headline and the photo of Big John Hammer and his perfectly imperfect wife. Rage and disgust swelled, blocking his airways, holding him immobile for an interminable moment. When he had gained control, he said, "He won't be in the race much longer."

"Do you have a premonition, Adam?" Rune's tone was gently mocking, but beneath that Adam heard a solid curiosity.

"No." He'd said too much. How unlike him. Elle's appearance in his life had done more than change his circumstances: emotions threatened his calm, memories swamped his mind, and the old failures taunted him. He recognized a corner when he'd been backed into one. He was the last man who should be caring for her, and yet he could protect her. *He* could protect *her.*

Angelica followed Tamalyn, and as she came through the door, she tripped. She glanced back and frowned, then placed a clothing bag against Elle's chair. In a low voice, she said, "I added some essentials."

Elle looked inside and wasn't surprised to see the neatly folded pairs of panties and two tan bralettes. "Thank you."

Angelica offered a tube of ointment. "For your bruising—Arnica is an unproven but effective topical remedy. Don't take it internally." Her fingers hovered over the bump on Elle's forehead. Retracting her hand, she smiled in that cool, superior way. "I'm sure you know how to read a warning label."

"I do remember how to do that," Elle said. "I'll see you soon."

Angelica nodded. "Yes. Gothic is a small town. Tamalyn..." She turned.

Tamalyn had skittered back into the store.

Angelica followed her in. She hesitated at the door, looked left and right, shook her head as if bewildered.

Elle placed her palms on the table and hefted herself up. "Rune, we'll meet tomorrow."

"Yes." Rune watched Elle go into the store and turned to Adam. "That woman is in need of empathy, and I worry you're not the person to—"

"I'm not. But I will keep her safe."

Rune ruffled the tarot cards. "You have good instincts. Follow them."

Also irritating. "They're not instincts in some woo-woo portents that float through the atmosphere. They're observations, usually peripheral, filtered through my experiences and presented to my mind as warnings."

"Right. Not instincts. How dare I suggest such a thing?" Rune did sarcasm well. "Do you have any gut feelings about the violence that drove her to Gothic?"

"Better than that. This morning, she told me what wakes her screaming. Her memory of that is clear, if limited."

"A starting point." Rune shuffled the cards and placed three on the table. "Excellent. And why didn't I ask that?"

"Because you were surprised by the news of the amnesia."

Rune looked up. "Do you feel comfortable sharing what she told you?"

Adam repeated, word for word as far as he was able, what Elle told him this morning. A man's hands gripping her throat, her screams trapped within. Square lights rolling as the floor beneath them rose, fell, tilted. Music throbbed inside the house, masking the violence outside from her friends who partied, drank and sang. And the storm, wind and rain lashing her face as he killed her.

Rune leaned back. "A ship? A boat? A dock on the water?"

"Or maybe her lack of oxygen created the illusion of square lights on a rolling floor. When I pulled her from the water, she had a flotation ring with her."

"Boat, ship, dock. These days they hang those things on railings everywhere. Did you research missing persons or—" Rune caught sight of Adam's face. "Of course you did. Something capsized out there?"

"Possibly. That would explain why there's no person-overboard reports to the coast guard, but that doesn't explain the marks on her neck. Someone tried to throttle her. Maybe he was interrupted and, to finish the job, he threw her in." Adam lifted his hands. "Suppositions. What I know for sure is that she's afraid of a big, hulking man."

"In general, women are afraid of men. Some are brutes with a tendency toward violence."

"I know. She's been traumatized by the attack on her. Yet I see flashes of the woman she was before. There's a spine of steel beneath the terror." Adam walked to the stairs, stood at the railing and scanned the hills. A shadow grew in his mind, an awareness of danger, a sense of being watched.

"Adam?" Rune got to her feet, wavered a bit, then moved to Adam's side. "What's wrong?"

From inside the store, Adam heard Elle call, "No, I've got everything."

Urgently Rune said, "Before she comes out, I need to tell you—her eyes are different colors, and that condition is called—"

"I know. Heterochromia iridum. Possibly genetic, possibly caused by her injuries. I'll watch for changes." Adam turned in time to see Elle take one step through the door, still clutching the newspaper. Then the second foot, the one behind the lead, seemed to catch. She rose on her toes, dropped the paper and fell hard, her hands outstretched.

Adam reached her before she landed.

21

"SOMETHING CAUGHT MY FOOT. I mean it, Adam. It was like I tripped over something." Although he had said nothing, Elle sounded argumentative.

Adam drove the ATV into the garage between his shop and house and parked it beside his four-wheel-drive pickup. "I looked. There was nothing there." That worried him. She'd shown no signs of concussion, but her clumsiness had come out of nowhere, and if he hadn't caught her, she might have seriously injured herself. "If I could take you to the hospital..."

"No! No."

He heard terror in her voice.

Then with a sigh, she added, "Anyway, I'm too tired."

"I know." But after she slept, they would discuss this again.

Although it was only midafternoon, the day felt long and fraught. He needed to use his hands, to distract himself from the swirl of violent emotions and that itch of uneasiness. He helped her out of the ATV, made sure she was steady on her feet, then walked her outside. He locked the garage. "I've got to go to work. In my shop."

"Okay." Elle looked at him in hope.

"Come on." He led her into the tall building beside his home. He lifted the oversize RV garage doors and illuminated the interior.

He had had this structure built to his specifications. The walls were a pale golden wood with skylights in the ceiling that bathed his shop in even light. A long pegboard with hooks and tools hung on the wall over the workbench. A small, intense propane kiln stood in the middle of the floor; he could start a hot fire and the flames could not spread to exterior walls, the grasses outside or the fragile countryside. "You can take a nap here." He pointed to the narrow cot against the wall. "But you have to wear ear protection."

"Ear protection? Why?"

"I work with metal. I fire it, I pound it, I—"

Elle caught sight of the tall sculpture he had created with the help of his old companion, despair. She walked around it in awe, like a person seeing the sunrise for the first time. "What is this? Definitely not tin cans. This is a piece of the ocean cut into a cross section that shows the beauty, the cruelty, the savagery." She would know. "*You* did this?"

"Sometimes I take a break from the paying work and do something that expresses—"

"Your soul?"

"No. Not my soul. The world in all its cruelty."

"No wonder they call you an artist. This is poetry in metal."

Other people said stuff like that. But somehow, it meant something coming from Elle.

He used his toe to unlock the wheeled stand, turned his sculpture in a circle and gave her the full experience. "It was a ship's prow. I stood the piece on the broad end, let it taper toward the sky, carved and polished cruel waves along its length."

"Yes… I can see what it was, and how you've used its shape to symbolize what happened—" she choked up "—to me." Before he could speak, she held up a hand. "I know. Not to me, but your creation seems so personal. I suppose it will feel personal to each one who sees it. That's why it's genius." She cleared her throat. "How did you get it off the beach, up the cliff to…here?"

"That effort involved my four-wheel-drive pickup, a winch and some creative swearing."

She reached out to one of the bright, glittering points.

He caught her hand. "No, Sleeping Beauty. It will prick your finger, at the least, and you have enough injuries."

"Oh." She examined the razor-sharp sculpture, and again examined him. "You're brilliant." She walked to the cot and sat down. "Brilliant." She faded onto the mattress on her side, tucked the pillow under her head. "Brilliant."

Maybe sleep would cure her clumsiness. He hoped that was the case, because he liked having her here—which wasn't what he should want. But she lifted his spirits, warmed his heart, helped him remember a time when the world was more than a messy wallow in the mud of guilt.

In his experience, he could want all he cared to. He'd wanted a lot of things in his day. Want availed him nothing. His common sense motto: Life's not fair.

It never was. It never would be.

"I'm going to take the food and your clothes into the house."

"Okay." She didn't open her eyes.

"You won't be afraid?"

"As long as you come back."

"I'll always come back." That sounded uncomfortably like

a vow, so he offered her foam earplugs and muttered, “Ear protection.”

She inserted them and was asleep before he returned, and she slept undisturbed by the roar of the fire and the pounding of his hammer.

22

THE SILENCE WOKE ELLE. Was Adam finished for the day?

Had he left her alone?

In that instant of panic, her eyes sprang open. She blinked at the light of late afternoon. She was facing into the shop, and Adam was there, stripped down to his shorts, posed with his long sword gripped in both his hands.

As she watched him, her terror eased, and she relaxed.

He raised the sword over his head, thrust it down, pivoted and raised the sword again. This time he slashed sideways, then sideways again. He was like a Nordic god, rippling with muscles, intent on victory, moving slowly, deliberately. The sun stroked him from the upper windows giving him a gilt glory.

He was so beautiful he brought tears to her eyes.

Painfully, she hoisted herself onto one elbow. It had been more than twenty-four hours since Adam had dragged her out of the ocean. How long would it be before different aches and pains stopped showing up?

Adam spotted her motion and stopped. He walked toward her, searched her eyes as if seeing into her soul…and said something.

She remembered the earplugs and sheepishly pulled them out. Even in her sleep and with the earplugs, she had been aware of muffled pounding. Even in her sleep, she had known Adam was nearby.

He indicated the sword. "Would you like to try it?"

"Yes! Yes, I would." Her scramble off the cot was more of a lurch and stagger, and he put a hand under her elbow.

She placed her hand on the sword's long hilt. She caressed the metal, in awe of the beautiful workmanship. A round knob of pounded iron topped the black leather grip. The guard was a crossbar of a dull gold material, and on each side was an indentation created for a specific purpose, and she knew what it was. "Where are the jewels that should fill these holes?"

"I made the sword to sell, not keep. The buyer will choose their gems, and a jeweler will attach them."

"But when you were practicing, it was as if you and the weapon were one."

"I am the sword's maker." He didn't sound conceited. More matter-of-fact.

"A thousand years ago, you would have been in demand as a swordsmith."

"I would have made a substantial living." Again, no hubris, but he looked at her sideways like a man offering a gift. "The blade is iron and steel, as it would have been in medieval times. Collectors who can afford my work are fussy about authenticity."

She put her second hand on the hilt and lifted the sword. "It's heavy!" The tip wavered.

He put his hand under hers and steadied her. "Four pounds."

"I should be able to lift four pounds."

"It's the way the weight is distributed. The hilt is ten inches, long enough to use with both hands. The blade itself is three feet. That's forty-six inches that you're controlling from your core. Altogether you're sixty-two inches? Sixty-four? The ratio causes the unbalance."

She engaged her abs and tried to lift the sword over her head—and realized at once she was in trouble. She was going to fall over. Or drop the sword. Neither was acceptable.

Suddenly he was behind her, her back to his front, his arms around her, both his hands over hers, and her arms and the sword were straight in the air above her. He said in her ear, "Now slash to the right." The sword sliced the air. "Slash left." The sword swung to the side. "Step forward with your right foot and thrust." She did, and he followed.

On his instruction, they moved, pivoted, swung, thrust. She was sweating with the exertion. She was pretty sure she was in pain. But for the first time since she woke on that beach, she felt strong, in control, powerful.

When they came to a halt, they stood like that, together, holding the beautiful sword, and he said, "It's like dancing to a music only you can hear."

"Yes." She liked this kind of dancing—with him.

"I'm going to let go now." He loosened his grip and stepped back.

The sword wavered again.

She sighed mightily.

He chuckled—the first sign of laughter she'd heard from him—and took it from her.

"Is it sharp?" she asked.

"No, but if you whack somebody with it, they're going to know they've been hit. The blade is solid. It could break a man's arm." He wiped down the blade, slid it into the scabbard and used the leather strap over his shoulder to carry it to a hook in the pegboard. "Swords like these are for display, or to strut around a renaissance festival or for use at a battle reenactment. That's what I'm doing next week. At the—" he squinted as if he remembered something he didn't want to "—GSPF."

She might have heard some humor in his voice. "What's that?"

"The aforementioned Gothic Spring Psychic Festival, designed to bring tourists to Gothic to buy crystals or tarot cards or get psychic readings, and drink and eat funnel cakes and organic pomegranate cookies and make merry."

Yep. This was definitely humor. "You told me that. But you didn't mention you're doing something with the sword. A demonstration?"

He hooked his arm through hers and led her at a slow pace toward the doors. "A mock battle between me and some other idiot who agreed to fight."

"So a dull blade to prevent accidents."

"And to prevent anyone who gets too much into the spirit of the fight from slicing open their opponent."

She could see that: two men who imagined themselves medieval knights, fighting a mock battle, losing their tempers and really going at it. "What is the sword's name?"

"It's a…sword."

"This sword should have a name!"

"Whoever buys it can give it a name."

"Let me think on it." She tapped her lip, then laughed. "How about 'S and P'?"

"Salt and pepper?"

"Sharp and pointy!"

"As I said, it's not sharp although it is—"

She rolled her eyes at him.

"Whoever buys it can give it a name," he repeated.

She put her hand on his wrist. "You will be careful, won't you? In this mock battle?"

He looked surprised. "Of course. I've been assured the other reenactor is a professional. It will be a sedate demonstration."

"I'd love to see that!" It struck her that, if she didn't improve, she might very well be here to see it. "My God. What's going to happen to me?" At once she realized that was selfish, and she added, "I can't stay and be a burden on you forever."

"You're not a burden." He pulled down the garage door and locked it. Taking her arm once more, he led her toward the house. "Today you made a breakthrough. Tomorrow we'll let Rune work her magic again."

The breeze off the ocean smelled like salt and the world made new and reinforced her feeling of strength and peace. Cheered, she said, "I'm not afraid right now."

"Right now, if your monster sprang out at you, what would you do?" he asked in a conversational tone.

Instant terror gripped her. *The hulking man gripped her throat with his strong, murderous fingers.* She was blind, helpless, immobile.

Adam took her hand.

Elle came out of her paralysis, but the joy in the evening was gone, replaced by the familiar gnawing fear, the pain in her throat, her joints, her ribs and hips.

"That, what you're doing now. Responding with panic." Adam's voice was calm, encouraging. "Don't do that. Keep your wits about you."

"I don't have any wits left." She wasn't even trying to be funny.

"You *do.* You have a bright spirit that was crushed in a moment of savagery."

"A bright spirit?" She had a bright spirit?

"The spirit's still there. You simply have to unearth it. Remember, bravery is being the only one who knows you're afraid."

"Is running away a good way to handle a fight?" she said, trying to joke.

"It's the best way."

That surprised her. "Really? Because I could be really good at that."

"This man, whoever he is, has big hands. I can tell by the fingerprints on your neck. You're in good shape. You lift weights."

Yes, he would know that. He'd viewed the whole package, and his assessment brought her fear down a notch.

He continued. "You're petite, and you're injured. You don't want to get into his grip again. But he also probably has longer legs than you do. So you'd want to disable him somehow, *then* run."

Her heartbeat kicked up again. "How would I do that?"

"Slam the heel of your hand upward into his nose. Pick up a pencil and stick it in his eye, in his ear. Stab his face with your keys. Scream as loud and as long as you can."

"I know how to scream." She put her hand on her throat and remembered the screams locked in by the monster's grip. "Given the chance."

"Yes, you do." He flung his arm around her as if she were a pal. "You are an excellent screamer, and in the right circumstances, it's a useful weapon."

She was cheered about the running and screaming and depressed by his offhand friendly attitude. Sure, she didn't remember her own name, but she was pretty sure guys liked her for more than her companionship.

He helped her up the stairs to the porch, unlocked his front door and gestured her inside.

Before he followed her, he stopped and scanned the area

around the house, then scanned the larger horizon, up toward Gothic and down toward the Pacific.

He seemed obsessed with locks and making sure no one observed them unnoticed, and Elle was blinded by the memory of those hands tightening around her throat. "What is it?" She could barely speak. "Do you sense something? Someone?"

"The neighbors. It's the neighbors." Adam shrugged as if shedding a load off his shoulders.

In a hoarse voice, she asked, "Do you think the man who killed me is out there on a hill watching me?"

"I think the man who tried to kill you threw you into the ocean believing he had finished you. He has no reason to hunt you."

Adam's cool response made sense, but it didn't explain why he remained vigilant. Except...today she had learned more about him. Adam Ramsdell hid dark secrets from his past. What menacing presence did he fear?

23

"YOU'RE RIGHT. OF COURSE you're right." Yet the idea of someone making a corpse of her, tossing her into the Pacific Ocean and thinking he was done with her, hurt and disturbed her. It was her death they were talking about!

Adam followed Elle inside his home. He shut the door, he turned the lock at the top and bottom and slid a slender metal bar into a socket.

She stared at him, trying to shake off the leaden remembrance of sinking, drowning, dying.

But she didn't really remember...did she? Breathing in the salty ocean, the bone-chilling cold of the Pacific waters, the knowledge that death swam with her and would claim her when she was done struggling...

Adam seemed unaware. "Shall we eat? We have the Live Oak leftovers, and Angelica gave us Asian tofu lettuce wraps, Szechuan green beans and pork with garlic and ginger on rice."

The description of the food brought Elle's consciousness back to the present. Her struggle with death sank into the depths of her mind. She might be moving slowly and aching in every joint, but she was hungry—again. "Yes, that sounds great."

"All of it?"

"Sure. That's one of my favorite meals." Elle heard the echo of a woman's voice. *By God, there's nothing wrong with your appetite.* She tilted her head, trying to catch the wisp of memory.

"Elle, are you all right?" Adam took her arm. "Do you feel faint?"

He yanked her out of her reverie. "What? No, I was just..." She didn't want to tell him she'd been close to remembering something. A woman speaking to her in an amused, proud tone. "I thought I heard something. The ocean. I'm not used to having it so close."

He considered her as if he didn't believe her. "The sound *is* a constant reminder of our mortality."

"Really?" She laughed in his face. "I thought it was a constant reminder to run to the beach and play!"

He relaxed. "I suppose. If you are of a frivolous nature." Now he laughed.

She followed him into the kitchen. They were going to be okay.

He pointed to a kitchen chair. "Sit while I put dinner on the table." He placed the lettuce wraps on the table and helped himself to one.

"As much as I'd like to loll around and watch you, I need to look something up. May I use your—" she almost said *phone*, then remembered the kind of cell he carried "—computer?"

He glanced toward the newspaper that sat folded on the table. "Of course. Will you need help?"

"I'll holler if I do."

When she came back, Adam had opened the takeout boxes,

prepped the food and set the table. He was obviously a man used to doing for himself.

"Did you find what you needed?" He sounded neutral.

"I did. I researched Angelica Lindholm."

"Oh. Angelica. Yes." He held her chair. "When she saw you, she had an interesting reaction."

"You mean she dropped something." Elle sat and he pushed in her chair. "When I took the Cheery Freeze cup, it was sweating, slick. It slipped in my grip. I steadied it. It occurred to me then that Angelica didn't even try to catch the cups. It was like her hands had lost their strength."

"A spontaneous reaction from Angelica Lindholm."

"Even having just met her, I thought that was odd. I wondered if perhaps she'd been abused at some point." Elle pointed to her face. "That I was a painful memory."

"I'd forgotten about how bruised you look."

"Many people would see only the injuries and not the person beneath."

He loaded her plate and his and delivered them to the table. "Those kinds of judgments lead to trouble."

"I'm living proof of that. Obviously I made one huge mistake in judgment." She picked up her fork. "Anyway, the whole Lindholm story is interesting. Her great-great-great-grandmother, Maeve Lindholm, was a major 1930s movie star who drove north up the coast along the newly completed California State Route 1, took a right on Nacimiento-Fergusson Road, stepped out on the top of Widow's Peak Ridge and announced, 'I will build my home here.'"

"I guess I *should* have bought a copy of Freya Goodnight's book."

"Right. *Gothic, California: A Haven for Lost Souls.* I'll bet it's all in there. Anyway, the area ranchers, males all of them—" Elle pulled a face at him "—laughed and sold her the worthless land for the Tower and the town. They stopped laughing when they found out she was a ballbuster."

He found himself enjoying the story. "I'll bet that *was* a shock."

"You bet, because Maeve was a beautiful, blonde bit of Scandinavian fluff." Elle smiled a savagely pleased grin. "She knew what she wanted, and she had the money to get it. She designed and built the town. She decided which buildings would line that road and what they would be used for." She sobered. "What she didn't intend—would never have wished—was that her lover would fall to his death from an unfinished rampart of the Tower."

"Ah, the tragedy that cursed the castle."

"In the end, she had no one but her daughter, Hazel." Elle took her first bite.

He dug in, too. "What happened to Hazel?"

"Hazel was a minor actress, and she produced a daughter named Rosabel. Rosabel was also a minor actress, and she produced a daughter named Audra."

"Minor actress?" he guessed.

"Right. And Audra had Angelica. Sadly, that's when the juicy gossip ends. As far as I can tell reading Angelica's unsanctioned biography, her early life was charmed, and she's such a savvy businesswoman she's made a fortune. She seems to be living her perfect life. Except that she's estranged from her son, but it's a widely held opinion that she's a force of nature, and if she cared to, she could reconcile with him. He was, from all accounts, a pleasant young man."

He got the point. "Angelica's reaction to you was more than just spontaneous. She acted as if she knew you."

"Exactly. She did act as if she knew me. So I asked her. She said no. She looked me in the eyes, and she said *no* emphatically." Elle held out her hands in a helpless gesture. "Of course, I don't remember her."

"No. You wouldn't. You couldn't."

"How irritating is that!"

"It's only been a little over twenty-four hours, and you've already retrieved a few bits of memory. I have great hopes for tomorrow." For a man with great hopes, he sounded remarkably composed.

She was making inroads into her dinner. "Who would have suspected the food in such a small town would be so good?"

"Gothic caters to the tourists, and good food brings them in."

"Was that the reason you moved here?"

"One of them."

"Food is really important to me."

"I can see that."

She considered pinning him with a withering glare. But the sticky pork mellowed her. "What are the other ones? Reasons you moved here?"

That seemed to give him pause. "I have room to work without disturbing anyone. The house and land were, for California, reasonable. But those aren't the real reasons."

She put down her fork and leaned her chin on her cupped hand.

He put his fork down, too. "I didn't mean to stop here. I was driving away from California. I meant to go north, to Oregon or Washington or even Canada. I was taking the back roads, taking my time, shaking off the..." He took a long breath. "Shaking off the grief."

She wanted to ask, *What grief?* but didn't dare interrupt.

"When I got to Gothic, I drove down those curves. I saw the For Sale sign here. I stopped and got out of my car, and for the first time in a year, I could breathe." He picked up his fork. "So I bought it."

She waited a few seconds to see if he would continue. When he didn't, she picked up her fork, too. "A good investment! It is lovely here, perched on the sharp edge of the continent. Are you sleeping with me tonight?"

He didn't look as if the prospect made him want to jump for joy, but he said, "If you want me to."

"Yes, please." The fearful knot inside her gut loosened a little, and she could breathe, too. "This evening, what do you want to do? After we eat?" She meant, did he want to sit together and talk, maybe kiss, figure out whether her survival and his rescue of her meant she was his lost soul?

Instead he said, "I'm not much for TV."

"Uh, no." He hadn't followed her train of thought at all. "Who is?"

"If I want to watch, and mostly I don't, I stream something on the computer."

He thought she might complain about the size of the monitor, but no—she zeroed in on the interesting part of his explanation. "Why don't you watch TV?"

"Nothing I want to see."

"You don't seem like a twenty-four-hour-news guy."

"No. The world runs without me, and there's nothing I can do to change the course of history short of—" He stopped so fast his voice got scratchy.

"Short of what?"

"Assassination." Probably not the best answer.

Elle stared at him, wide-eyed.

He struggled on. "People decide what they want to believe, then they go looking for corroboration. I can't… I can't change that, and I can't stand to witness such willful ignorance."

"I understand." She chewed a bite, swallowed and squinted

as if trying to see into her past. "I don't think I watch much of anything, either. I think I'm busy doing other stuff."

I'm busy would have been a better answer. Not as revealing. He wished he'd thought of that.

That night, they sat in his small living room. The front door faced west, and was open. The screen door was locked, and as intent as Adam was on security, Elle would not have been surprised if it was electrified. The scent and sound of the Pacific wafted in on the breeze, but the only illumination outside was the twinkling stars and, far out on the ocean, the glow of a ship's running lights.

Inside, she read the newspaper by the light of a standing lamp.

Adam studied a book on metallurgy in the Middle Ages.

At nine o'clock, he spoke softly to her, and when she lifted her head, he put his hand on her shoulder. "You're asleep in your chair. Let's go to bed."

"Asleep again?" She had the uncomfortable suspicion her jaw had been hanging open. "I need to shower."

"You don't *need* to shower. You smell fine."

"Silver-tongued devil. Stop trying to seduce me."

"You can shower in the morning." He directed her toward the bathroom. "Either in the tub or we can use the outside shower. That is, we can use it separately."

Can I watch you?

Best not to ask. After she had washed her face and brushed her teeth and put on the pajamas Angelica had included in her package, Elle climbed into bed. But she wasn't ready to sleep until Adam joined her.

He turned his back to her.

She snuggled up behind him, draped her arm on his shoulder, finding comfort in his warmth and strength, and smiled into the dark.

He had said she had a bright spirit.

A bright spirit. Adam Ramsdell, uncommunicative and austere, thought she had a bright spirit.

She remembered that compliment, sincerely given, and held it in her heart and polished and admired it.

She would do her best to keep the bright shining outward.

24

Aboard the Research Vessel Arcturus

DEANNA CHARGED THROUGH THE door of the sunlit comm center at the stern of the ship. "Has anyone seen that bitch Elladora Varela? She hasn't used her crawl time for two days, and if she's not going to use it, I want it. *My* project is a lot more critical than whatever secret mission she is on, and—" She stopped, aware that two pairs of eyes watched her, one pair coldly, the other wide with warning.

"Right now, the comm center is being used for important business. Come back later," said Stephen Penderghast's assistant, Zsóke.

Ryan Naidu, their ocean-currents study scientist, was the wide-eyed warning guy. And what was he doing in here? She had expected to find Daniel, the crawl-time superintendent and project-scheduling supervisor.

Ryan and Zsóke leaned over the massive, inclined tracking screen.

Somehow DeAnna had walked into a situation, and she made an attempt to salvage it. "Zsóke!" She fumbled with the pronunciation. To her ear, it sounded like *SO-key*, but when Stephen Penderghast said it, the name sounded Eastern European and harsher. "I hope Mr. Penderghast is doing well."

Zsóke gave a slow nod. "He lives."

With Zsóke's attention on DeAnna, Ryan jerked his head sideways, indicating DeAnna should leave *now*.

"Good. That's good. Give him my best wishes." DeAnna backed out and headed for the rear-deck helipad. Yes, there was the Penderghast helicopter, its rotor slowly rotating. She might have noticed its arrival, except her crawl time was in the middle of the night and she had to sleep sometime…

Zsóke appeared, black hair wild in the wind, walked briskly to the helicopter and got in the pilot's seat, making a check of the instruments in preparation to lift off. It figured that Zsóke was the pilot.

DeAnna turned and bumped into Ryan. "What was *that* all about?"

Even in the breeze, Ryan looked pale and sweaty, as if his encounter made him seasick. "Zsóke is interested in the currents around the *Arcturus* on the night Stephen Penderghast was hurt."

"Do you have that information? About the currents?"

"Not to Zsóke's complete satisfaction, but essentially yes."

Daniel sidled up, keeping out of sight of the rising helicopter. "Ryan, man, how did it go?"

"I just spent a harrowing hour outlining all the possibilities of where the currents surrounding this ship could have taken an object." Ryan looked over the railing. "If it had fallen into the ocean."

"I wondered why Zsóke wanted to talk to you in private." Daniel pulled them both into the shade of a lifeboat. When

DeAnna looked at him in surprise, he said, "We don't want to be seen discussing anything about Stephen or Zsóke."

"Ryan? What did they lose?" DeAnna asked.

Ryan shook his head. "I don't know. Zsóke wouldn't tell me what, if anything, had gone over the edge and didn't listen when I said where and how far the currents carry an object depends on its size and weight and…all the things."

Daniel thought it through. "That night, something went overboard, and they want to retrieve it. Something Stephen got badly hurt trying to save."

DeAnna took the next leap. "What's so precious Stephen was willing to die for it?"

"I don't know," Ryan said.

"Why didn't you ask?" DeAnna pressed.

Ryan whipped around to scowl at her. "Would you have the nerve to question Zsóke about *anything*?"

Remembering that still, focused, deadly face, DeAnna said, "No. Still, I wonder what was so important they'd go to such lengths to get it back."

"Or…or maybe that's the wrong question," Daniel said. "*Who* did they lose? Did Stephen Penderghast get hurt fighting with *somebody*?"

Ryan grabbed their arms. "Don't speculate!"

"Hey, that hurts." DeAnna pried his hand off her.

"Don't you two get it? Zsóke is scary. I don't know what went off the ship that they want, or who, but anyone who talks about it…might take a visit overboard, too."

"C'mon," DeAnna scoffed. "Not that scary!"

"Shut up and forget you heard anything." Ryan walked away.

"He's right," Daniel said. "I've got a baby on the way. I've got to be careful."

"Sure..." DeAnna struggled to comprehend. "As badly as Stephen was hurt, if it was somebody and not something, it had to be a guy. One of the crew?"

"Don't speculate." Daniel was low-voiced and insistent.

But DeAnna loved a good mystery. "Maybe someone was stealing research from the ship?"

"Keep talking, and you're going to get us all in trouble." Daniel walked after Ryan.

"Wait!" Her original complaint still stood. She hurried after him. "If Elladora Varela isn't going to use her crawl time, I want it. She's so top secret, we don't even know what she's doing. I know what I'm doing. You know what I'm doing. I'm mapping the ocean floor along the trench. I've found so many new features that Eric is reviewing my tapes, and he's excited about the new creatures I've captured on camera. Double the bang for your crawl-time buck. Geology and biology. You're in charge of the schedule. Give me her time."

"How many sessions has she missed?"

"Two in a row."

"Have you asked her about it?"

"We're not friends."

Daniel made up his mind. "Tonight the crawl time is yours."

"What if Elladora shows up?"

"Tell her I said she forfeited this evening. This equipment is too expensive to leave it idle."

"I'd say she forfeited tomorrow evening, too."

"There are other scientists who would like the time."

"I asked first. The squeaky wheel gets the grease."

"Yes, but whatever it is Elladora is doing, she's intense. She'll show up." This time, Daniel walked away without a backward glance.

He was right about that. Elladora was intense about her project. Like it or not, DeAnna supposed she would show up.

But DeAnna had tonight. She walked away, smiling.

She liked being the squeaky wheel.

25

ONCE ZSÓKE HAD THE information from the *Arcturus*, finding Elladora Varela was ridiculously easy. The ocean currents could have dropped her only on a limited area of Big Sur shoreline, and on a hill above those beaches a tiny speck of a town existed: Gothic, California.

A moment of internet research took Zsóke to the neighborhood social-media page where the residents of Gothic posted updated information about the continued Highway 1 road closure, warned of area cougar sightings and reminded each other that the recent storm had created a lush growth of grass and brush that would burn all too well during the fire season.

Caution should be taken.

Luckily for Zsóke, the posts also churned with gossip about the newest celebrity at the Live Oak Restaurant and Inn and buzzed about the town outcast who had driven up the main street with a young, heavily bruised woman.

The outcast's name was Adam Ramsdell, but no one knew the woman's name or where she came from.

Amid vehement denials from Adam's apparent friends, speculation ran rampant that Adam himself had administered the beating. Other people of a less vicious mindset offered a claim that the young woman had come in with the storm and the aftermath of fog and that she was a lost soul, which was one of the area's weird and persistent superstitions.

Zsóke leaned back in the office chair.

It would appear Stephen was right. But who would have thought that that delicate little scrap of a woman would survive both Stephen's fury and a stormy night in the Pacific Ocean?

And why hadn't she called the police about her assault?

Zsóke speculated that, rather than bring charges against the well-respected Stephen, she had chosen to conceal herself, at least until she knew whether he would live or die.

A good plan, but doomed to failure.

Now, how to get into this small, close-knit village without being spotted?

Another scan of the posts gave the answer.

Really, people shouldn't put their entire lives online. That made a distraction so easy to create.

Elladora shouldn't have chosen to shelter with this Adam Ramsdell.

Because now they both would have to die.

26

THE NEXT MORNING, A knock on the back screen door brought Adam's and Elle's heads around to the open door.

A uniformed man stood there, a police officer, a man in his thirties holding a computer tablet and wearing a serious expression. "Hi, Adam."

A cop. Elle took a deep breath to still the sudden wild thumping of her heart.

Adam put his hand over hers. Softly he said, "You've done nothing wrong. Maybe he has information for us. Probably he's here for some reason unrelated to you or me. Dave's a friend. He probably came for breakfast."

Just as quietly, she said, "I hurt the man with a shiny pole. I'm sure I did."

"Is that still all you remember?"

She nodded.

"Because you don't look as if you won the fight. Even if that's why Dave is here, and I doubt it, it's clear you merely defended yourself against an attacker. Be calm. Say little. Listen much." Adam rose, unlocked the screen door and opened it. "Hi, Dave. Come in."

The officer stepped inside, and his gaze skipped Adam and zeroed in on Elle. "Hello, miss. I'm Deputy Dave MacLean. Most people call me Deputy Dave."

"I imagine they like the alliteration." She stood, too. "I'm Elle. Would you like some breakfast?"

Deputy Dave glanced at Adam's meal: a parfait of Greek yogurt, frozen blueberries and whole-grain cereal.

Elle had fixed herself a less organic breakfast: five strips of bacon, two soft-boiled eggs, a piece of toast (multigrain) and a bowl of fresh ripe red cherries. "I fried plenty of bacon," she assured him, "and it's nothing to fix an egg."

"I'm a sheriff's deputy. Last time I turned down a meal, some idiot partygoers built a firepit on the Crosswinds Ranch, and I spent the next twenty hours helping evacuate thirty people and two hundred sheep. By the time that was over, I was starving and had been butted by every ram right in the—" Deputy Dave cast his gaze downward with a pained expression. "Please, may I have my eggs scrambled?"

"I remember that fire." With heavy irony, Adam said, "Good times." While Elle whipped up a robust meal, Adam set a place. "Toast? Multigrain or sourdough?"

Deputy Dave poured himself a cup of coffee and sat. "I'd rather have sourdough, but my wife has me on a strict diet of whole grain. I eat so much fiber I could pass wicker furniture."

Elle did a double take, then laughed so hard she bent over at the waist.

"I like her," Deputy Dave told Adam.

"Because she likes your jokes? Don't flatter yourself. She likes to laugh." Adam lowered a slice of multigrain into the toaster, and when it popped up he passed the finished breakfast to Dave.

Before Deputy Dave took the first bite, he said with great gravity, "I am here on official business to check out a complaint from the neighbors."

"Oh. A complaint from the neighbors." Adam nodded reassuringly at Elle. "What kind of complaint?"

"Apparently the last couple of nights there's been a woman screaming like she's being murdered."

Adam turned to Elle, gestured toward Deputy Dave and turned back to his breakfast. He had explained to Elle that in a few days he was going to fight on the field of battle. He needed to fuel himself correctly.

Reluctantly, she put her fork down. "I have nightmares. I scream. But I only screamed once last night."

"Once was enough," Adam said.

"Once was better than the night before," she told him.

Deputy Dave concentrated on Adam. "The complaint suggested you'd given her those bruises."

"No!" Elle's eyes flashed. She turned to Adam. "You didn't tell me you had malicious neighbors."

"Not malicious," Adam said. "Concerned."

"Nosy," Elle insisted.

Adam gave a shrug, one shoulder only.

"That takes care of the official complaint." Deputy Dave grimaced at his multigrain toast, smiled at his bacon and eggs and went to work. After the first few bites, he said, "This is good! What's your name, miss, if I might ask?"

At once, she felt tense, defensive. "I told you. I'm Elle."

"That's all? Elle?" Deputy Dave kept his gaze on the eggs.

"Yes."

He glanced up. "How did you get those contusions? The marks on your throat?"

"Adam Ramsdell has never hurt me."

Adam patted her hand. "Take it easy. Deputy Dave is one of the good guys."

She yanked her hand away. "I'm not going to get you in trouble for something you did not do."

Deputy Dave asked, "Would you like to tell me who *did* do this to you?"

She bent her head and shook it.

"Sometimes victims are ashamed of what's happened to them. They blame themselves. Whoever hurt you deserves the blame and deserves to face a judge and be convicted of abuse. My father was a guy like whoever gave you those bruises, and my mother died at his hand."

"I am so sorry," Elle murmured.

"People get into law enforcement for a lot of different reasons. That's mine." Deputy Dave finished eating, put his dishes in the sink and poured himself another cup of coffee. "I have only empathy for you and your ordeal."

"Thank you." Elle flashed him a smile. "I appreciate your candor. But I can't tell you what happened. All I can tell you is that Adam Ramsdell rescued me from a watery death and let me stay here with him. Whoever is complaining about my screaming—I'm sorry, but I can't help it. Believe me, I wish I could."

"I figured Adam for the good guy. Don't worry about the screaming." Deputy Dave put his business card by her elbow. "I'm always around if you want to talk." Something whistled like a teapot, and with massive good humor, he unbuttoned his shirt pocket and retrieved his phone. "That's a text. I imagine I'm back on duty. But I got to finish a meal!" He read the text, and the way he moved, the expression he wore, made it clear he was indeed back on duty.

"What is it?" Adam asked.

"A body was found on Bustier Basin Ranch." Deputy Dave

looked into Elle's eyes, then Adam's. "Either of you know anything about this?"

Elle stood and put her hand on Deputy Dave's arm. "What? Who?"

"Male in his midtwenties. Found naked and in a shallow pit. Battering to the face and body. Throat slashed." Deputy Dave read from his phone. "According to the reporting officer, killer was determined and efficient."

"That doesn't seem as if it would have anything to do with me," Elle said.

Adam wanted to tell her not to look troubled, that Deputy Dave would draw conclusions. "Who is he? Have they taken fingerprints?"

"Yes, but no identification as yet. White, blond hair, six foot plus and fit. Very fit, according to the officer, emphasis on *very.* Whoever killed him is a master at attack and weapons. The victim has lost everything—clothes, money, credit cards, ID—so it's probably a robbery." Deputy Dave turned to Adam. "Time of death is within the last twenty-four hours. Can you account for your activities during those hours—"

Adam kept his expression neutral. "Why would you suspect me?"

"Because there aren't many people in this area who could kill a tall, fit man in such a manner. According to the media, you can." Deputy Dave had read the stories.

Not surprising, but Adam once again knew distaste of being the center of a cruel scandal.

"I can vouch for Adam." Elle spoke up without hesitation. "He's been with me every minute. Or rather, I've been with him. The only way to keep the nightmares under control is to be with Adam."

The deputy frowned. "Where was he last night when you were asleep?"

"He was sleeping with me."

"You're sleeping together?" Deputy Dave looked between them as if he hadn't expected that reply.

Elle threw open the door to the bedroom. "You decide."

The bed had two pillows with indents, two full-length marks in the mattress, and a tousle of sheets and blankets. Deputy Dave looked in and repeated, "You are sleeping together?"

"Yes." Elle was definite.

"Yes, but we're not having sex." Adam was just as definite.

Deputy Dave examined them suspiciously.

Elle had her chin stuck out.

Adam crossed his arms over his chest and appeared as if he could barely refrain from rolling his eyes. "I picked her up off the beach. I'm not going to make her pay for my lifesaving services by taking advantage of her."

Elle turned on him like a fury. "I wouldn't let you take advantage of me. If and when we have sex, my friend, it will be something we both consent to. In the meantime—thank you for helping me *sleep*."

Deputy Dave said, "I guess she told *you*."

Adam nodded sagely. "She does that very well."

27

AFTER PROMISING TO BE around if Elle needed him, and assuring Adam the sheriff's department planned a law-enforcement presence at all times during the Gothic Spring Psychic Festival, Deputy Dave headed back over the Nacimiento-Fergusson highway.

On their way to their appointment with Madame Rune, Adam and Elle collected Mr. Kulshan, who came out of Mrs. Kulshan's house a little spryer than when he went in, and while Elle transferred to the back-facing seat, Adam helped Mr. Kulshan into the front passenger seat.

"Good morning, folks!" Mr. Kulshan said. "Always good to spend time with the old bat. She's got a way about her that makes a man remember…how to polka."

Elle looked forward to the front seat. She observed Adam's horror and laughed out loud.

The old man cranked around to look at her. "That sounds good," he said. "I'll bet the wind caught that laughter and carried it up the hill to catch in the olive trees where it will linger, whispering in the gray-green leaves."

"Mr. Kulshan, you're a poet!" Elle exclaimed.

"Once upon a time I was, before the war knocked it out of me. Women like you and the old bat bring it back."

Elle asked cordially, "Out of curiosity, what's the *old bat*'s name?"

"Her name is Irene."

"A lovely name. Is there a single reason you shouldn't use it all the time?"

Mr. Kulshan looked as if he was torn between fight and surrender. Wisely, he surrendered. "Young lady, you win. From now on, I'll call her Irene."

Adam pulled up to Mr. Kulshan's house and helped him out. While Elle made the transfer back into the front seat, she gave the gent a kiss on the cheek. He patted her arm. "You look very sunny in that shirt," he said and went up the walk singing "Goodnight, Irene."

"My mother used to sing that to me," Elle said dreamily, then looked at Adam sideways. "That's all I remember about it. Her voice singing that song."

Only when Mr. Kulshan had climbed the steps and opened the door did they drive away.

"*I* like your laughter, too," Adam said. "And your shirt."

She grinned at Adam. He had sounded so...competitive. She enjoyed that, and the warm breeze in her face. "Are you going to write a poem?"

"No."

She laughed again, then her smile faded. If not for the sense of loss that haunted her and the terror that stalked her, right now she would be completely happy. She needed to recover her past. Soon. Now.

They reached the top of the curves where the Live Oak occupied the outer curve and Madame Rune's Psychic Readings the inner curve. Adam parked, and before he could come around, Elle got out of the ATV.

"You're moving better today," he observed.

"Still a little stiff—" she gently rubbed her hip and her ribs and grimaced "—but the more I move, the better it gets."

"Good." Adam searched her eyes. One was brown. One was blue. Condition unchanged. "Good," he murmured and opened the shop door for her.

A jingling bell announced their arrival.

Elle stepped across the threshold, and with heartfelt awe she said, "Wow."

The wide front windows glittered with rock crystals, crystal balls and globes of the universe with the horoscope stars lit from within. Built-in along the side walls was a knee-high enclosed painted chest shelf with locked, sliding doors underneath. On top of that shelf, glass eyeballs filled a basket labeled *Eye of Newt.* Next to that, small packages of cookies filled a bowl labeled *Figs of Newton.* Clocks with crooked arms and reversed numbers cluttered the walls, interspersed with self-proclaimed magic mirrors of every size and style. In the front corner, wizard staffs made of a variety of knobby, polished woods rested in a tall umbrella stand.

The long, narrow room was immaculately clean, and the scent of lavender and sage perfumed the air. On the back wall, a sign hung over an entrance to a small, dimly lit room: *Library. Enter at your own risk. Knowledge within!* Beneath that was a card that said, *Palmistry, tarot, rune-reading, horoscopes performed by Madame Rune herself.*

Rune bustled through the beaded curtain and into the shop in the full fortune-teller getup: gathered skirt, fringed scarves, dangling earrings and her long wavy gray hair hanging loose around her shoulders. "Darlings! Welcome to my shop, the home of my heart. I predicted you would be here early."

"Ten minutes early," Adam said, "and we have an appointment."

Elle was willing to be impressed. "Ten minutes is ten minutes, Adam."

Testily, Adam said, "I'm always ten minutes early for an appointment."

Coins jingled as Madame Rune waved an arm and intoned, "Many are the ways of divination."

Adam set his teeth and watched Elle wander along the shelves.

Behind a sign that read *Divination Objects*, stacks of tarot cards in various sizes and with exotic paintings were scattered on the shelves. Small velvet bags clanked with (naturally) rune stones. Elle shook out the small black dicelike rocks into her palm and stared at gold scratchings carved in the sides.

"No idea," she muttered.

Scattered on the shelves were sheep, large and small: sheep figurines, sheep painted on pottery plates, cute and cuddly stuffed sheep. A miniature hardback book stood on the shelf: *Buddhism for Sheep.*

Elle picked up a skein of wool from the cubbyhole beneath the shelf. A warm gray color, the wool was thick, soft, inviting. "Why sheep?"

Rune replied serenely, "I like sheep. I sell yarn sheared, colored and spun from the backs of local sheep."

"I don't believe in the supernatural, but I do believe Rune is one helluva businessperson," Adam told Elle.

Elle nodded. "I love this."

"Most people do. Unless they don't, and then—" Adam stopped.

Clearly, Elle was intrigued. "Then?"

Rune filled in the blank. "Adam rescued me once."

28

“**UPSTAIRS IS MY CONSULTATION** room. There I read palms, crystal balls, tarot cards, auras, and rune stones—” Rune used her best dramatic tone “—tossed by seekers of knowledge to reveal their destinies.”

Elle turned to Adam. “You rescued Madame Rune? Upstairs in her consultation room? I’m not the only one?”

“A coward tried to stab Rune for being…” Adam couldn’t remember the exact words.

Rune filled in. “A false prophet.”

“Mr. Kulshan called me, yelling. By the time I got here, Rune had disarmed the intruder.”

“In the process, I broke his arm.” Rune shuddered. “That’s a sound I’ll never forget. The breaking, and the screaming.”

“When I ran into the shop and up the stairs, the customer—”

“The asshole,” Rune insisted.

“Is that official psychiatrist talk?” Elle asked.

"Madame Rune's words are many and varied," Rune deadpanned.

"When I ran in," Adam repeated, "the customer was insisting Rune had tried to rob him."

"Adam told me to show them the video of the visit."

Elle turned her head from side to side as they talked.

"By the time Deputy Dave arrived, the customer had been reduced to spouting some prophesies of his own, including that Rune would be stricken by the seven plagues." Adam looked Rune over from head to toe. "Which apparently hasn't happened yet."

"No frogs. No boils. No lice. I've already had the pestilence."

"That was one helluva day." Adam shook his head at the memory.

"So much for not having friends." Elle laughed. "You are finishing each other's sentences."

"We were both there," Adam explained. "We had different points of view."

Elle exchanged glances with Rune.

"Come. Let's go to the consultation room." Rune locked the front door and flipped the sign in the window from *Open* to *Closed to allow the spirits to visit.* She pulled the shades down on the door and the front windows, then bustled to the beaded curtain and pushed it back to reveal the shadowy stairway. She led them up the steps and into the small, sunny room. A wide window faced onto the street, and smaller windows in each of the side walls were hung with burgundy brocade drapes. An antique side table was set with candlesticks of silver, ceramic, pewter, and two tall ones that gleamed like gold. White candles had burned and left lacy beeswax drippings.

Elle hurried to the centerpiece of the room, a small square table painted with a large square of iridescent copper paint.

An extravagant design of checks and swirls spilled off the sides and down the legs. She smoothed her fingers along the edge of the copper. "I love it!"

"I knew you would," Rune said in satisfaction. "Adam hates it."

Irritated, Adam said, "I never said I hated it. I said it was a shame to destroy the intrinsically organized square-upon-square with the foolish madness of the rest of the design."

Elle grinned at him. "You would."

He felt like a fuddy-duddy, yet he heard the warm affection in her voice.

She ran her fingertips over the flocked wallpaper, fingered the gold ropes that held back the drapes and petted a stuffed sheep on a shelf as she faced out the front window. "This room is comfortable."

Adam thought it was bizarre, like a throwback to some magical dystopian preteen novel. But what did he know?

"I'm glad you think so. Before we start, let's handle the business end of this." Rune rattled the fringe of coins on her scarf. "I'm a fortune-teller. You have to cross my palm with silver."

Elle looked stricken. "I don't have any money."

Rune turned to Adam. "C'mon, buddy, you're sleeping with her. Pop with a few coins."

Adam's well-disciplined temper rose. "Damn it to hell. Did you talk to Deputy Dave? What did he tell you?"

"I haven't seen Deputy Dave today. What makes you think I have?" Rune's voice developed a pleased, singsong tone.

"You know that we… Wait, is this one of your guesses?" Adam had been conned. Conned!

"Madame Rune does not guess, she divines."

Adam was already tired of that line.

Rune continued. "Since you're sleeping with Elle, you should cough up the coins."

"We're not having sex," Elle informed her. "When I sleep alone, I scream."

Adam wanted to tell her to stop feeding Rune material. Because Rune looked so wickedly pleased.

"I knew that." Rune took her hand and kissed it. "You can pay me when you find out who you are and can access your funds." He shot a look at Adam. "Or Mr. I'm-Not-Paying-for-Lunch can do it in advance."

She went toe-to-toe with Rune. "Adam doesn't support me. He doesn't own me. Tell me what you're charging, and I'll see you're paid back. Or if you're charging a lot, I'll leave and figure this whole amnesia thing out for myself."

Rune backed up like a Doberman under attack from a Pomeranian. "I'll take an IOU."

"I don't want to put you out." Elle wasn't taking bullshit. "I don't need any favors." She poked her finger at Rune's chest. "How? Much?"

Adam crossed his arms and leaned against the sideboard. *Now* he was enjoying himself.

"I can't guarantee success, so—how about forty dollars for the first half hour and twenty dollars every half hour after that?"

"Wowza." Elle was taken aback. "Do you really make that much?"

"More. You're getting the friends-and-family rate." Rune stood on sure footing. "I'm good at what I do."

"I'll pay you when I'm recovered, which I will do—" she was fierce in her determination "—either in one lump sum or in payments as I am capable. For what it's worth, I don't think I'm wealthy—I know I'm good with a budget—so it'll probably be payments." She offered her hand.

They shook. "That's settled. Let's start. If it's all right with you, I'd like to shut out the rest of the world, light the candles.

The contrast of darkness and light gives us a more focused experience." Madame Rune pulled a velvet drape over the front window. "Elle, only if you're comfortable with the idea."

Elle looked inside herself and considered the question seriously, and Adam remembered how much she feared the dark and the monster man who had attacked her. He was about to offer his opinion—*No, definitely not*—when she nodded. "That will be fine."

In a reassuring tone, Rune said, "If at any time you wish to welcome the sunlight, it's only a curtain pull away."

While Rune closed the drape beside the sideboard, Adam walked to the window that looked up and out of town. An olive grove was clustered on the west side of the slope, and he scanned it, looking for movement.

There. A flash as if someone had been watching with an eyepiece. A movement as if someone had slipped back into the shadowy branches.

Rune came to stand beside him. "I should have asked. Is it all right with you, Adam, if I enclose us?"

Everything about this situation irritated Adam. "What's the purpose of darkness? It's not a séance."

"In its way, it is. We're going to attempt to explore something far more complex and fascinating than the beyond. We're going to attempt to bring light to the fog that obscures Elle's mind."

Put that way, it made some kind of sense. "Do it."

Rune shut the drape. A glass sheep-shaped night-light in the wall plug-in popped on. "I take every opportunity to defeat the darkness." She lit candles at the side table. "We must never allow it to get an upper hand. Please, take a seat."

Four antique straight-backed chairs sat waiting for them, and she watched as Elle chose the one facing the street. Rune brought candles over, two by two, until they had six burning on the table in front of them. "Adam?" Rune gestured to the chair beside Elle and seated herself on the other side.

Elle touched the gold-colored candlesticks. "These are extraordinary."

"Yes." Rune watched her as if she had said something of great interest.

"Twenty-four karat gold?"

"Eighteen."

"Tiffany, early twentieth century?"

"Exactly. You have a good eye."

Now Adam knew why Rune scrutinized her. Elle's knowledge of those candlesticks revealed something about her background. But what, exactly? Was she a jeweler? A person of wealth? A thief? Someone who had been robbed of valuables, choked and thrown in the ocean?

"Do you trust me?" Rune asked Elle.

"I do."

"Are you willing to let me hypnotize you?"

"I am."

"Let's try this, shall we?" Rune held up his hand, fingers spread wide, palm toward Elle. "Focus on one of my fingers. Just one. Which do you choose?"

"The finger with the entwined gold vines ring. That's beautiful."

"Thank you. Great choice. Now, concentrate on that fingertip."

"When I know who I am, I'm going to celebrate by buying a ring like that."

"That's an admirable goal. We'll get you there. All you have to do is relax and focus..." Rune's voice got smooth, warm, gentle.

She nodded and kept her gaze on his finger. "I am."

"Focus and breathe."

"I am." Her chest rose and fell.

"Where are you?"

"I'm here with Adam and Rune."

"That's right." Rune intently watched her.

Adam saw her go under. Then she sat straighter and took a long breath, and she seemed to see a different vision.

In a soothing tone, Rune said, "Elle, I'll take you to the past. To that moment you want to forget. What do you remember?"

Elle sat up even straighter, and at that moment Adam knew what was going to happen.

She screamed, loud and long and shrill.

29

ELLE'S SHRIEK LIFTED THE hair on Adam's neck and warned him that fear was primal and here on the doorstep.

"No! No! Let me go!" Elle fought with an invisible attacker. "How could I have been so wrong? I'm going to die! I'm going to die!"

Adam lunged at Elle, wrapped her in his arms, held her and murmured, "No one can hurt you. Not now. Not here."

Elle snapped out of her trance. She looked into Adam's face, saw him, knew him, whispered, "I'm fine. I'm fine."

"Whoever he is, he can't get to you. You're safe." Rune's voice was soothing, but she scooted her chair back as if she needed distance from that ferocious onslaught of terror.

"I tried to defend myself. I know I did." Elle put her hand on her chest. "But he could not be defeated."

Rune stood up, went to the window and started to pull the curtain open.

"No!" Elle shouted. "No light. I can't see...in the light."

Rune seemed to understand. She went to the shelf by the

window and picked up the stuffed sheep, stroked it, then handed it to Elle.

Elle clutched it to her chest, bent her head into the fleece and closed her eyes.

"You're all right?" Rune put her hand on the back of Elle's chair and leaned over her. "Elle, you're all right?"

"I'm fine. I just… Could I have a glass of water?"

"You bet." Rune hurried into the tiny restroom off the consultation room and came back with a water glass of swirling colors of blues and purples.

"That's so pretty." Elle smiled as she took the glass and sipped.

"You stopped my heart." Rune put her hand to her chest.

"It's terrifying, isn't it?" Adam was irritated. "I warned you, Rune."

"I believed you, Adam." Rune was just as irritated. "I just didn't think we'd go there so soon."

"I didn't mean to go there. It's that…as soon as I let loose of my consciousness, there I am, helpless, fighting him." Elle lifted her hands and let them drop. "He's choking me, and I'm dying… I know I'm dying… Slowly…"

"We'll forget the hypnotism thing." Adam was relieved. And determined.

As thoroughly as Rune and Elle ignored him, he might have saved his breath.

Rune said, "The way I led you into the trance was ill-advised. I should have thought it through. It was a man's hands that hurt you, led you to death, revival and a loss of memory."

Elle caught on before Adam did. "You won't have me concentrate on your hands again?"

"We're going to try again?" Adam couldn't believe it. "After that?" He flung out a hand toward the past…wherever that was. "Now?"

"Why not now?" Rune asked.

"At the least, she needs time to let her fear retreat," Adam insisted.

"No. Not now." Elle hugged the lamb tighter and looked into the candle flames. "Something else now. Rune!"

"Yes?" Rune stroked the length of gray hair that hung over her shoulder.

"Tell me how you came to the City of Lost Souls. Tell us how you became Madame Rune and opened your shop here."

Adam enjoyed seeing Rune try to collect herself. He was willing to bet that not even in Hollywood had Rune seen such drama as Elle presented.

Rune saw Adam's amusement and glared, then in a soothing tone said to Elle, "After my divorce, the failure of my business, the loss of my health and friends, and my personal fall from grace… I had to find property I could afford, and in California that's not easy. My darling grandmother died—that was an awful year—and left me an inheritance. I drove around the state and ended up here, the City of Lost Souls." Rune wandered toward the candles on the sideboard, hovered her hand over the heat of the flames and watched intently. "I bought the shop from the psychic who wanted to retire, because what did I do as a psychiatrist but help people realize what was bothering them so they could work it out for themselves?"

"But why such a distinctive change?" Elle asked.

"The new voice gave me a head start on that. I wanted to try life from a different perspective."

"The height and shape and five-o'clock shadow don't tip off your clients?" Adam was sarcastic.

Rune walked into a corner, almost out of the reach of candlelight. "For some people, my look can create an initial double take. People who visit a psychic want scarves, a trance, the gypsy legend with all its promises and enchantments and dangling gold coins. A little chin stubble doesn't throw them off. I am still a lost soul, but at least I'm in good company." She looked meaningfully at Adam.

Adam didn't believe he was a lost soul. He believed he had lost his soul. A not-subtle difference.

Elle leaned toward Rune. "I like you."

"I like you, too." Rune came out of hiding, back to the table, and patted Elle's hand. Without looking around, she said, "Stop glaring, Adam. I'm not putting the moves on your girl."

"She's not my girl."

"Your boarder, then."

"I'm not a boarder. I don't pay him." Elle's fierce interruption collapsed into a pile of wretched uncertainty. "I'm a coward who's afraid to leave. I'm afraid *he'll* find me and I won't know him until it's too late."

Rune and Adam exchanged glances, then the fortune-teller assured her, "The trauma and the loss of memory you've suffered has naturally resulted in emotional highs and lows, and what you now experience is not cowardice. You'd be a fool not to feel a natural wariness."

"True," Adam said. "As long as you stick close, whether you recognize him or not doesn't matter. I have a nose for trouble."

Rune glanced toward the window where Adam had earlier been standing. "You do, don't you?"

"Not always soon enough." Like Rune, Adam seemed to withdraw into the darkness—but without moving a muscle. "Elle, I have promised to help you. To the best of my abilities, I will keep my promise."

"I don't doubt you, Adam. But I don't want you hurt, not for my sake." Elle scooted her chair closer to the table. "I'm calmer now. I want to try hypnosis again. I need to know *something* about that night."

"I know I can help you. You like the swirl of color in the drinking glass. I've got something similar. Let me get it." Rune went down the stairs into her showroom.

Adam knelt beside Elle, took her hands. "Elle, you don't have to be hypnotized. Rune said you could answer questions, talk your way through your memory loss."

"She did, but she also said that's conventional therapy. While I have respect for traditional routes, I don't have the time it takes to chip away at my mind's barriers. I need to know what happened to me and why I'm so convinced this man will find and destroy me." Elle patted Adam's hand as if he were an anxious nanny. "We didn't really fail with the hypnosis. If anything, we succeeded too suddenly. Rune's theory about her hand holds merit."

Leaning heavily on the rail, Rune climbed the stairs holding up a pendent necklace on a black cord. "This flowing form is created from blown glass shimmering with cool blue and lavender iridescence—"

"Won't that remind her of the ocean?" Adam felt he was being logical.

"And etched with tiny vines and leaves." Rune glared at him.

Elle cupped the pendant in her hand. "Rune, this is beautiful. You have exquisite taste!"

Rune beamed. "I carry local artists, and here in the City of Lost Souls talent congregates, irresistibly drawn by the swirl of spiritual beauty."

"That is such bullshit," Adam said.

"Like you aren't here and a great artist," Rune answered.

"I'm a *metalworker.*"

"You listen when the metal speaks."

Elle coughed softly.

The two turned to face her.

She clasped the pendant in her palms. "Yes. I'd like to use this."

Rune took the pendant, seated herself across from Elle and swayed with it, back and forth, back and forth.

Adam sat down and watched and for the first time realized how well hypnosis could work.

"Elle, you're here with Adam and me. You know that. At the same time, you remember what you fear. You remember..."

"Yes. I remember."

She couldn't breathe.

She couldn't scream.

She couldn't see anymore, nothing but flashes of light that flared behind her eyes like fireworks. She was dying. Dying. She kicked with increasing feebleness and clawed at his arms, at his sleeves.

She flung out her hands, slapped the wall—and touched cold, hard metal. A rod of some kind.

Inspiration joined with instinct. She grasped the handle, wrestled it free from whatever held it. It was heavy. It was long. She lifted it above his head and, with her last strength, smashed him in the back of the skull.

Cursing, he released her and staggered away.

Gasping, breathing, she collapsed where she stood. As she drew in great breaths, she could see squares of light. Windows. A door. A house.

Safety.

She tried to crawl toward them, but the world tilted and spun, and she rolled away into the darkness. A splash of cold water slapped her face, bringing her back to true consciousness.

Somehow, she still clutched her weapon. Some instinct had warned her to hold it tightly, and she would not relinquish it now. She held it up to the light; the metal shone like stainless steel. She saw the length of it: it was as long as she was tall, and the end curved like a cane back toward her, terminating in a barbed hook.

Thank God she had retained her weapon, because silhouetted against the careening light, a dark, menacing form moved toward her.

She tasted salt and terror.

Him. He stood between her and the house where there was help, light, life.

He was returning to finish the job.

30

ELLE TOOK HER GAZE away from the pendant, leaned back in her chair and sighed. "I had a weapon. I used a weapon. That makes me feel so much better to know I hurt him at least a little."

Adam was stunned by the clarity of her revelation, and even Rune looked not so much pleased as amazed.

She put her hand on Rune's. "Can we go on?"

Rune reached into her capacious skirt pocket and pulled out a velvet bag. "Let's consult the runes."

Adam groaned. Did they have to go through every phony supernatural device known to mankind?

Rune shook the stones out on the table—they looked like finger bones—and studied them. "The runes say we should postpone our next hypnosis, give Elle some space before she tries again."

Elle grasped the edges of the table. "But I'm remembering!"

Rune dropped her fortune-teller persona and became the therapist. "You stopped remembering at that point for a reason. Let your subconscious rest and gather strength for the next revelation."

Adam might scorn the psychic, but the therapist obviously knew her shit.

"There might never be another time!" Elle was almost crying in frustration.

Once again, Rune delved into her pocket and presented Elle with a journal bound in turquoise leather and stamped with an imprint of rope tied in an intricate knot. "Do you know what that is?"

Elle traced the impression with her forefinger. "A Gordian knot. Alexander the Great was presented with it and was told no man could loosen it except he who was destined to be ruler of all Asia. He took out his sword and cut the knot in half." She peered at Rune. "Is that a message to me?"

"Sometimes the direct way is best. I suggest you start journaling. First thing in the morning, write down anything you feel like—the weather, what you think of Gothic and its inhabitants, what you'd like to see happen in your day-to-day life here. You could even write what you think of grumpy ol' Adam." Rune walked to the windows and opened one curtain after another. "Writing has a way of shaking loose thoughts we aren't expecting."

"You think it'll help me recover my memory," Elle said.

"Your memory would be an added bonus, but it's not the only goal." Rune looked out the stained-glass window toward the hill above Gothic. "It will help you recover *yourself*."

"That makes sense. With no memory, I feel like a jigsaw puzzle that got dumped out of the box with pieces missing." Elle inched her chair back, groaning at the stiffness in her joints. "That makes me frantic."

Adam stood and leaned over her. "I have a suggestion of my own. After you've recovered more, the bruising fades and your pain has eased, I'd like you to take self-defense from Bendy Wendy."

"Bendy Wendy?" Elle grinned at him. "Really?"

"Wendy is Gothic's yoga instructor, physical trainer and self-defense artist."

"*You* can teach me self-defense," Elle said. "I know you can."

"You heard what Rune said about not trusting men."

"I trust you!"

"You have trust issues, well justified, and you're not going to learn as well from me or any other man as you would from a woman." Adam looked into her eyes, and he projected warmth and comfort. "I've taken Wendy's classes myself. She's an excellent teacher."

"Journaling. Self-defense. Both of those are good choices, paths that can lead you from fear and back to who you really are." Rune half turned from the window. "If all goes well, we can return to the process tomorrow and—"

The window shattered.

Glass flew across the room.

Rune screamed, spun and fell.

As if swatted by a giant unseen hand, Adam flipped sideways onto the table, then landed on the floor with a thump. He shouted, "Gunshot! Drop! Drop!"

31

ELLE DOVE UNDER THE table. Her hip, joints and neck screamed for her careless disregard, and for a brief moment, she doubled over, holding her ribs, light-headed with pain.

Rune slid under the table like a runner going for home base, jostling her and hurting her more. Black spots danced in her vision, and she found herself leaning on Adam. When she caught her breath and focused, she saw red.

Blood speckled Rune's face.

It oozed from Adam's upper arm.

Rune had been struck by flying glass; *Adam had been struck by the bullet.*

Elle reached for Adam. "You're shot!"

He craned his neck to see. "It's not bad."

"You mean it's not life-threatening."

He pulled away. "In the world of gunshot wounds, that's a vital distinction. More importantly, are we safe? Are we out of sight?"

Rune shoved the table, blocking any view through the window. "Yes. Yes!"

"Adam, let me see your arm."

Adam rolled up his sleeve and held still for Elle.

Rune glanced at Adam's wound and turned subsequently lighter shades of pale. "Elle, you need to cover that. He'll bleed to death!"

"No, he won't." Elle could breathe. Blood was flowing, but it looked like no more than a long scratch.

"Good." Adam sounded the complete opposite of the way Rune looked: calm, firm, sure.

"Use this!" Rune dragged a velvet scarf from around her waist.

Elle plucked the scarf from Rune's trembling hands and wiped at Adam's wound. She grimaced at the slippery, shiny material and, thankful Angelica had given her a bra, pulled her T-shirt over her head. With a wistful sigh of regret, she pressed the lemon cotton to Adam's wound.

He looked appreciatively at her.

Yeah, to hell with death.

Rune pulled her phone from her pocket, tapped in 9-1-1 and spoke frantically. "A gunshot! Into my shop in Gothic! I'm Madame Rune. Yes, I'm sure it was a gunshot. The window shattered. Yes, someone was hit! We need medical attention ASAP. This is Madame Rune. Send cops. Send EMTs!"

Elle plucked the phone from Rune's fingers. "Madame Rune is injured. Send help quickly." She ended the call.

"I'm injured?" Rune lifted a hand and touched her cheek. "My God, I'm bleeding! Was I shot?"

"You have a shard of glass embedded in your cheek. And one in your forehead. Maybe more." Elle caught Rune's hand. "Don't touch. Right now, the glass is stanching most of the bleeding."

"Right." Rune was wild-eyed. "Someone shot at me!"

Elle looked her over thoroughly. "They didn't hit you. Why did you fall?"

"The bullet caught my hair." Rune showed her a short hank of hair with shriveled ends. "My hair! Why would someone shoot my hair? The force of the bullet knocked me off my feet, and my scalp—" she touched her head, looked at her fingers "—it's bleeding, too!"

"When you were looking out the window, did you see anything or anybody?" Adam asked.

"No." Rune seemed to catch fire. "Those damned illegal hunters in their stupid camouflage!"

"I doubt it was a hunter," Adam said. "A single shot through a window that came very close to blowing your head off—" Rune moaned in fright "—and wounded me indicates either a high degree of luck or amazing accuracy. We need to move."

"Move? We'll be exposed!" Rune was frantic.

"We need to get out of sight, somewhere the sniper can't target us."

"A sniper? You think it's a sniper?" Rune gestured toward the shattered window and banged her knuckles on the top of the table.

"A sniper," Elle repeated faintly. "I never thought..."

"A definite possibility. If it is a sniper, either a mercenary who needs the kill to be paid or someone with a grudge, well...if his target isn't in view, he might switch to a semiautomatic and spray bullets into the room." Considering Adam was discussing their imminent demise, he continued unruffled. "The table won't protect us. Elle?" He indicated Rune.

Rune had her hand to her chest while she breathed in great gulps.

"Right." Elle pulled herself together and put her arm around Rune, and her voice was now as comforting as Rune's had been to her. "Where can we move to? Madame Rune?" She shook the fortune-teller to get her attention.

It worked. "We can do that. See that velvet drape?" Rune pointed toward the wall where they had entered. "Behind that is my home—living room, kitchen, bedroom and bath. The drapes are closed, so we won't be seen. But the walls there are no thicker than here." Her composure fell away, and she shook as if suffering a hard chill.

"Bathrooms and kitchens have thicker walls for the pipes," Adam said. "Important in cases of earthquake and gunfire."

"How do you know this stuff, man?" Rune shouted.

"I watch PBS," Adam said.

"Rune, you go first," Elle instructed.

"Me? Why do I have to go first?" Rune was decidedly testy.

"The first person will take the shooter by surprise." Adam sounded as if he knew what he was talking about. "The second and the third will be the targets."

"When you put it that way..." Rune stared at the velvet curtain and gathered her skirts in one hand.

Elle instructed, "Dash to the door and open it, leave it open for us and get inside to the bathroom."

"Bathroom. Exactly. Interior room." Rune cleared the table, ran low and fast and, pushing the curtain away and opening the door, rushed into the shadowy interior.

"You next." Elle took Adam's hand and pressed it to the T-shirt on his wound.

"You next," Adam answered. "You have injuries that make it difficult for you to move."

"Right now, I can't feel my injuries." Weird, but true. "The longer you argue with me, the greater likelihood that we'll both be shot. You've lost blood. You might need help making it to the door. I'll be hot on your heels and ready to assist. Now, go."

In Adam's eyes, she caught a glimpse of the immensity of what drove him to dwell in bleak solitude, and for a moment, she thought Adam was going to shake her.

Or kiss her.

Or something.

Then, like a man unimpaired by injury, he slipped from beneath the table and vanished into the waiting open door.

She didn't hesitate. Even pumped full of adrenaline, she wasn't as coordinated or as swift as Adam, and the eight feet to the door seemed to stretch forever. She ran, and at last she was inside Rune's apartment.

Adam pulled her into his arms and held her, and he was breathing hard as if he had just finished running a marathon.

Well. This was more like it.

32

ELLE COULD HAVE STAYED right there, nestled in his arms, but Adam picked up the bloody T-shirt, turned her and urged her toward the bathroom.

With her and two large men, the tiny room, with its sink, shower and toilet, was tight quarters. Elle used her hip to bump Rune aside, dug into a small cabinet and found a new roll of toilet paper. She lowered the toilet lid and pointed at Adam. He seated himself. She took the shirt away, dropped it on the floor and used a wad of the paper to blot Adam's wound. Dampening a clean washcloth, she washed the smear of blood off his skin. "The bleeding has already slowed." Her frantic heartbeat had slowed, too.

Adam was not seriously wounded. He would recover.

"I clot well," Adam said with dry amusement.

Rune fluttered her hands and moaned. "How bad...?"

"He was grazed, nothing more," Elle said reassuringly. "Four inches, and the heat of the bullet cauterized the edges of the wound." Turning to the medicine cabinet, Elle scanned the shelves and located a roll of sterile gauze and tape. "If we butterfly the deepest part together, someone can easily stitch the edges."

"You seem to know what you're doing," Adam observed.

"I do, don't I?" Elle thoroughly washed her hands, then went to work opening packages of gauze and tearing tape to fit.

"Can *you* stitch it?" Adam asked.

"You're not serious!" Rune was horrified.

Elle got her knees and examined every inch of the wound. "I could try."

Rune wrung her hands. "If you'll wait a little longer, the sheriff or a deputy and some kind of emergency crew will be here."

"Maybe Elle's a doctor," Adam said. "Have you thought of that?"

"No." Rune seemed quite definite. "She's not old enough. I've known a lot of doctors, and she isn't the type."

"There's a type?" Adam teased Rune gently.

"Adam, with your free hand, can you pull the edges together?" Elle turned to Rune. "Do you have silk thread?"

"Yes, I have to repair my shawls and—" Rune took a breath and slowed down. "Yes. I do."

"Can you get some for me?" Elle asked. "And a fine needle?"

"Yes." Rune stuck her head out of the bathroom door, pulled it back like a turtle, peeked out again and left in a rush.

Elle worked quickly, creating the butterfly bandage and applying it to the leading edge.

Rune returned with a sewing basket decorated with faded plastic flowers. Opening it, she pulled out a thread organizer, found the spool she wanted and handed it to Elle.

"Now a fine needle," Elle said.

"You really intend to…" Rune faltered.

"Yes." Elle already knew where Adam was going with this, and it would be ungrateful of her to refuse to help him.

Rune found a needle and a small pair of sewing scissors. Her hands shook when she offered them to Elle.

"Adam, can you thread the needle?"

He did.

"I wish you'd wait on the professionals," Rune fretted. "They'll be here soon."

"He doesn't want to wait." Elle made the first stitch. "He doesn't intend to tell anyone he was hit."

"*What* are you talking about?" Rune waved her arms and banged her hand on the glass shower door. "Of course he has to tell everyone he was hit. The police are going to ask."

Elle said, "In a general way, perhaps, but—"

"You'll never succeed in stitching it—" Seeing Elle's competence, Rune changed direction. "Adam, you need an injection. For infection."

"I have everything I need at home," Adam reassured her.

"Of course you do. Doesn't everybody stock their own penicillin?" Rune wrung her hands.

"If they're smart," Adam said.

"Rune, you must be feeling less frightened." Elle smiled as she completed the last stitch. "You're sarcastic. Hand me another gauze pad and tear off four four-inch pieces of tape, would you?"

Rune handed her a gauze pad in its wrappings, took it back, opened the package, tore the strips and returned them. Leaning both hands on the sink, she sagged and closed her eyes, then opened them and caught sight of her reflection. "Look at me," she moaned. "Why am I even concerned with you two when I've got window glass in my face?"

"Because you're a kind and caring person." Elle pressed

the dressing to Adam's arm. "Six stitches, nicely done if I do say so myself."

Rune risked a glance and muttered, "Maybe medical school."

"You've got a steady hand." Adam took a look at Rune. "You, not so much. Do you have a shirt I can wear? An old shirt, blue or brown, some color that won't show blood if I bleed through? Button-front?"

"In the back of my closet."

"Can I use it?"

Before Rune could answer, Elle said, "Also, if you've got a T-shirt I could borrow?" She nudged her bloody shirt with her toe. "This one's ruined. Angelica would not be pleased."

Rune took a breath and whipped out the bathroom door.

As soon as she was gone, Elle sank onto the floor and put her head on her bent knees. Now that the stitches had been dealt with, her fears were realized and the adrenaline that had kept her on her feet faded, she trembled like a leaf in the wind. Tears hovered on her lashes, and she fought a losing battle for composure.

Adam placed a gentle hand on her head. "Thank you. You did a wonderful job."

She nodded.

"Queasy now?"

She nodded again. The trauma of the last few moments left her fighting a battle with her breakfast, and of course Adam knew. She took long breaths, got herself under control and met his gaze. "I'll buck up for Rune's sake."

Adam petted her hair as if she was a cat. "The letdown is always difficult."

"Letdown? From the danger just past, sure. But what about my attacker? What about your constant watchfulness? What about Hammer?" She didn't shout, but she wanted to. "It's all piling up, getting worse and worse, one thing after another, more threats, more fears, more—"

Rune stepped into the bathroom holding two shirts and grumbling, "Safest place to be is in the bathroom so *I'm* rummaging in my closet."

Elle took the T-shirt, rolled her trembling fingers in the material and remembered she had promised to buck up for Rune's sake. "You're very brave."

"No, I'm not." Rune helped Adam ease his arms into the sleeves.

Adam buttoned it from the top down. "You're a good and true friend."

"That I am," Rune agreed.

Yes. For Rune's sake. Because Rune made her smile. Elle held up the women's size-small turquoise shirt: good material, expensive brand. She raised her eyebrows at Rune.

"It was my wife's. I kept it as a souvenir. Put it on. This is a better use for it." Rune said the right words, but she brooded as she watched Elle pull it over her head. "Now what? As far as I can tell, no one's fired another shot."

"That's the good news." Adam stood and extended his good hand to Elle.

With his help, Elle got to her feet. "Rune, let me clear the splinters from your face. Adam, assist me?"

Rune took Adam's place, and while Rune grumbled and winced, Elle used tweezers to remove the glass shards from her cheek and forehead. As she did, Adam applied pressure, then while she bandaged the wounds, he handed her tissues, Band-Aids and gauze. In a conversational tone, he said, "While we wait, let's talk about who the shooter was aiming at. Rune, what about the guy who cursed you with the seven plagues?"

"That was three years ago," Rune said. "Took his time about coming back for vengeance."

"He might be out of prison now." Adam was nothing if not practical.

Elle pinched the lovely material of the T-shirt she wore. "What about your wife? Ex-spouses sometimes take the breakup badly."

"Jessica?" Rune snorted. "She took everything. Why bother to kill me?"

"She was your wife, important because of *you*, wealthy because of *you*. If life hasn't gone well, wouldn't she blame *you*?" Elle gazed inquiringly at Rune.

"You, young woman, have a future writing screenplays." But Rune had a pucker between her brows, and she stroked her bullet-sheered hair.

"Everything's possible," Adam agreed. "Of course, we know someone could be after Elle."

Elle staggered as if the words were a bullet that could kill.

Adam rubbed her shoulder. "Although the odds are that whoever strangled you and left you in the ocean to drown believes you're dead and thinks he has no need to look for you. Or maybe you did enough damage with that weapon you picked up that he is badly hurt. In the hospital. Or—" He stopped short of suggesting she might have killed her attacker.

"I don't think so." She responded to his unspoken thought. "If I'd killed him, I wouldn't be in such terror, believing he is immortal."

"She's right, Adam," Rune said.

"Too bad," Adam said regretfully. "Last obvious choice, someone could be gunning for me."

"Who, Adam?" Rune still frowned. "Who would hate you enough to try to kill you?"

"I've made enemies. Who hasn't?" Adam looked at his wristwatch. "It's been twenty-seven minutes since the shooting, probably twenty minutes since Rune called 9-1-1, and

I'm sure they were inundated with Gothic calls. We should go out to meet law enforcement and give our version of events." Adam shot a look at Rune. "By that I mean, give a truthful recital and neglect to mention my injury." Rune's shirt was big on Adam, and that disguised the careful way he moved out of the bathroom and toward the door.

Elle followed.

Rune stayed where she was. "I respect Elle for all her good traits, and the stitches looked admirable, but why don't you just tell the EMTs you were hit? They'll give you the best care."

Elle turned back. "It's a gunshot wound. Law enforcement is required to treat a shooting very seriously, with emergency transportation and multiple reports and follow-ups."

"Yeah, so?" Rune said belligerently.

"Didn't you hear what Adam said? He believes this was not a random act of violence, not some careless hunter but a targeted attack on one of us." Elle came back to the bathroom and halted on the threshold. "Probably not you. Women don't usually resort to assassination. Except for the rampant gossip in the village of Gothic, I've kept a low profile, and as Adam said, my attacker probably believes me dead. So logic leads us to the fact that Adam thinks this has to do with him."

"Then, *logically*, why not talk to law enforcement? For protection?" Clearly, Rune didn't get it.

"Adam is a survivalist." Elle had had her suspicions before. After today, her belief was rock-solid. "I trust him to protect me, and that means he can also protect himself."

"No one can protect themselves from a well-aimed bullet!" Rune said.

"No. But if you make your way down to Adam's home and look around, you'll see that there's no cover for a sniper. I suspect that is one of the reasons he chose that property."

"I could tell the cops the whole truth!" Rune directed her

voice toward Adam's shadowy figure, waiting beside the outer door. "What do you say to that, Adam?"

"I don't seem to be involved in this conversation. Why include me now?" Adam's voice was, as always, composed, but as he descended the stairs, he left a cool breeze in his wake.

Elle offered her hand to Rune. "Come on. Let's go down and see whether anyone else was hurt or, God forbid, killed. That would destroy all my theories and give you more ammunition for your argument."

Rune grumped all the way down the stairs.

In the shadows at the bottom of the stairs, they found Adam, three wizard staffs in hand, surveying the sunlit, empty shop.

The sight of him seemed to trigger horror in Rune. She clapped her hand to her throat. "Adam, are you right-handed?"

Adam glanced at her in amusement. "Ambidextrous."

"That's good." Elle looked confused at Rune's distress. "Isn't it?"

"He needs both hands to swing the long sword. And he's been shot, disabled!"

"Now we get down to it." Adam peered through the windows at the empty street, and he grinned. "It's the Gothic Spring Psychic Festival Rune is really worried about."

"That's not true. I'm worried about you!" Rune was indignant, then conceded, "*And* the Gothic Spring Psychic Festival. The Pacific Coast Highway has been closed for months. If the festival doesn't come off as scheduled, most of the businesses in town will fail. People will lose everything."

"You'll be fine," Elle reassured her.

"Of course I'll be fine. In an emergency, I do online video-direct psychic readings. I keep my website updated with the stock in the shop. Online ordering comprises a good part of my business. I really will be fine," Rune assured her.

Adam cackled and handed each of them a staff.

Elle twirled her staff first one direction, then the other. "Well-balanced," she commented.

Adam shot her a sharp glance.

Rune's staff more than matched her height, and she leaned on it heavily. "My God, when word gets out to the paying public that there's been a shooting..."

Looking at Rune with the bright sunlight behind her, Elle saw something glittering in her hair and on her shoulders. She brushed at it with one hand and pulled back with a wince. "You've got glass everywhere. You need to shake out your hair and clothes and be careful until you can get cleaned up." She plucked a sliver from her palm. "This stuff will put a hole in you every time."

Rune shook herself like a horse, and tiny shards struck the floor.

"We'll take shelter in the restaurant," Adam said.

Elle looked across the street at the Live Oak. "The lights aren't on."

"It's the lunch hour. Someone's in there. Someone who knows to get away from the windows and turn off the lights." Adam led them out the door.

Elle followed close on his heels. "Is it safe to be on the street?"

"We'll find out."

33

"REASSURING," RUNE MUTTERED.

The fear that had been waiting to ambush Elle spread like an instant release of poison. But this time, the fear was not for herself: she looked at the two people who had fought for her memory and her sanity, and she feared that dash across the sunlit street. The memories echoed in her mind…

Of Adam asking her, "What's your name?" and her blank panic when she realized she didn't know herself.

Of Rune sharing her own story to lead Elle to a memory of her grandmother and a sense of herself.

Of Adam sleeping with her to calm her nightmares.

Of Rune horrified by her screams, yet proceeding undaunted with the hypnosis which gave her the gift of knowing she had fought her attacker.

Out of the goodness of their hearts—and for the friends-and-family rate—these two had cared for her physically and mentally. She couldn't bear to think of them dead on Gothic's main street.

"Adam, maybe we should stay here rather than exposing ourselves to this…sniper." Elle tried to sound sensible. She feared she sounded high and quavery.

Adam put his hand on her shoulder and led her farther into the shadows. "Once the shot is fired, a sniper doesn't stay in place. They know law enforcement is on their way."

"You think the sniper packed up and left." Elle relaxed. Not completely, but enough to realize her breathing had been short and tight.

"I would bet my life on it." Adam put all levels of meaning in his voice. "In addition, I don't like this place. If there's still an active shooter, he knows we're in the building. If they are someone who is, shall we say, less than logical and on the way down here intending to finish the job, I don't want to be trapped upstairs. The back is our logical exit, the door he would expect us to use, and it would be easy to pick us off. We can't stay in the shop and wait. The windows are large, the sun is shining and there are no blinds to hide us."

"Note to self," Rune said. "Install blinds."

"Our best bet is the front door. It's not visible from the shooter's original location, it's our least likely exit, and we have shelter across the street."

"He makes it all sound so rational." Rune shook her hair. More shards fell.

"Until I know the shooter's motivation, assuming they have one, nothing about this is rational," Adam said. "It's merely educated speculation. I could be wrong, and that could be fatal to one or all of us."

Rune groaned.

Adam continued. "Nevertheless, I recommend leaving, and soon. Elle, you help Rune. She's not feeling well."

Elle shot Rune a glance. She swayed as if today's events had exhausted her.

Adam left the shadows and strode purposefully through the shop.

Elle tucked her hand under Rune's elbow, and they hurried after him.

"Get across the street and inside as quickly as you can. Go!"

Elle and Rune headed out.

Adam said, "I'll be right behind you…after I make a stop at the ATV."

Elle started to turn, but Rune tugged at her. "He's collecting his weapons."

"Of course he is." They were at the restaurant door. They opened it and stepped inside. Blinded by the sunlight, Elle blinked, then heard the reassuring babble of voices.

Inside, a dozen Gothic citizens sat and stood huddled against the back wall and inside the alcove that led to the restrooms. Señor Alfonso and Ludwig held gleaming chef's knives.

"Come away from the window," Ludwig commanded.

Señor Alfonso said, "Where's Adam? He will know what to do next."

On those words, Adam came through the door carrying a black nylon belt and holster. His measured stride seemed deliberate, as if he wanted to calm the others. "Now we wait for law enforcement."

Elle suspected his movements were calculated to hide his pain and started toward him, to support him.

"Elle, go to the back," he commanded. "I'll help Rune."

She didn't think he was in shape to help anyone, but she knew better than to focus attention on his careful motions, and she hurried toward the wall.

"Was that a gunshot?" Freya Goodnight eyed his holster. She seemed incredulous and inclined to disbelieve.

"Yes." Adam assisted Rune to a chair at the back.

"I told you that was a gunshot!" Mr. Kulshan was annoyed

at having had his word questioned. "I was in the military. I *know.*"

Mrs. Kulshan patted his hand and murmured soft words that made him close his eyes and relax into his chair. "Shell shock," she mouthed to Elle.

"Was someone hit?" Señor Alfonso asked.

"Look!" Ludwig pointed. "Rune was hit!"

"I'm not badly injured." Rune touched her bandaged cheek and forehead. "The shot came through the window in my consultation room and—" Elle held her breath, and Rune glanced at Adam "—and sprayed glass everywhere." She held up a lock of her hair. "The bullet cut my hair!"

"Wow." Justin Scharphorn from the *Gothic Times* got his computer tablet out of his backpack. "You were there for the shooting! Can I get an exclusive?"

"I… I suppose. Sure." Rune looked at Justin, and Elle saw the spark of realization: handled correctly, this could be good for the psychic business.

Elle found herself unexpectedly grinning.

Adam grinned back at her and indicated the holster and pistol draped over his arm. "Would you help me put this on?"

"Sure. Although I don't know what I'm doing." She pushed a chair toward Adam. "Sit down."

Adam slowly seated himself. "It's a shoulder holster. I'll explain as we go. The pistol safety is on, so you don't need to worry about it accidentally discharging. Be careful, um…"

"I know." She knelt beside him, and she kept her voice low. "The arm."

Señor Alfonso touched the point of his knife with his finger. "Does this have anything to do with the body found at Bustier Basin Ranch?" He looked to Adam for an answer.

"I don't know." Adam indicated Elle should put the strap over his right shoulder. "Anything's possible, although the description Deputy Dave gave doesn't match this crime. He said the body suffered battering to the face and body, and the cause of death was a slash to the throat. The recent shot was a high-powered rifle."

"Told you so," Mr. Kulshan said to Freya.

Freya ignored him for all she was worth.

The belt went around Adam's chest, the holster slid on the belt, and everything fastened with Velcro. Self-evident, except for the location of the holster and pistol.

"But a body found in the morning?" Señor Alfonso was doubtful. "Then a bullet shot in early afternoon?"

"This is Gothic. Things like that don't happen here." Freya glared at Elle. "Or they didn't until she arrived."

The venom made Elle slide back. "Adam said..."

"I said it's unlikely that whoever attacked Elle and tossed her into the ocean could have followed her here, or would see any reason to do so. I'm afraid, Freya, if you're going to blame someone in Gothic for the gunshots, I'm a more likely candidate." Adam sounded absolutely reasonable—and he left no doubt in Freya's mind he was not pleased.

"For that matter, it could have been me. Or Señor Alfonso." Ludwig held his knife with the skill of an assassin. "Our lives have not always been as dull as they are now."

"Any of us, really." Rune's coins jingled as she swept around at the group. "No matter how blameless you imagine your life to be, someone will find a reason to hate you."

Freya tried again. "I'm just pointing out—"

"Put a sock in it," Mrs. Kulshan snapped.

Freya did.

Elle knew Freya and her beliefs could hardly compare to the recent shocking events, and she had more important things to do, like finish helping Adam into his holster. With Adam's left arm injured, he would shoot with the right, so for easy extraction she slid the holster around to the left side.

"Perfect. Thank you," he murmured. "You are a marvel."

She looked up into his face; he looked at her as if she was the lost soul he'd sought his whole life. The sounds, the light, the fears died away, and only the two of them existed, caught in a moment crafted from tragedy that had come too near and the promise of joy that hovered ever out of reach. He leaned toward her and—

They heard the thud of footsteps running down the stairs from the penthouse. Elle stood and swung to face the door, her fists up.

Adam touched her arm. "It's all right. For the moment, we're safe here."

Elle felt foolish. Who did she think she was? Superwoman?

Clarice and a party of two men ran into the restaurant; Clarice held a short sword pointed toward the floor. In a low voice that projected throughout the room, she said, "I saw him. I saw him!"

Señor Alfonso stared at her, his eyes widening. "Who?"

"The shooter!"

34

AS ONE, THE PEOPLE faced Clarice.

The two men who followed Clarice were in disarray, their hair mussed, their clothing creased, and both looked like the kind of people who would normally take care with every aspect of their appearance.

One was basketball-player tall with shoulder-length black hair and brown eyes and lashes Elle coveted. His complexion was perfect, acquired with the help of a dermatologist, a tanning salon and expensive serums. His jeans fit him so perfectly Elle wondered if he'd had them altered, and his white starched shirt was open at the throat. His rolled cuffs displayed magnificently muscled forearms.

He was a god… He must be an actor.

"I was on the roof," Clarice said. "Gregoire was coaching me on voice."

The tall one bobbed his head. So, he was Gregoire.

The other fellow had wildly exuberant, brilliantly copper hair with black roots, a drooping black mustache, eyes of such a dark blue they were almost violet. Although he was a good five eleven and built like a rock wall, next to Gregoire he looked short.

These people had recently arrived in this bucolic town and unexpectedly faced a deadly situation. They were vibrating with horror—and excitement.

Clarice continued, "Sarcha was measuring me for costumes. I was holding the script out, looking over the wall, across the countryside, projecting my lines as Gregoire would have me say them, and I saw a man step out of the olive grove above town." Clarice waved her hand toward the east.

"What did he look like?" Adam slid his hands in his pockets, a movement disguised to hide his pain.

"He wore a casual jacket and a broad brimmed hat. Seen from a distance, I thought both were leather. Then...jeans, I think." Sarcha's tone expressed profound fashion disappointment.

Clarice nodded at him. "Right."

"But what did he *look* like, Clarice?" Adam asked again. "This man in a jacket."

"Solid. Well-built."

"Skin tone. Pale? Tanned? Dark?" Adam insisted.

"Tanned. I couldn't see his features, though. His hat protected his face."

"Age?" When Clarice started to squirm, Adam said, "Young? Middle-aged? Old?"

"The prime of life. His white shirt looked... Well, it was too far away for me to see." Clarice met Adam's severe gaze. "All right. It looked crisp, starched."

Adam nodded, a thank-you that acknowledged Clarice's acute observations. "Go on. What happened?"

"He was holding... I thought it must be a walking stick. He took off his jacket, fiddled with the stick, then put it to his shoulder. I realized… I realized what it was, a rifle. He aimed. He took his time. No hurry…and I thought it was pointed at me. I thought… I thought…*he's going to shoot me!*" For the first time Clarice's hands trembled, and her voice faltered.

Right, Elle thought. She's famous, an actress. She might have been the target. Whoever did this might be her paparazzo.

Elle looked around. Where was he, anyway, this Bruno? What a suspicious time to be missing…

Sarcha took up the tale. "Clarice yelled, 'Get down!' and dropped like a rock, flat on the ground."

Elle looked at Adam. Exactly as he had done.

"The gun blasted. I thought she'd been shot!" Gregoire had a decidedly French accent and a stammer, an almost imperceptible hesitation in his voice, and that took him down from a god to someone not quite good enough for the demanding profession of movie acting.

"They didn't drop." Incredulous, Clarice gestured to the two men.

"I didn't think… Who would want me dead?" Gregoire gestured at Sarcha. "Then he fainted."

"I can think of a lot of people who want *me* dead." Sarcha wasn't defending himself. He was stating what was for him a plain fact. "But you—you imagine yourself a hero!"

Gregoire advanced on Sarcha. "How dare you? Don't slander me. I am no hero. I'm a voice coach!"

Elle hid her smile. She met Adam's gaze. He had that twist of pain between his brows, but he was amused, too. These men were so dramatic.

"Gregoire and I crawled around on the floor," Clarice said.

"Dragging his unconscious ass close to the wall," Gregoire chimed in, "looking him over for bullet wounds—"

"Which is why I look so disheveled!" Sarcha flung a scornful hand toward Clarice and Gregoire.

"Disheveled?" Elle whispered to Adam. "That's disheveled?"

His mouth quirked, but obviously he was adding Clarice's story to the previous drama, and Elle knew that he was weighing events and coming to conclusions.

"Once we decided he hadn't been hit," Clarice said, "we debated whether the wall would protect us from further gunfire and if we should take a chance and see if the shooter was still out there."

"I woke up, and they were debating over my body about lifting my head over the top of the wall to see if the shooter took it off!" Sarcha bellowed.

Gregoire lounged, hands in his pockets. "Woke you up, didn't it, mate?"

"Self-preservation!" Sarcha calmed. "My God, we were shot at!"

"No, *we* were shot at." Rune subsided in a chair, put her elbows on her knees and breathed as if she couldn't get enough oxygen.

Elle hustled over and rubbed Rune's shoulders.

"I'm sorry, Rune. Your poor face." Clarice seemed honestly sorry for her, because the possibility of scars could be disaster in her profession.

Adam brought them back to the moment at hand. "Did you look over the wall?"

"I did," Clarice answered. "The shooter was gone without a trace."

Adam pulled out his phone and made a call.

The restaurant grew hushed.

"Dave, it's Adam. You're on your way to Gothic? Watch for oncoming cars. We've got a description of the sniper—male, tanned, well-built, prime of life. White shirt, brown jacket, wide-brimmed hat. Since it seems unlikely he's local or he's going to stick around, and there's no way out except on the highway, he should have to pass you. I know. I know I should have told you before." Adam raised his voice. "I didn't know anyone had seen him!" He looked at Clarice. "You didn't see a vehicle?"

She shook her head no.

Adam spoke into the phone again. "We've taken shelter in the Live Oak Restaurant. Okay, see you in a few minutes." To the assembly, he said, "Sheriff and ambulance will be here soon."

The group released a collective sigh of relief.

In a low voice, Clarice said, "I'm worried. Faith went for a walk."

"Who's Faith?" Elle asked.

"My acting coach. Faith Moore. She's famous in the business, and she's out there somewhere." Clarice cupped her forehead in her hand, then self-consciously removed it, flexed it. "Is there anything we can do to find her?"

"No one is going out. Until the area is secured, it's dangerous." There was no doubt that Adam was in charge. "I'm sure she took refuge somewhere."

The restaurant door rattled. A woman with cropped curly platinum-blonde hair that frothed around her beautifully made-up face peered in the window.

"That's her!" Clarice cried, ran to the door and unlocked it. "Faith! You're all right."

Faith scooted into the room. "I am." Her voice conveyed warmth and assurance. She wore a pressed cotton sheath that perfectly fit her petite figure, her bare arms and legs were toned and tanned, and her sandals looked both comfortable and stylish. She scrutinized the crowd, observing people's reactions and interactions exactly as Elle expected an acting coach would do. Elle thought, also, that Faith's gaze lingered on her a moment longer than on anyone else, and that caused a twinge of discomfort.

Did Faith recognize her? Was she going to see pieces of herself, bewildered by her loss of memory, in Clarice's next role? Or, Elle wondered, was she hypersensitive about every observer?

"All my people are here and safe," Clarice proclaimed. "We're protected. I'm blessed."

Faith put her arm around Clarice. "You're the talent. We will take extra special care of you."

Gregoire was quick to add his bit. "Besides, Clarice, worrying could cause wrinkles."

"Can't have that," Clarice muttered.

Sarcha chortled and poked at Gregoire. "We're supposed to be her support team, not the team that causes wrinkles by warning her about wrinkles."

Gregoire scowled.

The small crowd was so intent on the Hollywood drama they failed to notice the white Mercedes that sped down the street and parked in front of the restaurant. But they couldn't miss Angelica Lindholm as she burst through the door. Her hair was mussed, and her white jacket was askew. Her gaze zeroed in on the people huddled at the back of the restaurant. She gasped and spoke. "A gunshot? There was a gunshot?"

35

"YES, MRS. LINDHOLM, AND we don't know if the shooter is still out there, so if you'd move away from the window…" Señor Alfonso said.

"Here? In Gothic?" Angelica seemed frozen in place, her hand on her heaving chest. "I thought we were safe here."

"Mrs. Lindholm?" Ludwig started toward her.

The movement seemed to wake Angelica from her trance. "Of course. I simply… When I heard them saying there had been shots fired in town, I was naturally horrified! It was a mistake, wasn't it? No one actually was… Madame Rune!" She hurried toward her. "You were hit! But of course not with a bullet or it would be more than Band-Aids…" She was babbling.

Glances were exchanged.

Elle thought no one had ever seen Angelica Lindholm so discombobulated. Only she had, when she had dropped those Cheery Freezes.

"Where were you? In your upstairs room? Oh, no! The

glass must have made a terrible mess… Not that that matters as long as you're alive. Although it will be difficult to clean up. Consult my team. They know how to clean everything. Was there anyone with you?" Angelica seemed to hang on a breathless hook.

When Adam said, "Elle and I were with Rune," Angelica's knees trembled.

Ludwig thrust a chair under her.

She sat down hard. "I'm sorry. No reason for a sensible woman to be so upset. But with the Gothic Spring Psychic Festival coming up, this is disaster!"

Rune waved an arm at Adam. "See? I'm not the only one."

"We can't go forward when there's a madman taking aim at Gothic," Angelica said.

Adam placed a chair next to her and gestured for Elle to seat herself. In a tone of utmost sensibility, he said, "While it is possible Gothic is the target of a madman, it's also possible that the shooter is randomly targeting remote coastal villages knowing he has little chance of being apprehended, or even that he was shooting because he thought it would be funny to stir up the town."

Elle noted he didn't go into any possible reasons someone was targeting her or Rune or him.

In a low tone, Angelica asked, "Elle, you aren't hurt more than…before?"

"I came out of today's incident unscathed." Elle patted Angelica's trembling fingers. "Not to worry. As far as we know, there was one shot, everyone's fine and law enforcement is on the way."

A tear trickled down Angelica's cheek, and she blotted it with her sleeve.

Elle sensed the group's amazement. Where was Angelica's tissue?

Mr. Kulshan whispered, "Maybe she's got a heart after all."

Mrs. Kulshan chided him. "Shush, dear."

A group of six elderly women passed in front of the restaurant windows. One of them opened the door, and they all filed inside, accompanied by a wail of oncoming sirens.

"Hi, I'm Tammy White," one said, then indicated her friends. "We're the Shivering Sherlocks. We won the online auction to stay the week at Angelica Lindholm's castle."

Angelica leaped to her feet. "Excuse me, I've got to powder my nose," and she rushed for the ladies' room.

"Look, Rita, that was her!" One of the ladies nudged the another.

Rita bolted after Angelica.

"You can't follow her!" Tammy said sternly.

Rita never stopped. "Try and stop me. I've got to *go*!"

As one, the stunned Gothic citizens looked again at the group of women.

"The Shivering Sherlocks?" Adam, at least, sounded calm.

"We solve mysteries," a woman with smiling brown eyes said. "It's our mystery week, and it will wrap up during your Gothic Spring Psychic Festival."

"We're supposed to lunch at the Live Oak before we go up to meet Angelica." This woman had the unsmiling countenance of a math tutor. "And we most assuredly have a reservation."

Slowly Ludwig went into motion. "I'll set the table."

A short bald red-faced man in a white shirt and flamboyant purple velvet waistcoat caught the door before it could close. "Hey, I'm looking for some guy named Rune. We've got the first truckful of equipment to set up for the—" he consulted a clipboard "—Gothic Spring Psychic Festival."

Rune came to her feet. "Aren't you a day early?"

"Yeah, we packed up the Ren Fest real fast, didn't have another gig, so we came on up. Man, that highway is a bugger." The man looked Rune over from top to toe. "Sorry, ma'am. I'm Eric. You look like a fortune-teller."

"I am."

"Ooh, Candy!" one of the Shivering Sherlocks said brightly to another, "that's Madame Rune. She organized the raffle. She's going to tell our fortunes!"

"Hey, Madame Rune," Eric said. "Our fortune-teller for Ren Fest found her fortune in federal prison. Embezzled from one of her clients. If you need a job—"

"I'll let you know after the festival is over." Rune walked toward the door. "I may need a new job then."

"Don't worry," Mrs. Kulshan said to Elle. "She always says that before festival weekend, then she rises to the occasion."

Señor Alfonso clapped his hands. "All right. Enough fear. We have the Shivering Sherlocks, and it sounds as if very soon, the sheriff's department will be here and need to be fed. Clear a table for interviews, and anyone who actually saw the shooter gets to talk to the cops first. Let's go, let's go!"

People scattered, and Adam and Elle sat down to wait for their chance to talk to the police…and tell them as little as possible.

36

AS SOON AS ELLE and Adam walked into his house, she asked, "Where's the antibiotic?"

He started toward the bedroom.

She put her hand on his arm. "Sit down. I'll get it. Tell me where."

"The roles are reversed." He laughed a little and sank onto the love seat. "In the bedroom, in the closet, on the shelf to the left, in a black backpack. It has everything we need."

"Provided you don't get an infection." Now that the immediate crisis was over, she felt a mite snappish. "You have to promise me that if things take a turn for the worst—"

"I know. You want me to promise the same thing you promised me. Yes, if the wound gets infected or I develop a fever, I will go to the hospital. Although, like you, I know that explaining what happened will be complicated."

"Right." In the bedroom, she grunted when she pulled the backpack off the shelf: it was heavy, laden, she was sure, with everything Adam needed to survive an evacuation, an illness, an attack, any eventuality. When she came back to the living room, he had removed his holster and placed it on the table beside the lamp. He sat very still with his eyes closed, taking slow, deep breaths.

When he heard her, he opened his eyes.

"Meditative pain relief?" she asked.

He nodded and extended his right hand.

She put the backpack on the floor out of his reach. "Tell me what I'm looking for."

He looked amused, but he gave directions, and in no time she was sticking a needle in his very fine buttock muscle. She placed a small bandage over the puncture and helped him pull up his shorts.

"You have definitely had some kind of medical training." He took the pain reliever she offered.

"Yes, but not…nothing more than emergency stuff. The only real in-depth knowledge I have of anatomy is that the shin bone's connected to the knee bone."

This time he laughed a real laugh.

She grinned, pleased she had entertained the chronically serious man. "When those ladies walked in, did you see the look on Rune's face?"

"And Señor Alfonso's? And Ludwig's? The arrival of those women had completely slipped everyone's mind."

"Poor Rune. Between talking to the police and the guy there to set up the festival and getting stitches in her face and having to keep her mouth shut about your wound, it was not her day." Elle unbuttoned Rune's shirt and slipped it down Adam's arm. "Hm. Blood is seeping into the bandage, but I don't think it's excessive. I vote we don't disturb anything until tomorrow."

"I promise, I heal well."

"That's reassuring." She pulled the shirt back up. "I'm pretty sure the Shivering Sherlocks thought they'd fallen into a *real* murder mystery. I was sure when they heard a shot had been fired and the shooter was free, they'd want to skip town. Instead, they sat in the restaurant and listened to the witness statements. When I said something to Patty about leaving—she was the lady with the umbrella—she told me it was too late for them to die young."

He laughed again. Then his smile disappeared as suddenly as it had come. "Do you still have the newspaper?" he asked. "The one Angelica gave you?"

"I finished reading it—" all of it, and she marveled at how little she knew of national and local happenings "—so I stuck it in the trash can in the kitchen."

"Did you read about Big John Hammer?"

"Yes," she said cautiously. "Scary guy."

"More than you know. Did Angelica tell you that Hammer and I have a past?"

"She mentioned it, yes. But I didn't think... Oh. You think he's the one who shot at us." That fit. "He's the enemy you've collected."

"I have others, but most of them are linked to the Amazon trek."

Puzzled, she said, "I didn't read anything about any Amazon trek."

"Then you should. Go do your research. That will explain a lot about me—and Hammer."

"First I'll see if I can trace Big John Hammer's location today around noon."

Adam leaned his head back on the couch. "Brilliant! My God, I love you."

He didn't mean that, she assured herself. He didn't mean to say he loved her... Well, maybe he loved her. He could. She was worth loving. But he was hurting and worried and maybe feverish. The best thing to do was nod, do the research and figure out what they should do next. Because someone *had* shot at them, and they needed to figure this out. "I'll be back. In the meantime, would you rest? That bullet might have merely grazed you, but you were shot and had stitches, and I can see you're in pain."

"Yes. I'll rest." He lowered himself full-length on his side on the sofa.

She tucked a pillow under his head. "I wish you would allow me to give you that injection for pain."

"It would knock me out. Someone is out there. I need to be able to respond, and we need to talk."

"Okay. I'll be quick."

"Take your time." He closed his eyes.

When he opened them again, she sat in the chair opposite, watching him and wishing she could stroke his forehead, take away the anguish she knew he felt, assure him that what had happened was not his fault...and she knew, too, he would not argue, but he would not agree. He was one of the responsible men, the kind who took seriously the task of caring for those who couldn't care for themselves. "This afternoon, Big John Hammer gave an interview from his palatial home in Santa Barbara."

"So either the shooter was not him, or a helicopter lifted him out and transported him from somewhere near the olive grove to Santa Barbara."

"He has a helipad on the grounds. More likely he hired out the sniper job."

"That's not his way. It was either him or someone with a different agenda. So...shooter currently unknown. Did you do your research about the Amazon trek?"

"Yes, which is why I agree he's probably the sniper."

"Did you look at the pictures and watch the videos?"

"I did. I took it all in. I don't believe any of the slander. Did you think I would?"

"No."

"Tell me what really happened."

37

"HELP ME." AS ADAM sat up, he leaned on Elle and, when he was upright, held her a little too long.

She let him. She liked it.

When he started talking, she stayed close to him. This wouldn't be an easy conversation for either of them.

"You guessed correctly. I was—am—a survivalist. When I got out of high school, I worked my way around the world, doing whatever I needed to get by, and at the end of two years I had learned a lot. I established my company, sold my services to corporations—the kind who send their people into wild, dangerous places of the world. I'd take small groups, two or three people, into the mountains or the jungle or any place where nature was indifferent to suffering and death. I taught them to survive, and I was good at it, too. I was in demand. There was simply no one else who did what I was doing."

"Find a need and fill it. And, I think, follow your heart?"

"Yes. I... Yes."

She thought for a moment he was going to tell her why he'd

chosen such an unusual, dangerous career. None of the news stories had given a hint of what forces drove Adam Ramsdell.

Instead, he continued the story he had begun. "The first thing I told my students was the secret to survival is preparation. I guided them through the thought processes that illuminated possibilities. Could this happen? Is there a possibility that the consequences could be fatal? If so, what would you need to survive?"

He was in full-lecture mode, and she knew how his students must have felt.

"Together we explored every possibility they could think of, and I pointed out the ones they didn't. Then we prepared. We had lists. We packed backpacks. Some items were unique to our destination. Housing, clothing, footgear. Some were universal. Weapons, medications."

"Fascinating," she murmured. "Did you ever do caving?"

"That was a specialty I did not teach. Why? A memory?"

She nodded, squinting as she looked into her past. "Darkness and…lights shining. Rock walls and paintings, beautiful work. Then—an earthquake! But I wasn't afraid because—" she realized he was watching her intently "—we were prepared." She spread her fingers helplessly. "I wish there was more. But I want to hear the rest of your story."

"Yes. Now that I've started, let's finish." Looking down at his hands, he deliberately loosened his clenched fists. "I was hired by an international medical corporation to train two of their employees to safely explore the Amazon basin. Baptiste was my age, twenty-four, enjoying the hell out of the adventure that was his life. Nevaeh was the smartest human being I ever met and—" He paused.

"I know. They both died."

He inclined his head. "We were packed and ready to go when the CEO called. He wanted me to take Hammer with us. I said no, but the CEO was a good judge of character, and he assured me Hammer was a good man. As it turned out, the CEO was a wrestling fan and wanted to do Hammer a favor. My mistake for not delving deeper. Hammer was late for the rendezvous. The helicopter that was dropping us at the upstream site couldn't get back before dark, so we had to delay a day. That night, the backpacks were…tampered with. In the book Hammer wrote—" Adam used air quotes "—he said he wanted to survive without all the modern conveniences."

"He sabotaged your preparations."

"Yes. I had used the pilot before. I believed him to be trustworthy. Now I speculate Hammer bribed him to unlock the helicopter where I had stored the backpacks." Adam met Elle's gaze; his eyes were a stormy wash of guilt and remembrance. "I should never have trusted anyone. I knew better. But a massive storm system was moving in. If we didn't get off the ground, we would be stranded for a week waiting for the weather to clear. I rushed. I didn't check every item in every backpack. Two people died."

He took responsibility for those deaths. She would not be able to dissuade him, because he was the man he was. Because he was the man she admired.

"We rappelled out of the helicopter into the Upper Amazon. Baptiste walked behind me, Nevaeh behind him. Hammer brought up the rear. Before the end of the first day, we left the Andes foothills for the jungle. It was the dry season… but the front moved in, and it rained. A deluge, twenty-four hours a day, every day. The first casualty came when we were crossing a tributary to the Amazon River—a creek in a normal season—and Baptiste was swept away. I ran miles downstream and found him caught in the branches of an uprooted tree, floating toward the Amazon. He was conscious. I swam out to him and dragged him to the shore. He seemed fine, just weak with the struggle to stay above water. Breathless from his time underwater, I thought, but fine."

"His backpack?"

"Was washed away."

"I suppose that was inevitable."

"No one's fault. The price we paid for Baptiste's survival. I knew what it would mean in terms of supplies, but to find Baptiste alive—that was a miracle. We met Hammer and Nevaeh slogging toward us. I decreed we should trek back upstream as quickly as we could. I was afraid of the Amazon River rising fast and engulfing us. We sank waist-deep in mud. Trees fell in slow motion around us, trapping us in their branches. We no more than gained the high ground when an anaconda dropped out of the tree onto Hammer. I reached for my knife and—" Adam touched his side as if the sheath that held his knife still resided there "—it was gone, lost in the river. *I thought*. Hammer had his knife, and he slit the anaconda down to its gullet."

"He took your knife?"

"The knife he used wasn't my knife."

"No. I mean, he removed it from the helicopter?"

"To this day I don't know. If he had stolen it before the helicopter set down, how did I miss that it was gone? It could have washed away in the river, and yet in view of events... I failed to check sufficiently before we set foot on the ground. I was in too much of a rush to beat the storm." Hectic color blotched his cheeks and forehead. "Excuses."

"You had no reason to believe you would be sabotaged!"

Adam looked at her, his eyes weighted with guilt and misery.

She didn't want to hear any more. Her research had told her the bones of the story. But to hear it from Adam, to watch him reveal his past and the grief that had sent him into hiding... She could hardly bear it.

But he needed to tell her, so she asked, "What next?"

"That night, Baptiste fell ill. Desperately ill, maddened, suffering. His eyes bled. He raged in pain. I opened my backpack, searched for the homing beacon that would bring in anyone within range. It was gone."

She suggested, "Possibly washed away in the river?"

"Impossible. It was zipped into its own pocket. That was when I first looked at Hammer and thought, *What is he doing here?*"

"A sensible question."

"Or the start of my paranoia. I searched Nevaeh's backpack. Her beacon was also gone. Hammer claimed he had never received a beacon."

"Sure. Paranoia."

"Baptiste died, swearing at me, condemning me for assassinating him. Afterward I found out he was the grandson of an elderly Frenchman who had been a Nazi sympathizer. Baptiste had been a target his whole life."

"You were five hundred miles from the nearest place you could call for help."

"At some point on the struggle to gain solid ground, Nevaeh was gashed by a thorn. A branch. She said nothing. Baptiste was so sick, she didn't want to make more trouble. I noticed she was limping, so I asked about it. She showed me the wound, red, infected, swelling. I injected her with antibiotics from my pack, then from hers."

"What did Hammer do?"

"He watched. He watched as her wound turned septic. He refused to give up his antibiotics for Nevaeh. He allowed her to die in agony."

"You despise him."

"Oh, yes." Adam's eyes became slits of molten hatred. "It wasn't until we—he and I—had made our way at last to the village where I knew we could be rescued that I realized the demon I had brought on our journey."

Elle held her breath. "What happened?"

"He pulled his phone out of his backpack and started transmitting the photos and videos he'd taken on the trip."

38

ADAM'S VOICE GREW HOARSE with fury. "While I was fighting for our lives, he was *filming*. That phone... I could have used it to transmit a rescue signal to a satellite. I could've saved Nevaeh and Baptiste."

Elle had read the accounts of what had happened next, and there were many of those: Big John Hammer's and Adam's and the witnesses' and the people who claimed to be witnesses, and the opinions of people who talked to someone who claimed to be a witness. She believed only Adam, but she asked because he wanted to tell her. "What did you do?"

"I picked him up over my head—adrenaline surge—walked to the end of the dock and threw him into the Amazon River."

"Good for you."

"He lost his phone. Whatever photos and videos you saw came from his phone before the dunking. At least there is that."

"Good for you," she repeated. What else was there to say?

"Like a river monster, he charged out of the water, all froth and self-important vengeance. He didn't believe I could best him. He thought the first time was a fluke. He's a big man. Fit. A fighter. But he learned to fight for money, fame, glory. I learned to fight to survive—and I was livid. I picked him up and threw him back into the river, and this time, every camera and phone in the vicinity was focused on us. I made a fool of him, and the whole world saw it." Adam sighed wearily. "I'm proud to say he's hated me ever since."

She had no doubt that even if Hammer killed Adam, Adam would always be proud of the damage he'd done to the fighter's reputation.

Adam's bitterness was almost tangible. "Two people had died, and to him they were nothing more than a video opportunity to tell his story in a way that made him a hero. He's no hero. He's nothing better than a murderer. He made me a murderer."

"No," Elle murmured, but in his mind, Adam would forever bear the responsibility of those deaths. "I have a question. If Hammer is a sharpshooter, if he's as good at it as you say he is, wouldn't he have killed you today?"

"The glass in Rune's window is—was—old and wavy. Distorted." He looked out of the glass of his own old windows and considered. "But you're right. It seems unlikely he would have only grazed me. When he had realized he'd missed, he would have taken more shots."

"Yes. Obviously he's not worried about shooting me or Rune by mistake." Odd, that she could face with equanimity the possibility of a gunshot tearing into her flesh, but the dark specter of the man with cruel hands made her scream in terror. The idea of dying slowly without breath, without hope, sent her into a frenzy.

Possibly because she'd experienced the intimacy of being

choked. To death, according to Adam. "Collateral damage is merely a word to Big John Hammer."

"The deaths of others are interesting to him in a clinical way. He has no empathy. No kindness." Adam's voice grew thin. "He likes to watch."

"Then, perhaps Hammer is not the one who fired the shot." Was that better or worse? She wasn't sure.

"Or he has an ulterior motive for wounding me." Adam flexed his shoulder. "I believe I'll sleep now. You have no reason to worry." He lifted his wrist and showed her the watch again. "I have alarms set up on the perimeter. No one will sneak up on us tonight."

"I'm not worried." She meant it, and not because of his perimeter alarms. She had someone to care for, and her own pains and fears had diminished.

"In the morning, you might consider going to stay elsewhere, with someone who is not a target."

"No."

"Think about it overnight."

"No." She stood, offered her hand and helped him to his feet. "And no."

Later, after she had fussed over him, helped him as much he would allow, and they rested in bed on their backs with the lights out, Elle said, "One thing I don't understand. If Hammer did shoot at you—and we both know that can't be discounted—why now? What would drive him to kill you now?"

"Oh. That. The timing."

Once more Elle heard grief in his voice.

"The raging river we crossed, the river that swept Baptiste away, was the breeding ground for a rare parasite which enters through any orifice. Mouth, nose, eyes, anus or any wound. Once inside a body, they find the organs, burrow into them and breed. And spread. Left unchecked, they'll consume liver, heart, lungs, kidneys..."

Elle sat up in dawning horror.

"The return from the Amazon was ghastly. Publicity. Reporters wanting to interview me on camera. Civil suits from the families of Baptiste and Nevaeh. All the while, those parasites consumed me bit by bit."

"Adam..." She rested her palm on his chest, felt the heat of his body, the pump of his heart, and realized how close she had come to losing him before she'd even found him.

He paused, breathed as if he needed the assurance that he could breathe. "I realized something was wrong, but not soon enough. They caused permanent damage to my lungs. I spent almost a year in treatment to eliminate the parasites."

She was almost afraid to ask. "A terrible, painful treatment?"

"Yes." His voice was clipped. Clearly, he did not intend to elaborate. "I contacted Hammer, told him he should be tested and treated. Instead he announced his candidacy for governor, escalated his appearances."

She felt consumed, too, by disbelief, shock and the dawn of fear...for Adam. "What does this mean? Why should he try to kill you *now*?"

"The brain is the organ the parasites relish. Soft, blood-engorged, oxygen-rich. I suggested to my doctor, and she conceded that it was possible, that Baptiste went mad because he tumbled down a river of parasites in search of a host. Water was forced up his nose and into his eyes and mouth."

She knew that sensation. She feared it, and her fingers curled and clutched the material of Adam's shirt.

Adam put his hand over hers. "Baptiste almost drowned in that river, and when he came out, the parasites were already gnawing at his brain, driving him mad, making him imagine conspiracy and ultimately killing him."

"You think Big John Hammer is insane," Elle whispered, "and he's coming after you."

"The parasites are chewing on a brain that already housed a dangerous personality, and yes, in the best of circumstances, he would never have forgiven me for tossing him in the river. But as he gets closer to his goal, to the office of governor and that video circulates more and more widely to more people who fear him or long to mock him… I suspect he's coming for me." With terrifying finality, Adam said, "And he won't fight fair."

39

ZSÓKE STEPPED OUT OF the stairwell and up onto the Live Oak's roof and looked up at the stars, twinkling so brightly in the midnight sky, and laughed. Who would have thought everything about this job would be humorous?

Zsóke dialed the private hospital, asked for Stephen Penderghast and was put through far too hastily. He must be acting up, and of course, if he was recovering, he would be.

Stephen answered the phone with a snap. "What?"

"How are you doing?"

"This surgeon is an arrogant ass. I'm in pain, and he doesn't care. He's gloating. Why? Because he saved my life? That's his job. I should be well by now. As soon as I can get off oxygen, I'm getting out of here."

"Darling, don't. You were badly hurt." A faint trail of smoke rose from the firepit where earlier the acting group had gathered to discuss Clarice's role.

"Yes. I was. That bitch. Who knew that short shrimp of a thing could manage to bring me to my knees. Report!"

He barked the command like a military dog. "What do you know about her?"

"You were right. She made it to shore."

"Of course I was right." He was savage in his satisfaction.

"You'll love this. She doesn't know me."

"She only met you once, and briefly."

Zsóke prepared to deliver the punchline. "She has amnesia."

Stephen's snort was loud, explosive, disbelieving.

"Seriously. You know I wouldn't tell you if I didn't know it was the truth."

Stephen mulled that over.

"They call her Elle."

He riled right up. "I don't give a fuck what they call her. I don't even give a fuck if she has amnesia…" He calmed again. "Although, yeah, that's kind of funny. She must have hit her head. I didn't do that, though."

"Definitely hit her head. She's still bruised, and Clarice tells me she looks better than the day after she came ashore."

"Clarice? Who's Clarice?" Stephen developed that possessive, jealous note.

Which was fine with Zsóke. Jealousy kept him distracted and less irritable. "Clarice Burbage. Actress. Gothic is a provincial town with one road in and out, and everyone knows everyone. I came in as one of Burbage's team."

"Right. Of course you did. You and that dumbass job."

"That dumbass job keeps me busy when you don't." Zsóke was used to Stephen's contempt, but *that dumbass job* brought in a lot of money, and one never knew when one would have to escape just ahead of the police. Stephen would not care. He was as cold as his father, as hard as the gold statues he sought, his only interest in the attention he would receive when he brought them forth from the ocean.

"Tell me what you've accomplished. Tell me Elladora Varela suffered—" Stephen's voice grated with cruel desire "—and is going to be dead."

"Elladora's not dead—yet. But soon, I promise." From one of the chaise lounges by the firepit, Zsóke heard a faint gasp.

"Why not yet?" Stephen snapped. "If she doesn't know you—"

"She's made friends, and it's impossible to get her alone." Zsóke stepped to the short wall that rimmed the building and looked down. Perfect: night vision had stabilized.

"Shoot her friends. Knife her where she stands."

Zsóke was not so foolish as to think Stephen would hesitate to sacrifice the person who he'd once purchased as his best friend. "If I do that, I'll be arrested. And if I'm arrested, our relationship, yours and mine, will come to light. Your injuries and her injuries, and your proximity to her the night before she washed up on the beach. You would be implicated."

Stephen was silent as he struggled against the truth he had to face. If Zsóke took the action he demanded, he'd be revealed. In a low guttural voice Zsóke recognized as rage, he said, "Never mind. I will get out of here and kill her myself."

"Really? How? Because I saw the doctor's report, and today you collapsed trying to walk by yourself to the bathroom."

"Who gave you that report?"

"No one. You know I have my ways." Turning, Zsóke faced the roof and casually scanned the herb garden, the grape trellis, the groupings where the acting team worked and the firepit. There. On the chaise lounge, wrapped in a down comforter…

Zsóke brought up the subject that truly prompted this call. "Darling, I do not like to think you double-crossed me, your very best friend."

"What are you talking about?" He had struck the right note: Stephen sounded confused.

"I'm here on the scene in Gothic, preparing to do your will. Then a sniper tries to kill her."

"Kill who? Elladora Varela? A sniper—"

"Yes. A sniper."

"There? What the hell? Shooting at Elladora Varela? With what?"

Not that Stephen Penderghast couldn't act as well as any Academy Award winner, but Zsóke thought, in this instance, he was truly flummoxed. "A sniper shot through the window and into the room where Elle was visiting with her friends. The police dug the bullet out of the wall. The weapon was a B14 HMR."

"The hell you say. Elladora is not dead?"

"There's some doubt that she's who the sniper was shooting at."

"So who's dead?"

"Nobody."

Now Stephen sounded truly angry. "You thought I would hire a sniper so lousy he couldn't make a kill?"

"I thought perhaps you hired a sniper to hurt but not kill her." Over by the firepit, Zsóke could see small motions, as if someone was shivering in cold and fear.

Wise. Very wise.

"Whoever that sniper is, he fucking better not make my kill. I want that woman to bleed internally, like I did. I want her to suffer, like I did. Amnesia? No. I want her to remember me and what she did and know she's lost everything. Family and reputation. Friends, too. Kill them all. Take everything."

That sounded like the Stephen Zsóke knew. Time to soothe the savage beast. "Don't shout. Stay where you are. I'll take care of matters here. You'll hear from me soon. You know me. The woman is as good as dead." Zsóke tapped the phone off and headed for the door that led downstairs.

Open the door. Don't leave. Close the door. Wait behind the grapevine trellis.

The person beside the firepit unzipped the sleeping bag and stood.

Zsóke could see the outline of Clarice Burbage. She had been up here, sleeping or thinking or concentrating on her upcoming role, and she'd heard everything. Wrong time, wrong task, wrong place. Now she tiptoed toward the door, no doubt hoping to get to her room or down to the street to call for help.

Zsóke allowed her to touch the knob before grabbing and twisting her arm and saying in her ear, "I'm sorry you overheard that conversation."

Clarice groaned when Zsóke pulled up on her arm, putting pressure on elbow and shoulder, pressure that threatened to rupture ligaments and break bones. "I didn't hear anything." Her voice was high, frightened.

She was right to be frightened.

"I have to keep an eye on you. You understand that?"

Clarice shook her head. "I didn't hear—"

"Here's what we're going to do. Every night, I'll sleep with you."

"I won't tell—"

Zsóke twisted again, not enough to break anything, but enough to make Clarice writhe as she tried to escape the pain. "No one will think anything about our tryst. In this little hamlet, every person imagines the actress is sleeping with every member of her team. That's the way provincial minds work."

"No. No," Clarice whimpered. "Who are you?"

"You know who I am. You simply don't know all that I am. You don't know that to take this job, I had to eliminate one of the original members of your team and take his place. He was a big guy, strong, but I killed him, stripped him and left him in a ditch to be a feast for coyotes." It was time to take control of Clarice and all her future actions. "Your little sister—"

Clarice took a frightened breath.

"Mila is so young. So vibrant. She's barely started her career. Next month, she will attend the premiere of the picture you two did together, *Sisters in War.* I am an expert with a stiletto, and I could stick a blade in her back and pierce her lung, and she would die a slow, inevitable death..." Zsóke contained Clarice's struggles. "No? There are other ways, some more terrible than others. So remember, you and me, we sleep together. We eat together. We never leave each other's sides. When I've finished this job here, I might let you live... and you might remember to never mention my name to law enforcement. Because if you do, they won't catch me...but I will remember your sister."

40

ADAM WOKE FROM A dream of water, death and madness to a morning of bright sunlight—and no Elle in the bed beside him. In one movement, he flipped over and onto his feet. He caught his breath at the surge of pain his careless movement caused, shook it off and rushed into the living room.

Elle wasn't there, nor was she in the kitchen. He ran out on the front porch—and found her, seated sideways in the swing, her back against one armrest, her feet propped on the other. In her lap, she held the leather journal Rune had given her. Her pen was poised over the half-scribbled page.

How dare she scare him half to death, yet be the picture of relaxation?

Looking up, she smiled as if the sight of him gave her pleasure. "Good morning. Are you rested at all? Or did the nightmares exhaust you?"

"What nightmares?" he asked automatically.

"The ones that had you twitching and moaning all night." She swung her legs over and patted the seat beside her. "It was a reversal of roles. I didn't scream because you were in such turmoil. It gave me a different perspective. Nice to think of someone else for a change."

He didn't know what to say. Or do. It was his immutable policy to do his suffering in private. But now he was sleeping with a woman, here to protect her, to give her a sense of security, and they'd reversed their roles, and he was the…not the weakling. Because he never thought of her as a weakling. But in the dark of the night, his subconscious had succumbed to memories that had shattered him.

He removed his focus from her, from himself. He remembered yesterday's bullet and their possible danger, and he scanned the horizon.

"You don't need to worry about someone with a rifle." Elle pointed at his binoculars sitting on the small round wicker table before her. "I brought them out and periodically I do reconnaissance. There's no cover and no one out there. Of course, I haven't looked toward town—" she pointed toward the back of the house, uphill and east "—but I don't know what I'd see there except maybe a lot of neighbors pointing their binoculars in avid interest at us." She grinned at him.

Now that the adrenaline that drove him out of bed had faded, his arm hurt, his head ached, and the nightmares she had described hovered on the edges of his consciousness. With a sigh, he slumped on the swing beside her. "How's the journaling?"

"Interesting. I was describing yesterday, and either I remembered more than I realized or I was making things up. I have details about Rune's shop, about the hypnosis, about that scream, and then the gunshot. Then," she said as she leaned close to his face, her unusually colored eyes alive with excitement, "then I remembered my mom's voice giving me instructions on what to do in case the rebels came in shooting."

"Your mom? The rebels?" He was dumbfounded. "Shooting?" Great. Dumbfounded and repetitious.

"I am tucked in bed. The curtains are closed tightly. I see Mom tucking them into exactly the right position so no light leaks out. She sits beside me, holding my hand." Elle groped for his hand and clasped it strongly. "I see her face in the dim light. I can hear people shouting in the street below. I hear gunshots. There's an insurrection."

She spoke as if she could hear everything at this moment, and he responded accordingly. "Where are you?"

"I don't know, but it's somewhere familiar and—" she reconnected with him "—and Adam, in my mind, I see my mother, and I hear her voice!" She squeezed his hand. "I have a mom. I know her. I love her. The memory is like having a platform to stand on, to reach all the rest of my memories."

"That's great." Not really. That didn't help him get her to safety. "Do you have any idea what your mother's name is?"

She grinned at him again.

"I do. Mommy." He leaned back with a groan he didn't mean to release.

"That sounded painful. Let's look at the arm." She unbuttoned his shirt, and she seemed to be paying more attention to his chest than the buttons.

He supposed that made a kind of sense. Buttons weren't that interesting, and in his day, he had had women spend more than a little time stroking his—

His watch vibrated and snapped him out of his reverie. He heard the thudding sound of swiftly running feet.

Elle heard, too, and half turned to the side, and they both saw a tall woman, six feet if she was an inch, round the porch and stop at the bottom of the stairs.

She looked up at the two of them on the swing, him with his shirt hanging open, Elle with her hand on his shoulder, and the woman said, "I didn't mean to interrupt an intimate moment." She got a cockeyed grin on her face.

"You must be Bendy Wendy." Elle got to her feet, walked down the stairs and offered her hand. "I'm Elle. I called this morning and asked for an evaluation."

"I had a cancellation so I ran down." Wendy shook Elle's hand. She was a handsome woman with brown eyes, black hair and a sculpted body. Wendy had created a lifestyle that challenged her every day. "How are you, Adam?"

"Good. Elle called you for an evaluation?"

"Self-defense," Wendy said.

Elle had called for an evaluation? Based on his advice?

He answered himself. Yes, and on her own good sense.

As he got to his feet, he buttoned his shirt. "Use my shop. There are workout mats. I need breakfast. I'll come after I've eaten." He had absolute faith in Wendy's ability to assess Elle's fighting strengths, and he knew without a doubt that Elle would perform better if he wasn't watching.

Breakfast was the usual: Greek yogurt, whole-grain cereal and fruit. At times like these when he was anxious and in pain, he freely admitted he fantasized about the Live Oak and Señor Alfonso's gourmet meals. But no more running up there, not until he was healed. Damn, this arm was badly timed and inconvenient.

Breakfast took precisely thirty minutes. Then he was outside. He snagged the binoculars and slowly scanned the horizon.

Nothing.

He walked around the house toward the shop and scanned up toward the town. He couldn't see the olive grove from here, yet he could see the bends in the road, the houses and buildings, and nothing looked unusual. After all, the flash of binoculars from the Hardlings' *was* usual.

But then, he didn't expect to see the sniper coming. Not if it was Big John Hammer.

Adam stepped inside the shop.

Bendy Wendy stood, hands on hips, watching Elle go through the third tae kwon do form.

Adam walked to her side. "What's the situation?"

Bendy Wendy gestured at Elle. "As you can see, she has some self-defense experience. She can't make a karate movie—"

"Thank God for that."

"But she's proficient enough to take care of herself against a single attacker in most situations." Wendy squeezed an imaginary throat. "So what happened? How did the bastard get to her?"

"She said he was big, and she said she trusted him."

"Long arms, and he got close before she realized his intentions."

"I suspect."

Bendy Wendy looked him over. "You're not going to say anymore."

"No."

"You're a good man, Adam. You know how to keep secrets."

"I thought people in town complained about that."

"We'd all like to know *your* secrets, and it would be your right to tell them. But her secrets are not yours to tell. Some people don't comprehend that concept." Wendy turned to Elle, who had paused, feet firmly planted, hands raised. "What's the matter?"

"I don't remember any more," Elle said.

"You got through the sixth form of international tae kwon do, and that's great. I teach world tae kwon do, which is different than the forms you were using, and you're still pretty battered, so I hesitate to teach you right now. But I suspect in a fight with an attacker you'll be able to injure him and get away."

Elle nodded. "Okay. Thank you. I feel better knowing that."

Bendy Wendy didn't question her. "When you're recovered, if you want a refresher class, give me a call and we'll set up a private lesson."

Elle came to Bendy Wendy and shook her hand again, and Adam took note of the height difference, thought of the added self-defense challenges of being five foot three and said, "A refresher class is a good idea."

Wendy had satisfied herself about Elle's proficiency. Now she addressed the question that concerned her personally. "Adam, do you have any thoughts about yesterday's shooting? Anything you can share?"

"It's worrisome."

Elle smiled at his brevity.

Wendy continued. "Did you hear that law enforcement searched for the sniper's location and found trampled grass, but no shell casing and no sign of a vehicle in the vicinity?"

"Gothic's neighborhood social media page reported that."

"If that spot in the grass was where he stood, the shot was two hundred and fifty yards!" She flung her hand in the direction of the sniper's location.

"I saw that, too."

Bendy Wendy calmed under his low-key tone. "The sheriff released the scene this morning, and now every person around Gothic who owns a metal detector is headed up there to scan for the casing."

"I don't think that's particularly safe." Adam glanced toward town and imagined the buzz of excitement as everyone joined in the search.

"How do we stay safe from a sniper except by apprehending him?" Wendy demanded.

"I will repeat what law enforcement no doubt has said. Civilians apprehending a sniper is unlikely, and civilians apprehending a sniper without being hurt is highly unlikely. Somebody's going to get hurt."

"I know, you're right, but I don't like jumping when someone pops their bubble gum." Bendy Wendy leaned close. "Do you think Rune was the target?"

"Without knowing who the sniper is, how do we tell?"

"Right. Well. Back to the studio. I've got a yoga class in twenty minutes." Bendy Wendy waved and took off running uphill as fast as she'd come down.

"She's in amazing shape. Did you see her at the restaurant yesterday selling yoga classes to the Shivering Sherlocks?" Elle was in awe. "She swooped right in there."

"She's an astute businesswoman. Did they go for it?"

"They were delighted. Apparently they work out together *all year* so they can do these mystery weekend jaunts. They're a bunch of spry old ladies!"

He wouldn't have thought he could smile this morning, but he smiled at Elle. "When you're an old lady, you'll be as spry."

Reaching up, she took the ends of his shirt collar, pulled him down and kissed him. Just a light kiss. A friendly kiss. Nothing that should have encouraged or worried him. Yet he was encouraged…

But he should not be. He had no right to be. Not about this, about her.

In a fierce whisper she said, "That's right, so let's get all this figured out, and we'll be spry old folks together."

Together? A giant vise squeezed his chest, and he couldn't catch his breath. She was talking about a future. The two of them together forever. Based on what? Extreme trauma, moments of extreme fear, long hours spent together for safety, the knowledge that even under stress, they got along well. They really did, and that, he knew, meant more than a night of passion…although the mere idea of sex with Elle brought tears to his eyes.

"Are you okay? You look a little like I must have when you pulled me out of the ocean." She nudged him. "Take a breath."

He did, then in his most cool, reasonable tone, he pointed out, "We don't know whether you have someone else you love, someone who deserves all your loyalty. A husband. A lover. A child."

She observed him with narrowed eyes. "I'm unattached."

"That's not good enough for either one of us."

"You're right. I'll see what I can do." She took his hand. "Come on, we've got to clean your wound and get you into a different shirt before our next visitors show up."

"What visitors are those?"

"Everybody who wants to know what you think of yesterday's shooting. Trust me. They will come."

41

WHILE ADAM LEANED AGAINST the bathroom sink, Elle finished taping his wound. "You're going to have to take it easy for a week or so, but all in all I'm pleased to say it looks pretty good."

"You're smug."

"Yes, I'm smug. I do have some talents, after all."

"You're a scientist. Of course you have talents."

"We'll stay home for the next few days, away from town where there's cover for a sniper." She helped him into a button-up shirt and came around to fasten it. "I'll call and order groceries at the Gothic General Store." She finished and stepped away. "Do you have anything in particular you want to eat? I warn you, I may have talents, but I suspect gourmet cooking is not one of them."

"Let's stock up on Angelica's prepared meals. The menu is tacked on the bulletin board." He handed her his phone. "The number is programmed in."

She called and made the order for the next four days, then

hung up. "We have food on its way. What do you want to do now?"

Adam went out to the shop, Elle trailing behind. "I'm going out to practice for the GSPF."

"The sword work? Now?" She wanted to ask if he should wait at least one day before indulging in such vigorous physical activity. But he was Adam. He had promised to perform at the Gothic Spring Psychic Festival, and he would do so to the best of his ability.

He took the sword off the wall, grasped the handle in his left hand and gave it a swing. The long, heavy sword was weighted for a two-handed grip, but Adam lifted it and thrust as if the sword was an extension of his arm. He moved so gracefully, Elle forgot his injury and watched for the pleasure of seeing him move. And thought hungrily that a man who moved like that would be a pleasure to dance with… and make love to.

Should she be so seriously considering that development? She, who didn't even remember her whole first name? In the first days of fear and recovery, only her own emotional recovery had mattered. Now as her world expanded beyond her own self-awareness, she wondered, Did she have a family somewhere? A husband, a lover? Someone besides her mother who she loved and cherished? *A child?*

She needed to know, and she needed to know now before she got more involved with him, as she so deeply desired. Taking a breath, she closed her eyes and searched her mind for the shadows of emotions.

She stood on the top of the highest mountain. Other mountains surrounded her, rocky, snow-capped, frozen. She breathed in the frigid air and knew she had achieved the height alone, without the help of anyone. She depended on no one but herself. No one depended on her. And she straddled that peak without fear and with pride. And she waited for—

The peak collapsed beneath her. She plunged into the turbulent ocean, down, down, down to the bottom. Desperately she wanted to rise to the surface, and something in the murky water beckoned her, and she floated forward, past skittering crustaceans and evil-eyed fish. The ground beneath her was rising, rising. The sediment in the water seemed to dissipate. Plants grew here, verdant otherworldly seaweeds that waved to the rhythm of the fierce currents. She reached out. She parted the fronds—and she saw two faces, frozen, staring at her... without eyes.

She gasped in surprise and horror.

But she couldn't breathe. She couldn't breathe.

Elle woke, struggling to suck in air. Her lungs sucked in oxygen so urgently, she knew she'd been holding her breath.

"Elle, are you all right?"

She opened her eyes to see Adam kneeling before her. Was she all right? "Yes."

Yet those faces, hidden behind the fronds in swirling, murky water, staring without eyes, accusing her of...of what?

Adam put his hand on her waist and steadied her. "You were unconscious. What happened?"

She put her hand to her chest and breathed again, taking the time to note the act and how much it eased her terror. "I wanted to know if I had more family, besides my mother. So I thought about emotions and connections, and I saw..." Words failed her.

Rune appeared behind Adam.

Where had she come from?

"She hypnotized herself." Rune rubbed her own forehead.

"Can she do that?" Adam demanded.

"Of course. Self-hypnosis is a tool I teach—taught—my patients." Rune pulled up a chair. "How long was she out?"

"Not long, but I don't know for sure when she went under. She didn't tell me she was going to do such a—" Adam stopped himself precipitously.

"Such a risky thing?" Elle suggested.

Adam picked up her hand and kissed it. "You scared me."

If he was going to kiss her hand, she supposed she'd forgive him for whatever unfortunate thing he said. "I didn't scream this time," she told him.

"No, but I almost did."

She wasn't sure Adam was kidding.

Rune nudged Adam out of the way and looked into Elle's eyes. "Quickly now. Tell me what you saw."

"It wasn't real. It was more like a dream populated by symbols. A vision."

"Did you see if you do have a family?" Adam asked.

Rune turned on Adam. "Shut up! These memories fade quickly. She needs to recount everything while she recalls it."

Elle ignored Rune and stared firmly at Adam. "The only family I have is the family I grew up with. I have no partner, no children. I'm alone in the world."

"Seriously?" Adam sagged with relief, then caught himself. "A vision isn't a guarantee." He turned to Rune. "Is it?"

"If you'll let her talk, I'll give you my expert opinion. And never doubt it, Adam—it *is* expert." To Elle, Rune asked, "Now, what did you *see*?"

As Adam paced and Rune listened intently, she told them about the mountains. Every detail was etched clearly in her mind, as if she'd really been atop of that mountain gazing at the other mountains that peopled her life.

When she finished, Rune turned to Adam and nodded.

"She's reading that absolutely right. She has no one who depends on her."

Adam stopped pacing. "Could her subconscious lie to her?"

"Unlikely," Rune said.

"No." Elle looked at them both. "I went looking for shadows. There were none. The light was pure and bright and uncomplicated."

"Good. That's good." This time, Adam allowed the relief to lift him.

Rune looked at the two of them alternately. "That *is* good news. I can see we're relieved to hear it."

Elle swallowed. "The shadows are in the water. In the ocean."

Rune settled more firmly into her chair. "That is where they would be."

"But not because of the near drowning. It's not like that." Elle told them the fearful vision of murky water and terrible creatures and tried to explain the fear and anticipation she had felt. Then…the flat faces. As she recalled them with their empty, staring eye sockets and prominent lips, she had to again put her hand on her chest to calm the beating of her heart.

"Can you clarify what you saw?" Rune asked. "There were two people looking at you in the water?"

She squinted into the sunlight pouring through the windows. "They were leaning against a…a rock. A rock that rose out of sight. The root of the mountain."

"That makes sense. You had been at the top of a mountain. Then you were at the very bottom," Rune said.

"The faces," Adam said urgently. "They had a nose? A mouth?"

She nodded. "Ears that stuck out at an odd angle. But no hair. No bodies that I could see."

"And no eyes?" Adam wanted that to be very clear.

"Their eyes had been scooped out, yet they stared at me as if I were responsible for the agony of their loss. They didn't move or speak." She swallowed. "I suppose they were dead."

"But not decomposing."

Rune hushed Adam.

"No. No decomposition, and their skin was a dull yellow. They scared me so much I woke up." She looked to Rune. "What does it mean?"

Rune rubbed her palms against her skirt. "Let me tell you what I hear. Elle, you went looking for the shadows of existing relationships and found that you are free. But your subconscious heard not only that question but another—*what* are you responsible for? And showed you those two faces."

"How can I be responsible for dead people?"

"Maybe they're not people," Adam said. "Maybe they're—"

"Excuse me!"

Elle jumped and looked toward the open garage door.

Tamalyn stood there, hands on hips. "I went up to the house but no one was there." She stared accusingly at Elle, as if being in the house was a duty she had shirked. "I brought your grocery delivery."

42

ELLE STOOD ON THE porch of the house and watched Tamalyn bicycle laboriously back up the road toward the store. "That kid has issues."

"She's in love with Adam," Rune sang like a delighted second grader.

Adam picked up two of the grocery bags and headed into the house.

"Of course she is." Elle picked up the remaining bag and followed. "But it's more than the usual teen angst. I recognize that. She's angry about something."

"That you're living with Adam," Rune said.

"Maybe. There have to be underlying issues." She put her bag on the table beside Adam's and watched him put groceries away.

"Sure," Rune said. "She's a teenager."

"You're the psychic. What's wrong?" Adam asked.

"I don't have to be psychic to know. It's the usual. Her father died. Her mother remarried, the new family moved here from Silicon Valley. Her stepfather is a noted novelist who gets a lot of attention. Her mother is the head of a computer-development team. She works remotely, and she had a baby—" Rune developed that sloppy grin people get around charming toddlers "—who is currently the cutest eighteen-month-old I've ever seen."

"Tamalyn is displaced," Elle said, "feels ignored and lonely—"

Rune continued. "She also used to write angsty poetry, but since her stepfather is a commercial author who rakes it in, she gave it up with the fury of an artist betrayed by reality."

Elle winced. She had written her share of teen poetry.

Rune watched the food disappear into the cupboards and the refrigerator. "I never ate breakfast," she said wistfully.

"Hey, Rune, want to stay for lunch?" Adam asked, and at Rune's nod, he began to make sandwiches.

Elle laughed at Rune. "Subtle!" She hummed as she assembled a vegetable plate and opened a tub of Angelica Lindholm's Own Curry Dip. When she saw Adam looking at her in surprise, she sidled up to him. "We've got company!"

Adam looked at the egg salad he had spread on a piece of bread. "It's only sandwiches."

"And chips!" Elle pulled a bag out of the pantry and turned to the observant Rune. "Can't you make Tamalyn talk to you?"

"I'm a psychic, not a magician." Rune was more than a little sarcastic. "No one forces a teenager to talk."

"I remember." Elle froze for a moment, then laughed. "My mother married when I was a teenager. He was a good guy, I liked him, but before I had had *all* my mother's attention and then...not so much. I suffered. I really did. I moped around and inflicted dramatic sighs and long silences on them. He paid attention to me, making up for my mother's distraction.

Things smoothed out and—" She interrupted herself in exasperation. "Would you please tell me why I can remember that kind of anguished adolescent stuff that I don't want to remember, and not who tried to kill me?"

"Ain't it hell?" Rune didn't seem concerned.

Adam jumped in. "No, really. Why does she remember stuff that is so unimportant—" He caught himself, turned to her and said, "Not that I'm dismissing your teenage years. They helped make you the person I admire."

Elle grinned at his polite nod to her past and filled their water bottles. "Thank you, Adam."

Adam turned back to Rune. "But we've got problems here, and what she knows would help us focus on how to resolve them. Why can't she remember?"

"Adam, her mind has to recover on its own schedule."

Adam picked up the laden lunch tray and strode out onto the porch.

Rune followed. "Please realize she's doing well. The wonderful thing about the memories she has recovered is that they indicate a healthy brain." Picking the leather-bound journal and pen off the porch table, Rune smiled at the scrawl of ink on the pages and placed them on the railing.

Adam put the tray down.

Elle came out carrying two stacking tables from the living room. "I have no brain damage?"

"When you consent to go to a doctor, we'll have tests run." Rune settled into a wicker rocking chair, hung her beaded handbag on the arm and draped her shawl behind her. "As badly as you were hurt, an injury to the brain is a dreadful possibility and could have horrible repercussions."

"As I told you," Adam said.

"Repeatedly," Elle agreed.

"Having Elle remember her teen angst is reassuring and, may I point out, the return of memories is accelerating," Rune said.

"There is that." Adam stepped back to allow Elle to place a stacking table beside Rune and hand her a paper plate. "Help yourself."

Rune took a corned beef sandwich and a handful of baby carrots. She nodded at the notebook and pen. "I see you've been journaling. Did it help? Do you remember any more about the night you were attacked? More than the lights and the hulking monster?"

Elle stared with narrowed eyes at the turquoise leather. "Yes. I remember how badly I hurt him."

Somehow, she still clutched her weapon. Some instinct had warned her to hold it tightly, and she would not relinquish it now. She held it up to the light; the metal shone like stainless steel. She saw the length of it—it was as long as she was tall—the end curved like a cane back toward her, terminating in a barbed hook.

Thank God she had retained her weapon, because silhouetted against the careening light, a dark, menacing form moved toward her.

She tasted salt and terror.

Him. He stood between her and the house where there was help, light, life.

He was returning to finish the job.

His rage gave him an implacability she had never imagined from any man and certainly never from him. She never imagined he would turn on her. Never.

He had been a paternal figure, her mentor, her friend.

She held the rod so tightly her fingers ached. But she held it in the middle, not by the handle, and she needed every inch of length she could bring to bear. Clumsy with cold and terror, she walked her hands up the slippery metal to the vinyl grip.

Quick. Quick!

He loomed over her and…

She swung. She hooked him behind the back and yanked, burying the barb into his flesh.

Even with her impaired senses and through the roar of the wind, she heard him scream. Breathing, gasping, using the railing, she dragged herself to her feet.

Still screaming, he staggered, clawing at the metal rod. He grasped it, braced himself and pulled.

She couldn't believe it.

Like a giant fish hook, that barb must have torn flesh all the way out, and he just…did it.

He should have been on his knees.

He should have been dying.

He looked at Elladora, huddled against the rail. He looked at the hook, shiny and deadly. He adjusted his grip. He started toward her again, and the whites of his eyes glinted with madness or satisfaction or pleasure.

Now she realized he was a monster, a zombie, impossible to kill.

And he would murder her in the most painful way possible.

Elle finished her story. She looked at Rune, who was frozen in astonishment.

Then at Adam, who wished fervently he had been there to help her. No wonder she suffered from nightmares.

"Before you ask," she said, "no, I don't remember what his name was or what his face looked like or where I was."

"I wasn't going to ask." Yet Adam didn't know if he was telling the truth.

"What I remember is grasping that metal and knowing killing him was my only chance to survive. I remember thinking, *I trusted him.* At the time, I was grieved to know I had been so wrong." Elle took a deep breath. "I'm furious that he was such a bastard. I don't care what happened, how I came to be a victim. I did nothing to deserve dying in such a cruel way."

As if in agreement, the breeze off the ocean ruffled the pages of the journal. The pen rolled off the porch railing. The wind picked up, and the journal rocked, then toppled into the rosemary hedge below the porch.

"Excuse me. I have to get that." Elle jumped up.

"I can get it for you." Adam felt as if today he needed to do something to help her, because he hadn't been there in the past.

"No! Let me get it." She pushed her way past him. "My brain is fine. There's nothing wrong with me." She headed for the stairs.

"Give her a moment, Adam," Rune murmured.

Adam watched her take the first three steps at a run, as if she was trying to escape the last painful moments. As she took the last step, she caught her foot on something. On nothing. With flailing arms she fought to recover and failed. She fell hard, down the last step and flat onto the ground.

43

BEFORE ADAM COULD GET to her, Elle climbed to her feet swearing virulently. "That wasn't my fault. I tell you, I tripped on something!"

She had grass stains on her knees, she wiped at her palms, and he was sure the fall had jarred her healing ribs. But she was moving fluidly; he judged she had not been badly hurt, so he turned to the steps and searched, doing first a visual, then running his hands along the edges of the boards.

She came closer. "What are you doing?"

His fingers encountered what he expected: he jerked the thumbtack free and held it up. "Looking for this."

The thumbtack had been embedded into the side of the wooden step. Dental floss was wound around the pin. He felt sure he would find another tack on the other side of the step. With dental floss stretched between them, it formed an effective trip wire that snapped when activated and disappeared from sight.

Elle figured it out immediately. She stared in shock. "She… Tamalyn…"

Rune peered over the railing and saw what Adam held. "Oh, hell."

The three adults gazed at each other in consternation.

"Now what?" Adam had seen Elle fall and caught a glimpse of the floss as it whipped around, but to find himself holding a homemade snare… He was a survivalist. He knew what to do in every imaginable situation. But not this one. Not in an attack by an angry adolescent.

Elle pressed a hand to her ribs. "I'm going to talk to that kid right now!"

"No." Rune pulled the phone out of the pocket of her skirt. "Let me handle it." She dialed the General Store and spoke in a voice that trembled. "Tamalyn, darling, I know how you feel about Adam, and I didn't want you to hear from anyone else. He fell coming down the porch steps. Just fell! No reason."

Adam heard Tamalyn's high-pitched squeak.

Rune continued. "He broke his neck. He's dead!"

Elle covered her mouth in horror at Rune's audacity.

"I have to go now, to close his staring eyes that will never again gaze on a starry sky and cover his still-warm body with a blanket. Good-bye!" Rune hung up. She nodded at Elle and Adam. "That should do it. Let's sit down, have our lunch and wait for her to get down here. It shouldn't take long."

"That is harsh!" Elle protested.

"She set the trap for you without ever thinking her beloved Adam could very well have tripped. Or me. People die taking falls." Rune watched Elle grimace as she pressed her ribs. "You're lucky you weren't badly hurt."

Hastily Elle took her hand away.

"Tamalyn already got away with that stunt once. Remember when you fell at the store? Angelica tripped, too. If Angelica ever discovered what Tamalyn was up to, that young woman would be out of a job. Her mother would be afraid to allow her near the baby. Everyone in town would view her with suspicion, and she'd be shunned until the day she left for college." Rune enumerated all the reasons Tamalyn needed to learn a lesson. "She's getting off easy."

Elle couldn't argue about that. But she'd lost her appetite. She waited, tense and uneasy, until Adam lifted his wrist. "She's coming," he said.

Elle heard the sound of bicycle tires racing down the gravel driveway and a faint, constant sobbing interspersed with panicked words like "No!" and "I didn't mean..."

Tamalyn skidded around the corner of the porch, dropped her bike, ran toward the bottom of the stairs. She stared at the worn grass there, then lifted her gaze to the porch where Adam, Elle and Rune watched her. The blood drained from her face. She gasped out loud. She stammered, "You...you lied!" She pointed at Elle with a shaking finger. "How dare you scare me like—"

Elle could not believe she was getting blamed.

Adam stood, walked to the railing and held up the thumbtack dangling from the floss.

Tamalyn stopped in midsentence. She turned her palms up and spread her fingers, as if trying to disassociate herself from the deed. "I didn't mean to—"

"Kill anyone?" Rune questioned her ruthlessly. "That wasn't a cute practical joke. You could have killed any of us. Do you understand you could go to prison?"

Tamalyn switched her attention among her audience.

Adam folded his arms and stared without speaking.

Bursting into tears, Tamalyn ran for her bike.

They listened as she rode away, sobbing wildly.

Rune sighed and placed her plate on the table at her elbow.

"I guess I'd better head after that child and make sure she doesn't do herself an injury."

"Tell her we won't tell anybody," Elle said.

"As long as no one else trips," Adam added.

"I'll do a good lot of counseling while I'm at it. Thank God I'm feeling better today. This is going to take a while." Rune gathered her shawl and handbag.

"By the way, why did you come down today?" Elle asked.

"I wanted to discuss what happened yesterday, share more thoughts about who shot at us and why, and talk about how to protect ourselves." Rune flung her shawl around her shoulders. "That'll have to wait. What's on the agenda for you two?"

"We're staying here, lying low, recovering from the trauma of the last four days." Now that the incident with Tamalyn was over, Elle could nibble on a celery stick. "I'll journal and practice self-defense. Adam will no doubt test the limits of his strength to get in shape for the Gothic Spring Psychic Festival."

"We're going to concentrate on not dying." Adam surveyed the horizon.

Rune headed for her ATV. "Stay away from windows. I intend to."

"Let us know what happens with the girl," Adam said.

Rune lifted a hand in a wave of acknowledgment.

Two hours later, Adam handed Elle his flip phone. "It's Tamalyn. She wants to talk to you."

44

ELLE BRACED HERSELF, TOOK the phone and in her most soothing tone said, “Hello.”

“Hi, Miss… Hi, Elle. This is Tamalyn.” The girl’s tone was low, as if she wanted no one to overhear. “I wanted to say… I really do want to say this. No one’s making me. In fact, no one knows I’m calling. Except Adam, and he won’t tell. Will he?”

“He isn’t a tattletale, Tamalyn.”

“I know. Listen. I never, ever thought of killing you, I swear! I did want to hurt you for moving in with Adam and the way he looked at you…like you were…special and nobody ever…” A long, wet sniffle followed.

“It’s okay.” Elle had never felt so inadequate. Even without her memory, she knew that.

“Forgive me. I will never do anything like that again to you. Or anybody. My mom’s coming to check on me. Bye.” Tamalyn hung up before that last word was finished.

Elle flipped the phone closed. She cleared her throat. “She apologized.”

The phone rang again. Adam grimaced, took it and answered. He listened for a moment, then placed it on the table and put it on speaker.

It was Rune. "About Tamalyn. I got to the General Store. Veda met me. She said Tamalyn was crying hysterically in the back room, so I headed there and handed her tissues. When I didn't say anything, she started talking in between crying fits. She said she was a bad person. Not because she tried to hurt you, Elle, or because she loved Adam, but because she was jealous...of the baby."

"Uh-oh." Elle got a sinking feeling.

"She kept assuring me that she loves the baby, but everyone coos about the baby, and nobody even notices her unless she's got a pimple the size of Everest on the end of her nose. Her term, by the way—the size of Everest."

"Glad you didn't make that up," Adam said.

"Poor kid." Elle really felt for Tamalyn. "She's jealous, and she's guilty."

"That about covers it," Rune agreed. "She's mad because the baby calls her Tammy, so her family now calls her Tammy, and the kids at school heard it and started calling her that, especially when they realized she hated it."

Adam began, "That's no reason to—" and stopped when Elle glared at him. "That's major."

"When you're sixteen, it is," Elle told him.

"I said a few things, barely got into who I was and who I'd been and we could talk anytime, and her mother walked in." Rune made it sound like doom.

Elle tensed. "Oh, hell."

"Right. She came sweeping in with the baby on her hip. Tamalyn looked at me like I was scum." Rune sighed. "She thought I had tattled on her to her mother. Then her mother said Angelica's assistant had called, and she'd dumped work to get to the store, and what was wrong? Had someone hurt Tamalyn? I got a dirty look from Mom, too."

Elle couldn't help it. She laughed. At once she said, "I'm sorry, Rune, but you are…unique."

"In a good way, right?" Rune wasn't really checking. She didn't care what anyone thought.

Adam made his contribution to the conversation. "You're absolutely the most normal psychic I ever met."

Elle poked him with her elbow. "Stop that!" To Rune she said, "What happened with her mother?"

"Tamalyn started crying again, crying hard, and the baby started crying, too, and her mother handed me the baby and put her arms around Tamalyn. Which was exactly the right thing to do. But the baby didn't want me—and I've held her before, she likes me, she likes everybody. She wanted Tamalyn. I offered her to Tamalyn, and the baby flung herself into her big sister's arms and wrapped her chubby arms around her neck and kissed her face and wiped her tears and hugged her and kept saying, 'Tammy, don't cry, don't cry, Tammy.'"

"Ahhh." Elle felt as choked up as Rune sounded.

Adam looked alarmed.

"That got everything under control. Her mother privately asked me to tell her what happened. I refused and asked that she not ask Tamalyn, either. I told her my background in therapy and said I'd be glad to assist when I could." Rune coughed. "She seemed more impressed when she thought I was a psychic."

Adam gave a crack of laughter. "Therapist or psychic, which is worse?"

"I know. What was I thinking?" Rune's fluting voice grew wry.

"I'm thinking you're doing very well," Elle told her. "Tamalyn called and apologized to me."

"Did she really?" Rune got anxious. "Did her mother make her?"

"Her mother knew nothing," Elle assured her.

"That must have been a hard call to make and shows real contrition and more maturity than most adults I know." Elle heard a bell tinkle, and Rune was suddenly brisk. "Now I'm back at the shop, the Shivering Sherlocks just walked in, and this is going to be lucrative. Talk to you later!" She cut the connection.

"Another day, another crisis, and one that's ended well for all." Adam wiped fake sweat off his forehead.

In a burst of affection, Elle hugged his arm. "You are a nice man. Now, how long do you think until the next crisis arises?"

He pulled back in dismay. "Good God, woman, don't challenge fate."

"Sorry! You're right." She rested her head on his shoulder and said wistfully, "I really would enjoy a few days of peace so we can rest and recover."

"Me, too." He had never meant anything so much.

The following four days were everything Adam could have wished. The weather was perfect. The horizon remained clear. The sense of being watched had vanished. No bullets flew, and no one fell down the stairs. He and Elle had conversations about what foods they liked, discussed metallurgy and how Adam created his armor and weaponry, and discovered they both liked reading suspense novels while rocking in the porch swing.

They did not have conversations about their pasts—because she didn't remember one more single darned thing and Adam refused to discuss any time earlier than his arrival in Gothic, especially not the deep, inner meaning of his art. In fact, he told her there was no deep, inner meaning.

What he couldn't figure out, what didn't make sense to him

was how she managed to wear clothes that always looked as if she was naked underneath? He knew Angelica had brought Elle bras and panties: the first few days, he'd washed them. Then she'd taken over her laundry. He also knew that the panties Angelica had brought Elle covered her butt. At least, he'd seen no evidence of a thong.

Where had those panties gone? Because as the days passed, temperatures climbed and Elle had taken to wearing her dress every chance she got. When she walked, a subtle friction of what looked like her silky skin against cotton cloth distracted him, and once he noticed, he was obsessed with her butt.

Not only her rear; in the evenings, he examined her breasts for a bra. A bra would keep her warmer than she appeared to be, assuming that he remembered correctly—it had been a long time since he'd had personal experience—and nipples got hard when chilled. He worried she was going to catch him checking her out, but she never did. She seemed oblivious to his interest.

He couldn't decide if he was a disgusting beast or a man with a scientific question that begged to be answered. Luckily for him, his control had been honed by hardship and pain, and no matter what she said, he would not take advantage of a woman under his roof and protection.

All in all, he thought that for two people who had known each other so briefly, they were doing pretty well.

Then came the night of the big storm, and all hell broke loose.

And all heaven, too.

45

AS THE SUN SET, the clouds built in bright pinks and golds, higher and higher, then darkened with the promise of menace. The wind sang in soft soprano tones, then gained the strength and despair of an operatic tenor who had lost his love. The storm rolled in with a bluster that turned to a threat, and Elle found herself staring at the journal in her hand, pen motionless, waiting in terror for the moment when the ocean closed over her head and she saw those faces again.

Adam's hand gently plucked journal and pen out of her grasp. "Want to watch a movie?"

She stood. She walked to the middle of the living room. She listened to the storm arrive fully onstage and blast a melodramatic operatic climax that shook the house. She put her hands over her ears. "I can hear voices in the wind."

He wanted to scoff, to tell her she was imagining things. But he heard voices, too. Voices of the past. Voices of reproach. "On nights like these, when the storms brew and the fog waits, lost souls visit Gothic and sometimes…they stay."

Why the hell had he said that to her, when she stared with eyes so wide and her face so pale? What could he do to ease her fears, to make her realize others shared the fears she suffered? That *he* shared the fears she suffered?

Taking her hand, he led her to the couch. Putting his hands on her shoulders, he looked into her tearful eyes. "We've all got secrets. You don't remember yours. Sometimes I wish I didn't remember mine."

"If you can tell me—" she put her hand on his shoulder "—I'd like to hear."

She gazed into his eyes and she looked so…sincere. Like she cared. Who would care? He gave an incredulous crack of laughter. "What makes you think there's more than the Amazon debacle?"

"No one becomes a survivalist based on a happy childhood."

His brief spurt of bitter amusement faded. How did she know? "I can't tell you. I'm not the strong man you imagine me to be. Every time I remember, I break a little more. If much more of me crumbles, there'll be nothing left."

He had warned her, and still she hugged him. She was affection and kindness, and he…he was painful memories of a lost and broken childhood. "I'm here for you, and you feel solid. This house won't fall in. Its foundation will hold us here on the hill. The furnace is working."

She was reassuring him. When had the roles reversed?

"We're warm," she said, "and the voices in the wind aren't really voices. It's a storm off the ocean, and it, too, will pass."

As if in protest, the wind shrieked like a soprano as she died a terrible stage death. Rain slammed against the windows and rattled the front door. Elle gasped as if a salty wave had slapped her face, and she was back on the boat…

★★★

She swung. She hooked him behind the back and yanked, burying the barbed point into his flesh.

Even with her impaired senses and through the roar of the wind, she heard him scream. Breathing, gasping, using the railing, she dragged herself to her feet.

Still screaming, he staggered, clawing at the metal rod. He grasped it, braced himself and pulled.

She couldn't believe it.

Like a giant fish hook, that barb must have torn flesh all the way out, and he just...did it.

He should have been on his knees.

He should have been dying.

He looked at her, huddled against the rail. He looked at the hook, shiny and deadly. He adjusted his grip. He started toward her again, and the whites of his eyes glinted with madness or satisfaction or pleasure.

Now she realized he was a monster, a zombie, impossible to kill.

And he would murder her in the most painful way possible.

Wildly she looked around for an escape.

The wind paused. The rain ceased. For one moment, far away and high toward the east, she saw a light. If she jumped into the sea in hopes of reaching shore, she would likely not survive.

But if she stayed onboard the ship, she was going to die a terrible death.

Grabbing a flotation ring, she climbed the railing and flung herself into the violent churn of the Pacific Ocean.

"You *jumped* into the Pacific Ocean in the middle of a violent storm?" Never in his wildest dreams would he have believed this woman had deliberately gone into the sea. "My God, what courage! And you survived."

She sniffled, wiped her nose on the back of her hand and

peered up at him with big, sad eyes of brown and blue. "You said I died."

"You revived." Right. Sure. That was obvious.

"The more I recall, the more solid I feel, as if I'm reassembling the body I have always been."

He handed her the box of tissues from the table.

She used one to dab her eyes and blow her nose. "Of course, it was you who brought me back to life."

"Rune is right. I was meant to find you." Adam put his arm around her, hugged her, and somehow...somehow their lips met. They kissed. He brushed the tears off her face. And they kissed.

The best kiss he'd ever received. Ever enjoyed. *Ever...* They slid off the couch onto the floor. The floor was the best he'd ever kissed on. He climbed on top of Elle and kissed her. That body was the best he'd ever kissed on. Worshipped on. Welcomed into the exploration of his own body.

Her voice murmured in his ear. "Adam, maybe it's been a while for you. But this works better if you don't wear your boxers."

She was tugging at his pants.

Right. Get rid of them.

And slide her dress up her leg, up her thigh, to her hip, grope for her panties to bring them down...

"Aha!" It was not so much an exclamation of surprise as satisfaction. No wonder he hadn't been able to discern panty lines. She wasn't wearing panties.

She laughed throatily, sat up and pulled her dress over her head.

No bra. No panties.

No restraint.

Well. Except for the one. Groping in the end-table drawer,

he found the condom he had so hopefully stashed there and pulled it on.

Elle chuckled. “Always prepared.”

“Always.” He flipped her onto her back. “Let me love you. Let me taste you.” He was babbling.

She was miles ahead of him. She straddled him, guided him into her and called the tempest inside.

They held each other, screaming as the winds swept them, the rains washed them. They raced across the ocean, confronted the heart of the storm, lost themselves in pleasure and need and vanquished the darkness.

As they finished, the electricity went out.

Of course it did. They’d blown the circuits.

But the generator kicked on, and one by one, the night lights it powered illuminated the living room.

It looked almost like candlelight.

Elle lifted herself off Adam’s chest.

He was aware of several things.

1. He’d managed to remove his pants, but his shirt was open and still on.

2. When a man was making love, he was supposed to be restrained and give his partner encouragement. That would enable her to achieve climax.

3. He was pretty sure Elle had beaten him to the finish line.

4. Man, he was tired. His arm throbbed, and he was aware that he’d spent many wakeful nighttime hours contemplating the conundrum of Elle’s elusive panties.

5. But Elle was eying him like a slab of grilled steak. Who was he to complain?

“This floor is uncomfortable,” he said. “Let’s see if we can ride the storm…in our bed.”

46

THE NEXT MORNING, ELLE slid out from underneath Adam, grabbed his shirt off the chair and padded naked and barefoot to the bathroom.

He watched until she shut the door, then rubbed his face. There were many ways to work out and condition himself for the big fight.

That was the best one.

She came out buttoning his shirt over her chest. "What were you going to tell me about those faces? The ones I saw underwater? Yesterday, you were going to say something when Tamalyn interrupted."

"Oh." Adam remembered. "I thought from the way you described them—no eyes, protruding ears, flat faces, prominent lips—that they weren't real faces. They sounded as if they were masks."

"That's it!" She pivoted toward him, alive with interest and agreement. "That's right, they are. Masks from an ancient civilization. South American. Peruvian. Moche."

"Put that together with your memory of an insurrection and your ability to speak Spanish, and that makes sense. You knew about the ancient civilization that made those masks. You *knew*." Adam stood, pulled on his underwear and headed to the computer.

The internet was down.

"Stupid technology. Happens every time!" Elle huffed like a dragon who had lost her pilot light.

Adam didn't care about technology. This revelation was about Elle, and her past, her memories, her scientific background. He picked up his cell phone. "We're going to call Rune. We're going to talk to her about getting another session of, er, psychic evaluation for you. Maybe that'll break the dam that's holding back your memories."

"That would be great." Elle's face lit with relief.

He flipped open the phone, tried to dial, sighed and shut it again.

"It's dead, too?" If possible, Elle now looked more frightened than before.

"Even on clear days, here on the edge of the continent, it happens." He reached into the cupboard beside his desk. "That's why I have this." He brought out an old phone with a tangled cord between the base and receiver and a flat cord between the base and the wall.

"Right." She sat in the office chair and waited while he dialed the number.

Connection. Right away. He gave Elle the thumbs-up and said, "Hey, Rune, how's it going?"

At the blast of speech, Adam held the phone away from his ear. Rune shouted, "We had a storm. The Gothic Spring Psychic Festival is setting up on Angelica Lindholm's lower lawn, one of the tents blew over and the pole shattered a window in her greenhouse. The fryer for the ice-cream balls arrived broken. Also the knight who is lined up as your opponent in the mock sword battle called, and he is one weird guy." Less frantically and more reflectively, Rune said, "Of course, all the people who set up and run a festival are weird. I don't know what I expected. A little more discipline, I guess."

Elle took the phone. "Adam has discipline. He's been working with the sword two hours every day."

"Not necessary! You're not trying to win. It's a mock battle." Rune lowered her voice. "Although, how are the stitches?"

"They look good," Elle told him. "I'll remove them on Thursday. That way everything should be healed, and Adam can practice with both hands. I mean, more energetically than he is."

Adam took the receiver. "I have to practice, not to win but to assure I don't accidentally injure my opponent."

Elle smiled at him and thought, *He's the best man I ever met.* Even though she didn't remember the other men who had passed through her life, she knew it was true.

"Everyone should have your sense of responsibility." Rune didn't actually sound pleased. More like irritated. "You didn't call to hear me complain. What's up, there?"

"Elle had a tough time with the storm. She knows some stuff, not memories, but knowledge that seems unlikely for most folks to have, and we were wondering—"

"If later today I can set aside time and we can do an online session?"

Elle yanked the phone out of Adam's hand. "Come down now. You can take a break, have breakfast, talk to me about my rebellious brain. We'll listen to what's happening with the Gothic Spring Psychic Festival, and it'll be a friendship hour."

"Elle, I can't. With less than three days left until the moment we open the gate, and psychic readings lining up, and the shop being so busy, I just..." Rune stopped talking.

Elle held her breath.

"All right, I will!"

Elle grinned at Adam and gave him a thumbs-up.

Rune continued. "I deserve an hour doing nothing but eating and talking with friends. I'll bring rolls from Firm Buns Bakery."

"That sounds great, Rune. See you in a few." Elle hung up, turned to Adam and kissed him right on the lips. As if he deserved all the kisses. She talked close up to his face. "I don't know if Rune is my psychic, my therapist or a friend, but I love that she feels as if she can come to our house and relax."

Adam loved that Elle called this place *our house.*

He had begun to think that when she left, the heart he thought he no longer possessed would shatter into a cosmos of loneliness.

"You're the cook," Elle said. "What shall we fix Rune for breakfast?"

47

IN THE BRIGHT, NEWLY washed morning, in a corner of the control center, DeAnna squared off with Daniel and Liam and angrily whispered, "I'm the one who realized we had extra crawl time. I'm keeping it!"

Liam turned the red color of frustration. "That's not fair, Daniel. I realized Elladora had disappeared almost as soon as DeAnna did. I thought we should give her a chance to show her face before I—"

DeAnna pointed a finger in Liam's face. "Loser!"

"You've got no more right to that crawl time than anyone on this vessel."

"Let's shout it out to everyone and see how fast those times fill up." DeAnna raised her voice. "I thought we were whispering about this for a reason."

"Keep your voices down," Daniel said. "You know if anyone else aboard finds out there's open crawl times, you're going to get bumped."

The three of them squared off, stepped back and pretended

to be civilized people when in fact they were researchers fighting for their places in the scientific world.

"Anybody hear how Stephen Penderghast is doing?" Liam paced away.

"He's still alive. He's rich. You can bet he's had every expensive drug that every top doctor in the country could give him." Daniel was patently bitter.

"I don't care how many doctors he's got. I saw him leaving the ship," Liam said. "I'll bet he's already dead and they're lying about it until they can get his affairs settled—and kick us off the ship."

Gloom descended on the small group.

"Did you hear Elladora's mother called the captain?" DeAnna said.

"You're kidding." Liam was agog.

"Mommy said she hadn't heard from her for days and wanted him to find her," DeAnna reported.

"And?" Daniel waited.

"He said he wasn't a babysitter and that when her daughter wanted to call her, she would." DeAnna wore a wary expression, as if she wondered what would happen if she disappeared.

"Seems a little cold," Daniel said.

"Elladora's mother has been calling every day since. Captain won't take her calls." DeAnna turned on Liam. "Have *you* seen Elladora?"

"No." He started backing toward the galley. "Haven't seen her. Barely know her."

Daniel stood his ground. "I haven't seen her, either."

Liam fled. Apparently his crawl time wasn't as important as staying away from conflict.

"Has anyone?" DeAnna asked.

"I went to her cabin to check on her." Daniel looked sideways at DeAnna. "The cleaners were in there wiping it down, every surface as if they wanted to erase all trace of her."

"That's not good. That means... No, it couldn't have been her who tried to kill Stephen," DeAnna argued as if Daniel had said something contrary. "He's a big guy. She's short and skinny."

"Stephen said he fell on the hook. Maybe she got caught by a gust of wind. It was really blustery that night. He was grabbing for her, she went over the edge—"

"Sure, that's possible, but why keep it quiet?"

They looked at each other in alarm.

"Something funny's going on. Something...not good."

"I'm going to ask around and see if anybody's seen her or knows anything," DeAnna said.

"Be discreet," Daniel warned.

"No kidding. I don't want to go overboard, and I really don't want a hook in the back."

48

RUNE SAT AT THE breakfast table and talked, an outpouring of frustration. "I hired Melinda to come in and help with the shop. I need help during the festival. Right? That makes sense, doesn't it? I can't run the shop, do my regular psychic readings and the tourist readings and keep on schedule with the festival setup. Melinda's always been dependable, and she has her own fortune-telling costume, and she dyes her hair pomegranate-red which really adds a wild vibe to the outfit." She tugged at the strand of hair shortened by the bullet's impact. "When I called to give her her schedule, her voice mail said she was on vacation. She didn't even call me! Honestly, people! Show a little concern for your commitments!"

Elle handed Adam a plate piled with silverware and he loaded the dishwasher.

"My shipment of Magic 8 Balls has been delayed. I've got four fortune-tellers lined up, one to read palms, one to read runes, one to read a crystal ball and one to run the machine that spits out fortunes. Miss Crystal Ball doesn't want to sell *my* products. No, she thinks she should get to sell her own. You'd think if she really was psychic she'd know that's going to get her fired faster than anything." Rune sucked in a breath. "You wouldn't happen to know a fortune-teller who wants to work at a psychic festival, would you?"

"I can safely say you're the only fortune-teller I know." Adam shut the dishwasher door and set the cycle. "How about you, Elle?"

"I can safely say Rune is one of the few *people* I know." Elle sat back down at the table.

Rune blinked, glanced at her watch and dabbed her mouth with her napkin. "I'm not here to complain. I'm here to see if I can help Elle recover more of her memory. Shall we try hypnosis again?"

"Yes, please." Elle sounded very sure.

"What was it you learned last night?"

"That after I hurt the monster who had attacked me, I jumped into the ocean to escape."

"Into the jaws of the storm." Rune turned to Adam. "What a woman!"

"She had no choice," Adam said.

"I assure you, most women, most people, would die for lack of nerve."

"I know." Adam knelt beside Elle. "I do know."

Elle smiled into Adam's face and touched his cheek.

"Let's use something that's *not* my hand to help you go under. Ahhh." Rune sounded as if she'd discovered something satisfactory. "Do you have your glass pendant?"

"I'm wearing it." She lifted it from under her shirt and over her head.

"Elle, since you're willing, let's begin." Rune spoke in that soothing voice Adam had come to equate with hypnosis and dangled the necklace in front of Elle. It swayed, back and forth and back and forth. "What do you remember?"

Elle watched the movement, but Adam could see she was fighting to relax. Her hands rested on the table, and they twitched, trying to close into fists, and he wanted so badly to help her. He was about to say, with another fair amount of logic, that this should wait for another day.

Then in a voice a little higher than before, she said, "Mommy."

Rune exhaled with satisfaction. "Who is your mommy?"

"She's my mommy!" Elle sounded like the child she had once been. "She loves me. She hugs me all the time. She teaches me stuff."

"What kind of stuff?"

"Math. Spelling. She showed me how to dig. We read together every night." Elle's smile faded. "Sometimes she's not happy."

Adam sat down at the table. He would have asked about digging.

Rune went for the emotions. "Why isn't she happy?"

"She says sometimes it's hard to be a woman alone." With that, Elle sounded more mature, more like her present self.

"Where's your daddy?"

Elle set her chin. "I don't have a daddy."

"Your daddy isn't alive?" Rune asked.

"I don't know. Mommy never talks about him. When I ask her, then she's unhappy. So I don't ask." Elle rubbed one eye as if she was tired—or as if the tears of long ago threatened to return.

"What about digging?" Not that Adam didn't sympathize with Elle and her mother, alone in the world, but *digging* was a clue.

"It's fun. Once I found something. Everybody gathered

around. Mr. Kheifets wanted to take over, but Mommy said, 'No. Let the child learn.'" Elle grinned. "Mommy said Mr. Kheifets was acting like an old lady, twisting his hands and walking up and down."

Rune and Adam exchanged glances.

"What did you find?" Adam asked.

"An early Moche ceramic bird, circa 300 CE."

"Moche?" Rune mouthed to Adam.

Rune might be the expert on hypnosis, but here Adam was on sure footing. "So you and your mommy were excavating in the Peruvian Andes?"

"Yes!" Elle waved a hand and looked around as if she expected to see the mountains—and just like that, she saw where she really was. The child dropped away, and for a moment she looked confused. She took a long breath.

Adam thought she was going to scream and half stood.

But her gaze fell on the blown-glass pendant, and she smiled. "My mother." She took Rune's hand. "Thank you. You truly gave me my mother, all of her."

Adam's relief passed, and he wished she was under again. He hadn't asked all the necessary questions. "Your mother's an archaeologist?"

"Yes. We work in Peru in their summer, and stay at Grandma and Grandpa's in summer here. Here in the northern hemisphere."

"Right. The seasons are flipped in the northern and southern hemispheres. I know that. I really do." Rune had obviously suffered a confused moment.

With every passing second, they moved further away from the revelations Adam needed. "What is your mother's name?"

Elle opened her mouth to reply—and stopped.

Adam's heart sank.

Then, in a childlike, singsong voice she recited, "My mother is Sofia Neely." The adult Elle appeared again, and looked at Adam. "My mother made me memorize that."

Adam went to his computer. The internet seemed to be back. "Sofia Neely, American archaeologist working in Peru. We can find her."

"That would be good. I know she's worried to death." Elle came and hung over his shoulder. "My mom. If I can talk to my mom, I can find out where I was when this all started."

Adam felt the tremor of excitement that ran through her. Although, since she had landed on the beach and come alive in his arms, she'd been totally his. To have the rest of the world engulf her…

"What are you waiting for?" She nudged him. "Type!"

"Right." He entered *Sofia Neely* and her occupation into the search engine, then narrowed the search to Peru. "Why aren't I finding her?" he asked. "Why aren't I finding any archaeologists working in Peru?"

Rune joined them. "You're hitting an information block?"

"That's right." Elle was remembering again. "To discourage looting, Peru no longer releases information about its archaeological sites."

"But she should be somewhere!" Rune protested. "She grew up somewhere! She went to school somewhere!"

Adam said, "One problem. Sofia is a common name in South America. Another problem is that she may have married and changed her last name. Elle? Any thoughts about that?"

"She married my stepfather. I told you that. Did she take his last name? I have no idea." Elle lifted her hands helplessly. "I had to tap the little girl Elle to come up with her name in the first place."

Rune's phone rang. She looked at the number, excused herself to answer it and went out on the porch.

From inside, Adam and Elle heard a rapidly escalating conversation that ended with Rune bellowing, "Not only are you not selling your own products, you're fired! Yeah, sue if you want to!" Quiet followed, then a muttered "For all the good that's going to do you." Rune stuck her head in the door. "All hell's breaking loose. I've got to go. Thank you for breakfast and a few minutes of respite spent among friends. I'm so happy for you both!"

What the hell did that mean?

"Thank you."

"Rune, wait a minute." Adam went into the bedroom.

Elle put her hand on Rune's arm. "I'm coming to work for you, to tend the store while the festival is on."

"What? No! I wasn't hinting. Anyway, you can't. Adam would never stand for it. My store has been the only target for the shooter. Here you're safe."

Adam came back out and handed Elle a phone. A flip phone, of course. "I activated it," he said. "My number is in the memory. Rune's number. The Live Oak. The Gothic General Store and Deputy Dave. You know how to dial 9-1-1."

As he spoke, she ran through the controls. "I can figure it out. I'm set."

"Adam, what are you thinking?" Rune asked. "She's not completely recovered. And I know you're worried about her."

Elle went electric with irritation. "I'm not going to do anything stupid in your shop."

"I didn't mean that!" Rune said. "I meant he's worried *you're* the one who the shooter was aiming at."

"Oh. Hm." Maybe she was oversensitive about the memory loss/brain damage issue. She smiled weakly. "Right. I think the last few days of relative peace have convinced us both we should get on with our lives."

"She'll stay out of your consultation room, won't you, Elle? Which is the side of the building that faces the olive grove and provides cover for a shooter." Adam wasn't completely comfortable with this, but Rune needed help and Elle needed occupation, and who could hurt her while she was in a busy shop?

Okay, lots of people, but if he figured percentages, the probability was lower than her being a target out here.

Rune took a few breaths, then exhaled excitedly. "If you're absolutely sure, this would solve such a dilemma for me. Thank you, both! Elle, if you're ready, I'll drive you up and acquaint you with the workings of the shop, then abandon you to sink or swim." Her smile disappeared. "Sorry! That was absolutely not a phrase I should have used!"

Elle laughed, kissed Adam on the cheek and headed out the door.

As Rune drove Elle up the road to Gothic and her psychic shop, Elle turned and waved at Adam.

Of course Adam was watching and waved back.

He was glad to have the afternoon to himself.

49

ADAM HAD WORK TO catch up on, work he'd put aside during the turmoil surrounding Elle's lost-soul appearance in his life. Today he would start the creation of a nineteenth-century fencing sword, an épée, something that required all his concentration. Going to his kiln, he fired it up. As it heated, he went inside to further research Elle's mother.

Nothing. Peru had clamped down on archaeological information, and he didn't have the contacts or the hacking skills to get the information. In his mind, he ran through his old contacts, people he had worked with before the Big John Hammer scandal, people with whom he had ceased contact. Although they'd never indicated anything but staunch support, he had told himself they wouldn't want to be burdened with knowing a man with his now-doubtful character. But right now, one of those contacts in South America could possibly assist in finding Sofia Neely.

For Elle…

He painstakingly typed an email to Ezra, his old friend,

asking for help and sent it off. He started to turn off the computer when a reply arrived in his inbox. Warily he opened it to read an enthusiastic, excited reply from someone, he realized, who had been missing him and his friendship. Maybe he had taken this retreat from the world a little too far. He wrote back, explaining the situation, and got an assurance Ezra would search his contacts for Elle's mother.

Adam logged out and glanced at the clock.

Elle had been gone forty-seven minutes. Not that he was counting.

Secure in the knowledge that within days they would know the location of Elle's mother, he went to his shop and chose the pieces of metal for the épée. This was exactly what he needed to calm his turmoil after last night's riot of ecstasy.

What had he been thinking, making love with Elle?

He hadn't been thinking.

Feeling. He'd been feeling, with his hands, his tongue, his dick. She had touched him, he had touched her. Last night, emotions had not been involved. Had not. Today he wasn't so lucky.

He wondered how it was going in Rune's shop, whether Rune would spend enough time teaching her the ropes or whether one of Rune's festival emergencies would call her away and leave Elle hanging.

He walked out of the shop and looked up the road.

This was ridiculous. Except for losing a fight with a much larger opponent, Elle had proved to be very capable.

He went back inside and returned to heating and pounding the blade into shape, then repeating the process.

Being killed had put a dent in her self-confidence. Naturally. What if the bastard who had done that to her showed up in Rune's shop? What then?

He didn't usually mind when the heat of the furnace and

the afternoon sunshine combined to take the temperature in his shop to over one hundred degrees, but today he pulled his T-shirt off over his head, used it to wipe the sweat off his forehead and wished Elle was here to appreciate his buff, damp body by running her tongue over…

Enough of that. He was using an iron mallet. He didn't need his cock sticking out there asking to be hammered.

He checked the clock on the wall. An hour and twenty-two minutes. Eighty-two minutes total.

That couldn't be right. She'd been gone longer than that.

He checked his watch. There. He knew it. Eighty-three minutes!

It was going to be a very long afternoon.

50

AT 4:02 P.M., ADAM gave up. He put his shop in order and sprinted into his outdoor shower, holding a change of clothes, to do a fast cleanup.

Mistake! Memories filled the space: the day he'd found Elle, given her a shower, seen her body, caressed her—

No. He had not caressed her. He had behaved like a civilized, compassionate human being and washed the poor, injured woman.

He looked down at his dick which didn't remember the civilized part at all, only the feel of her boobs beneath his palm. Thank God that mallet remained on the workbench in the shop, although he did need to be careful he didn't bump into anything. Like the far wall.

By 4:23, he was dressed, in the ATV and headed for Madame Rune's as if the place was on fire. He parked and hopped out, took a breath and casually sauntered in.

When Elle saw him, she smiled, but she was talking to Clarice's acting coach, Faith Moore, expounding on the large geode Faith held in her hand. She peered at Elle intently, listening, nodding, not smiling. She didn't seem a very cheery sort of woman.

Gregoire and Sarcha were there, too, each holding a staff while discussing the various ways they could be used to take out an attacker.

Clarice stood in the back corner, holding her arm close to her chest. She neither looked at Adam nor spoke, and when he called out a greeting, Gregoire broke off his discussion to tell him, "She's not allowed to speak to anyone. It's an important part of her role preparation."

"Huh." Adam stuck his hands in his pockets. That was stupid, but he supposed Clarice had agreed to that stipulation when she took on the job.

Elle led Faith over to the cash register, rang up her purchase and thanked her for her business. When the Hollywood gang had filed out, Elle grinned at Adam. "Rune is going to be so pleased, and so will Hartley and Sadie. That was an amethyst geode, the largest one they ever found, and it is one expensive rock!"

Yay. "You're having fun?"

"I am. Except I tried to talk to Clarice and got soundly told off."

"By Gregoire?"

"No, by Faith. I feel as if they're torturing her, I guess to get the best acting out of her, but this seems cruel." Then she said exactly what he'd thought. "Although, I suppose she agreed to it, or she wouldn't be doing it."

"Right. You'll work again tomorrow?"

"Yep. I can't wear Rune's clothes, but she said something about loaning me a few of her scarves to tie around my head and hips." Elle slid her palms down from her breasts to her thighs. "That'll look good on me, don't you think?"

He was so busy staring he forgot to answer.

She laughed throatily and greeted a couple who wandered in. "Welcome to Madame Rune's Psychic Readings and Bookshop. Can I help you find something?"

"If you're so psychic, shouldn't you know what we want?" The husband was irritated, feeling foolish and out of place.

"Harry!" the wife exclaimed.

"Roberta!" he mimicked.

"I can't know when you don't know yourself," Elle answered sensibly and set a stool beside the display of scientific desk toys: kinetic-art asteroids, perpetual-motion swinging steel balls, a light-up plasma ball. "When the shop's not busy, I play with these. Why don't you do that while I speak with your wife?"

The wife explained she didn't really believe in all this psychic stuff, and Elle showed her the glass necklaces and stone rings and slipped her a book on how to read palms, and by the time they left, the husband had acquired three of the scientific toys. "For the grandkids," he said, although Roberta rolled her eyes at Elle.

As they left, Elle wished them a fun time at the Gothic Spring Psychic Festival, then turned to Adam. "I didn't think he noticed her looking at the stone-winged butterflies, but he paid for it and slipped me their address, and asked if I could wrap it for their anniversary. What a nice man! Another expensive sale."

Adam began to think Elle would do very well at Madame Rune's. "What time do you close?"

"Six."

Which Adam knew because he'd looked at the hours when he walked in.

"Rune said she'd come back to help me. She already showed me the back room and the safe behind the counter, in case

I sold so much in cash I needed to put the bills out of sight. There's another safe back there for the jewelry. She keeps cheaper stock out here." Elle showed him the sliding doors beneath the wide chestlike shelf on the side walls. "Lots of storage. She's going to show me what to lock up and I suppose stuff like lowering the blinds—did you see? She got some installed right away."

"Being shot at will induce immediate action." Adam glanced around, trying to figure out what he was going to do for another hour. "Do you want to go out to dinner at the Live Oak?" Not that he wanted to dine out, but women liked good food, candles and white tablecloths, and here in Gothic, there was only one place for that. And Elle had said food was important to her.

"No, I'm a little weary. I'd rather go home with you." She moved closer and said suggestively, "Maybe we could eat and go to bed early."

"So you can sleep?"

"Sure." She placed her hand on his chest over his heart and looked up at him with sultry desire. "Afterward."

If working at Madame Rune's put her in a sultry mood, he supposed he would put up with it…for the time being.

"Eh!" From the doorway, Rune made a sound like a trainer correcting a dog.

Elle jumped away from Adam.

"None of that in Madame Rune's Psychic Readings and Bookshop." Rune waved as if trying to air the room. "The surroundings will absorb the passionate vibrations, and couples who enter will find themselves unwisely entangled!"

Adam gave a disgusted sigh.

"Don't give me attitude, Adam Ramsdell. I've had a stressful day." Rune sat on a stool, nudged the dragon snow globes aside and put her feet up. And moaned. She looked at Elle. "How did you do?"

"Here's the day's total." She ran a printout and handed it to Rune.

Rune's painted-on eyebrows shot up. "Wow! You can sell in my shop anytime. Although… I might ask whether you could help tomorrow setting up the festival." She was looking at Adam rather than Elle.

Elle didn't wait for Adam to reply. "I'd love to! But what about the shop?"

"I'd only keep you in the morning to run errands for me."

"I can do that." Elle put her hand on Adam's arm. "I'll drive the ATV."

"We don't know if you can drive," Adam said.

"I'm an American. Of course I can drive."

"I'll drive her up," Adam told Rune.

"If you do that, I'll put you to work, too."

Adam put his hand on his arm and whispered piteously, "But my stitches…"

Rune's expression was horrified. "I'm sorry. I forgot! How are they?"

Elle chuckled. "He's fine. The man heals very well. I'm taking the stitches out tomorrow night."

"Not funny, Adam!" Rune put her hand to her back and groaned. "Not when I feel like death on toast."

"Aren't we a threesome?" Adam said jokingly.

"I am fine," Elle said firmly.

Rune looked at her. "She is looking better. Bruises almost gone."

From outside somewhere, they heard a scream that lifted the hair on Elle's arms. "What was that?"

Rune groaned again. "She's starting early."

"Who?" Elle stared wide-eyed.

"Clarice and her acting coaches. Once the group got together, they really got down to business. They order all their food up from the restaurant. They practice the role all the time, and sometimes Clarice screams like..." Rune shook her head. "But usually at night."

Two tourists stepped through the door, hands on their chests and laughing in nervous spurts. The guy said, "That scream was something else. We both jumped about a foot. When you people do a psychic festival, you really know how to raise the bar."

"That's what we do best," Rune said. "Can we help you?"

51

THE NEXT MORNING, ADAM turned onto the road to Angelica Lindholm's home. As they drove through the gate, he told Elle, "That is never open unless there's a reason. Angelica reveres her Queen of the Mountain solitude."

"I'll bet. Why does she allow the festival to set up on her lawn?"

"This area is all hilly, and the land around the Tower is terraced. Flat. You'll see."

"Yes, but even so, why would Angelica—"

"Without the festival's concentrated influx of income, especially with State Route 1 closed, most of the shops would go out of business, and Gothic would be a ghost town."

"She doesn't need the income from the building rentals."

"Certainly not. But whatever else you can say about Angelica, she has a proprietor's pride in her inheritance. She won't let the town disappear on her watch."

Yes, Elle could believe that about her.

They drove up and around a corner lined with crepe myrtles now leafing out, and as they rounded the last curve, Elle exclaimed in amazement.

Adam stopped at the fork in the road to allow her to take in the sight: the Tower, a romantic ruin, the attached English manor house and the gardens in front of the building with vast sweeping lawns and beds of flowers preparing to burst into bloom.

Even though Elle had viewed the Tower from Gothic, this was so much more, with cherished touches of wildness, suggestions of the early twentieth century, and Angelica Lindholm's own vastly civilizing influence. "Spectacular."

"I know. I was told that when Angelica inherited the Tower and the mansion and the land, the whole of it was in bad shape. Somehow she managed to hold herself back from her obsessive tidying and simply enhance what she was given." Cynically he added, "Probably because to get a building permit, she had to retain the structure's historical parts."

A sign read *Festival Parking This Way* with an arrow that led away from the Tower and toward a lower tier of lawns, and from there Elle heard a cacophony of hammers, drills and shouts. "Doesn't the festival leave the place a wreck?"

"The first year it did. After that, Angelica paid for fencing which keeps all but the most determined within a specific area." Adam drove down and around, and they found themselves in the midst of the creation of a medieval village and marketplace.

"How interesting!" As soon as Adam parked beside one of the trucks advertising Ye Olde Festival Awnings, Tents and Paraphernalia, Elle was out of the ATV and rushing toward the oblong arena that occupied the center of the lawn. A corral-style wooden fence surrounded the enclosure, and on one end, a raised dais held seating for the privileged few. There

Rune sat on a gilded velvet throne, speaking to Angelica's assistant, Veda.

In the past, Adam had made it a point to never get anywhere near the festival, a solid decision he wished he had maintained. But after a critical look around, he hurried after Elle. Seeing her here, among strangers, reminded him of the gunshot through Rune's window and Elle's close encounter with death. He should never have given her a phone and agreed to her helping Rune in the shop. Yes, she practiced her self-defense, and yes, her memory loss was easing, but her life force burned so brightly she shone like a beacon, and everyone on the grounds noticed. Tools stopped, suspended in midair. Voices calmed. Every eye appreciated her…and Adam knew that attention led to danger.

Someone knew who she was. Someone who wanted to kill her.

So Adam observed which of the men and women stared too long and too fiercely and made mental notes of each one. By the time Elle and Adam made their way to the foot of the dais, Eric was shouting at his crew to return to work and the sounds of hammers and drills once more filled the air.

Veda leaned toward Rune, gesturing at the greenhouse's shattered window as if her job depended on her righting this wrong. As maybe it did.

"Hi, Rune!" Elle waved at the beleaguered fortune-teller.

Veda straightened up, focused all her concentration on Elle, then in a flurry she ran to the edge of the dais, jumped three feet to the ground and ran up the path toward Angelica's mansion.

Adam watched her with thoughtful, narrowed eyes. "That young woman should have her blood pressure tested."

"That young woman should get a less stressful job," Elle said.

Together, they climbed the dais toward Rune, who was ruddy-cheeked, fiery-eyed and snarling. "Every year it's the same mad rush to set this thing up, but this year! Adam! Elle! What was I thinking to take this task on again? We've got to be ready in three days, and this festival is a train wreck!" Rune waved her arms and spoke in italics.

Elle ached for her. "It's not so bad. All that has to be done is—"

"Everything!" Rune put her hands on her knees and gasped for breath. "And oh, God, here comes Her Highness again to complain that her greenhouse isn't repaired and her orchids are suffering. Priorities, lady. Priorities!"

True, Angelica Lindholm was steaming down the same path her assistant had run up. Her linen starchiness stood in contrast to Rune's wild froth of scarves, fringes and coins, and Elle and Adam's casual California attire.

"She's going to wither me with another stunned reproach," Rune moaned.

Instead, Angelica stopped at the edge of the dais and smiled up at Elle and Adam. "How delightful that you've come to visit. Won't you come to the house and enjoy some refreshment? I'd love to give you a tour."

Again the entire grounds quieted. An incredulous murmur arose, then at a signal from Eric, died away, and the hammering resumed, although at a lower decibel level as everyone strained to hear.

Elle looked at Adam, surprised and uncertain. "Um, sure. That would be interesting. Adam? Shall we?"

He nodded. "Sure. I've been here five-plus years and never been inside the Tower."

Elle shot him a *Shut up* scowl and added a *What's wrong with you?* glare.

Adam wandered down the steps, offered Elle his hand and helped her down. "Lead the way," he said to Angelica.

To Rune, Angelica said, "If you need any help, ask my assistant." As Veda rushed up, Angelica added, "Veda will do whatever you ask. Won't you, Veda?"

"Yes, Miss Lindholm, if you want me to." Veda sounded as gobsmacked as anyone at this new direction. Surely Angelica demanded efficiency from her assistants, and before the end of the day, Rune would be breathing easier.

Rune's eyes narrowed as she turned to Veda. "Right. Let's get this done."

Adam gestured for Angelica and Elle to proceed up the winding path, and he followed, his hand hovering under Elle's elbow. In a voice pitched to reach her ears only, he said, "You've lost your job as Rune's festival assistant."

Out the side of her mouth, she said, "I think you're right."

Angelica started talking, tossing information back to them like an experienced tour guide. She told them about Maeve Lindholm choosing this location, the house's square footage, the famed decorator who had furnished it, and the exotic 1930s Hollywood galas. Elle listened and murmured appropriate replies while avoiding Adam's gaze because...damn, this was weird.

At the top of the trail, Elle paused to look, and the gardens and mansion took her breath away. The mansion itself ranged between one and three stories, building toward the four-story Tower on one end. Ornate carvings along the roofline decorated the sandstone facade. Wicker furniture offered an invitation to relax on the wide veranda.

Adam, of course, seemed uninterested in the beauty of the home. Instead, his gaze assessed their surroundings, and he paid particular attention to any cover offered by trees, foliage and outbuildings.

They crossed the broad, flat lawn to the cast-iron double doors. With the panache of a true showman, Angelica flung them open and stepped back. "Welcome to the Tower. *Mi casa es su casa.*"

52

ON THE ROOF OF the Live Oak, Clarice knelt before Zsóke, clutched her hand close to her chest and wept. This new pain was focused under the nail of her index finger, but so many places hurt she didn't know if she could bear to live. So many places hurt she probably wouldn't live. How could she survive, when her wrist had been twisted so hard the bones had cracked and her skin had been slashed and her joints broken?

"Shut up. I didn't hurt you." Zsóke stood over her, the thin stiletto flashing in the sunlight.

Clarice raised her tear-stained face. "Hurt me? Of course you hurt me!"

"No, I didn't."

She was in agony, and the other two on her acting team believed she had submersed herself in her role of the mad King Lear. When they praised her for her dedication and she might have tried to confide in them, Zsóke snapped at them to leave Clarice alone to brew her role.

Now Zsóke smiled a broad white smile and promised, "If you don't stop crying, I'll give you something to cry about."

How could Zsóke be so unreasonable? "You slid your knife under my fingernail. Three fingernails! You cut my—"

The stiletto suddenly pointed at Clarice's right eye.

Clarice gulped back her tears. "You didn't hurt me."

"That's right. I've never hurt you."

"You've never hurt me."

"I only punish you when you deserve it."

Clarice's mouth went dry. She couldn't repeat that. She couldn't. How could she agree it was her fault Zsóke tortured her with such skill and enjoyment?

Yet the knife tip was an inch from her face, from her eye, unwavering, glinting in the sun.

How had this all started? Up here, on the roof, that night when Clarice overheard Zsóke's intention to murder Elle. Elle, whose real name was Elladora, who had run afoul of Zsóke's boss and had almost died at his hands. Clarice had meant to flee the roof, warn Adam and Elle, call law enforcement...

Now when she saw Zsóke watching the street below, waiting for the opportunity to erase Elle from the face of the earth, Clarice couldn't bring herself to care. All she lived for was one moment free from pain.

"What do you say?" Zsóke embodied everything about command and cruelty.

"I said...you only punish me when I..." Clarice took a quavering breath. "You only punish me when I—"

Zsóke whipped around toward the back wall that surrounded the rooftop. "Shut up!"

At Zsóke's anger, Clarice wanted to curl up in a ball of misery and beg forgiveness.

But all Zsóke's attention was on that wall. The knife disappeared from Clarice's vision. Zsóke paced across the roof, intent on something...

Clarice wiped her tears on her sleeve. She couldn't see anything unusual; the view that direction was nothing but hills, grass and trees. Directly below the restaurant's wall was an oak tree and the back parking lot.

Yet Zsóke was swift and intent, stalking like a panther on the hunt.

A clicking noise. Clarice knew that sound. She used the arm of a chair to rise and noticed with a leap of hope three iron hooks were dug into the wall's plaster—a grappling hook—and between them rested something long and dark.

A camera lens. *A camera clicking, making a record of Clarice's torment.*

Who could have the guts to rappel up three stories of this building to take photos of her?

Only the paparazzo. Only Bruno. He was her ticket to escape.

Bruno crawled onto the wall and stood with his legs wide. His camera hung around his neck. His brown eyes gleamed with triumph, and he said to Zsóke, "I have pictures!"

Clarice wanted to scream at him, *Shut up!* Didn't he realize what Zsóke was? Hadn't he seen enough to know he challenged a monster?

Zsóke smiled. "I know you have pictures."

Bruno's glee faded. He teetered on the brink of realization and the edge of the wall.

"You're a witness—and I can't have that." With both hands, Zsóke shoved him over the edge.

53

ELLE AND ADAM WALKED into the foyer hung with a crystal chandelier and graced by a curving marble stairway, which was overshadowed by the view. The western wall was three stories high and all glass, and the farther Elle walked, the wider the vista grew until all she could see was the sweep of Pacific Ocean stretching to the faint blue horizon. At last she stood still, nose almost touching the sparkling windows, to absorb the wild beauty.

Beside her, Angelica watched Elle intensely. "This is the Great Room. This is what I've worked for my whole life, to be able to gaze every day at this view and marvel."

"There are no words," Elle said. Except *wow*, and that seemed too trite.

Adam stood on her other side. "I've heard about this, but no one could describe it with the eloquence it deserves."

His voice seemed to wake Angelica from her concentration on Elle. "I've ordered appetizers to be served in the sun porch. This way."

As Elle followed, she looked around at things she hadn't previously noticed: Angelica's carved walnut desk occupied one section of the Great Room, while on the other wall, trendy furniture surrounded a massive fireplace. A collection of antique bronzes shone with the patina only daily hand-stroking could produce. Elle turned to point them out to Adam and realized he stood behind Angelica's desk, holding a gilded picture frame and studying the photo.

"Mr. Ramsdell, if you would care to join us." Her tone was sharp. Angelica Lindholm, local landowner and self-proclaimed czarina.

Not at all abashed, Adam replaced the frame and strode across the room. Going to a closed door at the north end of the hall, he put his hand on the lever. "Is this the way into the actual tower?"

"Yes, but the door is locked. When Maeve Lindholm built her home, she planned for the Tower to be a crumbling ruin, silhouetted against the sky, what the English call a folly. Unfortunately, the deliberate decay introduced real decay. The Tower is the part of the house I haven't yet renovated, and sadly, no one's been in the structure for years—" Angelica's voice shook in emotion that was puzzling "—although the view there surpasses even this."

Curious. "Why haven't you concentrated on that remodel?" Elle asked.

"Construction will involve a complete inner restructure and will be noisy and expensive. It *is* on the agenda for next year and the year after." Angelica opened the door that led to the sun porch and stepped back to allow them to enter.

"It's a conservatory!" Elle exclaimed in delight. Plants and flowers filled every corner, and a garden of herbs grew in pots around the perimeter.

"Brava! Yes, I designed a traditional English conservatory

with all its lush glory, and a place where my cook can come and harvest whatever herb she wishes for meals." Angelica indicated they should take seats on either side of her. She poured tea and passed a platter of lemon-nutmeg scones, cheese Danish and miniature cinnamon rolls. "Elle, I imagine your parents must be worried."

"I'm afraid that's probably true." Elle bit into a scone and sighed with pleasure. "I imagine you heard Adam found me on the beach?"

"I heard something like that," Angelica confirmed.

"I'd been in the water for hours, and I had some gaps in my recollections." A tactful way to put it. Elle blotted her mouth with a cocktail napkin. "But some memories of my mother have returned."

"Ah." Angelica looked down into her teacup. "Not your father?"

"I believe I have a stepfather."

Angelica flashed a glance at her. "No relationship with your birth father?"

No doubt about it. Angelica was being weird. "No."

Adam felt it was time to insert himself into the conversation. "She doesn't remember her name nor anything that would lead us to her family or the man who strangled her."

Angelica shot him a glare—clearly, they weren't here on his account—then turned graciously back to Elle. "If I can help in any way, please let me know."

"Thank you. I don't think there's anything anyone can do." Elle changed the subject. "Where do the Shivering Sherlocks stay? Is there a separate wing for guests?"

Angelica expounded on the guest suites, the medieval-style dining room and the charming, mystery-solving Shivering Sherlocks themselves. She assured Elle that as the festival neared, more guests would arrive, and all rooms here and throughout Gothic would be filled.

Adam's watch vibrated. He looked at it in surprise.

"What is it?" Elle asked.

"I'm getting a phone call from the Live Oak."

"You?" Angelica was visibly surprised that he ever received a call.

"Yes. Excuse me." He answered on his watch and headed toward the door.

It was Señor Alfonso, and he shouted loudly enough for Elle and Angelica to overhear. "Adam Ramsdell, come at once. Clarice pushed the paparazzo off the roof."

"Clarice? *Clarice* did that?" Adam could hardly believe it.

"Yes, and he is dead!"

54

ADAM AND ELLE ARRIVED at the Live Oak Restaurant to find a crowd gathered on the sidewalk. As they got out of the ATV, the townspeople grew silent, except for Mr. Kulshan, who said loudly, "I tell you, that girl didn't kill anyone!"

Adam met his gaze and nodded.

"Yeah, you'll handle this right." Mr. Kulshan folded his arms over his chest and sat in the chair Ludwig had provided for him.

From behind the building, a vehicle alarm was going off, an indecent, irritating blare that Elle thought a fitting salute to Bruno the paparazzo. She followed Adam as he strode toward the noise, but before they rounded the back corner of the building, he turned to her. "You won't want to view this."

"No, but… Clarice might need someone to hold her."

"Then, try not to see, because you can never unsee, and with the trauma and the violence you've suffered, it might slow your recovery."

She nodded and muttered, *"Try not to see,"* and they walked behind the building.

A black Ram pickup's horn was blasting, and its lights were blinking. For a moment, Elle observed no sign of Bruno, only the cab's crumpled roof and the shattered windshield. Then she realized the object on top with the splattered appearance *was* Bruno, dressed in black and blending into the finish. He'd landed on his back, an impact that had instantly broken his body.

Elle turned her head away. *You can never unsee.* She knew it was true, but she knew, too, her mind remained strong. Nothing about the scene was similar to the attack on her. This was a tragedy brought on by a single man's greed and obsession. Clarice was the victim here, and it was she who needed Elle's compassion.

"He didn't suffer," Adam told her. "From three stories up, he was dead as soon as he landed."

"Bet he had a bad few seconds on the way down," she muttered.

"Yes."

"How did he get up there?"

Adam had already assessed the scene. "Grappling hook and climbing rope." He left her to speak with Señor Alfonso and Ludwig.

Elle gathered her courage and glanced at the back wall of the restaurant. There the rope dangled, and at the back door stood the huddle of Hollywood. The triangle formed by Gregoire, Sarcha and Faith protected Clarice, and they rubbed her shoulders and spoke in comforting tones. Elle hurried toward them, but when Clarice caught sight of her, she turned her head away.

Elle stopped, hurt by the rejection.

Gregoire and Sarcha stepped forward, shielding Clarice

from Elle's gaze, and Faith held her hand up in a stop gesture. "Miss Burbage will see no one."

"I'm not a reporter. I'm a friend." Softly Elle called, "Clarice..."

Faith repeated, "She says she'll see no one."

From beside Elle, Adam said, "She'll see me. The sheriff is on his way, and he's asked me to take Clarice Burbage's initial statement."

Elle was astonished to hear Adam's lie. Yes, she knew people called him in an emergency while waiting for law enforcement, but she *knew* he hadn't spoken to the sheriff. She looked around, trying to see what he saw. What had he observed that made him think all was not as it had been reported?

Faith didn't take her gaze off Adam. "Gregoire! Come here. Listen to this."

Gregoire strode over. "I'm not merely Clarice's voice coach, I'm a lawyer, and I'm in place to protect her in case something happens." He gestured at the broken body sprawled on the truck. "What is it you want to know?"

Elle could see Adam gearing up for a fight. He wanted to hear Clarice's statement before law enforcement got into their investigations and the lawyers got into their repudiations. She peered around Faith, Gregoire and Adam and caught sight of Clarice poised to make a run around Sarcha, who was wildly ogling the horrific scene, and toward Señor Alfonso.

Elle met Clarice's gaze, and together they silently made a decision. Elle headed toward a carefully cultured clump of manzanita beneath the wide live oak that gave the restaurant its name, and Clarice slipped from behind Sarcha and, hugging the wall of the restaurant, met her there.

"What happened?" Elle asked.

Clarice grasped Elle's arm and pulled her down into a crouch behind the bush. "That stupid man. Stupid, stupid man." Clarice glanced over her shoulder. "But I didn't do it! I didn't kill him. I tried to save him. *Check under the truck.*"

Elle glanced at the still-blaring and flashing truck. "I will." From far up the highway, she heard the wail of the police sirens.

"Clarice, darling, you shouldn't be over here talking to a stranger." Sarcha used the soothing voice used for speaking to a vulnerable individual.

Clarice gave him a single, dismissive glance. She grabbed Elle's shirt, yanked her close and said, "Bruno wasn't so bad. Tell Adam I said Bruno wasn't so bad."

Elle put her arm around Clarice. "Don't be afraid. I'll tell him."

Clarice winced away from Elle's embrace and stood to meet law enforcement—and a roar of publicity such as the actress had never seen.

55

"THANKS, DAVE. I APPRECIATE the update. Yes, Elle is Clarice's friend, and she'll be relieved to hear the situation. And yes, it was good of Elle to point out the camera under the truck... It was smashed, but the memory card has to be there *somewhere*. Right, another sweep tomorrow in the full daylight." Adam closed his phone.

The evening was quiet and cool, with the ocean breeze rippling the grasses and a few thin, silvery clouds lit by the setting sun. He leaned back in the porch swing beside Elle and filled her in on events. "After the sheriff arrested Clarice, her little group of cohorts followed her to the courthouse. Gregoire acted as her attorney, and she has been released on a hundred thousand dollars' bail. The general consensus, according to Deputy Dave, is that the whole thing was a dreadful accident brought on by Bruno's stupid stunt of climbing up the side of the building and standing on the wall to take photos."

"I suppose I should be sorry about such a gruesome end

for the man—but he deserved it." She gave the swing a hard push with her foot. "What a creep."

"Clarice is back at her suite at the Live Oak. I wish I'd been able to speak to her." Adam looked at Elle meaningfully. "I saw you talking to her."

"She sent you a message."

"I hoped for just that."

"I didn't understand it, or why she didn't just explain what had happened, but—" Elle recounted every word Clarice had said.

Adam asked to confirm, "She said 'Bruno wasn't so bad'?"

"Yes."

"She had previously described Bruno as a slug who crawled out of the mud and consumed everything in his path. This is definitely a message." One thought haunted Adam. "What truly concerns me is the loss of the memory card. When the camera shattered, the card could have flown anywhere." He pictured the area behind the restaurant: the paved parking spots, the foliage on the outskirts and the massive oak tree.

"The parking area was thoroughly swept to gather evidence and remove the windshield glass." Clearly, Elle was reconstructing the scene in her mind, too. "It's not impossible for the card to have flown somewhere no one looked, but odds are someone would have found it. Is the memory card truly lost, or did someone retrieve the camera and remove it, then fling it under the truck?"

"Who? And why?"

"Seeing the photos Bruno took will illuminate the time leading up to his fall."

"Someone doesn't want that evidence produced." Adam hummed with the need to do something. "The crime scene is closed, or I'd go search myself."

"If it's there, we could find it." Elle leaned her head on his shoulder. "I wish Clarice could have told me more."

"I wish I knew why she couldn't be specific." He pushed the swing and thought that, at this moment, he had everything he wanted. To be here, with Elle, at his house while the light faded and the stars popped out and the ocean roared in that grand rhythm that spoke of life and love, loss and eternity. "We're both uncomfortable with the chain of events as described."

"Clarice despised Bruno, but she wouldn't have killed him unless her own life was threatened."

Logic demanded Adam point out, "You only met Clarice a few days ago."

"Ten days ago!"

"In the span of a lifetime, that's not so long, and you've spent only a few moments in her company." He regretted pointing out those germane details. "You don't actually know. You can't speak to what she's capable of doing."

She seemed undeterred by his good sense. "Haven't you ever met someone and immediately recognized a soul mate?"

"I don't believe in soul mates." Although, if he did, that would lend credence to the City of Lost Souls legend…

"Of course you don't." Elle sounded snappish to Adam. "No matter what you believe, I knew immediately Clarice was my friend."

Adam remembered how the women had bonded over lunch and nodded. "I could see why you would think that."

"I want to help her and… I don't know, Adam. There's something very wrong in the suite occupied by Clarice and her team."

In the gathering darkness, Adam could clearly hear the trouble in Elle's voice.

She stood. "I'm going to go look them all up."

Startled by the abrupt call to action, Adam asked, "*Them all* who?"

"Faith, Gregoire and Sorcha. I'll even look up Clarice. Read their official biographies, read any gossip about them, see if there's a hint of wrongdoing." She took a step toward the door, then turned back to Adam. "No, not *wrongdoing. Murderous intentions*. This isn't like the man who tried to kill me." She corrected herself. "Who did kill me. Nothing about this points in that direction. Does it?"

"Not that I can see."

"But now that I've suffered that terror, I can't sit still and allow Clarice to suffer when I know, I *know* she didn't do it." Elle was fierce in her determination and her courage.

Adam stood, and with the binoculars, he looked along the horizon, empty of everything but trees and grass, and up the hill, the town of Gothic topped by The Tower. When he followed Elle, he shut and locked the doors and set the alarms. Because, although she was intent on protecting her friend, he could not forget the bruises that still faintly rimmed her throat or the danger she faced, until she completely recovered her memory.

At the computer, he sat beside her, read the acting team's bios, looked at the photos, and when they had finished and found nothing amiss, he said, "I know you're feeling ferocious in your defense of your friend. I do understand that. But this is a second violent incident in a town that is usually bucolic and without violence. Tomorrow, I don't want you to..." Carefully he rephrased his desire. "Tomorrow, I would prefer if you did not go to work at Madame Rune's."

"I agree. So does Rune."

"You spoke to her?" Adam asked in surprise.

"While I was watching them take Clarice away, Rune caught up with me. She doesn't want to open the shop until afternoon, to avoid the gruesome curiosity seekers. Then apparently when Angelica heard I was working in the shop, she got a pinched look, like her lemon zest wasn't freshly grated."

He grinned at the apt description of Angelica and at his own relief that Elle would remain home with him.

Elle continued. "And she has assigned Veda to Rune for the duration of the festival."

"Rune must have done some fancy talking to pull that off."

"I don't know. Angelica is a highly strung woman. Rune told me since Veda has started helping her, I didn't have to work the shop at all ever again." She glanced around the small house.

He glanced around, too. Did she see his house as a home? Or a prison?

"But I like it. I'm good at it, and I need something to do besides watch you work, try to recover more fragments of memory and brood about the cruel bastard who strangled me and who might very well be dead from the wounds I gave him in return. I *did* defend myself. I *did* hurt him. I hurt him badly. When that hook sank into his flesh, I didn't flinch away, I thought only of survival. Bendy Wendy says that's huge." She drew a breath, stopped trying to persuade him and asked, "What do you think? Is it safe to work in Rune's shop?"

"Logically, being in town surrounded by people is safer than our isolation here. That is, assuming that the man who attacked you isn't willing to commit a crime in broad daylight. Or, even better, if he's dead." Adam fiercely hoped the guy was dead, and even more, he hoped he had suffered. "If you enjoy working the shop, you should. But not tomorrow."

"Right."

"Rune can use Veda up at the Gothic Spring Psychic Festival. Isn't she short a psychic? Maybe she can dress Veda up and have her read a crystal ball." Adam was joking.

But Elle opened her arms to him, grabbed his face and kissed him on the mouth. "That's perfect! It's fate! You genius!" She picked up her burner phone and called Rune. "Guess what Adam figured out for us!"

56

THE NEXT MORNING, ELLE leaned on Adam's chest. "Let's go play on the beach."

"Play? At the beach? Where I found you?"

"Yes, play. It's this thing you do when the sun's shining, the water's cold and sloshy, the sand is hot and waiting to be made into a castle and you've got the day off." She leaped up, tugged at his hand until he was on his feet, and less than an hour later, they had loaded two backpacks in the ATV, one with a picnic lunch and one containing the emergency supplies Adam deemed necessary for any trip, especially to the beach.

Elle hopped into the driver's seat. "Let's settle your mind about whether I can drive." She grinned at him.

"Yes. Let's." He did not grin back. Allowing someone else to drive him rubbed against his possibly overdeveloped need to be in control.

She pushed the starter and put the ATV in gear, and they headed down the road.

It took less than a minute for him to realize she most certainly did know how to drive, and in fact at some point in her past she'd probably had experience with an ATV like this one.

He'd been unaware of signaling his lack of confidence, but as soon as he relaxed, she patted his thigh. She read him too easily. "Where did you find me? Show me the spot."

He directed her to the area above Nora Beach. She parked the vehicle and leaped out. Wearing the backpacks, they skidded down the steep slope to the sand. Elle laughed and talked all the way.

As they neared the spot where he'd pulled a black plastic bundle from the waves and Elle had come to life in his arms, Adam felt the tightening of his nerves. He thought she might react, as he did, to the shadows of the past.

Instead Elle pulled off her sneakers, leaped from the rocks onto the sand and shouted to the Pacific, "I'm here!"

Whatever trepidation he felt at challenging the elements, she blithely dismissed. She ran toward the ocean, arms and legs flailing with enthusiasm, let the first wave roll over her feet and ran back to him shrieking at the cold. "Isn't it gorgeous? Isn't it grand?" Her laughter blended with the sea breeze, and she once again ran toward the ocean.

Eleven days ago, she had drowned in this water.

Today it was her playmate.

He picked up her shoes and carried the picnic backpack to a sheltered spot at the base of the cliff. He spread their wool army-surplus blanket on the sand, then dared to look away from his mundane tasks and into himself…where he feared to go.

Elle made him see things as if he was viewing them for the first time. In the ocean he'd seen only the monster that drove the storms. She made him see the froth and the foam, the blues, the greens, the shadings in between.

Where before he'd heard only the roar of the deep, the

constant drive to batter and destroy the land, she helped him hear the seagulls and eternity rolling in the waves.

Change had inexorably rolled in on the waves that had carried her to shore. He wasn't the same man he'd been eleven days ago. As he walked toward Elle, the dry sand shifted beneath his soles, then a frigid wave frothed around his ankles, his calves, his knees. The cold water splashed his shorts, and hers, because she squealed, caught his arm and ran backward, away from the assault of the ocean. As soon as that wave began its retreat, she dragged him forward again, challenging the Pacific. Her eyes shone, and her hair stood up as if electrified with joy.

She made him feel things, things that terrified and exalted him.

He felt love.

He stood stock-still.

Please, God, no. Not love. Never in his life had he been tempted to play with that shiny, sharp emotion. He'd been sliced open by betrayal, bled every day from the lingering infection of sorrow and guilt.

But love—oh, God. He knew from observation a man could die of love.

He didn't even know who she was. *He didn't know her real name.*

Despite Rune's assurances, and hers, he knew the chance existed she could be involved, married, have children. Be a criminal. Or even a nun.

Or she could be… She could be the lovely, joyous creature she appeared to be, and he would love her every moment, and someday she would die, and he would be alone, and all the music and beauty in the world would die with her.

"How great is this?" she shouted at him. "We're alone at

the edge of the continent, you and me. Now you know what I want to do?"

"Have lunch?" That seemed like a logical guess. She ate all the time.

She laughed at him. She seemed to do that a lot, too.

"I want to do this." Gripping the front of his shirt in both hands, she pulled him close and kissed him, an openmouthed, tongue-seeking kiss that knocked him off-balance.

Then a wave hit, and it did knock him off-balance. Her, too, and they fell over. The water tumbled over them, shoving them up on the beach, then began its retreat and sucked them toward the ocean's maw.

Stupid! He knew better. He should have been watching. *Never turn your back on danger. Never disregard the ocean.*

But she was already on her feet, grabbing his shoulders and dragging him up on the sand. She wasn't big, but she was strong, and she was determined. And laughing. Again.

He staggered to his feet.

She pushed him toward the hollow against the cliffs where he'd placed their blanket and their lunch.

He had a faint glimmer of her intentions.

Okay, a huge glimmer.

Okay, what she wanted tumbled out of her in words and deeds.

She tugged at his belt. "Come on, Adam. I have plans for you!"

57

ELLE WIGGLED AROUND ON the blanket as if she was scratching her back. "The old saying is true."

"What saying is that?" Adam watched the white wisps of clouds race by against the deep blue backdrop of sky.

She lifted one bare leg and brushed at her thigh. "The damned sand gets into everything." She chuckled.

He watched the edge of the cliff and wondered if they should move out from beneath its shadow and farther onto the beach. Storms such as the recent events loosened rocks and boulders, and here they were in danger of being crushed. Of course, here they were safer from any possible onlooker or shooter…

"I thought it was funny. And apropos. What's wrong?" She rolled over and propped herself on his chest. She did that a lot these days. "Did we hurt your arm?"

"No. Why?"

"You look like you've got indigestion." She lifted herself

to look in his face. "Which, let me tell you, is not at all flattering."

Slowly he disentangled himself and sat up. "Each time I've made love to you is a shining moment, the best of my life."

She sat up just as slowly. "But?"

"What?"

"I heard it. *But.* The best moment of your life, but...?"

"Life is uncertain. Love is treacherous. Believe me. I know." He looked down at the blanket. All that bouncing had encouraged the arrival of sand, and he absentmindedly brushed at the wool. "I have seen the world in all its cruelty and terror, disease and peril."

"Yes, but you went looking for the cruelty and terror, disease and peril." She gestured like an opera singer projecting a famous aria. "Look around. The world is beautiful." She slid her arms around his neck and looked into his eyes. "And some parts of this life are glorious."

"Yes. The best moments I've ever had have been with you."

She kissed his lips, a gentle pressure that eased the heartache he felt. "We came for a picnic on the beach, and you're sad. Tell me why."

"I found you here, rolling in on the waves, a corpse that came alive in my arms."

"You saved my life. Now you're responsible for it." She poked him playfully. "So they say."

"You, everything about you, makes me happy." He looked out at the rock that thrust its way from the cliff into the water and there faced the crashing waves. "But on the day the fog carried you to me, I was walking out there. I was headed to oblivion."

She didn't understand. "Oblivion? Where is...?" Then she did understand. "Suicide?" She sat back on her heels and looked out at the ocean, then back at him, and he could see her choosing words with care. "You wouldn't want to do that. Drowning was the hardest thing I've ever experienced, and I can tell you, until you've lost it, you don't understand how sweet and rare life is."

He could hardly contradict her. She had been where he had not: to death and back. Beneath all the joy and light-hearted laughter, this woman was not a frivolous creature. She had faced challenges—still faced challenges—that he could barely comprehend.

"Do you believe in fate?" she asked him.

"No." Fate was an intangible, created by people who sought hope.

"Well," she said as she tucked her hand in his, "if you did, I would point out that had you thrown yourself into the sea, two people would have died—permanently—that day."

"Yes. That's true." A hopeful thought, one he hadn't previously considered.

"You keep trying to tell me you're older and wiser. Yes, you look tons older and you're probably wiser, but I'm younger and smarter."

She laughed so much, he thought she must laugh now.

But her face was intent; her voice was sure. "What I know is, you have to take the life you're given and shape it, moment by moment, into an existence that keeps you busy and makes you happy. Being with you makes me happy. But being with me seems to make you unhappy. And the closer we get, the more time we spend together, the unhappier you seem to be. Can you tell me why?"

"People…die."

"Yes. They do. I know that. But since you dragged me out of the ocean, two wonderful things have happened to me. I got to know you, and I remembered my mother." Elle concentrated all the strength of her clear determination on him. "Adam, do you have any family?"

Somehow, she'd sifted through this conversation, or maybe through all the conversations, and come up with the right question.

"No."

"Did you ever have family?"

She was getting close. "Just my parents."

"How did they die?"

He couldn't help it. The bitterness crept in. "Stupidly."

"Tell me what you're afraid to say."

58

GOD, NO. ADAM DIDN'T want to tell her. But for some reason known only to his subconscious, he'd begun this conversation with his confession. Now he would follow through, and when he was done, Elle might finally see why he was the best man to keep her safe—and why he was the man to avoid ever after. "You wondered why I was a survivalist. Why I make every preparation for every possible disastrous occurrence. Why I watch the horizon and listen when my instincts warn of danger."

"I suspected a difficult childhood."

"Yes. *Difficult.* That's one way to describe it." It was close to noon. The sun shone on his shoulders and on hers. Overexposure to sunshine could lead to dangerous burns and potential skin cancers. "When I was a kid, eight years old, my parents decided to abandon civilization and live off the land."

"Oh!" Clearly, she hadn't expected his story to start like this.

He pulled a long-sleeved shirt out of his emergency backpack and helped her into it. He placed a broad brimmed hat on her head. Then he did the same for himself. "They found a decrepit log cabin in the Colorado mountains. Later I found out it was deep into Forest Service land. For three years we lived undisturbed except for the occasional hiker or biker, and when they got a look at us, they fled."

"You looked scary?" Her voice contained a fair amount of caution.

"After a few months, my dad looked like a wild mountain man, tangled hair and beard. I was growing so fast, I grew out of my clothes and my legs and arms stuck out like… One biker called me a hillbilly." He handed her a tube of sunscreen.

She looked at it as if she didn't remember what SPF 50 meant.

"We planted a garden, hunted illegally, chopped wood, made candles—no electricity for us!—and we survived the first winter. And the second. My parents had brought clothes and food staples to help them through the first winter. Good thing, because my mother never got the knack of tanning hides. We ate beans, root vegetables, venison and bear meat." He looked sideways at her. "In case anyone ever offers you bear meat, keep in mind it gets bigger the longer you chew it."

She squirted sunscreen into her palms and everything not covered by clothing got a thorough treatment. "I don't remember much, but I'm pretty sure I've never eaten bear meat." She offered him the sunscreen.

He took it and followed her example, then tossed the tube in the backpack. "Year three…was the bad year. We had snow in July. Autumn started at the beginning of August. The garden barely happened. My parents knew we faced disaster. But they wouldn't admit they might be wrong. That nature was cruel and indifferent." He spoke with the surety of a man who knew that to be the painful truth. "It was cold and snowy in early September, then some sunshine. We harvested a few carrots, potatoes." He took a long breath. "Then the arctic winds swept south and in two hours froze everything solid."

"You didn't know it was coming?"

He wanted to tell her it did no good to protest the past.

But she wanted somehow to make it right, and she argued with him. "I understand you didn't have electricity, so no computer or… But what about a weather radio or—"

"We did not have contact with the world. My parents believed that in the good old days—" said with air quotes "—people survived in the roughest conditions. Which was true. But they also died." He closed his eyes.

Elle's hand clasped his; she tangled their fingers and held their palms close together.

He opened his eyes and looked at her fingers entwined with his. "We lost every remaining bit of our garden. I was out fishing, and I almost didn't make it back with my string of trout—and I wasn't coming back without those fish, because I knew… I'd grown up during those years. I wasn't a kid anymore."

"You were eleven!"

This was hard for him to tell and perhaps hard to hear, too. "Do you want me to stop?"

"No. I want to know…need to know what happened." She gripped his fingers harder. "Please, tell me."

"Every day my parents had pounded their beliefs into me, but I didn't trust them anymore. I understood what this kind of cold meant. We had insulated the cabin with natural materials. It wasn't enough. We had collected downed trees and chopped wood for our rusty stove. That wasn't enough. We brought the livestock inside. I slept with the goats." He laughed a little, then sobered. "A mother goat and her spring kid. The kid died, and I swear to you, the mother died of grief. My parents didn't want to eat them. They thought of the animals as part of the family. So did I, but I was the only practical person in that cabin. I cleaned the animals, hung the meat and made the first stew."

"I can't even imagine..."

"I had to learn to cook somewhere."

"I didn't mean the cooking, I meant..."

He knew what she meant: she couldn't imagine an eleven-year-old butchering the animals he loved.

"I burned the stew. We ate it, anyway." Adam tried to recall why he'd started this, what he'd hoped to accomplish. An examination of Elle's face told him that. She had wanted to know him, really know him. Before this was over, she would, and that pity he saw on her face would never dissipate.

The last thing he wanted from her, from anyone, was pity, but the damage was done, so he kept talking. "After that stew, my mother took over the cooking while my father paced. By Christmas we'd been in the cold and dark for three-plus months with no hope we would make it to spring before food and fuel ran out." Before Adam got into the worst of the story, he took a moment to breathe, to regain his composure. "One morning I woke to hear my parents arguing. My father intended to go for help. My mother said he didn't have a chance. When she couldn't change his mind, she dragged out the heavy coat she'd brought and hidden in case of emergency and made him put it on. He came over to my bed, kissed my forehead and smoothed my hair. By now, I was so angry at him, I pretended to be asleep."

"Oh, no," Elle whispered.

The old guilt racked him. "You're right. I never saw him again."

Tears sprang to her eyes. She slid her arm around his shoulders. "You were a child. You didn't realize—"

"I attended a brutal school, and I became a pragmatist." He didn't lean against her or yield to her affection. If he allowed himself a crack in the wall of his defenses, he would do what he intended before. He would fling himself into the ocean.

"After Dad left, storm after storm roared over us." He turned to face the ocean breeze. "I didn't hear voices in the mountain winds. I heard death rattling the logs, bringing the cold to eat our toes one at a time. When the snow buried the cabin, I had to struggle out a window and onto the roof to shove the weight off. Days, weeks, months, I couldn't tell how long we'd been there in the endless dark watching our supplies dwindle."

Elle shuddered and moved closer, and squeezed his hand hard enough to make his knuckles hurt. "Keep going," she urged.

"One sunny day, Mama woke me and told me to go for help before I was so weak I couldn't make it." Words poured from him now. Memories. Pieces of his heart and his mind he thought the long years had banished. "She told me she couldn't come. There weren't enough warm clothes for both of us. She stitched me into the few hides she had managed to tan. She had even made knee-high boots. She hugged me, told me she loved me. I walked for about a mile, and as the cold air cleared my mind, I realized that she'd given me all the food in the house. She was sacrificing herself. I couldn't leave her to die alone. She was my *mother.* I rushed back… She was already gone, out into the snow. I followed her tracks and found her, frozen to death in her thinnest summer clothes…"

Elle broke down in tears.

"I brought her body back to the cabin. I placed her on her bed, covered her with blankets and set fire to the place." Softly he said, "I wanted her to be warm at last."

Elle's tears hiccuped to a stop. "What about you? What did you do?"

"I stood there and watched it burn and figured I'd die beside her pyre."

She stared, teary-eyed. "But?"

"The huge plume of smoke alerted the Forest Service. A helicopter came to see what was going on. They wrestled me onto a stretcher—I was both charred and frozen—and took me to the hospital. They recovered my mother's fragile remains. In the spring, hikers found my father's body still wrapped in the coat."

"What happened to *you*?"

"I became a reasonably civilized human being who doesn't go camping for fun." He was not trying to be humorous. "Years later, I found a black-and-white photo of a disheartened woman who lived in the Dust Bowl and saw Mama as she was in that last year."

"You keep a copy of that photo on your desk." Elle had wondered why.

"It's the nearest thing I have to a picture of my mother."

And now she knew.

59

ADAM HAD NO MORE words to say. He waited to hear what kindly comment Elle would make, what platitude she would express.

Instead, in a prosaic voice, she said, "For a moment, when you said you were headed to oblivion, I thought you meant it was a place. You know. Like Gothic."

He thought, then chuckled. "That does make a kind of sense."

"I'd share my childhood story, but it's probably not as wrenching as yours. Also, I don't remember it."

"Pretty sure I win the wrenching-childhood award."

Now she chuckled. "Yes. But it is interesting that you're not really a survivalist. It's not you you're trying to save. It's your mother. That's why Big John Hammer drove you to rage. He killed your mother all over again, and you couldn't save her."

Adam sucked in a breath. "Not my mother—"

"It's not difficult psychology, Adam. Every person you teach to survive the winter is your mother. On the Amazon trek, when you lost those two souls, you were eleven years old again, finding your mother frozen in the snow. You broke your vow, you failed in your goal and since then, you've been wandering, lost. You blame yourself, just like you did when you were a kid caught up in circumstances beyond your control."

"On the Amazon trek, I was an adult, and I was responsible."

She thrust her face into his. Her eyes burned, and her voice crackled with anger. "No, you were not responsible! It was Big John Hammer staging his autobiography. He is the one who should suffer, not you. Never you. Stop blaming yourself *now*."

For someone so diminutive, she spoke with great authority. "How do you see so clearly what I can't?"

"You're a huge tangle of emotions, and I'm Alexander the Great."

He'd never thought of himself as a Gordian knot.

She pulled on her T-shirt and tightened the hat under her chin. "I'm going to go play in the ocean. Want to join me?"

By that he assumed they were done talking and he was to do what he'd been told—get over himself. "Aren't you going to put on more clothes first?"

"There's nobody around!"

"No, but..." He cast an eye up to the top of the cliffs.

She stood, leaned down and kissed him, a hard, enthusiastic kiss, and ran a few steps, then paused. "When you get your life figured out, come on. It's fun!" She dashed toward the Pacific.

Somehow she'd managed to get sand all the way up her calf, up her thigh and onto her right butt cheek. Which was so cute he wanted to brush it off slowly and with great care. Using an artist's brush. No, using his fingers.

That was not any way to relieve a surging erection.

Reluctantly he tugged on his underwear and shorts, buckled his belt and watched her.

She opened her arms and flung herself at the oncoming wave. It splashed around her in a joyous spray, engulfing her to the belly. She shrieked, ran backward away from the wild Pacific, shrieked again. She ran sideways, lifted a piece of driftwood out of the foam, threw it as hard as she could into the waves, then as the ocean brought it back, she chased after it.

He could hear her laughing.

The towering white clouds brushed the blue into the sky. The sea roared and foamed, comforting in its consistency, with a deep green warning glint of danger. And she—she was thin, too thin, with a straight and supple spine and long legs. She was young, glowing with color, her dark hair wild where she'd rolled with him on the blanket. He had never seen anything so beautiful in his life. So free. So joyous.

How could she do it? Return to the ocean that had robbed her of her life and take such pleasure in a simple pursuit? He didn't understand that kind of resilience, courage.

He thought he had recovered from his childhood and used his experiences to make a living where no one else dared. But she said he'd been pursuing a goal, saving his mother, and failed. Failed because he'd been set up to fail. Yes, he would always bear responsibility for those deaths on the Amazon, but was it time to put it all behind him and go on? Use his gifts and his skills to help others? Release the past and find happiness…with Elle?

With her, he sensed life, realized for the first time in too long that he was more than a shell empty of emotions. He now had no choice: he wished as fervently as a child blowing out birthday candles that they could be together forever. Forever!

He came to his feet, intending to go to her, talk seriously about—well, not forever, he hadn't changed that much that quickly. But about their options, and with so many unknowns, there were a lot of options, some of them even hopeful.

The waves rolled in, rose, foamed, divided on something—a rock or a log—and there she stumbled and fell.

He headed toward her.

She got up, bent down into the waves and tugged at something. A wave knocked her backward. She disappeared into the ocean.

He ran.

She bobbed up twenty feet from where she started and waded determinedly back.

He paused and watched.

She seemed to grope with her feet under the foam, then she reached down, grabbed something and tugged again, working hard. She had a grip on it, and although she strained, she hadn't the strength to raise her discovery. She dragged it bit by bit up onto the dry sand.

He caught the first glimpse of her find. As he suspected, she'd found a piece of a ship long-lost off the coast. A piece moved by currents and earthquakes onto this beach.

She knelt beside a single side of the steel prow, the bowsprit thrusting forward and broken off. The metal was corrupted, eaten by salt and water currents and years of work laboring through the sea before it sank beneath the waves.

But what focused his attention was Elle, the way she stared at the prow, the way she breathed as if desperate for air, the defensive hunch of her shoulder...the change from a carefree woman to someone with a burden too heavy to carry alone.

"Elle." He hurried to her side and touched her arm.

She looked up at him. "My name is Elladora Varela."

60

"I'M AN ARCHAEOLOGIST." ELLE wrung out the damp hem of her T-shirt and hurried up the beach to their blanket. "As is my mother and my stepfather, and as were my grandparents and great-grandparents." Without grace or care, she shook the sand out of her shorts and pulled them on. "My great-grandparents..." She sighed as she tried to gather their stories. "In the sixties, the greats, under the direction of the brilliant Peruvian archaeologist, Renzo Rojas, discovered a Moche site in the Andes, untouched since the Moche walked away in the eighth century."

"In light of your other memories, this makes perfect sense." He offered her half a cheese and pickle sandwich.

She shook her head.

He hardly knew what to think. Elle, refusing food? With the return of her memory, had she changed personalities? Because he liked the hungry Elle.

"The team tried to keep their discovery secret. The Moche were expert metalworkers. To find an untouched ruin meant...

not merely objects of archaeological interest—" her voice grew strong with excitement "—it meant gold, copper and silver art that, if the local warlords confiscated it, would be sold to the wealthy. That's how the evil of the world finance their wars."

"That's one of the ways." Adam looked at the sandwich, shrugged and took a bite.

"Sadly, inevitably, word of the find leaked out, and Rojas got word that the warlords were on their way."

"So your great-grandparents and Rojas had to hide the artifacts?"

"Hiding everything wasn't possible. The find was too big. Rojas begged my great-grandparents to take the best pieces, the silver masks, the statues of solid gold, to the US to be stored in an American museum." She watched him chew, plucked the sandwich out of his hand, took a bite, then passed it back. "Rojas led my great-grandparents out of the mountains. Every step was treacherous. When they reached the coast, they hired a boat and a crew. Not the most seaworthy of vessels, but they had no choice."

"They were desperate. In a hurry." They polished off the half sandwich, then Adam handed her the container of kale chips.

She ate one without noticing, then grimaced and handed them back. "Exactly. Rojas helped load the artifacts onto the boat. My great-grandparents set to sea and headed north, staying close to the coast. They stopped in Mexico and took on provisions, and my great-grandmother sent a letter to her parents describing the situation and their intention to sail to San Francisco and safely store the artifacts until Rojas could retrieve them from the museum." Elle looked down at her feet, dug her toes into the sand and buried them. "The boat was sighted off the coast of California, foundering, struggling to get to shore before the full wrath of a storm struck." She wandered over to the rusty prow, knelt and ran her hand over the metal. "They didn't make it. All hands were lost. A few pieces of the wreckage washed up on shore."

"Where on shore?" he asked, although he knew the answer.

"Here. Along this stretch of coast." She met his gaze. "It is, after all, the City of Lost Souls. Some are more lost than others."

"That is a tragedy. Do you believe this—" he touched the prow "—is part of the vessel? That would be an amazing—"

"Coincidence, yes. Whether it is or whether Gothic really is a source of mystical energy doesn't matter. I know who I am, I know what happened, and I know why it happened." She had a toothy smile that boded ill for someone. "I remember everything."

61

ELLE TUGGED AT ADAM'S hand. "Where can we hide this piece of my great-grandparents' boat until we can retrieve it?"

Adam knelt beside her. "We can't know if this really—"

"Adam." She sounded firm, like a schoolteacher reprimanding a six-year-old.

He wasn't going to fight because, well, it might not be as sensible or logical as the old, more cautious Adam would like, but the Adam who stood here believed Elle had found exactly what she had been brought here to find. "I've got a place in the rocks. Later, we'll bring the truck and winch it up the cliff."

"Does it speak to you?" She leaned in to him, her hand on his chest in that way that spoke to his heart. "Can you make something out of it?"

This piece interested him. He would be glad to take it into his shop and use it to create a piece of art that spoke of a terrible past, of violent storms, of a desperate and fearful death. "Oh, yes."

Together they lifted the odd, oblong metal prow and carried it to a protected spot and piled driftwood on top of it.

Elle stood up and wiped her hands. "Do you know the name Stephen Penderghast?"

Adam had to cast around in his mind before he recognized it. "He's a wealthy philanthropist of some kind?"

"Renowned for his support of the sciences. He funds a research vessel, the largest of its kind, that's currently off this stretch of the coast."

"Ah." At last, all would become clear.

"Marine biology and geology, meteorology, any kind of science that can be best studied from a ship are carried out aboard. The equipment—telescope, current sensors, underwater unmanned crawl vessel and the single-occupant submarine—are all top-notch. Scientists fight to be rewarded time on the *Arcturus*." She looked around as if seeking something to keep her hands occupied.

Adam followed her as she charged toward the blanket. "You did say you were a scientist. You knew the story of what rested in the depths of the ocean. Are you a marine archaeologist?"

"No." She started packing up. "I'm an archaeologist who had familial knowledge of the wreckage and a perceived claim to the lost treasures."

"Perceived?" Now it was getting interesting.

"The artifacts belong to the peoples of Peru. When Stephen Penderghast came to me and offered me a spot on the *Arcturus* and a chance to search for the lost Moche artifacts, I explained that to him."

"He agreed?" Adam took the lunch container away from her, extracted half a caprese sandwich and handed it to her.

She looked at it as if she'd never seen filling between two pieces of bread. "Yes. He badly wanted to recover the sunken boat. Locating lost treasure, *known* treasure, is the kind of find every archaeologist dreams of. The added interest of knowing my great-grandparents risked their lives to save those artifacts… I should have asked more questions. Done all the research on Stephen Penderghast."

"What did he do?" Adam asked as he ate.

"First, it's what he *had done* thirty-some years ago. As a young man, he discovered the Caribbean location of a sunken seventeenth-century Spanish treasure ship. Massive amounts of precious metals, particularly coins, were recovered, along with jewelry. Colombian emeralds—"

"Right. I get the idea. A valuable find." Adam sat on the blanket.

She sat beside him.

To Adam, it seemed as if her newly returned memories had so overwhelmed her, she didn't know what to do with herself. She could only copy him. So he finished his half of the sandwich, watched as she consumed hers and asked, "What happened after Penderghast found the sunken treasure?"

"He was seventeen, rich and handsome, and he catapulted into fame. He was on the nighttime talk shows and featured in the science magazines. His fame grew even greater when, after a legal fight that awarded him the find, he gave most of it to the Smithsonian."

"The value must have been…"

"Unimaginable. He kept only a few mementos—very expensive mementos, but nothing compared to the value of the whole treasure—which he displays at his Florida home."

Adam leaned on his elbow. Watching her following on the path to her realizations, coming along with her and coming to his own conclusions… "Penderghast wanted to make another find."

"Because nothing in his life has brought him as much fame."

She smiled crookedly. "I received a lot of insights while he was killing me."

"*You* found the treasure? You *found* the treasure?"

"I did. Whenever he was on the ship, and he was there quite a lot, he watched over my shoulder, gave me advice on how to manipulate the remote crawler, what to look for. He told me repeatedly that after seventy years underwater, most artifacts wouldn't be recognizable."

"He annoyed you."

"Not at all." Clearly a lie. "I had done an instant simulator class on how to run the remote crawler and studied everything I could about underwater archaeology, but I was raised on South American sites high in the Andes. The exact opposite of the underwater mission. I kept thinking Stephen would have been better with someone who was experienced in underwater archaeology. It didn't add up. I admit I had niggling doubts."

"What did the other scientists think?"

"They didn't know what I was doing."

"What do you mean?" Adam sat straight up. "You were on a secret mission?"

Elle looked at Adam in exasperation.

Enlightenment dawned. "Of course you were. Stephen Penderghast didn't want anyone to know what you were searching for."

"The other scientists complained. They were sure I was doing frivolous science. They said I was taking too long. They had hoped I would get out so they could spend more time with the *real* sciences." She looked sideways at Adam.

"Marine biology and geology?"

"Right. And astronomy, although some cast doubts on how valuable astronomy could possibly be. But I couldn't say no to the job, and I was getting better at everything. I really was!" She leaned close to Adam and stared insistently at him.

"One day when Stephen Penderghast wasn't on the ship, one of the other guys asked what I was looking for. I figured why not tell him, because Ryan Naidu was piloting an ocean-current study. I didn't explain the details, but I said it was a shipwreck that had foundered close to shore."

She seemed defensive, so Adam soothed her with his tone and the gentle stroke of his knuckles across her jaw. "A guy who knows ocean currents was exactly the right person to ask."

"I didn't ask. I…explained things." Definitely oversensitive. "Ryan told me all the currents of the Pacific Ocean converged on this beach. He said if someone on land had spotted the foundering boat, prevailing currents would have swept the boat closer to shore. He suggested I search among the sea stumps."

"Stumps?" Adam looked out to sea.

"There." She pointed. "Those are sea *stacks*, pillars of stone that stick out of the water. Sea *stumps* are what are left when the stack is eroded. Ryan said if I was going to find anything, the stumps would have caught the remains. The next night I launched where Ryan directed—" she looked up at a flock of white seagulls that called encouragement as they swooped onto the firm, damp sand "—and I found wreckage. Scattered metal from the hull and, propped up against the stone of the sea stump, two solid-gold Moche heads. Gold doesn't corrode, so after so many years underwater they were just…there, noble and serene." She clutched a fist to her chest. "What a moment. I thought, I will never forget this."

"But you did." *Way to point out the obvious, Adam.*

Elle shot him a glare. "I remember now."

The first sign of irritability he'd seen her exhibit. The new, memory-enhanced Elladora would not be the Elle he had known. And loved. Who still, regardless of her irritation, attracted him and made him fear…for her.

"I sent Penderghast a message saying I had news. The next day he arrived ahead of the storm. His helicopter landed. He disembarked and went to his cabin. I waited for him to contact me, but first he arranged for a party for the researchers. He said since the storm was starting to roar, the teams should, too. By the time he texted me, it was after nine in the evening. I met him on deck." She inched away from Adam, sat up, looked into the mounds of white sand. "What a sucker I was."

He prodded her with scorn. "Alone on the deck? Without telling anyone you were meeting him?"

She sat up straight, in a flurry of anger at him. "Why would I tell anyone? I believed he was a philanthropist, a man interested in promoting the sciences, who took personal interest in the recovery of important archaeological finds."

"I withdraw the question."

She wasn't done defending herself. "He wanted to keep what we were doing quiet. I thought because it involved artifacts of great worth. He wanted to make sure no one stole them before we could preserve them. Pretty stupid, huh?"

"Not stupid. In light of Stephen Penderghast's reputation, it makes sense."

"That's right." Her shoulders relaxed. "I told him I had found the treasure. He smiled."

"Did he?"

"Like the Cheshire cat. Then I explained Ryan's advice, and he said, 'You told someone?'" Her voice hit a new high.

Adam recognized the incipient horror.

"He went mad. I had this one moment where I thought, I'm in trouble. But I didn't really believe it. How was it possible? Stephen Penderghast. He was one of the good guys! I didn't react when I should, the way my karate master taught me. Penderghast grabbed me by the throat and he—" Tears leaked from her eyes. Then she broke down and cried, and in a broken tone she said, "How could I have been so wrong? I knew I was going to die. I knew he was going to kill me!"

Adam located the napkins and thrust one into her hand. "You didn't die."

"You said I did." She wiped her cheeks, blew her nose, and wadded up the napkin and tossed it in the garbage bag.

Adam put his arm around her, hugged her close. "Not permanently."

She smiled a wobbly smile, then put her head and one hand on his chest. "That's what matters now. Ryan said all the currents meet and push toward this beach. That's why you found me."

Adam put his other arm around her, too, because she liked it and he liked it, and they were better together. "I found you because I was meant to."

"Maybe my great-grandparents held me up when I would have drowned."

"Maybe they did." Adam looked out to sea.

The wind blowing, ruffling their hair, cooling their skin. The ceaseless waves, always the same, every one different. The blue, every color of blue, in the sea and the sky. The smells of salt, fish, shells, wet sand, ancient rocks ground to sand and earth movements bringing new stone to grow beneath their feet.

God, he loved this place.

He loved this woman.

He was alive again.

Elle put her hand into the crook of his elbow. "When I realized what was under the water, buried in the sand, a spark ignited in my brain, and I remembered…everything. But Adam, it was you who laid down the fuel for the fire. You've kept me safe, given me a chance to heal, and you told me the story of your survival, your love for your mother and your father, your continuing quest to bring people to safety, to make the world a better place… You teach me." She leaned her head onto his bicep and sighed with satisfaction. "You're the person we all dream of being."

He loved to hear this. Who wouldn't? But in all honesty, he had to remind her, "People have died under my care."

"People have lived, thanks to you." She smiled up at him. "Gothic looks to you as law enforcement because when there's a shooter in the hills and the sheriff and deputies are a half hour away, you're sensible, you have experience and you care. Some people, if they lived through those winters with your parents, would lose their humanity. You have the compassion your parents taught you."

"My parents?" He was startled. "My parents taught me not to be a damned idiot, and they did that with their deaths."

"Your parents made a fatal mistake, and in the end, they knew it, and they sacrificed themselves for you. That's what you learned, Adam." She seemed to think it was so simple. "That was the lesson your parents taught you. If the cause is good, you don't shy away from sacrifice. Do you know how rare that is?"

He looked out at the horizon, to that space where the edge of the turbulent sea met the pale blue of the sky. Ever since he had escaped those mountains, he'd been angry at his parents for putting him through hell, for leaving him to grow up alone. He didn't brood about it: he was, as Elle said, too sensible for that. But it had been there, a niggling bitterness on the edge of his consciousness. Now she had shined a light on the whole of those years, and he remembered the good times: Dad watching his mother as she taught Adam his lessons, his eyes shining with love, Mama helping the two of them in the metal shop and creating her own joyful art to place around the cabin, evenings of making music and telling stories. He had talked as he had never talked to anyone…until Elle.

"You know what no one else knows, and you see more than anyone else sees."

"I see who you are. I like what I see. The story you told, about Big John Hammer, that confirms my belief that you're the greatest man I've ever met."

"Why? I failed."

"You could have made yourself into the hero of the story. That's what Hammer expected you to do. That's what he was prepared for. Instead you stood in defense of your dead, and you made a fool of him in the process. Turning aside from the cheers, telling the truth and knowingly plunging yourself into the quagmire of his lies."

He felt as if he should argue. But why? If Elle wanted to believe he was a great guy, he'd be a fool to dissuade her. "The revelations about you prove how strong you are."

"So we're a good match."

He liked how smug she was.

She turned serious. "I don't like what happened with Clarice. It worries me, but I don't see how it could have anything to do with…" She waved a finger at her neck.

"Nor do I."

"Nothing more has occurred that's threatened me." She lightly touched the place on his shoulder where he'd been shot, the place where she'd only a few days ago removed his stitches. "I believe it's you who's in danger."

"Constant vigilance is the rule." He walked them away from the waterline, and only then did he turn his back on the Pacific to scan the edge of the cliffs. "Still, I wonder if anyone else was diving with Stephen Penderghast when he made his first undersea discovery. Someone who didn't survive. Someone who died as he meant you to."

Elle nodded. "Sounds to me like something to investigate."

"Agreed. We should."

62

ELLE STRAIGHTENED. "CAN I use your phone? I need to call my mother."

"A reminder, there's no cell service here at the edge of the continent." Adam put his arm around her. "Let's pack up and go home. We can retrieve the prow of your great-grandparents' boat later."

She smiled, as if she liked that he'd declared this prow belonged to her family.

They collected their blanket and backpacks and hiked up the path to the highway and the ATV. Adam handed her his phone, and she flipped it open—and hesitated.

With dry wit, he said, "It's old-school, but you still simply press the numbers."

"Mom is in my Contacts, so I'm not sure about the number. But when I was a kid, she made me memorize it... I think it's the same." Elle dialed hesitantly, put the phone to her ear.

Adam could hear it ringing—and the message starting.

After the beep, Elle said, "Mom, it's Elladora. I know you

don't recognize the caller so you're not going to answer, but please call me back at this number. I'm okay, Mom." Elle's voice wobbled. "I really want to talk to you." She hung up. She sighed, sniffled, blotted her nose on the hem of her T-shirt. "It's two hours earlier there."

"You want to drive?" he asked.

"No. I want to talk to her when she calls me back." She got in the passenger's seat.

"Where's there?" He joined her and they started up the road.

"Peru. We talk at least twice a week, and it's been, what? Eleven days? She must be worried to death. We're close." As he drove, she talked. "I never knew my father. He abandoned Mom when she was pregnant. We were together, alone, for thirteen years, working mostly in South America. Then she met my stepfather, and he wanted to marry her. She wasn't going to marry anyone until I was in college, but he really loved her so he asked me. I said yes. It hasn't been perfect, but Dad's been a good stepfather and—"

Adam's phone rang.

Elle jumped so hard she lost her grip on it.

With one hand, Adam caught it before it hit the floor, flipped it open and handed it Elle.

"Mommy!" Elle sounded tremulous and happy.

A squawk of indignation blared from the earpiece.

Elle winced. "Mom, it wasn't careless disregard. Mom, I had to jump off the ship. I was a mile off the coast and barely made it to shore… Mom, I swear, I was in bad shape. No, Mom, listen! I lost my memory!"

He heard another explosion of language from the other end, and the words he could pick out made it clear Elle's mother was worried and angry.

Elle held the phone away and looked at him apologetically.

"She's excited." She brought the phone back to her ear. "I was pulled from the ocean by a man named Adam Ramsdell. He saved me. He's been wonderful through the whole ordeal... Mom, he hasn't done anything to me. It was...it was Stephen Penderghast. He tried to kill me. Yes, I know you said something was wrong about the job. Yes, Mom, you were right." Elle looked at Adam as if she knew he would understand her exasperation. "Yes, I'll say it again. *You were right.* He tried to strangle me... Yes, that's why I jumped off the ship. Oh, you want to know that, do you?" Elle was teasing now, and she chuckled at her mother's low murmur coming from the phone. "Yes, I found the treasure. No, seriously! All of it? I don't know. But the gold Moche heads were there, staring at me through the camera. It was a moment like none I've ever experienced." She glanced at Adam. "Mom, not to worry. He's not going to kill me for the find. He is such a great guy... In his thirties?"

Adam nodded.

"Good looking."

Adam nodded again.

"Once, yeah... Okay, once *today.*"

Adam didn't want to nod, to look, to find out what he had done today that Elle had told her mother about. But he couldn't help it. He turned.

Elle was listening to her mother and grinning at him. "It's okay, Mom. I'm going to marry him."

Adam turned back before he ran off the road.

"I'm in this little town on Big Sur—yeah, Big Sur, California—just up from the beach. It was really quiet when I first got here, but they're having a psychic festival and... Yes." Startled, Elle asked, "How did you know that?"

Adam surmised her mother knew the name of Gothic.

"I can't get on a plane and get out of here. For a lot of reasons. For one thing, I'm still kind of beat-up. For another... Mom, why? Well, for instance, why do you know Gothic, and why don't you like Gothic? It's a great little town... That's right, the City of Lost Souls." Elle listened to her mother's explanation with an increasingly puzzled expression.

She listened long enough that Adam's interest became active curiosity.

When Sofia stopped, Elle spoke in a slightly hostile tone. "Then, you come here." She lit up. "Really? You will? I wish you would. Mom, I've been so scared."

Adam could bear witness to that, although lately, as time went on and nothing happened, as she practiced martial arts and made friends in Gothic, she'd been gaining courage and strength.

"If I hadn't had Adam, I would have curled up and cried all the time." Elle sounded like she had on the first days: sad, fearful, lost. "Did you call the ship about me? What did they say?" She listened so hard she leaned into it. "That's not good. Yes, you should have." She looked at Adam and raised her eyebrows meaningfully, although he had no idea what she meant. "Send your flight information to my email address. No, my phone is at the bottom of the sea, but Adam has a computer, and now that I know who I am, I can access email. I love you, Mom. See you soon." Elle hung up and relaxed against the seat. "She's flying to the States. She's coming here."

What did you mean when you said, "I'm going to marry him"?
"I guessed. When?"

"As soon as she can."

What did you mean when you said, "I'm going to marry him"?
"She called the ship to ask why she hadn't heard from you?"

"She called me, didn't get me, didn't think too much of it until I didn't return the message. After a couple of days, she got worried I was sick. She called the doctor, who said he knew nothing. After another day of waiting, she called the captain, who said he wasn't a babysitter, that I was a grown woman and I'd call when I felt like it."

What did you mean when you said, "I'm going to marry him"?

"That seems fraught with possible legal issues. As captain, he faces repercussions if someone goes overboard and he doesn't report it."

"The times I met him, he didn't seem cold. But Penderghast... Yes, of course the captain would be afraid of Penderghast. Penderghast put his hands around my throat, looked in my face and squeezed." Her voice grew hoarse, and her gaze lost its focus. She was back in that moment of her death. "I was frantic. I couldn't believe he meant to do...what he was doing. He'd always been polite, although lately he'd grown—" she hesitated "—impatient."

Adam pulled to the side of the road and parked. "Because you hadn't discovered the treasure?" He turned to her, placed his gentle hand on her shoulder.

She didn't face him, but she didn't flinch. She was caught in the memories. "Yes. Yes, he tried to hide his irritation, but I watched his hands. Big hands. Strong hands. Long fingers. He would clench them like he wanted to grab me and...hurt me. That's why I asked Ryan to help me."

Of course Elle would recall more details now, details of the events leading up to the night of the storm. Adam supposed that was good. The details would unnerve her, and fear would help her maintain vigilance. "You were already a little afraid of Penderghast."

"A little. Not enough. Simply worried that he would call in his helicopter and I'd leave, and the treasure would remain at the bottom of the ocean, and my great-grandparents' loss would be all for nothing." Elle glanced at Adam, and self-derision clouded her usually clear gaze. "He was so intent on finding the treasure, I thought he'd dismiss my indiscretion with Ryan, maybe lament the time we'd wasted by not bringing him in. But when I told Penderghast, he went—"

"Mad," Adam supplied. She'd said this before, but she needed to put it all together, one event at a time.

"Yes! He choked me and choked me. Then he loosened his grip, and I thought for a moment I was mistaken. I thought he didn't mean to hurt me like that. But all he did was adjust his grip and…smile."

Adam slid his arm around her and brought her close.

She leaned her head against his chest. "The Pacific may have taken the last sparks of life, but Penderghast murdered me, *murdered me*." She sat up and settled back into her seat. "It's okay, Adam. Don't worry. I know that I hurt him badly, maybe killed him back."

"No regrets?"

"None. I'd do it again if I could." She was calm and cold.

Good girl. But Adam was wise enough not to say that. "Penderghast has people working for him in any capacity he might need. In the case of the captain, I suspect someone on his team laid out the situation and the possible repercussions of investigating your whereabouts. Dismissal or violence." He scanned the horizon again. It was one thing to know Stephen Penderghast had attacked Elle with the intent of killing her. It was another to know the details, that he'd taunted her with the possibility of life, then gleefully denied it. The man had people covering up his crime and possibly his own death. As always, Adam's own surveillance was as thorough as possible, but Elle's story served as a reminder that no surveillance was impregnable, especially out here.

He started up the road, intent on getting them home.

"Anyway," Elle said, squaring her shoulders, "Mom said if

she didn't hear from me within the next few hours, she was going to call the coast guard."

"That would have been a wise move. Although—" His words halted in his throat. He couldn't believe what he saw coming down the road toward them.

The Shivering Sherlocks were piled into two ATVs, and as they whipped down the road, he heard them whooping and hollering. They waved their beach towels as they passed Adam and Elle and shouted, "Going to the beach!"

Adam and Elle waved back.

Elle waited until they passed. "That was a close one."

Adam was appalled. "Two hours earlier and they would have seen my bare butt!"

"I'm almost sorry they missed it."

He slammed on the brakes and turned to her. *"What?"*

"It is an awfully nice butt, and those old ladies would have thoroughly appreciated it." Elle looked completely serious. "Two of them are widows, you know, and one has been divorced so long she says she's having a romance with her washer when it's on the spin cycle."

He wanted to ask her how she found this stuff out. But he knew: she talked to people. If only she would refrain from telling *him*.

"I suppose we should call Deputy Dave and make a report about Stephen Penderghast." She didn't sound as if she was looking forward to that.

"Hm." He drove on up the road. "Not necessarily. Or at least, not until I've done some research."

"I thought more than anything you wanted to take this—me—to the police."

"That time has passed." In fact, he couldn't remember a single reason he would want such a thing. "Stephen Penderghast lives in the stratosphere of the rich. You stabbed him with a boat hook, possibly killed him." He turned into their driveway and parked in front of the workshop.

"He was murdering me!"

"I understand. It was self-defense. Nevertheless, there were no witnesses. If Penderghast dies, or if he's dead, there may be repercussions for you. And if he lives, it could be very dangerous."

Elle paled. "He'll come after me."

"Or send someone after you. Don't worry, I'll protect you." *Not simply because you said you were going to marry me. Because that is what I do.*

"I know you will." Leaning over, she put her hand on his thigh and kissed his mouth. "But you can't be with me always. Let's go in and do our research. We have a lot to discover."

63

ELLE SAT IN A chair beside Adam at his desk while he searched for Stephen Penderghast. She pressed against him, her chest to his arm.

He found a report that Stephen Penderghast had been injured, was in critical condition in a large Los Angeles hospital and was headed into surgery. Then, a week later, the smallest piece of news, a piece they were lucky to find: amid speculation he needed constant and specialized care, Stephen Penderghast had been moved to a posh private hospital.

After that, no information was forthcoming.

"He's not a celebrity," Adam said.

"Not anymore," Elle said. "But he wouldn't have been moved if he was dying, and certainly he's not dead. That would have hit the media."

"Agreed. The news cycle isn't concerned with him as an injured person, but they *would* report his death." Adam stared at the screen and sorted his thoughts. "I don't know how to interpret this silence."

"How would you assess my situation? Am I anonymous here in Gothic? Not at risk? Or am I a sitting duck for Penderghast's assassins?"

Adam considered her in surprise. "Why would you think he has his own personal assassins?"

"Do you think I'm exaggerating his power, his reach or his corruption?"

"No. You suffered at his hands—and died."

"Temporarily," she reminded him with a smile.

"Temporarily," he agreed, but he didn't smile. His expression promised trouble for Penderghast if Adam had the chance. "I doubt he has his own personal assassins, although…it's possible. More than that, wealthy men can manipulate perceptions."

"And hire assassins."

"Not if he's dying or in a coma, and his financial team doesn't want to say for fear his company's stocks will drop."

"I don't know about that." Elle could barely wrap her mind around the thought. "I didn't think about the consequences of his death to his financial worth. I don't think that way."

"That's why you're not a billionaire."

"Is that why?" Elle asked with wry humor. "I thought it was because I chose to become an archaeologist."

Adam paid no attention to her wit. "You think you hurt him badly."

"I promise you I did. I wish I could forget how it felt when I grabbed him with the hook and sunk it into his flesh. It was—" she felt queasy "—gross."

"But you don't think you killed him right away."

"He stayed on his feet, ripped the hook out, stalked toward me like Frankenstein's monster." She could remember so clearly now. "He saw me jump off the ship."

"All right." Adam faced her. "I would not dream of assuring you that you have no reason to be afraid. I suggest caution and vigilance in every move you make."

"But you always suggest caution and vigilance. That's who you are."

"Since you arrived, we've had one occasion of gunfire with one person hurt."

"You!" She lightly touched his arm.

"If that shot was fired by a Penderghast assassin, he missed his target, and he hasn't followed up on his failure. Therefore, the shot wasn't aimed at you, and for the moment, we're not going to law enforcement. There's too much about this situation they're ill-equipped to handle. I'm afraid they'd want to take you into custody."

"Because I attacked Stephen Penderghast. Or killed him?"

"Definitely a possibility. Or for your own protection. Which makes you a sitting duck for an assault."

She puffed out a sigh of relief.

Adam continued. "We're going to lay low until we can find the status of Penderghast's health."

"You really think he might be dying?" That cheered her immeasurably, and at the same time, she realized she had to find out whether or not anyone on the ship realized that her disappearance was related to his injury.

They did know she was gone, surely?

Adam checked his email and gave a crack of laughter.

"What?" Elle asked.

"I just got a reply from my friend letting me know he found out your mother's name. It's—"

"Sofia Neely-Varela," they said together.

Elle laughed, too, then nudged him aside. "If you're done, I need to use the computer."

"What are you going to do?"

"Contact somebody on the *Arcturus* and find out what's going on out there."

64

THE NEXT AFTERNOON, ELLE stood with Adam at the top of the cliff and observed as the winch brought up the prow of her great-grandparents' boat. Retrieving it from its hiding place on the beach and getting it into the wire basket had been nerve-racking. Watching it swing and scrape against the rocks was even more harrowing.

"How was work?" Adam was trying to distract her.

Wasn't going to happen. "Good. Busy all day. The day tourists are showing up for the festival and shopping, and the tourists who have taken vacant rooms in people's houses or in bed-and-breakfasts are buying out the shop. Oh, and Justin came in."

"Justin? The high-school kid? What did he want?"

"To interview me about Bruno's fall." She never took her gaze off the prow as it slowly rose toward Adam's truck. "He was quite disappointed to find out I was nowhere near when it happened."

"Interview you? Why? Oh…for the *Town Blab*."

"That's right. I believe he sees a profit in writing it up for the newspaper and selling copies to the tourists—and except for glimpses on the restaurant rooftop, no one has seen Clarice or her crew since they returned from the sheriff's department, so they can't talk."

"That kid has a future in reporting."

"Or harassment. He really didn't want to hear that I had no intention of talking about what I did see. I had to get in his face to get him out the door."

"I'll speak to him."

She thought about that. "While usually I prefer to handle matters for myself, in this case I'll say thank you. I suspect your reputation will intimidate him now and in any future incidents. Of which I hope there are none."

"When is your mother getting here?"

"She lands late tonight. She'll drive down tomorrow."

"In time for the festival."

Elle grinned at him. "If we're lucky, she'll see you in action."

"Oh, God." Adam hadn't considered that his first introduction to Elle's mother might be while he was duded up and stomping around an arena waving a sword. "You never told me why she knew about Gothic."

"Oh. She always knew she wanted to be an archaeologist, so for her graduation trip, her parents brought her to California to the spot where her great-grandparents disappeared with the Peruvian treasure. They spent a week in Gothic." Elle shook her head. "She never did explain why she didn't like the town, though."

"Maybe simply the loss of family and heritage." Adam looked out over the ocean toward the horizon. "What have you heard from your contacts on the ship?"

"No one is answering me."

That brought his attention right to her. "How many people have you emailed?"

"There's sixty scientists. When we came onboard, they assigned each of us an email address and gave us a directory with those and the pertinent onboard staff: captain, executive officer, doctor. I wasn't good friends with anybody—"

"How is that possible?" he asked smartly.

Startled, she asked, "What does that mean?"

"You've been in Gothic twelve days and you're everybody's best friend." The prow hit the crumbling edge at the cliff top. Adam caught the winch wire and guided the sea-scarred metal onto firm ground. "How could you have been onboard a ship for five weeks and not know everyone's favorite ice-cream flavor?"

"Oh. That. A couple of reasons. The scientists are competitive in ways I've never witnessed before. Every mechanism on the ship is assigned for use every minute of the day, and each person is working their own thesis, theory, experiment. They often have contempt for every science but their own, and to get more time on the equipment, they're always shoving, usually verbally but sometimes physically." She smiled to see the prow safe and sound and ignored her own hurt feelings.

"I thought scientists wore pocket-protectors and carried Pentel pencils and calculators everywhere."

She crossed her arms and glared. "What do you know?"

Adam subdued a grin. "Nothing, obviously."

"Stereotypes," she said scornfully. She helped him free the prow and lift it into the back of the pickup, then dusted off her hands. "In my case, I was working on a secret mission, and Penderghast repeatedly warned me not to confide in anyone. On a ship with that many scientists, speculation and gossip is the lifeblood. They'd talk to me, ask questions, I'd brush them off... I got a reputation as being standoffish."

Adam snorted and finished reeling in the winch.

"To add to the problem, when Stephen was on the ship, he spent most of his time with me. Which created professional jealousy."

"Because they thought you were lovers?" Adam held the pickup door for her.

"I don't think so. Well, yes, of course somebody said that. But Stephen Penderghast's goals aren't sexual. If his passions were linked to a heart-rate monitor, it wouldn't beep. The line would be flat." She hoisted herself up into the cab and waited until he came around to the driver's seat. "I need to know what the scientists have been told about me and about Penderghast. I tried to contact the ones who I believe are honorable."

"Honorable?"

"Not likely to notify Penderghast's people that I'm alive. I've received no answers. I hesitate to contact the captain or crew. I'm guessing there's some firewall set up to block emails to the ship, and I don't want to alert the people who get their paychecks from Penderghast that I'm alive and asking questions."

"Aren't they all getting their paychecks or funding from him?"

"We're talking grants as opposed to paychecks, actually. It's like the difference between being a subcontractor and being employed."

"Are you using the email they assigned you? Because—"

"No, no, no. I created a new email with a pseudonym. That got me nowhere."

"The timing of this blockage is suspicious."

"I know. What is it the Stephen Penderghast Scientific Foundation doesn't want them to know?"

"At a guess, what's really happened to Stephen Penderghast and where his favorite scientist has gone."

65

ON FRIDAY, BEFORE THE sun rose, Elle went right from sleeping to sitting straight up in bed.

Naked and half-awake, Adam leaped out from under the covers, prepared to defend her against all foes.

She paid no attention to him. "I've got it!" She leaped with equal excitement, although for a different reason. "I know how to get in contact with someone on the ship."

Adam sank back onto the mattress. "Elle, I thought we were being attacked."

"Sorry." She grabbed her bathrobe and her phone and checked the time. "She'll be awake."

"Who'll be awake?"

Elle thrust her arms into the sleeves and hurried out into the living room, tying the sash on the way.

Adam pulled on his shorts and a T-shirt and followed. "Elle, who'll be awake?"

She started his computer. "Daniel—not that he's friendly, but he's an okay guy. Right before he left for the *Arcturus*, his wife found out she was pregnant. She emailed me, asked me to call her and gave me her phone number. She had learned the baby's gender and wanted the cook to make a pink cake to be presented to Daniel at dinner." Elle seated herself in the office chair and opened her email inbox. "Apparently he'd told her I knew how to keep a secret, so she trusted me to handle the presentation and to make sure I FaceTimed her in. Which I did. And there's the number." She picked up her phone.

"You're going to call her and ask if she's talked to her husband. Very clever way around that email block. She's on the East Coast?"

"Right. Three hours later. I want to know what she knows about the situation on the *Arcturus* and if she can get a message to Daniel for me."

"What if she won't tell you or won't convey a message to him?"

She smiled at him. "She owes me."

He put his hand on her neck and leaned down to kiss her cheek. "I guess that's worth waking up in emergency mode. As soon as my heartbeat calms, I'll make us some breakfast."

"Good. Thanks." She started dialing. "After that, if you'll take me up to Madame Rune's, I'll get it ready for another busy day. Maybe I'll open early. I enjoy talking to people, and I love showing Rune a good day's receipts."

He couldn't figure her out. "I thought you'd want to take the ATV."

"I do. It's so much fun to drive. But it uses a parking spot, and those are in tight supply—" She swung away from him and said, "Hello, Bev? This is Elladora Varela… Yes… Really? That is exactly what I called about."

66

DANIEL HAD FINISHED HIS daily run around the shipboard track and slowed to a walk when DeAnna hurried up behind him. "Got a minute?"

"Sure, I'm cooling down. What's up?"

"I found out something about Elladora Varela."

He glanced around. "We agreed to be discreet."

"I didn't have to be discreet or indiscreet. I was just down in the lounge, talking to Ryan, and without me asking a thing, he told me—" she glanced around and lowered her voice "—do you know what Elladora Varela was using the remote crawler for?"

"It was a such big secret, I figured it was some government-conspiracy-related thing."

"Not even close." In triumph, DeAnna said, "She was searching for sunken treasure!"

"Oh, bullshit." Knee-jerk reaction, but definitely bullshit.

"That's what I said. I mean, really. Why would Stephen Penderghast okay *that*?"

"I had to jump through hoops to prove my study was worthy."

"Me, too. But Ryan showed me on his phone. In 1958, a boat carrying South American artifacts sank not far from here."

"You're shitting me! Elladora Varela has been wasting precious crawl time looking for...gold?" Daniel scratched his head. "Why would Ryan know anything about this?"

"Because she told him what she was doing. She wasn't getting to the right location, and she needed help reconstructing where the boat would have gone down."

"Did he help?"

"He doesn't know. After she disappeared, he looked, but her crawler films are encrypted. All he knows is that after he talked to her, when she got done, she sent for Stephen Penderghast."

"She's the one who got Penderghast here that night he was almost killed?"

"Apparently."

"Is the sunken treasure what Zsóke was on the ship looking for?"

"I asked Ryan that, too. He said no, definitely not. Zsóke was looking for something that went overboard. Apparently Ryan hinted he knew about those statues..." DeAnna made the wide-eyed horror face. "He broke a sweat telling me about it. He's still freaked about what Zsóke might do to him."

"If he's so freaked out, why tell you?"

"Because." She made a drinking motion with her hand.

Daniel groaned. "He keeps talking, he really is going to get in trouble."

"I told him that." When Daniel looked at her, she said, "Yes, I can be as smart as you! Anyway, he seems to think since I know what happened with Zsóke, he can confide in me. It's not like I believed him right off the bat, anyway. Once I knew who I was looking for, I found Elladora online. She's an archaeologist based out of South America. Guess why *she* was doing the search?"

Daniel shook his head. "No idea."

"The people who were piloting in the boat were her great-grandparents."

Daniel sped up to a fast walk, then slowed down again. "I don't care. I don't believe in a treasure hunt. Penderghast is rich. He doesn't need gold. What he doesn't have is the brain-power that goes with the smart sciences."

DeAnna made a scoffing sound.

"Why else does he hang around on the ship so much? He loves to have us fawn over him, explain what we're doing, justify our existence. He loves to play God, and we let him because this is one plush situation and the only place in the world I can actually *complete* my study."

"All that. But think. *Think*, Daniel. Who does he hang with most?"

Daniel started to answer and froze with his mouth open.

"That's right. Stephen loved to sit in the crawler room with Elladora Varela—and not because he's hot for her. I mean, you can tell. The old man's as cold as ice. He's only hot for that treasure." She brought up the bio of Penderghast on her phone. "Look!"

Daniel scanned the part about young Penderghast's part in recovering the ship in the Caribbean. "What do you suppose happened between him and Elladora?"

"I think they were up on the deck together. He told her he wasn't going to fund her search anymore. She tried to kill him with the boat hook. He pushed her overboard. That would explain why no one from Penderghast's organization is talking about what happened to him. You wouldn't want to say a little shrimp like Elladora Varela took out that big guy's kidney. Even if she did, shoving her over the rails is still murder."

"It's not murder if she's still alive." Daniel ripped the towel from the belt loop on his pants and stuffed it in his mouth, then looked chagrinned and used it to dab at the sweat on his forehead.

DeAnna grabbed his shirt. "What do you know?"

"Nothing! How could I know anything? They cut off our email."

DeAnna pounced on that, too. "They *cut off* our email? The official word is it's a *malfunction. What do you know?*"

"All right. Quiet down." Daniel glanced around. "I talked to my wife…who had talked to Elladora Varela."

"She's alive?"

"Shh!" He pulled DeAnna into a corner under the stairs. "She survived long enough to get to shore. She says Penderghast tried to kill her—"

"Come on!"

"You said it. If she found the treasure, he may have wanted to claim credit."

DeAnna thought hard. "Yes. Possible. Yeah."

"Apparently, she's freaked out about him finding her now. I told Bev to tell her the reports about his health are sketchy, but I saw him that night, and I'm stunned he's survived this long. If he really is still alive. I told her to tell Elladora to keep an eye out for Zsóke."

"For her sake, I hope you're right." DeAnna started to walk away.

This time, he caught her arm. "You tell no one! As you said, shoving someone over the edge is attempted murder—and it's already happened once."

On Friday evening, for the second time, Elle spoke to Daniel's wife Bev, and when she got off the phone, Adam sat waiting for her report.

"According to Daniel, who saw Penderghast leave the ship, Penderghast is a dead man. He says if Penderghast *is* still alive, which he doubts, he's sedated, has had surgery and transfusions and is in ICU. He also believes that if Penderghast *is* dead, the foundation would keep his death quiet for as long as possible."

"As we surmised. It's been almost two weeks, so the possibility that he managed to arrange to silence you lessens with every day."

"Yes, but..."

"But?"

"Bev also said Daniel warned me about Sookie."

"Who's that?"

"The waitress in *True Blood*?"

Adam couldn't have looked more blank.

"It's pop culture, Adam." Elle sighed. "Honestly, I'm racking my brains, but I have no idea. Whoever Sookie is, she came on the ship the day after Stephen Penderghast's accident, and she was looking for something that went overboard."

"If she's looking for you, she's apparently been unsuccessful."

Elle smiled toothily. "I know."

Adam felt the release of tension. "Considering the time that's passed and the lack of action—"

"After that one shot was fired but hit *you*—"

"And I'm mostly fine. A little stiffness, a little pain." He shrugged his shoulder, worked it a little. "The stressful part of tomorrow will be donning the armor and brandishing a sword in a battle between me and some guy who *doesn't* have hemorrhoids." And meeting Elle's mother, but one thing at a time.

Elle burst into laughter, then leaned in and kissed him. "Looks as if there's nothing to worry about. Did you practice your sword work today?"

"Every day. Tomorrow at two o'clock, I will raise my sword."

"I suppose since it's a mock battle, the winner is already chosen."

Adam said nothing.

"Who's going to win?" She wanted to wheedle the answer out of him, but he only hummed. She said, "I have Rune's permission to close the shop so I can be there to cheer you on. Pick me up on the way?"

"Of course." Adam leaned back in the chair. "What about Veda? Can't she come down and relieve you?"

"Veda is doing such a good job as a reader of crystal balls, she has a line ten deep. Rune is not going to take her out of rotation for the shop."

"I was actually right when I suggested her?" he exclaimed in astonishment. "I wonder what *she* foresees for the results of tomorrow's fight?"

"I'm wondering about the result of *tonight's* encounter. What do you think?" Elle smiled at him and thought how very much she loved him. "Can you raise your sword tonight?"

"I promise, it's already raised."

67

ON SATURDAY, TOURISTS HAD been in and out of Madame Rune's Psychic Readings and Bookshop all morning, and Elle sold candles, books, orbs, herbs and velvet scarves with fringes and coins. She chatted with the enthusiastic, cajoled the disbelievers and at least a dozen times pointed out the sign that said *Unattended children will be given espresso and a drum set.*

One moment, the shop was full and she was racking up the sales. The next, in an excited rush, the customers vanished.

Elle checked the clocks.

In an hour, in the main festival arena, Adam and his opponent were due to battle each other for supremacy of Gothic. She couldn't wait to catch a ride with Adam, take a seat in the stands and watch the enactment as eagerly as any tourist. It was not like she knew what the results were going to be. No matter how she teased, Adam, darn him, refused to tell her.

She had started the preparations to shut the shop—the gems needed to be put in the safe with the cash drawer, the new blinds needed to be pulled, the scanners needed to be shut down—when the door to Madame Rune's opened. Elle turned to see if she could make one more sale—and Faith charged in, dragging Clarice by the arm.

Clarice, who looked miserable, cupped one arm in the other and stared fixedly at the floor.

"Can I help you?" The question was automatic, but Faith's rush surprised Elle. The woman always seemed so composed, so watchful.

Faith pulled the shade down on the front window. "Rune sent me to help you close the shop."

Elle's heart sank. "Is something wrong?"

"I don't know." Faith pulled the blind on the other window. "Rune's in a frenzy." She flipped the open sign to *Closed* and pulled the blind on the front door.

"Let me put the cash and the valuable pieces in the safe, and I'll lock up." Elle opened the register, took the money drawer and knelt to put it in the unlocked safe. "I'm going up there to watch the battle. Who do you think will win?"

"Who cares?" Faith said.

Startled by the hostile tone, Elle paused. What was that attitude? She grabbed the keys to the locked jewelry display case and bent to remove the real jewels: the diamond rings, gold necklaces and copper bracelets encrusted with colored gems. "You're right, the battle will be fun to watch no matter what. Two men in full armor with swords—"

The door lock clicked.

Faith was really presuming.

Irritated, Elle stood. "Don't do that. We have to go out that door." She didn't wait to see if Faith listened. Then an unexpected memory pulled Elle to a halt, a memory of the *Arcturus*, of Stephen Penderghast and his dark-haired assistant striding toward the helicopter. Faith was blonde but, yes, the same woman.

Elle jumped aside and turned. “Wait a minute. I know you!”

Faith’s upraised hand, holding a sharp, thin-blade stiletto, whistled past Elle’s face.

68

IN ADAM'S SHOP ON his central worktable, he laid out his chain-mail coat and hood and the leather gauntlets for his hands and arms.

What had he been thinking to agree to such a stunt as a mock sword battle? He feared someone in the crowd would recognize him as the man who had killed two people on a trek through the Amazon, and that horror would start again.

He donned the padding he wore beneath the mail.

Of course, Elle would tell him he hadn't killed them. She would insist that Big John Hammer had destroyed three lives with his egotistical search for publicity. But Adam knew what she did not: some people loved to think the worst, to take every opportunity for cruelty. His own experience was the real reason Adam had held her back from reporting her situation to the police. How could she understand the agony of being vilified by scandal-seeking reporters? Or worse, by ignorant onlookers who never performed any great deed, who spent their lives in a recliner, remote in hand, watching newsfeeds filled with fake scandals that encouraged them to make judgments? She could never realize how difficult standing straight and still and taking the abuse could be.

Because it didn't matter whether the truth could be spoken or shouted or conveyed in news tickers, those people were not interested. They loved to bolster their outrage, and they didn't listen. They never wanted to hear the truth.

With some difficulty, he lifted the heavy mail coat over his head and settled it around his shoulders and down his arms.

If Penderghast died—and according to the report Elle heard from her onboard contact, he was unlikely to survive—and his organization decided to accuse her of causing his death, she had photos of her injuries, but no witness to his attack. In a just world, she would have no difficulty proving her innocence. But Adam knew with some intimacy the world was not just.

Yet...somehow, someday, she had to come out of hiding.

He lifted the mail hood and settled it over his head and twitched it into place. The whole getup was hot and weighed over thirty pounds. Medieval knights had a squire to assist with these tasks, and Adam could have found someone at the festival to give him a hand. But the closer he got to the mock battle, the bigger fool he felt for agreeing to make an ass of himself. The chain mail was an imperfect disguise, yet the fewer people who recognized him, the better.

He removed his watch and placed it on the table, pulled on his leather gauntlets and flexed his fingers. He unhooked his scabbard from its place on the wall, pulled the sword free, and examined it as he had done every day before he used it. The blade was perfectly clean, without blemish, and with great pride he knew it was beautifully worked. He gave a few experimental swings.

Yes, he could move in this getup, albeit more slowly than

he would like. He replaced the sword in the scabbard and set it on the table.

On the table, his watch vibrated. He frowned. Someone had passed through the alarms onto his land. He stepped outside to see a couple pull up in a Mercedes convertible and park. Tourists. "Can I help you?" Which was his polite version of *What the hell are you doing here?*

"Are you the artist?" The young woman couldn't have been more than twenty, and she leaped out of the driver's seat with an eagerness that boded ill for his privacy.

"I suppose I am an artist," Adam acknowledged.

The young man climbed out of the passenger's side. "Told you so, Haley." To Adam he said, "That armor is awesome. Did you make it?"

Looking at them standing side by side, Adam realized they were brother and sister, twins. "I did, and I'm on my way to a demonstration of knightly skills."

"That would explain the breeches," Haley said.

Adam ignored her grin. "If you'll excuse me..."

Too late. Haley rushed past him and into the shop, and shrieked. "My God, Carlos, come and look! Daddy would love this!"

Carlos cast an apologetic glance at Adam. "Our father is notoriously hard to buy for."

Adam followed him in and barely caught Haley's hand in time. "Don't touch that. It's razor-sharp."

The sculpture he had finished on the night before Elle's arrival still sat on the wheeled trolley, waiting to be placed... somewhere. Somewhere he never had to see it again. Then the prow of Elle's great-grandparents' boat would take its place, and he would create another piece of art.

But not one like this. Not one with killer points and edges. When he remembered the history of that piece of metal, he thought it would bear a vaguely human resemblance, a suggestion of the people who had sacrificed their lives to save the lost art of long-dead civilization.

Haley's bosom heaved with excitement as she stared. "It's beautiful, like some deadly monster rising from the depths of the ocean."

Full points to Haley for perception.

"It *is* good." Carlos sounded surprised. "I wonder what the old man would say if we got this for him?"

"Are you kidding?" She turned to her brother. "Can't you see it on the pedestal in the foyer at the beach house?"

Adam didn't have time to stand here while they debated. "I really do have to leave." He walked toward the wide open door.

"Haley, I think this guy—" Carlos indicated Adam "—is one of the knights who's in the festival thing. If he's got to leave, we should—"

She turned to Adam. "How much?"

Okay, sure. There was more than one way to get rid of unwanted pests. He said, "Usually for my large sculptures, I charge—" and he named a figure more than twice his normal hefty fee.

Haley's eyes lit up with joy. "Carlos, think! Christmas present solved!"

So Adam added, "But because of the unusual nature of this one, and my attachment to it, I would charge—" He named an exorbitant sum. A ridiculous sum.

In less than ten minutes he found himself holding the crumpled, faded check that Carlos had excavated from the glove compartment—"Man, you really ought to get into digital banking!"—while the twins drove away, waving and smiling, promising to send someone to collect the sculpture sometime next week. Adam looked at the sum and thought that that amount would help toward Elle's legal defense fund. For that reason, he hoped Carlos and Haley didn't change their minds, and he placed the check in a locked drawer in the main worktable. He pulled on his leather armguards and gloves—and his phone rang. In the pocket of his breeches. Underneath his mail coat and his padding.

After a lot of fumbling, he dug it out and flipped it open. Before he could say a word, Rune squawked in his ear, "Have you heard anything from Elle?"

Adam went on alert. "No. Should I have?"

"Ludwig called from the restaurant. He told me the shop is locked, the shades are down, and some kind of disturbance is happening inside."

"A disturbance." Adam was already moving toward the ATV. "What kind of disturbance?"

"Glass breaking. Things being thrown. Yelling. *Have you heard from Elle?*"

69

ELLE DANCED BACKWARD, NEVER taking her gaze away from that beautiful, vicious face and the point of the knife that sliced the air inches in front of her chest.

Not Sookie. *Zsóke.* Faith was Stephen Penderghast's assistant Zsóke. When Elle had glimpsed her aboard the *Arcturus*, she had been dressed in a dark, form-fitting suit and was clearly subservient to him. She looked different now, dressed in a pink cotton shift and Jimmy Choo diamond sneakers. An apt disguise for an assassin.

"Give me a weapon, Clarice. Clarice, something!" Elle held out her hand.

"She can't hear you," Faith taunted. "She's so traumatized by my tortures and by Bruno's death, she won't even notice when I slit her throat. But unlike you, I'll make her death swift and painless."

Elle glanced at Clarice. She was looking around like a lost child in a horror show.

Faith continued. "After all, it's hardly Clarice's fault she was in the wrong place at the wrong time."

"I was in the wrong place at the wrong time!" Elle shouted.

"No, you were in the right place at the right time. You found the treasure, and you told Stephen Penderghast he was wrong. One of those would be a guaranteed ticket to the next world. But both?" Faith lunged, knife point outstretched.

With both feet, Elle jumped up on the display shelf that ran along the side of the shop, knocking a cup rack over, scattering psychic-themed mugs and tins of herbal tea leaves. She leaped toward the front display window. If she could get there, rip down the blind and fling herself through the glass, she would… Well, she'd probably bounce off the safety glass. A stupid idea, but—

She spotted the basket of glass eyes of newt, and as hard as she could, she kicked it toward Faith.

Ouch. Wrong day to wear sandals.

Brown, blue and green eyes rolled across the floor. It would be funny if—

Faith's feet went out from under her; she fell flat on her back.

Yep. That was funny.

The door rattled. A man shouted.

Help had arrived.

"Clarice," Elle pleaded.

Clarice looked at Elle as if she didn't know her.

"Clarice, if you'd just open the door!" Elle grabbed a heavy crystal-ball bookend off the bookshelf, lifted it over her head and flung it at Faith's chest.

She missed. Instead she hit Faith's belly and heard the air whoosh out of Faith's lungs.

Elle said, "Ha!" *No! Don't exult over a single victory when death could recover so quickly.*

Faith rolled, grabbed one of the eyes, round and heavy. She aimed.

Run! Elle stumbled over the displays of rune stones and seer teacups, trying to reach the window.

With the skill of a professional pitcher, Faith threw the eye.

It struck Elle's left shoulder blade.

Blinding agony.

Elle pitched sideways into the wall, and this time her plea was quieter, but more heartfelt. "Clarice, please, a weapon."

No time to look at Clarice.

Because Faith grabbed Elle's ankle.

Elle kicked at her with the other foot, a solid kick just the way Wendy taught her. She caught Faith under the chin.

Faith's head snapped back. But she didn't let go. With a yank, she pulled Elle off the shelf and onto the floor.

With a thump, Elle landed on her hip, which brutally reminded her that a few weeks ago she'd been limping and injured. She blinked away the black and red shooting-star shower that obscured her vision and saw—

The knife tip gleaming as it dove toward her.

Adrenaline roared through Elle's veins, vanquishing pain. She bounded to her feet in a crouch, under the blade, and smashed her head into Faith's chest.

Faith stumbled backward again, then charged forward again, knife dancing a deadly tango. She was like one of the perpetual-motion desk toys, created to go on and on until forcibly halted, and so far, Elle had not been able to do more than slow her down.

The front door rattled. Voices shouted.

Desperate, out of breath, panting, Elle screamed, "Clarice, open the door! Let them in!" She was faltering, and the thought crossed her mind not that she might lose but that she and Faith might battle to the death and the best that could be said was that she had fought the good fight.

If only Clarice would unlock that door!

Faith herded Elle toward the back of the shop, away from her goal. Elle briefly considered the back door, but Rune kept it barred and chained as well as locked, and she would never have time to get it open before Faith had finished the job she'd come to do.

Then, to her left, she saw movement.

Clarice stood holding one of the wooden staffs, the stoutest black walnut staff with the largest quartz crystal set in the head.

Thank God. With that staff, Elle stood a chance. She put out her hand and hoped Clarice gave it a good, steady toss—and at the last moment, some instinct made her take her gaze off Faith and the knife and glance at Clarice.

Clarice's gaze was focused, her eyes were molten with hatred. Holding the heavy staff by the bottom end, intent on the back of Faith's head, she swung with arms outstretched.

Elle hit the floor. She heard the staff whistle as it sliced the air, the crack as it struck Faith's ribs under her upraised arm.

Elle raised her head enough to view Faith's shock as her feet left the floor. Her head smacked the side of the shelf. For one moment, she struggled, then went limp.

The people outside battered at the glass in the door, at the door itself.

Clarice stood over Faith, who appeared to be unconscious, sprawled like a broken china doll. Like the warrior-woman she had proved herself to be, Clarice pointed the quartz crystal at the base of Faith's throat, and her attention never wavered. In a guttural tone she said, "Elle, get me rope."

Elle got to her feet. She wasn't sure she wanted to tell this Clarice that she didn't have a clue where or if Rune had rope. Whatever had happened between Faith and Clarice had left its mark in pain, terror…and was that madness? Perhaps, or at least fury in its purest form. She gestured toward the front door. “I’ll let them in.”

“Rope, Elle!”

In a panic, Elle remembered the ties on the velvet curtains in Rune’s upstairs consultation room. “I’ll get something!” She ran through the beaded curtain.

Behind her, she heard Clarice declare, to herself, to Faith, to whoever listened, “I will finish this myself.”

Elle hauled ass up the steps.

The room looked as it had before the shooting, with unlit candles and the crazed tabletop—and velvet curtains tied back with gilded ropes.

Elle didn’t hesitate. She snatched four ropes and their tassels off their hooks and took the staircase down in three jumps.

The glass in the door cracked. Help was almost here.

Clarice paid no attention. She concentrated on Faith’s still seemingly unconscious form, and she gave instructions in a firm tone. “Wrap her ankles first. But don’t be fooled. She’s got a wicked kick that could knock you across the room.” Her gaze flashed up at Elle. “Believe me. I know.”

Elle held the loop of cord and tassel in her hands.

In the midst of the spills, of the eyes of newt and the broken glass snow globes, was Faith’s knife.

Elle used the razor-sharp edge to cut off the tassel. Then, moving with the speed of a rodeo calf-roper, she wrapped Faith’s ankles and leaped back before Faith could kick.

The window shattered. The door burst open. People—Ludwig, Señor Alfonso, Gregoire and Sarcha—spilled into the shop.

“My God!” Gregoire exclaimed in horror.

Faith remained still.

“Clarice, no!” Sarcha said. “It’s Faith Moore!”

Clarice sneered. "Don't trust her. Never trust her. She—"

Faith lunged at Clarice.

Clarice slapped her in the throat with the staff.

Faith's hands flew to her throat and she held it, choking. As her paroxysm of pain faded, she looked up at Clarice. "I tortured you into submission."

"You didn't." Clarice pointed the staff right between Faith's eyes. "Bitch, that's why they call it acting."

70

WISELY, ELLE AND CLARICE had stayed well back while the police applied the handcuffs to Zsóke, aka Faith Moore. It was only when they were strapping her to the stretcher and loading her into the ambulance that Elle stepped close enough to look down at Stephen Penderghast's henchwoman.

Zsóke's face was swollen, her eyes were slits, her throat bruised.

There was justice in that.

"Is he alive?" Elle asked.

"Stephen Penderghast will never die." She used each virulent word the same way she had used the knife: to instill fear, to cause hurt. "He will haunt you to the end of your days."

The EMTs shoved the stretcher through the open doors. One climbed in to secure the stretcher. The other turned to Elle. "Scary, that one, and I wouldn't believe a word she said."

Elle nodded and hoped he was right, then went to join Clarice on the curb. She cautiously lowered herself—her new bruises were making themselves known—and they sat, arms propped on their knees, and watched the ambulance take Faith away.

"She really is a famous acting coach," Clarice informed her.

Gregoire and Sarcha squatted behind them, holding staffs as if to make up for their previous negligence, and both murmured, "Yes, famous. Always gets results. Thought it was an honor to work with her."

"I know. We looked her up, Adam and I." Elle shifted uncomfortably. Her hip hurt.

Ludwig and Señor Alfonso took turns coming out of the restaurant to hear the story. They were the ones who had first noticed the fracas, called 9-1-1 and begun the battle to bring down the door. "I would have shot the lock," Ludwig told Deputy Dave, "but I feared the bullet would strike someone within. After I almost broke my shoulder, Alfonso and I took turns with the meat mallet."

Deputy Dave had clapped Ludwig on the shoulder. "You did the right thing." He knelt before Elle and Clarice. He held his phone out, and with their permission, it was set on Record. "Please give us the details, everything you remember."

Elle wasn't so much talking to him as to Clarice. "The name I know her by is Zsóke. She's Stephen Penderghast's assistant—Stephen Penderghast is the guy who gave me the bruises—and until I got my memory back, I didn't know her. But trust me, she's one scary woman."

Clarice looked grim. "I found that out one night on the roof. Faith, or whoever she is, had given me homework, thoughts about the role she wanted me to work out. I wrapped up warm, went up top, stretched out on a chaise, and stared at the stars hoping in the quiet of the evening to work it out in my head."

"Go on," Deputy Dave encouraged her.

"She came out and made a call. She called the person on

the other end *darling*, and I figured it was going to be a loving conversation. I intended to keep quiet so when she left I'd be up there alone again. Which was my big mistake. I overheard that she intended to kill you." Clarice took Elle's hand in hers.

Her fingers were icy, and Elle exclaimed and used her other hands to chafe them.

"I must have made a sound, and once she realized I knew, that was it. She threatened me. She intimidated me."

"How did she intimidate you?" Deputy Dave asked.

"She moved into my bedroom, locked us in every night, took my bed while I slept on the floor. She twisted my arm so hard my elbow and wrist were swollen, and my shoulder ached so much I cried. To teach me to be quiet, she slid the tip of her knife under my fingernail." Clarice held up her other hand, the one she had resting in her lap.

Elle looked in horror.

Not one but three fingers were bloody under the nail, and the hand itself was swollen and had a bluish tinge.

Sarcha toppled over onto his butt. "We thought she was strict, but we never imagined… We thought you were doing what she said because it was your choice!"

Gregoire stayed in his squat, but his voice shook when he said, "We didn't know. I wish you'd told us. We would have helped you!"

Clarice turned to them, and while she was distant, she was also reassuring. "That's the thing. She assured me if I told you, she'd kill you."

With a flourish, Gregoire exclaimed, "I am a weapons master!"

"Yes, and she demonstrated her knife skills to me and on me more than once. It wasn't acting. She had real-life experience. If I had decided to tell you, while I was explaining, trying to make you believe, she would have struck without warning, and we would all have been dead." Clarice was fierce. "I know somehow she would have acted her way out of it, become the innocent victim of a random killer."

"Don't you think that scenario is a little extreme, Miss Burbage?" Deputy Dave asked.

Clarice pulled her neckline aside and showed him a long, thin, shallow scab that cut from her armpit to her breast. "It goes all the way to the nipple," she told him.

Elle clutched at her chest.

Deputy Dave swore in horror. "We've got to get you to the hospital." He started to stand.

"I want to finish the story." Clarice swallowed. "Then, yes, the hospital. I suspect I'll need surgery on my shoulder and on the broken bones in my wrist. Anyway, the torture was simply the first salvo in her arsenal. She told me if I said anything, if I went against her… I have a younger sister who just started acting."

"Mila Burbage," Sarcha and Gregoire said in unison.

"Yes, Mila. She's beautiful, talented, and she's on the cusp of fame. Faith knows her. Faith is a famous acting coach with access to every level of the business. If she had offered to teach Mila, my sister would have eagerly agreed—and she would have died. Faith promised that somehow Mila would die, but before she did, she would beg for death."

Ludwig grunted as if he knew something of that kind of torture.

Elle had tears in her eyes. "Clarice, I'm so sorry you got involved in my horror tale."

"This taught me a lot about acting." Clarice sounded calm and deadly. "Faith's objective, she said, was to make sure I loved her so much I would never betray her."

"That's crazy!" Sarcha said.

"That's brainwashing." Clarice flexed her hand as if trying

to get the circulation flowing. "The final test occurred when Faith and I were up on the roof. She was…hurting me, and neither of us realized that at some point, at the back of the building, Bruno had lodged a grappling hook in the top of the wall. While we were out there, he climbed the rope. He hung below the edge, where we couldn't see him. He had his camera lens resting on the wall, and he was taking pictures. Faith heard the clicking of the shutter, and she headed toward the wall. Bruno hoisted himself up. I suppose he thought he was a man and would be able to take her out." Clarice shuddered.

Elle put a gentle arm around Clarice's shoulders.

"I followed her. Then—" Clarice's voice rose, and as if she could see the scene, her eyes grew wide "—it happened all at once. She pushed him hard on the chest. I grabbed the camera by the lens. She used her knife to slash the camera strap. He flew through the air. I saw his face… So surprised." Clarice put her poor, ruined hand to her throat. Her words chased themselves, ever faster and faster. "He landed on the roof of his pickup. In that second, I realized if I hung onto the camera, she would destroy the evidence. So I dropped it." With both hands, she made the motion. "But when I did, I *acted*. I *pretended* to try to hang onto it. She raised her hand to me."

Elle's heart pounded as Clarice told her story with flair and drama.

"I dropped to my knees and begged her pardon. I said my hand wasn't strong enough to hold the heavy camera. She looked at me like she wasn't sure…" Clarice's hands dropped into her lap. "So I asked her to punish me."

71

ELLE FELT NUMB WITH terror, more terror then she'd felt in the store while dodging that knife. Looking at Deputy Dave and at Sarcha and Gregoire, she thought they felt the same. Clarice's ordeal had been so harrowing—and they'd never known.

"Faith slapped me—a slap was nothing to what had gone before—and dragged me down the stairs as fast as we could go. On the way down, she explained what we were going to tell the police. When we got to the ground floor, the truck alarm was going off and people were already there. She managed to get to the camera before anybody else did—everyone was so shocked—remove the memory card, smash the camera even more and toss it under the truck. When the police came, I said exactly what she had told me to. Our stories corroborated." Clarice nodded at Elle. "But I did manage to give you the message for Adam."

Deputy Dave leaned toward Elle. "What did Miss Burbage tell you? Why didn't you report it?"

"Miss Burbage told me that the paparazzo wasn't such a bad guy. What would you have done with that?" Elle was as tart as he was stern.

He acknowledged her comment with a negative waggle of the head.

"Later, we did recover the camera," Elle told Deputy Dave, "but the SD card was nowhere to be found."

"It's in my room." Clarice nodded toward the restaurant. "I can locate it for you, and there will be photos."

"Visual evidence." Deputy Dave radiated satisfaction, signaled to one of the other officers, and Clarice told the officer where to find the SD card.

Clarice picked up the last threads of her story. "You know what happened then. The four of us went to the police, Gregoire served as my lawyer. I was released on bail." She began to radiate satisfaction herself. "After we returned from the sheriff's office, after I had been accused of the murder she committed—she watched me. She began to think I was compliant, that I was her creature to command."

"Which is what you intended," Elle said.

"Yes. That is what I intended. I wanted her to think she had broken me...before she actually did."

Aching with sympathy, Elle stroked Clarice's fingers, wanting to somehow to convey a comfort she had not been there to give.

Clarice continued. "And Elle, every day she sat at the edge of the roof and studied the shop. Whenever you were here, working, she watched, waiting for the moment when you were alone."

Elle thought of Adam, ever-observant, eyes on the horizon. "I wish I'd paid attention."

"I wondered..." Gregoire said.

Sarcha nodded. "I wondered, too. I thought perhaps she

was infatuated with Elle, but she was sleeping with Clarice so… I figured she was polygamous?"

"It's all right." Clarice hushed them. "I don't blame you."

Sarcha wiped tears off his lashes with his sleeve.

"Today, for the first time, she saw the shop empty." Clarice's voice grew strong. "No one was on the street. She'd studied the festival schedule. She knew what was coming. Adam was going to fight. Everyone was going to watch."

"Actually, Adam is coming to take me to the exhibition." Elle looked down the road, surprised he hadn't yet arrived. "I was going to lock up as soon as he got here. If Faith had been a few minutes later, she would have been fighting Adam." On the other hand, Elle felt pleased with how she had acquitted herself. She might not have won the fight, but she'd put a dent or two into Stephen Penderghast's henchwoman. She turned to Deputy Dave. "Would it be possible for someone in law enforcement to search the records for Penderghast's whereabouts?"

"Since that woman works for him, yeah. Seems important." Deputy Dave stepped away to make the call.

Another ambulance pulled up. EMTs got out. They had come to give Clarice much-needed medical help.

Yet Elle needed one more answer before Clarice left. "Clarice, I believed all that stuff Faith said about you, that she'd broken you, that you wouldn't respond, couldn't respond. You just stood there! Why didn't you help me sooner?"

"I couldn't! I wanted the heaviest staff because I wanted to see her *hurt*—with the thickest one with the large crystal. I kept trying to pull it out of the stand, and one hand was fine and the other hand was swollen and the bones in my arm… I didn't have the strength. I was in a hurry, I was trying to keep an eye on what was happening, and I kept dropping the staff back into the stand." The remembered turmoil made Clarice's voice tremble and her hands shake. She took a breath and slowed down. "I finally realized I had to concentrate not on whether you were holding her off but on what *I* was doing, and I got that staff out of the stand and into my hands. But Elle, I cannot lie. I was never going to give you the staff."

Elle thought she understood. "You wanted to hurt her back."

"I wanted to kill her," Clarice corrected her. "I aimed for her head, used all my strength, but my injured hand betrayed me, my grip slipped, and I hit her lower."

"I heard the crack when you hit her ribs," Elle said. "The way she flew over like an airplane propeller… It was very impressive."

"Thank you." Clarice sighed in relief. "I think that's all, except to say—" she turned to Gregoire and Sarcha "—you will never see a better acting job than you've seen here."

Gregoire and Sarcha softly applauded.

Señor Alfonso said, "Brava!"

Deputy Dave turned off his recorder and pocketed his phone.

The main street was emptying again as the last people in town rushed toward the arena to view the upcoming battle.

"The studio was supposed to send a different acting coach. He has a good reputation, but he's not as prestigious as Faith. I was so impressed when she showed up instead." Clarice's mouth twisted. "Now I wonder what happened to Dvan Freitas."

Deputy Dave looked up sharply. "I know the answer to that. The body in the ditch was identified as Dvan Freitas."

Elle flinched.

The officer continued. "Word is just out from Stephen Penderghast's corporate office that he died today of injuries he acquired two weeks ago onboard the research ship *Arcturus*."

"Really?" Elle collapsed into a puddle of relief.

Deputy Dave looked hard at her. "Can you speak to the source of those injuries?"

She shrugged, tried to look innocent and kept her mouth firmly shut.

Sarcha turned to Gregoire. "You're the lawyer. If Dvan Freitas is dead, doesn't that change the charges against Faith, or Zsóke, or whatever her name is, from attempted murder to murder one?"

"If it can be proved she did it," Gregoire confirmed.

Clarice rested her head on Elle's shoulder and sighed. "I'm going to be very glad to study for my part alone."

"Sarcha." Gregoire stood. "I think that's our cue to pack."

72

A SPEEDING ATV ROARED as it drove down the road toward the small crowd.

Deputy Dave got out his electronic ticketing tablet.

Rune drove up, parked and in a flurry of scarves leaped out and ran toward them. Briefly she scrutinized them and, satisfied, said, "Everyone looks okay!" and ran to the broken door of her shop. She looked at the yellow crime-scene tape, pulled it off and walked inside.

Elle cringed when she heard the shriek.

Deputy Dave put the tablet away. "I'll let that one go."

From down the road they heard the roar of an ascending ATV and the screech of tires taking the curves too fast.

The officer got out the tablet again and faced that direction.

Adam, clad in his chain mail, drove up and parked.

Deputy Dave sighed. "Of course. A knight in shining armor come to rescue his fair maiden. Can't do it." Again, he put the tablet away.

Adam clanked as he moved. He wore his coif and leather

boots, his leather armguards and gauntlets. Unimpeded by the weight of the mail, he leaped out and pulled Elle up and into his arms. He kissed her, a desperate kiss, a promise kiss, a kiss that told Elle how important she had become to this lost soul.

He kissed her, claimed her, without hesitation, in front of everybody.

A long time later, she came up for air, leaned her head on his chest and smiled at the enthusiastically clapping audience of Clarice, her coaches, Deputy Dave, Ludwig, Señor Alfonso, the EMTs and a few Gothic folks.

Hands on hips, Rune stood in the doorway. “Way to make a declaration, Adam.”

“I love her,” Adam said simply.

“We’ll never be apart again,” Elle declared.

Adam’s arms tightened around her. “Not if I can help it.”

“No, seriously,” she said. “My hair’s caught in your armor.”

73

IT TOOK FIVE INTENSE minutes to get Elle free and bring Adam up to date on the recent battle in Rune's shop, and by that time Rune was standing there tapping her watch saying, "Adam, you're supposed to be fighting right now!"

"Right." Adam glanced toward his watch, but he'd left it in his shop. "Where's my sword?" Realization dawned. "I left my sword in my shop! Rune called me to ask if I'd heard from Elle and told me about the fight..."

"I'm sorry!" Rune said. "I got a report, and I called you."

"As you should." Adam was as agitated as Elle had ever seen him. "But I rushed out, drove up here as fast as I could and—"

Rune snapped at him. "That medieval reenactor is up there right now, prancing around in his shiny armor. Honestly, Adam, the weird guy shows up in a complete suit of armor, no surface left exposed, shiny plate mail all over. Except for the codpiece which is polished bronze."

"Seriously?" Clarice was sitting in the back of the ambulance, being checked by the EMTs, but she sounded interested and more than a little amused.

"Seriously," Rune assured her. "No handshake, stupid pointy-faced helmet so we can't see his face, walks around like Stud Knight, waving at the crowd. Gets them roaring."

Adam paid no attention, and his voice held a note of disbelief. "I don't have my sword!" Clearly, this time he and his preparations had failed to keep on track.

"It's okay." Elle kept her voice soothing. "I'll get it and bring it up to the festival."

"How could I forget? I don't forget. I prepare. I remember."

"You're in love," Rune said.

Adam stared, narrow-eyed, at Rune. "I know that! But—"

"Rune, I know that, too," Elle said. "Here and now is not the time to discuss it. In fact, it is none of your business!"

Rune put her hand on her chest. "Well! Who could have foreseen this?"

In soothing tones, Elle said to Adam, "You were naturally rushing, and it was on my behalf. I'll get the sword."

"It's not safe. Do we know where Sookie is?" Light dawned on Adam's face. "Ohhh. Zsóke… Sookie."

"Right," Elle agreed. "It's the telephone game. The more people who tell a story, the more changes are made, and Zsóke is an unusual name. Daniel's wife heard what she thought made sense. Of course, it's always possible there are other Penderghast minions nearby. But unlikely, right?"

"Right," Adam agreed grudgingly.

"Deputy Dave says that Stephen Penderghast's corporate office has announced his death." Elle made her pronouncement with a flourish.

Adam looked between her and Deputy Dave.

Deputy Dave nodded.

Gregoire handed Adam his phone. "I found the story online."

Adam speed-read through it. "Do we believe it?" he asked Elle.

"Unequivocally? No." Elle had had time to think this through. "Since the announcement came within minutes of Zsóke's arrest, I'm skeptical, but my suspicions are that he knows she's going to name him as an accomplice to Clarice's torture and the attempted murder of me, and he's being whisked out of the country."

Adam followed Elle's argument and nodded. He turned to Clarice. "Do you know, did Zsóke have backup in town?"

"Not that I ever saw, and we were together constantly." Clarice took a quivering breath. "More than once I heard her speak on the phone to, I believe, Penderghast, and she constantly urged him to stay in the hospital, to recover. She sounded as if she feared for his life. Maybe he is dead."

Elle gestured up the road and said to Adam, "The immediate threat to me just left for the prison wing in the hospital. You don't want strangers messing around in your shop. You and me, we're no longer strangers—"

Adam started to pull her in for another hug, then at the outcry of protests about his armor, her hair and the lateness of the mock battle, he refrained.

"I will get your sword." She pushed Adam toward Rune. "I'll be swift. I'll be careful. I'll bring it to you. Go on, go with Rune."

Adam kissed her again, twice, then he got in Rune's ATV and waved a farewell, and Rune drove like a bat out of hell up the road toward the festival.

Elle bade a swift, affectionate goodbye to Clarice, ran to Adam's ATV, leaped into the driver's seat and drove down the hill. A pickup drove up the hill toward her, and that surprised her. Who would be coming up the road now?

She looked into the cab. This guy looked like a janitor. He grinned genially and waved.

Sure. This guy went to the beach and realized he was missing the sword demo.

As she neared the shop, she realized the garage doors, the house doors, everything was open. She braked, backed up onto the road facing town and called Adam.

Inside the shop, his phone rang.

She half laughed. In Adam's hurry to get to her, he'd also forgotten his phone.

She called Rune.

When Rune answered, in the background Elle could the roar of the crowd. "We just got here," Rune said. "What's wrong?"

"Nothing's wrong. I don't think." Because if Adam had forgotten his phone, he'd probably forgotten to close up. As she sat there, she perused the area. "Ask Adam if he left everything open." She heard Rune consult Adam.

Adam must have taken the phone, because he spoke next. "Yes. Never mind the sword. I'm not wearing my watch. I can't verify the place is secure."

My God, how she liked this! To know he loved her so much he'd abandoned his phone, watch and sword, forgotten to close up and rushed to her aid. "Adam, I'm going in." He shouted, but she held her phone away from her ear and kept talking. "I've looked it over. To all appearances, it's clean. If I see anything at any time, I'll back out and get away. Stephen Penderghast's corporation has reported that he's dead. After the fight with Zsóke, who from his people would be here to threaten me? You made a mistake, you left everything open, but the danger is minimal, and I will be vigilant… *Yes, I will.* Count on me." She hung up before he could argue more. She felt pumped from the victory over Zsóke and, even though she doubted the truth of it, she wasn't foolish. She would be swift and efficient and careful.

She drove. She parked. She listened. She looked around.

Everything was still. Quiet. So quiet all she could hear was the low roar of the ocean waves and the high calls of the seagulls. She saw nothing out of place, and *she needed to get that sword to Adam*.

But she didn't run toward the shop, she *strode*. She projected confidence, as much for herself as for anyone or anything that might be lurking. She stepped inside and blinked at the change from bright sunshine to shadows. When her vision cleared, the first thing she saw was the sword—and Adam's phone and watch—on the table lit by a sunbeam radiating down from the skylight.

She chuckled; it reminded her of that scene in *The Sword in the Stone* where Arthur touches the sword and a light from heaven shines down its approval. To draw an absolutely absurd simile, it was as if Adam was a kingly knight, and she was *meant* to bring him his sword.

She put the phone and watch in her pocket, picked the sword up by the leather strap on the sheath, whirled to leave—and heard the click of a gun's safety.

Her heart stopped, then beat so hard her lungs couldn't function. Slowly she turned to face her nemesis.

He stepped out of the shadows at the back of the shop—tall, big-boned, but gaunt and pale—and pointed a pistol at her.

Adam would say she'd been careless.

She would say Adam was right.

In the deep, rumbling voice she remembered so well from her nightmares, Stephen Penderghast asked, "Are you going to slay me with that sword?"

74

STEPHEN PENDERGHAST IS DEAD.

They said he was dead.

Terror robbed Elle of breath and strength, and she wanted to scream and scream, to yield to her fear of pain and murder. Fear rooted her to the ground—and the ground reminded her what Adam, her mother and her own experience had taught her. She was part of this earth, she had a right to be here, and Stephen Penderghast had no justification or reason to vanquish her.

But somehow, it wasn't that lofty ideal that motivated her. It was the single, lucid thought that illuminated her mind: *I don't have time for this.*

Adam needed his sword.

She had to get it to him.

"I see you remember me. So much for your amnesia." Penderghast put a lot of effort into his disbelief and contempt.

Deliberately she placed the sword on the table in full sight of her killer. "I do remember you."

Yes, the tournament was a mock battle. Yet Adam had worked on that blade, he had trained with it. It deserved to be utilized, and Adam had overcome an injury to train. He deserved to use those skills to overcome his opponent and to triumph.

In that, she and Adam were alike.

She was still afraid, but she had found her focal point.

Now to figure out how to defeat a gun-wielding maniac.

"I remembered Zsóke, too, and I fought her. Law enforcement arrested her and took her away."

"Through this entire ordeal, Zsóke has been a disappointment." Penderghast dismissed his henchwoman. He had no interest, no affection, no love for anyone but himself. "I am impressed that you were able to take her, though."

It wasn't me who defeated her, it was Clarice. Elle swallowed back the words. *Don't tell him anything.*

Penderghast continued. "I suppose I shouldn't be, after what you did to me."

From the words he spoke and the way he said them, she suspected he might be carrying a grudge. "So being almost killed by someone who stands a foot shorter and weighs a hundred pounds less rankles you?" Not the smartest thing to say, but her current situation was hopeless. She might as well challenge him.

"Because of you, I have surgeries lined up for months. Repairs. You shortened my life." He pointed the pistol at her chest.

She trembled with a hard surge of terror.

"Does knowing that make you happy?" he asked.

She was going to die. Again. Die in agony. Leave this earth and lose everything. Love, life, happiness.

Adam.

Adam who had told her, *Sometimes there's no right way to go about disarming the enemy, and you have to go with your gut.*

Her gut writhed at the thought of that bullet tearing through her. But she took a breath. Because she could, because Stephen Penderghast's hands were *not* around her throat. She stood far away from him, and in that moment between breath in and breath out, she knew that this man's arrogance was the weapon he had placed in her sweat-slicked palms.

"Yes. Yes, to know you're going to be dead makes me very happy." She cocked her hip, put her fist on it. She looked him in his bloodshot eyes and in an insolent tone asked, "Are you going to try to strangle me…again? And fail…again?"

Hatred flared on his face. The pistol shook hard, then steadied on her, and in a moment, she thought she'd goaded him into a killing shot.

Very softly, Penderghast eased the safety on again. "Do you think I can't? Do you really think you incapacitated me so much I can't tear you apart with my bare hands?"

As if alarmed by his threat, she…

Okay. She *was* alarmed by his threat. Despite his hollowed cheeks, his stooped shoulders, she remembered those big hands choking her. The hands were skeletal now. He looked like death on legs. Death stalking her…

No! She had to strategize. She could do this. She knew how. This was *not* Stephen Penderghast's turf. Here, in Adam's studio, she knew more. Adam's studio where he created a sword, chain mail, a weighty metal sculpture…

That sculpture, the one that rested on a wheeled trolley, symbolized the cruel depths of the ocean and, if mobilized correctly, its razor-sharp points could kill a man.

She could kill Stephen Penderghast.

The idea of causing a death made her feel ill. Kill another person? No. No, she would use the sculpture to stop him and—

Penderghast took a step toward her.

She scuttled sideways to stand beside the sculpture. She would do what she had to do. She crouched, held her hands up like knives posed to strike. "I've learned karate since last time you hurt me. You can't get me now."

He laughed with real amusement. "Did you really think I would let you get the credit for finding the underwater treasure?"

"I never thought about that at all."

For all the attention he paid, she might as well have not said a word. "When you're dead, when I've choked the life out of you, when your weird-colored eyes roll back in your head and your face is turning black—"

Panic swept her again, and her whimper was real.

"When you're nothing but a body to be kicked aside, then no one will know what you discovered at the bottom of the ocean." His eyes burned with the passion of a fortune hunter. "When the gold faces rise to the surface for the first time in so many years, I'll claim them, and I'll be interviewed, toasted, exalted."

"No!" He didn't deserve it.

"When I'll gift the most important pieces to the Smithsonian, all will marvel at my philanthropy. They'll name the exhibit after me. It'll tour the world, and everyone will know me." Penderghast swayed with an almost-religious fervor.

"I won't let you," Elle shouted.

Penderghast snapped to attention. "You're going to stop me—how?"

"Those relics belong to Peru!"

"Oh, Peru." He callously dismissed the place and the culture that had created them. "Who's going to see them in Peru?"

All her doubts fell away.

She owed her great-grandparents credit for their bravery in saving the Moche antiquities.

She owed her mother for raising her with strength and principles.

She owed Adam her very life. She wasn't going to lose it now. The blood of generations of archaeologists lent her strength. "Whatever antiquities found on the site are the last remnants of a great civilization." Her voice quavered, but she said what needed to be said. "The Smithsonian won't take them because they belong in Peru."

"The Smithsonian will do what I tell them!" he shouted and took a second, swift step forward.

She leaped behind the sculpture. "Please don't hurt me!" She didn't have to fake her fear—or her determination.

At the sight of her peeking around the sculpture, Penderghast chuckled, then with a low, constant, mocking rumble of enjoyment, he took one slow step, then another, stalking her, dragging it out, deriving pleasure from her real, white-faced terror.

With the toe of her shoe, she unlocked the lock on the trolley wheels.

She could do this.

She wiped her sweaty palms on her pants and took a firm grip midpoint on the sculpture.

She could do this.

But she had never hurt anyone…except him. And he hadn't died.

This time, she could do this and finish the job.

She would not freeze. She had found a life with Adam. She would claim it.

Penderghast paced on, a weakened jackal on the hunt. He reached the halfway point. He paused.

She trembled with fear and horror. She knew what she had to do.

Penderghast took another step, then without warning—he charged.

With a warrior's shout—maybe it was a scream—she leaned her weight into the back of the sculpture and wheeled into the charge.

She rammed into Stephen Penderghast.

She heard the sickening, squelching sound as the scupture's points pierced his flesh.

His shriek of agony raised the hair on the back of her head.

The force of the collision sent her reeling backward.

She stumbled, righted herself, prepared herself to grab the sculpture and ram him again.

But when she looked, the man stood erect and immobile, impaled on the sculpture's razor-sharp points. Groin, belly, chest, forehead. Blood bathed him in wet, flowing crimson. He sagged at the knees.

Was he dead?

His limp weight pulled at the sculpture. The trolley wheels slid back and up. The heavy metal fell forward, on top of him. The points buried themselves to the hilt.

But the body still twitched, and the fall and the weight of the sculpture pushed the remaining air from his mouth, and an inhuman groan made her jump back in horror.

With that, the last suggestions of Penderghast's life disappeared.

Dead. Yes, dead. He was gone from this earth, vanquished.

She drew a quivering breath, wiped a sudden gush of tears off her cheeks. She had known the man but not realized that he was a monster of inhumane cruelty. He had sought to use her to find the treasure he coveted, and he never intended her to live long enough to see it rise to the surface of the Pacific Ocean.

Now she lived, and Adam waited.

She sidled forward without looking at the corpse. Picking up the sword and scabbard, she turned and ran to the ATV and placed them on the seat. Right this minute, as fast as she could, she wanted to drive up the hill to Adam.

But she'd learned a hard lesson.

She hurried back to the shop and locked up, leaving Penderghast's body alone and unmourned. After she had given Adam his sword, she would report to law enforcement.

Then she drove as fast as she could up the hill to the arena.

75

AT THE FESTIVAL SITE, beside the central arena, a tent of simulated medieval splendor had been constructed of cheap shiny cloth and moldering velvet curtains, and two banners waved atop the two peaks created by the tent poles. "Listen to the crowd. They're buzzing like a nest of giant murder hornets. If we don't get this fight going…" Rune dropped Adam off at the back entrance. "Get in there and get ready."

"I am ready."

"I know. I know. Chain-mail hauberk and hood, leather gauntlets and armguards and breeches. Everything but your sword." She glared. "Adam, how could you forget it?"

Once again Adam tried to comprehend how he could have run out without his weapon.

Such impetuosity was unlike him.

Falling in love was also unlike him.

He smiled at Rune. "Elle's an extraordinary woman."

"Making you forget something—she's a witch!" Rune lifted a finger. "That's it! I'll make an announcement. I'll say you're recovering from a bewitchment and will be out when you're given your magic sword. Make something up about the enchantress who ensnared you. I'll tell them a story they won't forget!"

As Rune drove away, Adam said, "Good luck with that."

Lifting the tent flap, he walked into the dim light.

He was alone. He heard half-hearted cheers; the other knight must still be in the arena, parading around, as Rune said, in shiny armor. He was welcome to all the adulation. What did Adam care?

He knew what was important. Elle was recovering from her ordeal at sea. She would recover from the fight she'd fought today with Zsóke. Elle was well worth the trouble she caused him. If he could, he would keep her close to cause him trouble forever.

He looked out of the peephole created by a tear in the curtains. The tent opened directly into the arena. Spectators lined the fence by the hundreds. At the opposite side of the arena, Angelica Lindholm, Mr. and Mrs. Kulshan, and the Shivering Sherlocks sat on the elevated dais.

Angelica was speaking to the elderly couple.

Mrs. Kulshan was paying no attention. Mr. Kulshan looked as if he was debating whether listening was worth the elevated view.

Striding up and down the length of the arena was Adam's opponent, waving his sword, encouraging the cheers. Rune was right: this knight was so shiny that he hurt the eyes. He was tall, massively muscled if the armor was to be believed, and wore a massive steel mesh belt hung with a mace and a battle-ax. And that codpiece! "Way to be subtle," Adam muttered. He would bet this guy in the armor drove a huge pickup, raced up behind every car and flashed his lights, and at every opportunity bullied his way through traffic, and life.

A sense of wrongness nagged at Adam, and he studied Mr. Shiny Pants.

Who was he?

The way the guy bent his knees, the way he moved his shoulders, was so awkward Adam thought his plate armor didn't fit correctly, or perhaps he'd gone the drugs and alcohol route before he'd shoved himself into his costume.

Tamalyn stuck her head in the back of the tent. "Hi, um, Rune said to tell you the crowd is getting more restless. Would you step out and prance around a little, give them something *else* to look at?"

Adam faced her and glared. "Prance?"

"Show yourself. Until your sword arrives." She started backing away. "Shouldn't be too long. You know Elle will get here as quickly as she can."

"I know." Adam debated, but Tamalyn looked so embarrassed and wretchedly hopeful. "I can do that."

Tamalyn was gone before he finished.

Adam steeled himself to step out and have people stare.

Why had he agreed to do this?

Oh. That's right. Rune had asked him to help Gothic.

In other words—blackmail.

Taking a breath, Adam threw back the tent flap and stepped out.

A roar of approval greeted him. The whole crowd had tired of Shiny Pants and wanted a new champion—and the locals wanted Adam.

Shiny Pants stopped strutting. His helmet turned in Adam's direction. A cone of shiny metal—Adam could not get over the shininess—with long slits where his eyes should be.

Adam judged that the helmet would badly limit his opponent's vision—not that it mattered in a mock battle—but wouldn't the guy trip over his own feet? Also, bad PR. No one could see what this guy looked like; everyone liked seeing a warrior they could put a face to.

Adam walked to the center of the arena and waved genially. He nodded at Freya Goodnight. He gave a special wave to Tamalyn, who now hung over the fence next to the *Gothic Times* reporter, high-schooler Justin Scharphorn.

Hm. That was an interesting development.

Adam turned and waved to the crowd on the opposite side and faced enthusiastic cheers from Señor Alfonso and Ludwig. They must have hustled all their customers out and closed the restaurant to be here for his mock battle.

Warning shouts rose from the crowd.

He turned toward the dais and saw Mrs. Kulshan pointing a shaking finger toward him. Behind him.

The Shivering Sherlocks were on their feet.

Mr. Kulshan shouted, "Look out, boy!"

Adam spun.

Shiny Pants rushed him, sword swinging toward Adam's injured shoulder. Adam had only a moment to wonder *How does this stranger know where to aim?* It was as if Shiny Pants had shot the sniper rifle that resulted in Adam's injury...

Oh.

Now Adam knew who was inside the knight's suit of plate armor.

The crowd hurrahed louder, thinking the demonstration had begun.

Adam lifted his arm and took the blow on his leather gauntlet. The force took him facedown to the ground, and his arm...

Pain. Stars speckled his vision. *So much pain.* The force of that blow, the unexpectedness of it, had not been for display. For whatever reason, this knight was after him.

A few people in the crowd seemed to know that the demonstration shouldn't be happening this way, with one knight unarmed and the other hacking away with his full strength. Those people screamed at Adam to move.

He had to move.

He rolled to the right, faced his opponent in time to see Shiny Pants lift his long sword and point it down over his head, prepared to use all his strength and the power of gravity to skewer Adam.

The crowd booed.

Adam rolled again, away from the blow.

The knight drove the sword blade into the grass.

Now Adam knew why his foe was so awkward, so clumsy, so driven and insane he wanted to kill Adam. Holding his injured forearm, he sprang to his feet.

The crowd cheered.

He also knew he had the advantage. Plate mail had been created for jousting. Adam's lighter chain-mail armor had been created for hand-to-hand combat and effectively blocked injury. More importantly, he had been trained in combat and practiced for this moment for years.

A hundred phones were held up, taking video.

The knight's helmet muffled his grunts and curses.

If only Adam had use of both arms... He shook his hand, trying to get feeling back into it, and that brought another wave of pain that sent him staggering backward.

Although Shiny Pants had other weapons hanging on his steel belt, he struggled desperately to free the tarnished blade from its planting in the ground.

To the knight, Adam said, "I tried to warn you."

Shiny Pants lifted his head, and Adam could imagine the glare of those mad eyes behind the helmet.

Rune shouted and gestured at Adam to come out of the arena.

Adam shook his head. If he didn't end this now, someone would die. It might be him. And by God, not now. Not when he'd at last found a reason to live.

He looked around for Elle, but she hadn't arrived with his sword.

No matter. He didn't need a weapon.

With a yank, Mr. Shiny Pants knight freed his sword. He stumbled backward.

Adam was behind him, waiting. He slammed his shoulder into the knight's back, sending him reeling the other direction.

The plate metal rang like a gong.

The crowd laughed, going from alarmed to amused in a second.

Shiny Pants swung around, sword extended, ready to slice Adam in two.

Adam danced away, off to the side, staying out of his limited vision.

Shiny Pants spun in a circle.

The crowd laughed harder, more riotously. For them, it was a comedy.

Adam heard the knight's muffled ranting, the constant stream of furious invective about Adam, his cowardice, his morals, his doubtful ability to get an erection.

When the knight had made a thorough fool of himself, when the crowd was jeering, Adam darted behind him and shoved again.

Shiny Pants stumbled forward, still slashing the air.

With his other hand, Adam tapped the knight's shoulder.

Shiny Pants swung toward him.

Directly behind him, Adam danced to the other side and tapped him again.

Shiny Pants turned, then anticipating Adam's next move, he swiftly turned back.

But Adam knew this man, his trickery, his lack of values.

He would reveal his identity, no matter the cost.

He stayed behind him, braced himself for the surge of pain, and with both hands, he reached up and pulled the polished helmet off the knight's head.

76

BIG JOHN HAMMER WAS REVEALED.

Gasps rose from the crowd. Murmurs that grew louder and louder. "Who is that?"

"Is that...?"

"Yes, it's him."

"What's he doing?"

"Are you sure it's him? He looks bad."

Hammer did look bad. His thinning blond hair dripped with sweat. His swollen face was purple with heat and rage. His wild and bloodshot eyes bulged, and his words rang out unmuffled by his helmet.

As he raged, the crowd quieted.

"I'll kill you," he shrieked at Adam. "You betrayed me. You know what happened. Nothing you say is true."

One of the men in the crowd shouted, "Not serious. Must be a trick!"

As Hammer's voice grew louder and more vicious, a slick of white foam crusted the edges of his lips. "You're a liar.

You told reporters I stood by while people died. You can't be trusted. You told the press I refused to give that woman my antibiotics. I'm a hero! No one can trust you. You worthless piece of shit, you fucking coward, fight me!"

Over the murmurs and protests and shouts of the crowd, Adam heard a slight, feminine voice call his name. "Adam!" Elle. At last, Elle had arrived. "Adam, your sword."

For the first time, Adam relaxed. She was safe. Now he knew this would come out well. And with the sword, he knew he had a chance of survival. He backed away from the raging madman who stomped his feet like a toddler in the throes of a tantrum.

"Adam, this way." It was a siren's voice, a siren's call.

The source of Elle's voice guided him; he didn't dare take his gaze from Hammer. Hammer, who vibrated like a volcano about to blow.

As Adam neared the edge of the arena, Elle spoke right by his side, her voice low and comforting. "Take your sword."

Adam turned to see Elle there, inside the arena, holding the scabbard with the sword's hilt pointed toward him. Urgently he said, "You shouldn't be here." He pulled the blade free.

Something about Elle caught his attention, a remnant of wide-eyed terror and shock—and triumph.

"What's wrong?" he asked.

A roar of warning broke from the crowd.

Adam took heed. "Run!" he said to Elle and turned to face the charging bull that was Hammer. He braced himself. He lifted the sword, deliberately baring his midriff.

Hammer zeroed in on Adam's vulnerability and slashed toward his belly.

Adam leaped aside and brought his sword down onto Hammer's stained steel blade.

Hammer's elbow bent at an awkward angle. His sword leaped out of his gloved hands. He gave a howl of rage or pain, an animal sound that stood out from the crowd's shouts, and fell sideways. He writhed on the ground in what looked like a seizure.

Adam stepped away, but he didn't take his gaze off Hammer.

In that evil man's face, he saw a flash of cunning.

Cunning. Of course. In the Amazon, Adam had seen that expression. He hadn't understood it then, but he understood it now. Cunning. Lies. Adam knew what to do. He had to present a visage of weakness. "I won!" he shouted.

He pulled off his helmet, dropped it, bared his face to the sun. He turned his back on Hammer and raised his sword in triumph.

The crowd roared their approval—then shrieked in warning.

Exactly what Adam expected. He whipped around.

Hammer knelt on one knee. He picked up his sword and thrust it at Adam.

Adam slammed his booted foot down on the blade, pinning it to the ground. With a swift transfer of weight, he kicked Hammer under the chin, knocking him flat on his back. Placing his foot on his chest, he leaned forward with all his weight. Pulling a dagger from his belt, he put the tip on Hammer's neck. "Don't move. You've lost."

"I should have shot you through the heart," Hammer shouted.

The spectators gasped. They turned to each other, murmured questions.

"What's he talking about?"

"When did Hammer shoot the other knight?"

"Do you understand any of this?"

A confession, as Adam suspected. Hammer had been the shooter, the man who had wanted to tip the fight in his favor. "That would have been too easy. If you hadn't shot me, you would have had to battle an uninjured man. I would have easily beat you."

Hammer's bloodshot eyes almost glowed with loathing.

Adam had only a moment to jerk the blade aside.

Hammer lunged.

Adam's dagger sliced Hammer's neck, barely missed his jugular. The blade clanked against the armor protecting his shoulder.

One of the female spectators shouted, "Did you see that? That bastard tried to kill our leader!"

Only one voice, but Hammer raised his arm in triumph. "I won!"

Of course. No matter the course of events, no matter how many people witnessed the events, the truth would always be what Hammer deemed it to be. No matter what vicious offenses he performed, his disciples were true to the illusion he created.

Adam glanced back toward Hammer's follower and saw Tamalyn fighting her way through the crowd to confront the woman. "You're *stupid*," the girl shouted and waved an arm. "Did you see what happened? Did you see how unfair Hammer was fighting? He's evil, and you're *stupid*!"

The woman leaped at Tamalyn.

Tamalyn popped her in the face with her fist.

The woman staggered back. She put her hand to her nose, pulled it away, stared at the blood and started screaming.

She didn't try to attack Tamalyn again.

Adam used his boot to slam Hammer onto the ground.

The crowd roared in admiration, disapproval and confusion. They didn't know what to make of this battle. Was it mock? Hammer was a candidate for governor. What was he doing, fighting like an inept movie villain?

The parasitic-induced madness took him, and Hammer disintegrated into a howling, shivering piece of flesh.

Rune opened the gate to Deputy Dave and the other officers working the festival, and as law enforcement rushed in to take Hammer away, he clawed at Adam's boot.

Adam backed away from the scene, and someone caught him around the waist, hugged him hard.

It was Elle. "You won," she whispered, but he heard her over the shouts of the crowd. "He's insane. He would have killed you. He would have killed us. You saved us."

Hammer shrieked at the police and cursed the EMTs who tried to stanch his bleeding.

Beside Adam, Rune spoke. "This sword smells funky." She held Hammer's sword.

"Don't touch the blade!" Adam said sharply.

Rune took a startled step back.

Adam removed his leather gauntlets and the protection on his forearms. "Have it tested. He's coated it with something."

Rune dropped the sword. "Something?" She held her hands over her head.

"Poison would be the simplest. If you'll give me a plastic garbage bag, I'll dispose of these in a way that ensures everyone's safety." Adam let the leather fall into a pile on the ground. "Because Hammer might have access to other, more deadly substances. He doesn't care how he wins."

Rune stared at the blade as if it was a cobra. "What did you do to make him hate you so much?"

"I saw him as he really is." Adam watched as the EMTs and police fought to contain the raging madman that was Hammer, to anchor him onto the stretcher, strap him down. "I did warn him. Now it's too late for him to recover. He'll die in agony."

Elle said, "I'll bet live videos are already all over the media."

"Let me get this straight," Rune said. "Big John Hammer arranged to fight you by bribing or intimidating the reenactor we'd first hired. Hammer replaced that guy with himself—"

"And shot at me in your shop with the intention of wounding me enough to give me a disadvantage." Adam had followed all the ins and outs of this sabotage. "But not so badly I backed out."

"He intended to win, and he knew he couldn't win fairly," Elle finished the explanation.

"He really is—or was—a very good shot," Adam said.

"That was one helluva gamble." Rune touched the strand of hair beside her face.

"I'm sorry about your hair, but Rune—this will be great publicity for the festival." Elle smirked at her.

Rune pointed her finger in Elle's face. "When this is over, we're going to have a talk about your wiseass attitude. Now, let me see if I can move these people along." She took a step away, then turned back, her face creased with concern. "Although, now I'm worried about Melinda."

"Who's Melinda?" Adam asked.

"Remember? Melinda was supposed to work the store while I was up here. I've always considered her absolutely reliable, but she just...didn't show up." Rune looked toward the ongoing struggle between the law officers, the EMTs and Big John Hammer. "I wonder if she was coerced." Rune lifted her hands and dropped them. "I'll talk to Deputy Dave about sending someone out to her house to check on her."

The EMTs loaded Big John Hammer onto an ambulance.

The door was shut behind him, and whatever villainy he had intended was done. He was finished.

Elle was safe.

Adam was safe.

Nothing could threaten them now.

77

RUNE HEADED FOR THE dais and used the microphone to announce Professor Marvel would be performing amazing feats of magic on the Mystic Stage near the tent of Veda the Seer and reminded them the magic performance was free.

Talking, exclaiming, discussing, the crowd dispersed.

Elle hugged Adam harder.

Adam turned in her arms to face her. "I now know the sword's name. It is *Veritas*."

"*Veritas*. Latin for *truth*." She nodded. "That's perfect."

Again as he held her, he sensed terror and triumph. "What's wrong? What happened?"

She wet her lips. "Stephen Penderghast."

He had believed he was finished with the battle. But hearing that name, his every fighting instinct came to the fore. "Where?"

"In your shop. I killed him."

Adam looked into her face, saw the knowledge in her eyes. She knew what it was to face off with the shadowy hulk that had hunted her—and triumph without guilt, without loss of memory. "Good for you." He ran his hands up and down her arms. "Are you hurt?" It was the only pain he cared about.

"Some bruises from the fight at Madame Rune's, but Penderghast never touched me." She gave a small snort. "He never had a chance."

"No more nightmares." Adam knew that from his own experience. "You vanquished your monster."

"Yes, but I need to tell law enforcement."

"An hour ago, law enforcement believed Penderghast was already dead. His corporation lied."

"Or they didn't know the truth."

"Definitely possible," Adam agreed.

"At least now when I talk to Deputy Dave and tell him about the attack on the ship and me jumping over the rail into the storm, he's going to doubt Penderghast's good reputation." The tight, worried knot inside her eased.

"I'm not saying law enforcement will fail to do their job, but after the attack in Rune's shop and the way you fought that bitch off—" Adam's voice grew savage "—Deputy Dave and his buddies will be prone to believe anything you say."

"I hope so, although when they see what happened in your shop…" She sighed. "Your sculpture is going to need to be cleaned."

Adam thought that through. "Ah. Well. Today I sold it for a lot of money. But I don't know. If it's involved with a killing, will that enhance the value or decrease it?"

"The sculpture's not damaged at all. I do suspect it will be confiscated as evidence, at least for a while."

"Yes. It will. When you speak with law enforcement, I'll be with you every moment. And Elle—" he hugged her, taking care not to tangle her hair in his chain mail "—I am so proud."

"Yes." Her voice trembled a little, but her chin was up. "We've both done good work today."

A woman's commanding voice spoke from the sidelines, breaking them apart. "Elladora, I could kill you for frightening me like this."

78

ELLE SWUNG AWAY FROM Adam. "Mom!" She turned back. "It's my mother!" Then, arms outflung, she raced to the railing.

The woman there, in her forties, beautiful, fiercely smiling, looked like Elle's older sister. She leaped the fence and ran to her daughter. They embraced, pulled back, looked into each other's faces and embraced again.

"Tell me again why you didn't call me?" Elle's mother shook her.

"I almost got murdered. I didn't remember you. Then, oh Mommy, it was wonderful and terrible and fearful, and Adam—" Elle extended her hand to Adam. "He saved me. He taught me to defend myself. I love him."

Adam felt the thrill of her words from the crown of his head to the tips of his toes. She loved him.

Elle's mother thrust her hand toward Adam. "Sofia Neely-Varela. And you are?"

"I'm Adam." He felt the powerful need to add, "I saved her from death."

"Twice," Elle said.

"Really?" Sofia's hand tightened on his.

"Really." Elle must have had her own need to impress her mother, because she added, "Except for the last time when I saved myself."

"She is so brave, and smart, and strong." Finally, Adam couldn't contain the question that had been rolling around in his mind. He looked at Elle. "And she said she's going to marry me?"

"When you ask me." Elle detached herself from her mother's embrace and smiled into his eyes.

He looked around. Most of the crowd who had watched the battle had dispersed, headed toward the magic show. Yet somehow the word had gone out—something new was occurring in the arena, and they drifted back, phones raised and pointed toward them.

He hated publicity. But that ship had sailed. Once more, fame had found him, and Elle deserved all the formalities. He knelt. He took Elle's hands and looked up at her. "Elladora Varela, will you marry me so we can be together forever?"

She knelt beside him. "Forever is a very long time…and even that won't be long enough for us."

This kiss was soft and sweet, a promise for tomorrow, and when they pulled apart, the Shivering Sherlocks were dabbing at their eyes.

Tamalyn had her hands clasped together while she smiled and sighed, "That's real romance."

Justin Scharphorn was taking notes and snapping photos.

Mrs. Kulshan had her arms around Mr. Kulshan's waist while he honked his nose on a white handkerchief.

Rune hung on the top of the rail, shaking her head and

muttering, "Even with the Pacific Coast Highway closed and only the Nacimiento-Fergusson Road open, this year will never be outdone."

Yet Sofia clearly was not happy, and she scoffed, "No one ever asks the parent anymore."

"Mom!" Elle glared. "Since when did you become a traditionalist?"

"Shh." Adam softly put his hand over her mouth. "I'll handle this." He turned to Sofia. "Mrs. Varela, may I have your permission to wed your daughter?"

Sofia put her hands on her hips. "You're going to marry her no matter what I say, aren't you?"

"Yes." Adam was quite definite. "But we would prefer to have your blessing."

"And Dad's," Elle added.

"He'll be thrilled," Sofia said to Adam. "My husband *is* the traditionalist. He has been fretting because Elladora is in her twenties and unmarried."

Adam stood, helped Elle to her feet and offered his hand to Sofia again.

She shook it, then hugged him and Elle. "You have our blessing." Still holding Elle, she looked in her eyes and asked, "You jumped off the *Arcturus* and landed here? Why here, Elladora? Of all places, why here?"

"What's wrong with here?" Another woman's voice, well-modulated, pitched exactly to reach their ears.

Angelica stood outside the arena's fence. Rune opened the gate for her.

Angelica strode into the ring. She looked solely at Sofia, spoke directly to her. "Why shouldn't my granddaughter be here?"

79

ADAM WASN'T AS SURPRISED as he might have been. He'd seen the photo of the young man on Angelica's desk, the only photo there, with an inscription, *To Mother, from your loving son, Bradley Lindholm.* Even more than the resemblance between Bradley and Elle, Adam had been struck by Bradley's eyes, one blue and one brown—and that explained so much about Angelica's behavior whenever she was around Elle: skittish, intensely caring and almost bewildered.

But Elle… Elle was shocked. She took a hard breath. She staggered sideways. "What? Why? Mom? What is she talking about?"

Sofia's lips were taut; she spoke as if every word hurt her. "I've been here before. I told you I came here with your grandparents."

"Yes."

"I was eighteen, newly graduated from high school. I met your father on the beach. I told him about my great-grandparents and the lost treasure and how they'd died offshore, and he told me about the City of Lost Souls. He was younger than me, but he'd attended a private school and he'd graduated early. Bradley was charming, smart, kind, loving. We had a summer fling." Sofia smiled at some distant, sweet memory. "I had my scholarships, I knew where I was going to college, and most of all, I was sensible. Once I met his mother—" Sofia shot a look at Angelica, standing straight and calm and listening without expression "—I knew nothing could come of our puppy love. But somehow, Bradley showed up at my college. He'd arranged to attend, and we fell more and more in love. At least I did, and I thought he had, too."

"Then you got pregnant," Elle said.

"Yes. We came to Gothic together so he could…tell his mother that we were going to be married. That we were going to have a baby. Instead, he…stayed with her." As if that memory was too painful, Sofia choked on the last words. But before Elle could reach for her, Sofia added, "Bradley abandoned me—and you—for his mother."

"What do you mean?" Angelica lost that constant, preternatural calm. She flushed and her voice rose. "He went with you. I never saw him again. And he didn't tell me—you never told me—I had a granddaughter. You didn't even give me a chance to be a grandmother!"

Sofia marched to stand in front of Angelica, a slim, petite, brunette facing off with the tall, strongly built redhead. "Liar!" Sofia's voice was loud and angry.

"Mom!" Elle sounded incredulous.

But neither woman was paying attention to her.

"How cruel could you be?" Angelica asked. "Whether or not I wanted him to marry you, how could either of you imagine I wouldn't love this child?" Tears glistened in her eyes. "As soon as I saw her, I knew. She looks so much like Bradley. And like you!"

"Which explains so much about the way Angelica reacted to me," Elle murmured to Adam.

"Yeah..." Adam kept an eye on the developing argument.

Sofia's fists clenched. "I didn't deny you your grandchild. Bradley knew I was pregnant. He promised he would explain to you and follow me, and I got on that plane hoping he could reconcile you to our marriage. Our love. Because he loved you, too. I knew that, and I didn't want him to be unhappy. *He never appeared.* I waited months. I didn't give up until I was alone in the delivery room holding our baby. I thought I knew him. I couldn't believe Bradley would leave me alone to bear our child."

"Don't," Elle said.

"Now you are the liar!" At last, Angelica's voice rose to meet Sofia's.

Both women were flushed, furious. They strained, ready to physically attack each other.

Elle leaped between the two of them and shouted at the top of her lungs. "Wait! Neither of you ever looked for my father?"

"Looked for him?" Sofia was still furious, but she took a step back. "He abandoned me in my time of need!"

"Looked for him?" Angelica put her fist to her heart. "He was my son. He should have come back and at least told me—"

"My father disappeared and is...nowhere?" Elle slowly and clearly articulated the words. "Where is my father?"

Both women stopped speaking. Adam thought they stopped breathing. They stared at Elle.

She stared back at them, hands outstretched, eyes hot and angry. "My father. My whole life, I've hated him for abandoning me. And abandoning my mother. But neither of you know where he is? Neither of you have seen him for twenty-eight years? *Where is he?*"

Adam had never seen such magnificent righteous indignation.

Nor he had ever seen two women as horrified as Angelica and Sofia.

Angelica turned her head to look up at her home. In a dazed voice, she said, "Oh, my God."

Sofia breathed, "The Tower."

From the dais, Mr. Kushan's gravelly voice arose. "I told you that place was haunted."

80

THAT EVENING, POLICE REPORTS had been given and taken, crime-scene tape surrounded Adam's studio and Rune's shop, and Hammer had been placed under arrest and was in restraints in the local hospital psychiatric ward. His perfect wife announced that he'd been insane for years, she'd wanted to divorce him but had been afraid for her life, and she would now take action.

Adam and Elle, and Sofia and Angelica sat in Angelica's well-appointed library, sipping wine no one could taste and nibbling appetizers no one wanted, waiting for Angelica to stop playing the proper hostess long enough tell them what she had found in the Tower.

Finally Sofia burst out, "You're killing me. Please tell me if it's true. If that's where he is!"

With trembling fingers, Angelica put down her glass. "You know. You know it is."

"In the Tower. His tower. But…how?"

Angelica closed her eyes and touched the center of her forehead with her index finger. "I am reconstructing his last moments, but if you'll bear with me and not…raise your voice unduly, I will tell you."

Sofia narrowed her eyes and in a forced modulated voice, said, "Please do."

Elle exchanged glances with Adam. Obviously, years ago these women had been fatally different. They hadn't gotten along then, and even now they still strained to find a common ground.

But with the news of his death, Bradley Lindholm had united them, and they writhed in anguish at the memory of their fateful, angry ignorance. They had failed Bradley, and they had failed Elle, and neither woman was accustomed to failure.

Angelica said, "Bradley's friend drove you and him to the airport—"

"That's right," Sofia affirmed.

"Where Bradley was to bid you farewell. He was *supposed* to come back here so we could talk while you took a plane back to your home in San Antonio and college."

"Also right."

"I never saw him again. I thought he had changed his mind and left on the plane with you. I thought he had never returned home." When Sofia went to interrupt, Angelica raised a hand. "In fact, he had returned home. He bypassed finding and speaking directly to me and went to the Tower. Probably to think." She turned to Adam and Elle. "That was where he always went when he was uncertain of his next move."

Okay, Elle had to admit Angelica's instructional tone made her want to claw the story out of her, and she could see her mother vibrating with frustration. She prompted, "The Tower was always unsafe."

"Not really. Not in the beginning. But time went by, property taxes rose, money got tight and the Lindholm family concentrated on keeping up the part of the house that was livable. Even that was difficult. Carpets got shabby, paintings were sold… It was almost ninety years before someone started earning enough to provide both upkeep and improvements." In a display of ostensible modesty, Angelica veiled her eyes.

"Yes. We've got it. You saved the family estate. What about Brad? What about…" Sofia took a fortifying breath, but she was wringing her hands. "What about Brad?"

Angelica observed her coldly.

No. No. Angelica was not going to play with her mother's emotions. Elle said, "She loved him. And I, too, want to know. What happened to my father?"

Angelica's gaze shifted to Elle, and she yielded to the pressure for information. "Bradley was my son, my only child, and he always loved the Tower just as it was. Aging, decrepit… He found it when he was four. Climbed the steep stairs to the tower room at the top and played there with his armies. He built Lego castles that looked like ours, and when he got older, he hauled a desk up there and did his homework while he looked out the windows to the sea. I homeschooled him, as well as some of the children around Gothic. Of course."

"Of course," Sofia accused Angelica. "He was lonely."

"He never complained." Angelica yielded. "But yes, I fear that's true. When he went to college, he left California, and I seldom heard from him. Because he was in love." She looked at Sofia. "He was too young."

"I was one year older! What did you think? I was a seductress? A temptress? He was my first lover!"

Elle covered her ears and hummed loudly.

"I loved him. We loved each other." Sofia spoke to Angelica and Elle.

"You were too young. Both less than twenty. I could not

approve." Angelica sounded and looked like a mature, sensible matron, not like a woman who had seen all hopes of love and family crushed.

"He loved me. He loved you." Sofia stood. "You made him miserable."

"Yes. Worse, when he brought you home, I treated you badly."

Sofia snorted. And sat.

Angelica looked her right in the eyes. "I'm sorry. I was wrong."

Sofia took a breath, let it out in a sigh and leaned back in her chair. "Apology accepted."

"He brought you home to meet me, it went badly, and he went with you to the airport and came back. He didn't come to find me. Or maybe he did. I tried to reconstruct those moments, and if my appointment calendar is correct, I was chastising an employee who… Well, not important. Not as important as my son. Bradley went up to his room in the Tower, to his desk, and started a letter to me." Angelica looked at Elle. "I know this because after we spoke this afternoon, I climbed the stairs, four stories, to the Tower room. I would not ask someone else to go up there if it was dangerous. As I now suspected it was."

Adam took Elle's hand and squeezed her fingers.

She clung to him.

Angelica cleared her throat. "Bradley was writing a letter that assured me that he loved me, that he loved you, Sofia, that he hoped and prayed we could be a family soon because you were going to have a baby—"

Sofia pressed her fist to her mouth and tears overflowed.

Angelica handed her a half-empty box of tissues. "I found the letter on his desk. Before he finished, he stepped away to look out the window—and fell through the floor. The boards had rotted. He fell four stories into the dark."

Sofia passed her back the tissues.

Angelica accepted them and stared at the box as if she didn't realize tears were sliding down her cheeks.

"His neck was broken as well as... Well, his neck was broken, so he died instantly."

Elle knew that was perhaps not true. But Angelica and her mother wanted to believe it, and Bradley Lindholm was long gone. So it was true because believing that hurt less.

"I rigged a camera and a light on a rope and lowered them into the depths. I found him." Angelica closed her eyes and frowned as if opening them would cause pain. "I saw...my boy..."

Sofia was sobbing steadily, sorrowfully.

Two women with broken hearts endeavored to come to grips with an old, hurtful truth: they had each believed the man they loved had betrayed them when his disappearance had been an accident, and only now were they facing the truth—and their combined grief.

"I have people who are retrieving his body. It's taking more time than I...than we would like, because they have to shore up the structure before they enter. I would not allow anyone else to risk their lives to get him." As Angelica had risked hers. "We'll bury him in the Gothic graveyard and I hope," she said and her voice strengthened, "I hope you'll accept the role of his widow... Sofia."

Elle's mother sobbed steadily now, and she nodded.

Angelica looked at Elle. "You'll be his chief mourner."

"No. I never knew him. The role of chief mourner is yours. I'll be my mother's support." At last, Elle's voice wobbled. "And yours."

81

THE GOTHIC SPRING PSYCHIC Festival ended on Sunday night with a round of drinks at the Live Oak, a financial accounting (between Rune's shop receipts, the profits at the restaurants in town and Veda's earnings from her crystal ball, it was the best year yet) and a promise to clean up in the morning.

On Monday, cleanup did indeed begin, on Adam's studio and on the festival grounds. Before the day was over the studio looked as if blood had never been spilled within its walls, the tents and magic shows had been dismantled and loaded into the trucks, and Eric and his crew had bid Gothic a fond farewell and taken to the highway. It was only after they left that Angelica discovered Veda had accepted Eric's invitation to come on the road as their fortune-teller.

Angelica was not pleased. Good assistants were hard to find, especially for someone as exacting as Angelica.

On Tuesday, most of the tourists had packed up and left Gothic's spare rooms and bed-and-breakfasts and returned to their homes with eye-popping tales of the most exciting festival they'd ever attended. Only a few hardy folk lingered to take the jeep tours, buy last-minute souvenirs and the remaining sensational copies of the *Gothic Times* with its Justin Scharphorn byline.

On Wednesday, in the Gothic cemetery, the entire town attended a tragic graveside service for Bradley Lindholm, and they cried. They cried for the loss of his young life, for his mother's grief, his lover's long years of sorrow and his daughter who had never known her father. That was a difficult day, one that would never be forgotten.

On Thursday, Adam Ramsdell and Elladora Varela were married under the oak tree behind the Live Oak restaurant. Elle's stepfather had flown from Peru to give her away. Elle wore one of Angelica Lindholm's own courturier dresses that Angelica herself had worked feverishly to alter.

Again, the entire town attended, and this time, everyone rejoiced both at the union and at the reception catered by Señor Alfonso and Ludwig. The high-school kids from across the area served as Live Oak Restaurant staff. Tamalyn proved to be a strong leader, and Angelica began to eye her in a new you-could-train-as-an-assistant way.

On Friday, Adam and Elle took a helicopter to the *Arcturus* to witness the moment when, because of Elle's find, the remote crawler brought up the first Moche artifacts from the depths of the ocean. Film crews broadcast the moment all over the world. Elle and her family were famous for approximately fifteen minutes, which was as long as they wished it to last.

Everyone in Gothic watched and celebrated.

Adam had the now-cleaned and newly polished sword delivered to Madame Rune's Psychic Readings and Bookshop as a talking point for the tourists who would come to see any relic of the now-famous battle between Crazy John Hammer and Adam Ramsdell.

On Saturday morning, when Rune entered the Live Oak, she fluttered her fingers at everyone in the restaurant. Locals, all of them, looking weary and satisfied and ready for a long rehash of the events of the past two weeks.

They had plenty to talk about.

Angelica Lindholm sat with Mr. Kulshan, discussing his arthritic feet.

She appeared pale and still sad.

He looked ruddy and annoyed.

Clarice was the only person who was not strictly a local… but Rune suspected that, after her ordeal, she had confirmed her status as a lost soul and, in between roles, would soon take up permanent residence. For now, she sat, arm in a cast and sling, alone with her script. She cast Rune a smiling glance, then returned to work.

Señor Alfonso stepped out of the kitchen.

Ludwig appeared at Rune's elbow.

Rune looked up, expecting to hear a recitation of today's menu.

Instead, Ludwig extended a plain white envelope. "Adam Ramsdell left this with me to give to you today. He was quite specific about the date, and that you should open it at once, here in the restaurant."

Rune took the envelope and weighed it in her hand. She smiled at the others. Angelica was helping Mr. Kulshan to his feet, Clarice looked up alertly, and Señor Alfonso drew close to Ludwig. "Let's see what's in here, shall we?" She popped the seal, pulled out the brief note and read it. "Well. This isn't news to me, but it might be a shock to all of you. It would seem Adam and Elle won't be returning to our fair City of Lost Souls."

Señor Alfonso groaned.

"What'd she say?" Mr. Kulshan asked Angelica.

Rune waited while Angelica loudly filled him in.

"Oh, hell," Mr. Kulshan said, just as loudly.

"Shall I continue?" Rune asked.

"Might as well," Ludwig muttered.

"I don't think we could stop her," Clarice said.

"Indeed, no." Rune shook out the paper and pretended to read. "For the moment, Adam and his new wife will be making their home in Peru. Elle will be working, as before, as an archaeologist with her mother and stepfather. Adam will be speaking to the locals, who are, after all, descendants of the Moche and expert metalworkers, to see what more he can learn of his craft and their art. Adam and Elle would like me to take charge of renting their house to the next lost soul who finds their way to Gothic and wishes to stay."

Mr. Kulshan extended a knobby, shaky hand. "Lady, I'm not saying I doubt your word, but let me see that letter!"

"Trust Mr. Kulshan to say what you were all thinking." Rune handed the letter to him, and he looked around for his reading glasses, which were back on the table.

Angelica snatched the letter out of his hands. "Give it to me." She scanned it, looked up and said, "Get your wallets."

This time, everyone groaned.

Mr. Kulshan dug a bunch of crumpled bills out of his pocket.

Angelica asked, "Do you take credit cards?"

Almost before the words were out of her mouth, Rune said, "Yes!" and delved into her bag and brought out an electronic card reader.

Angelica grimaced and produced her card.

Clarice turned to Señor Alfonso, who was also extracting his credit card. "Would you put this on my bill?"

“Yes, yes!” Señor Alfonso said.

Ludwig paid in cash, and asked, “How did you know that Adam would meet a woman and be leaving town?”

“Madame Rune knows all and sees all.” She grinned as she collected the winnings. “When will you learn not to bet against your fortune-teller?”

★★★★★

ACKNOWLEDGMENTS

AS YOU READ *POINT* *Last Seen*, you undoubtedly noticed the loving care I used in creating Gothic. I grew up in the San Francisco Bay Area. My grandmother and great-aunts, powerful women who were huge influences on me, were born and raised in Ben Lomond in the Santa Cruz mountains, and as a family we traveled and camped all around central California. As my aunt Sadie once told The Husband, "As long as a wheel's going to turn, we're going to go."

The first time my mother and I drove the scenic Pacific Coast Highway into the heart of Big Sur, we were captivated by its frothing waves crashing against rocky cliffs, wide stunning views and mystical forests that whisper and roar in the ocean breeze. A visit to San Simeon—Hearst's Castle—cemented my sense that here, in this place of wealth and wildness, anything was possible. There was and is an otherworldly ambiance to Big Sur, a sense that this ancient area is immune to civilization. For the most part, it remains untouched.

Naturally when I looked for a glorious, isolated spot to place a small, quirky, totally fictional town with a totally fictional legend, I thought of Big Sur. Being in Gothic gives me great pleasure; I hope you enjoyed your time there and will join me for further Gothic adventures.

Thank you to my editor, Michele Bidelspach, executive editor, HQN and Graydon House, who joyfully joined me on this trip and daily gives me her valued guidance. My thanks to Craig Swinwood, CEO of Harlequin and HarperCollins Canada; Loriana Sacilotto, executive vice president and publisher, Harlequin Trade Publishing; Margaret O'Neill Marbury, vice president, Harlequin Trade Publishing; and Susan Swinwood, HQN editorial director. It's a pleasure to be publishing with this talented, dedicated team.